Mr O Winds Back the Clock

Mr O Winds Back the Clock

I J BAKER

INTRICATE BOOKS

First published in 2024 by Intricate Books
Copyright © I J Baker 2024
The moral right of the author has been asserted.

ALL RIGHTS RESERVED.

Without limiting the rights under copyright restricted above, no part of this publication may be reproduced, stored in or introduced into a retrieval system, or transmitted, in any form or by any means (electronic, mechanical, photocopying, recording or otherwise), without the prior written permission of the copyright owner of this book. The views of the author belong solely to the author and are not necessarily those of the publisher or the publishing service provider.

A catalogue record for this book is available from the National Library of Australia

ISBN: 978-1-7635379-0-3 (hardback)
ISBN: 978-1-7635379-1-0 (paperback)
ISBN: 978-1-7635379-2-7 (ebook)

Cover design by Duncan Blachford
Text design and typesetting by Typography Studio

The characters presented in this work are fictitious.
Any similarities with real people, living or dead, are coincidental.

For Serena and Clea

For Serena and Cleo

"One of the marks of a gift is to have the courage of it.
If they haven't got the courage, it's just too bad."
KATHERINE ANNE PORTER, interviewed for
The Paris Review, 29, Winter–Spring 1963

CONTENTS

Unempayment   1

WINTER
1. All Those Fabulous Heads   15
2. If Some's Good, More's Better   29
3. The Generosity of Steve   51

SPRING
4. Another Saturday Night   77
5. Genuine Filter Coffee   99
6. Prognosticating with Pash   129

SUMMER
7. A Roll in the Hay   163
8. Bellyaching about Bob   191
9. Are You Happy Now?   219

AUTUMN
10. What Becomes of Us   239
11. The Soul and its Appetites   267
12. All Grown Up   295

What Are You Waiting For?   325

UNEMPAYMENT

I HAD NOT THOUGHT THAT MY EXECUTIONER WOULD BE Danny. I had assumed that Danny would be insufficiently senior. He was chief sub-editor, and therefore my supervisor, but he did not have an office, and mostly he left me alone. I had not even logged on. I had sat at my workstation, which was set a little apart from most others, next to the desk used by Helga, our spare layout sub-editor, who had been promoted from real-estate copy sub, and who came in three days a week and made every second page look the same. It was as though she had learned two ways to assemble the headlines and pictures and paragraphs, and had felt no desire to learn more. It used to impress me that she could sustain her two editorial designs across the multiple shapes that had been left her to fill, shapes defined by the ad people when they stacked small advertisements. She may see herself here, but I doubt she will sue. For one thing, I have not accused Helga of incompetence. Her behaviour was competent. She understood what she needed to do, and she did it. We would talk only a little. The incompetent worker was I.

Perhaps Helga had complained of the way that I smelled. Perhaps she had thought that I should have shaved more. And that I should have carried in with me each morning less support for the hypothesis that I had washed down my breakfast with whiskey. But this was newspapers, and we all made allowances. The subs, most of us old hands, believed that one of our number undertook a breath test each day in a room behind the front desk, and was no longer permitted to let himself into our building via the rear door with his electronic key. Perhaps I too would be forced to sacrifice my freedom of entry. That had looked like a prospect I could set to one side until my moment arrived. I allowed myself only one drink, sometimes two, since I had a long drive to work. A third drink would make sure I was late, and therefore it commonly led to a fourth. If I poured a fourth drink, and embarked upon a fourth cigarette, I would not go to work.

Had I taken three drinks that morning? I believe that I may have been late. Having sat down at my workstation, I had been trying to prise my reading glasses from their hard black case, so that I could see my monitor well enough to log on. Danny had loomed to my left. Danny is a little shorter than I am, and a little younger, and a little better-looking. His face reminds me of a kelpie's face, pointy and shrewd. And like me, he is slight. He stood beside me but behind the line of my shoulders. I had registered an approach, but I knew the approach was from Danny only because it had become his habit to approach me in this way, on those occasions when he chose to approach me.

I had wondered for a moment what he would ask of me. Would he request that I proofread a late advertorial insert, a job that I believed was a job for the ad team? Had a reader drawn his attention to an error in one of our titles? Danny had grown circumspect when drawing my attention to allegations of error. Mostly I could explain to him that the reader was wrong: that the alleged error was not an error but established house style, style that an ignorant reader might mistake for an error. I was the custodian of the Guide to Style, as Danny was happy to acknowledge. I was our last line of defence, our deflector of likely own-goals. They paid me just to catch errors, and what else I did was optional, mainly. I did not need to change headlines, except to correct errors. I didn't need to enhance readability. I did not need to rewrite whole paragraphs, paragraphs that some enthusiastic young reporter had written, and that a sub-editor might have rewritten before he sent them to me for review. And certainly, very certainly, I did not need to excise every contraction from any phrase that did not quote, directly, a source.

I am not sure even now why I had come to see such excisions as high priorities for my attention. No reader paid for these papers. We had them tossed onto residents' doorsteps, so that they could draw eyes to paid ads that they carried. If I were to return to work of this kind, I would no longer place such importance on the excisions. It was not as though somebody had told me to make them. To transform every *don't* to a *do not*, and every *you've* to a *you have*. Doubtless Danny had wondered why I was doing this, when he discerned that I was indeed doing this.

"Seamus, I need a word."

Danny.

"Word away, Danny," I said, resisting the temptation to ask him just which word he needed. It isn't difficult for me to remember how I responded. I did not even turn my head.

"In the meeting room."

This was a room on our floor that housed a round glass-topped table and four or five chairs. And our accessible archives: bound bundles of recent editions, stacked up against two of the walls. A rectangular window was located high on the long wall, trimmed with a venetian blind that was left all but closed. We subs never held meetings. On Monday nights, after we had finished the most widely distributed papers, which covered the relatively wealthy southern suburbs nearest the city centre, immediately on our side of the Yarra River, we would yell at one another over beers from our workstations, celebrating the end of the grind and an impending day off. I could not recall having entered the space Danny indicated except to look at past papers. But I could see little point in resisting. Had I intuited that this would be my moment, and had I received that intuition with relief?

Danny closed the door and selected a chair. From his manner, I guessed that I was not about to be commended, or offered promotion without commendation.

"I don't want to say this, but I have to."

People deny agency when arriving at all sorts of choices.

"We want you to take a bit of a rest. Take some time off. We'll keep paying you."

And so they would keep paying me. While I took some time off. I think I felt a moment of panic. A sharp stab of fear as I contemplated the prospect of taking time off. Of absenting myself not because I had chosen to, but because somebody else had decreed that I must. Somebody—and originally, this may well have been Danny—had made a judgment about the value of my presence in this office, and had adjudged me a net non-contributor. By implication, that judgment might be revised. Did I resort, in that moment, to hoping that it would be revised? I wonder whether, instead, I waited without hope, while the fear found a warm place at the base of my stomach and set up a small shack. An extended absence from this grey place of toil, while they paid me, sounded very appealing, were it not for the prospect that I might never return, and that they might cease to pay me.

"We'll keep paying you," Danny said, "but there will be conditions."

Oh yes. There always are conditions.

I HAD DRUNK FREELY of Jim Beam bourbon whiskey, and less freely of brandy and beer. I had allowed myself freedom in the smoking of cigarettes. But over the five months prior to my moment arriving, I had smoked only two bongs. I had smoked also four or five joints, two in company and the remainder alone, on the latter occasions combining tobacco broken out from a tailor-made cigarette with a ration from a small parting gift. I have smoked no bongs since. If I were to smoke another bong, I would smoke only for old times' sake, among survivors from those with whom I once smoked bongs frequently. The prospect of smoking a bong no longer thrills me, as perhaps the prospect of smoking a joint thrills a little. When you smoke a bong it is as though you smoke two strong joints in succession, and all at once, and all just for you.

When it was proposed to me that I write about happy experiences, as a means of direction, as a revisiting that might uncover a path that had become overgrown, it did not occur to me immediately that I would write about times when it had seemed good to smoke bongs. I had not previously thought of those times as times when I had felt extraordinarily joyful. At first, I had smoked bongs on evenings when I might have served myself better by studying. Or by sharing a meal with one woman or another whom I had lusted for but whose intimate company I had avoided. Is it true that to know what is best is to do what is best, as Socrates is alleged to have argued? I might have thought about offering an invitation to an object of fancy, and I might have thought about when I would offer that invitation, and then I might have told myself that a better opportunity would arise.

It might have seemed best to me then that I should seek out a friend, someone who might be at a loose end, and most enticingly my enterprising friend Roland Browne, with whom for more than a year I had shared a small house. It was with Roland in that house that I had first smoked a bong—inhaling and spluttering and soon afterwards raving. My raving inciting confusion in Roland's principal companion at that time, Stephen Hurtley, whose confusion soon turned to merriment. Even after Roland took up residence elsewhere, it seemed safe to assume that he had dope stashed away, and that it would be good dope and possibly great dope, and that he would pack me a bong and insist that I smoke it. And I would smoke it and forget about the task undone, or the woman from whom I had hidden my interest.

I might say then things that I never had thought I would say. And I would say these things in ways that assumed much goodwill. I am more able now to recognise how much generosity has been advanced to me, over decades, by Roland and by other people with whom I have smoked bongs. The value of this appreciation has exceeded its price: merely my livelihood, and the inflated self-regard that my visible means of support had abetted. The past year I can recall as a good year, even if it was not a year when, most of the time, I felt good.

It is not obvious to me even now just what drew me to begin reconstructing such occasions of intoxication. My guess is that, having been invited to reflect upon past periods of pleasure, I was reluctant to acknowledge that such periods recently had been few. And so as a way of denying a reward to the invitee—Ms Felicity, as I will call her—I began with a response that I thought very petty. It was not as though my companions and I had spent these times sharing personal problems and solving them. The settings in which we smoked varied but one theme persisted. The question perennially in need of an answer was how many bongs would we have—a question that in any moment reduced to the question whether one of us needed to smoke another bong. Perhaps we were sharing problems, and solving them. It appears from my recent reinhabiting of these moments that commonly it was I who felt he had most at stake when resisting an exhortation that he take another draught of fumes from the giggle-weed, as we described the intoxicant sometimes in those days. Usually we just called it dope. In my small circles it was rarely labelled mere weed, or grass, or pot, or hemp, or marijuana, and even more rarely cannabis, although we thought of cannabis as its botanical name. Hashish was available sometimes. And yet it was not always I who had most at stake when deliberating over whether

I would do better to rebuff a suggestion that I attend to a bong, even if I recollect myself as being the most deserving of censure, among those with whom I inhaled, for what I said when intoxicated. Bob Cottleman, arguably, when he was present, had more at stake than I did, for in our company his resistance to smoking became complete. And a fat lot of good that did him—but I pre-empt myself.

How did these occasions proceed, when we would banter for hours over nothing at all? I shall offer a scrap of dialogue that I reconstituted only in February, the eighth month of my enjoined recollecting. I had recalled my having visited Roland, at the cottage he had moved to in the inner suburb of Abbotsford, where he resided with his girlfriend, Debbie Marten, whom he would make his wife. The year of my visit was 1986. Debbie had not been at home, and Roland, as I had hoped, had presented me with a bong, telling me that the batch of dope from which he would fill its bowl had been acquired only recently, and that it was good dope but he was not sure how good. Implicitly, this had invited me to render a judgment. The bong had tasted delicious and I am sure I did not cough from smoking it. I would have taken another swig on my beer.

"How does that feel?" I believe Roland asked, as he gazed at me across a corner of his dining table.

"Nothing. I feel nothing."

"You feel nothing."

"Nothing. Nothing at all. I feel nothing. I feel very weird and silly but I feel nothing."

"It'll come on soon."

"I don't think it will," I believe I told Roland, rendering my judgment upon this batch of dope. "I think I've got used to it already."

"You probably have. So you can just relax and enjoy it. And then you can have another one."

"You are not going to get me like that, Roland. You are definitely not going to get me like that. When Steve was here, you might have got me like that. But Steve isn't here, so you won't be getting me like that. Probably ever again. You might never get me again like that ever again, Roland. But Steve might have got me like that. Probably would have done. You were a horrible pair, Roland. A horrible pair."

"We were a horrible pair." Roland's intonation was perfectly flat, a mere echo.

"You *were* a horrible pair. No, I can't believe I just said that. Of course you weren't a horrible pair. You were a great pair. A fabulous pair. There was nothing like the pair you were. Oh no. It is bad, Roland..."

"It's bad that we were a fabulous pair."

"No. It's bad that you aren't a fabulous pair any more. That you aren't a pair. Any more. I do say terrible stuff sometimes, don't I."

"You do say terrible stuff sometimes."

"But it doesn't matter, does it. It doesn't matter. It really doesn't matter. Does it?"

"It doesn't matter," I believe Roland said. "Well, it does, but there's not much we can do about it. I'll have this bong and then you have one and then not all that much will matter, after all."

"It's a bong *you* need to have," I told Roland.

"I'll have this bong, and then you'll have a bong," Roland said. "That's what we need. That's what this is about. I'll have this bong, and then it's your turn for a bong."

"I think *you* need that bong."

"I do need this bong."

"But *I* don't need another bong."

"That's where you're wrong. You do need another bong."

WHEN I RECONSTITUTED THAT conversation, it had been about ten months since my suspension from the sub-editing team at Southern Suburbs Newspapers. I'd been employed by Southern more or less comfortably for twenty-two years, having been taken on with little relevant experience by *The Bayside Post* about two years before that chain bought it. At the time when I engaged in the reported repartee with Roland Browne, I had no idea that I would be offered a job with the *Post*, or with any newspaper, and certainly not a job as a trainee sub-editor. Roland's Abbotsford house had been a single-fronted cottage on Turner Street. Under the influence of my long inhalation, I had been lamenting the death of Steve Hurtley, with whom Roland had pursued many adventures, most connected with the consumption of black-market narcotics. When Steve had been living, I never would have lamented the absence of his uneasy companionship. I had wished that Roland would not allow Steve to so clutter his waking hours. Between Debbie and Steve—and not forgetting the insistent Bob—Roland had been besieged in that period by attention-seekers whose attention to him I received as intrusive. Even when I had lived with Roland, sharing our two-storey terrace house in Keppel Street, Carlton, barely a stone's throw from the colleges of Melbourne University, there had been scant opportunity for me to commune with him alone. And so when lamenting Steve's death, some years later at Abbotsford, while communing with Roland alone, I would have been lamenting a loss that I had barely begun to experience as a loss. And I would have been lamenting that loss while confident that it would endure. If Steve had merely moved interstate, or had married a tourist and gone to live overseas, I would not have been telling Roland, even as addled from smoking as I must have been at the time, that it was sad Steve was no longer with us.

If a theme has emerged from these months of my reflecting unhindered, perhaps I have captured it there. When we view them from the future, our circumstances look different from how they appeared in their present. Steve, an invasive and threatening madman, looks after twenty-five years like a sad little boy. Roland, a rock-guitar rebel whose gifts I admired, is revealed as a marketing middle-manager on a pre-family fling. Bob Cottleman, daunting and driven, was lost even then. And Patience Moore, forthright and wholehearted, owning defiantly her high-school nickname, Pash, is exposed as concealing and delicate—if no less forbearing.

Such a shift in perspective has taken place for me even recently, as I have reviewed the recounting I compiled under coaxing from an insistent interrogator whom I had been obliged to see fortnightly. I say I had been obliged to see Ms Felicity but more precisely I had chosen to see her, since the condition upon which Southern paid me had been only that I engage with someone who would supply them with reports on my progress. I doubt that such largesse will survive in the news business. My first choice I had encountered as grey, dry, and humourless. Having opted to replace him, I don't know what led me to conclude that my second choice had earned my loyalty. Possibly her key quality in prospect had been her beauty, evident from her photograph. I may have thought that at least I could look at her, and perhaps that she must be stupid and so I could feel safe with her. At the time I would not have acknowledged the latter thought as a thought—I am merely attributing to myself an unflattering prejudice. Sometimes prejudice serves us.

WHAT DID I FIND as I returned to this personal history, approaching it as a reader might who had not lived my life? I found a record of an obsession that had engulfed my narrator, that had swallowed him whole, and without his having appreciated that he had been overwhelmed. That obsession was not directly with Roland Browne, who stands out prominently in what is recorded, or with memories of Steve Hurtley, or with other figures whom the teller recalls as companions in the consumption of bongs. Binding together the episodes of his narrative, a seam visible sometimes but hidden at other times, is the abrasive presence of Bob Cottleman, who is reported as having died in the previous calendar year. And less obviously, but more profoundly, the obsession had been with Bob's knowledge of Patience, whom my narrator had glimpsed at Bob's funeral, when for the first time since his twenties he had occupied a room that she occupied. The prior room had been the living room of Bob's house in Collingwood; the prior occasion a party marking the betrothal of Bob to the art student Jessica Faithfull, who would give birth to Bob's son and his daughter. My narrator had lived with Jessica and others in a tumbledown dwelling near the beach when he first came to Mornington, the bayside outer suburb where at the close of the narrative he resides still—albeit at a greater remove from the shoreline.

Who is this narrator, whom as he spun out his tale I had thought of as no one but I? Of course he is I, and yet he is someone whom I had not known well. There had been a time when I had seen him but had passed him by. If I had found myself standing near him in a queue, I would have refrained from greeting him. He had been an observer recording and assessing; an inner voice that I had heard but whose pointed conclusions I had not accepted; a stranger with a story to tell whom I'd dismissed as too likely to rave.

I have edited him for coherence and filled in some detail. His initial riposte shall remain unabridged.

WINTER

WINTER

I

ALL THOSE FABULOUS HEADS

LET ME JUST SAY THAT I WAS AS CONTENT AS I HAVE ever been late one evening at Carlton, in the terrace house where I lived with Roland Browne. We shared also with a guy called Greg Morrison, whom we got from an ad, but on this evening Greg did not feature. Steve Hurtley was with us, however. Bob Cottleman may have seen us at dinner, but after we had fed him he would have gone home. The house stood between two others like it, and was located about ten minutes on foot from Tin Alley, a lane that bisected the University of Melbourne, where I had enrolled in humanities subjects. It was the time of my second attempt to deserve a degree, and my last. Roland, Steve and I were in our living room, with its cream walls and its grimy, hashish-coloured carpet, and its gas-fuelled radiator, whose crumbling ceramic element would glow red but supplied little heat. We had smoked several bongs. Roland had hot-miked the room, erecting a stage microphone on a stand near his stereo and running its long lead to his tape recorder, a reel-to-reel four-track that he had carried awkwardly down the stairs from his bedroom and installed on the floor.

We had turned off the lights, but illumination reached us from a window between this room and the sunroom, a tacked-on extension that held our fridge, and from which you could see dimly our ivy-encrusted outdoor loo. Our space felt well insulated from the stark streets outside but I knew that my audience might extend beyond my two companions at Keppel Street. I remember myself as blissfully insensitive to that possibility, telling the other two whatever I wanted to tell them and however insistently. Roland and Steve smiled and laughed in the gloom. The former doubtless congratulating himself for having got this on tape, and the latter keenly supplying more bongs.

Possibly this night stands up for me, among the many nights when we did something like this, just because Roland recorded us. We replayed that recording the following evening, and parts of it more than once. Only I sounded stupidly loose. It was as though no one else had been intoxicated. Which should have bothered me, and yet that never bothered me. The others accepted that after a bong or two had gone down, I would ramble more freely than they would. It is also possible that both Roland and Steve that night had abetted more than usual my holding forth. Not that the mere fact of my having occupied the floor, metaphorically, for so long was in itself memorable or connected with pleasure of unusual depth. What appeals to me, if I have to think about times when I might have felt better, is the lightness of those few hours. It was as though a heavy burden had slipped from my shoulders: the proverbial millstone had cracked and slid from my neck to the chocolate-brown carpet, where it had crumbled into smaller fragments and vanished.

AND SO LET ME take stock. I still have a house, even if it feels a bit mean sometimes and stands on the wrong side of the highway, in _____ Place, among people who got here later than I did and who could not afford a place—pun intended—in the original settlement on the beach side. None of my neighbours has known this town for longer than I have known it. I am still getting paid, although for how long that will last I have no idea. Three months initially. I suppose I could take my long-service leave. Perhaps they are thinking that this way, if they can argue that they have helped me for long enough, they can rid themselves of me without paying redundancy. Do I care? I am not sure how much I care. I owe on my mortgage only $83,000, which I repay at $930 a month. My mean little house is worth $400,000. I can afford cigarettes, and I can still afford booze. I was better located before, when I was in Haig Street with Marge, from where we could walk to the bay with less difficulty than most people can walk to the shops. But you move on and you move. Should I have bought somewhere nearer the office? Got a small flat in Beaumaris or Sandringham? With a garage? I did not want to move so far. It would have felt like defeat.

When Marjorie left, she took our Peugeot, and so I got a Corolla and kept the Ducati. I did not want to sell the Ducati that I had ridden with Marge, not so much for what Marge had meant to me but for what the Ducati had meant to me. Things had been okay with Marge, I can acknowledge. Why we split, I do not know. And then again, I do know. We split because she was not happy. And she was not happy because I was not happy. I knew I was not, even then. But was it, so much, that I had not been happy with whom she had been for me? I do not know how much of my restlessness grew from dissatisfaction. Marge moved away. I moved to here. On the wrong side of the tracks, so to speak. But still Mornington. I can walk to the beach, if I have an extra half-hour. A long way when it is hot. But worth doing, even in summer, just to remind myself that this is something I do. I suppose I am attached to this old-fashioned town. Even to the Peninsula. I never minded the commute to Moorabbin. More often than not I would take the beach road. Less than an hour, and it was always a good hour. It helped that I did not have to arrive there till ten.

Mr O Winds Back the Clock

I AM TO REFLECT upon good times, and not bad times. I get it. I am to reinhabit the past. I am to re-experience occasions when life had tasted sweet, and perhaps even zesty. Occasions where I was having a very nice time doing something, and when I might have wanted to do that sort of thing more. Have there been moments when I have feared that life might be too short? If these were infrequent, then surely they would stand out.

Bob Cottleman has been on my mind lately, and for obvious reasons. You realise that someone you knew has made an end to his life and you wonder for how long he had been barely clinging to life. Not that I had asked myself that about Bob until recently. Bob had seemed to be doing so well. He had just about everything, I believed until recently. Plenty of money, as nearly as I could judge. A profession that people respected, and he had done well in that. An accomplished and beautiful wife. Two fine children, a girl and a boy, and a great place to live. Bob was set, as my father used to point out to me about this former schoolmate or that one, having heard a scrap of laudatory gossip after mass. I might recognise a former classmate if I encountered him in the street but no one would phone me and tell me that one of that number had died. My father might mention such an event when I visited, if he had heard about it from a fellow parishioner.

I am no longer certain that my father attends the church weekly. I know that the taint of scandal has repulsed him. He has developed some scepticism about what observances God could require. I believe he has doubts about my uncle, but I hold that belief mainly because Brother Ged has stopped coming for Christmas, and because no one has explained that he is no longer welcome, or that he is presiding over something more significant at the rural centre where he resides. I do not miss his earnest expressions of his devotion to God. I do not know that my father accused him of sex crimes. Probably what my father accused was the church. Which his brother defended. And on which they could not see eye to eye. Which meant that Gordon would no longer humour Ged.

But if Gordon had been told after church about Bob, in the early days after I became a sub-editor, he would have relayed to me that Bob too was set. Unlike me. Bob was making a lot of money, which was the main thing, and he had bought a nice house in town. He had married, again unlike me. And unlike my sister, who will stay at Heidelberg in the old house for life or until Charles and I force her out. At least my brother got away, like I did. Charles married. Charles has children. Unlike Charles, Bob had a degree, and Bob was a professional. All these things that my father thinks I should have, since he thinks I am brighter than Charles, and since he would deny that I might be less bright than Bob. And yet, as I look back at the Bob whom I knew, not so much lately but quite well in my twenties, I wonder whether Bob had been clinging to life like someone might cling to a cliff-top with his fingertips when the rest of him has slipped over the edge. To stay alive is hard work, and you can feel yourself sliding. Why not just let go and be done with it.

"DO YOU REMEMBER THAT time when you bought all those fabulous heads? And you wouldn't even say why you wanted them?" I should have asked that of Bob. I could have reminded him that he had looked like a fool. I might have said to him that everyone present had known why he wanted that wondrous parcel of contraband. That we knew him to be a lonely, miserly arsehole. That we knew he had wanted to buy our company with his dope. That we knew he was a mummy's boy and had to be in control. That I had enjoyed every second of his torturous obfuscating across Roland's dining table at Abbotsford, after he had taken a tiny step out of his superior zone and had sought to behave like a person who deserved to have pals. Even if he still had to have the best something. I could have insisted to Bob that it was long past time we exhumed these events and examined them.

And how far would I have got with that? I would have got nowhere. Bob would have deflected my opening. He would have spoken over me, so as to drown out my telling. And he would have justified loudly, at whatever length was required to accomplish my silence, the extended defending he had undertaken back then. "If someone else had bought it, and no matter how good it had been, do you think I would have been sitting there demanding they sell me some? And then in the end, when I was the one who missed out, *nobody cared*." Bob would have claimed he had every right to be distressed about the events of that evening, and he would have taken pains to construct for me an ironic moral: that in conspiring to deprive him of his satisfaction, we had all hurt ourselves more than him. Do I miss Bob? I do not. It must be ten years since I saw Bob. Is life better without Bob? It is the same.

MY NEIGHBOUR ON THE southern side, Jack—Jack Russell, I name him—looks at me accusingly across our low dividing wall when he comes home from work of an evening. Parking his black Ford with its lift kit and chunky tyres, RANGER embossed on the tailgate, ladders and cables stowed on the tray. He has lived here eight months. He has invited me to a noisy barbecue, a big bonfire event with beery blokes and other young families like his, or so I could guess from the banter and laughter that poured over the fence. I had told him they could make as much noise as they liked. "Taking it easy, Mr Cullen?" It will be only at times when I am sitting and smoking, with a drink, on the porch, looking out at my front yard, where the grass once again needs a mow but is too wet to mow. Am I taking it easy? It must look like I am taking it easy. Jack probably wishes that he could sit here like me. But maybe he thinks he might be well placed for looking at me over his sharp little nose, with his head tilted back a degree or two, blond curls swaying and jeering in the chill evening breeze, given that clearly I have not been out making money. Which of course is the First Commandment for our secular age: 1. *Thou shalt make money.* So that thou can keep the Second Commandment: 2. *Thou shalt not burden thy neighbour by drawing openly upon the proceeds of thy neighbour's taxes.* Jack probably wonders whether my ease is self-funded. Never mind that he labours each day wiring the nursing home 500 yards up the road that has sprouted and grown. And that will earn half its income from subsidies. Am I taking it easy? No Jack, I am fifty and very uneasy.

I am wondering whether I could live on unemployment relief, which Jack might think I am doing already. I imagine I could, should my savings grow thin. I have been there before. Telling lies to the government, repulsive in prospect, did not feel so repellent when confronted in practice. I do not want to go back to my job. And I do not know what else I could do. People like me do not get rehired. And the headlines in newspapers mean less and less. No one gets how sub-editors work. Our special sauce is too subtle. But if I am to be honest, what we called with affection *the dole* scares me these days. Newstart, in the insulting doublespeak that we used to smell instantly but no longer notice. As if there were nothing to life but a job. It was Roland who helped me confront my resistance to reporting a search for paid work that I had not conducted. "I just write that I looked in the paper," he told me at Keppel Street. It had shocked me that a statement so unspecific could satisfy the cold bureaucrats whom I imagined as scrutinising fortnightly my application for a cheque. But it had satisfied them in his case, and it would suffice in mine. The Unemployment Benefit sustained me for well over a year, paying my rent—fifteen dollars a week, as I recall it—and covering also household bills, food and some booze. It was the mid-1980s, when you could get four litres of wine for four dollars. The scheme's description in those days was plainer but even then doublespeak. I was not unemployed. I had plenty to do. As I thought of it then, I was just unempaid.

I AM EXAMINING AN imaginary image of the house on Queen Street that I moved to when I came down here in 1983. A white picket front fence that was overdue for a repaint, and showing plenty of splintery driftwood grey with the white. A cream weatherboard facade in better shape and with a maroon iron pitched roof and a double frontage and half a front veranda, a veranda that ended at the front room on the left as you faced it from the street, which pushed into the front yard past the door.

That house is long gone, replaced with something grander and much more sturdy in brick. I have been reminded recently, by Jessica Faithfull, of a cartoon series that we conceived of when we lived behind that white-and-grey fence. We had fancied that we might submit strips to the very paper that I ended up subbing on. Jessica's boyfriend, Sandy, drawing—he could draw really well, and I would bet he has done nothing with that—and Jessica helping with captions and moral support. A role reversal for those two that they did not sustain. A strip character ponders lazily, while lying in state as the morning progresses, upon the advantages that he enjoys from not working for pay. I had dreamed this up in that house with those two and the patriarch, as we thought of him, Zoom. One of the best things about living on the dole was—the punch line of that particular strip: "You can't go any lower." A punchline decorated with an asterisk, which referenced a note at the foot of the frame: "*Unless you get kicked off the dole." We never submitted the strips. We told ourselves that the paper would never run something so wicked. The dole was a moral burden, and getting kicked off was always a worry. You could indeed go lower. We had fallbacks. I could have petitioned my father. But it had been good on the dole. We had carried the moral burden together, Jessica and Sandy and I, and when we carried it together it had felt very light. We were on the dole together, and living the dream. None of us had dreamed about getting a job. Jessica is living her dream still, in so far as I understand what she dreamed of. With help, of course—and this fact tastes bitter—from Bob.

I CAN PICTURE MYSELF standing on Roland's veranda, on a crisp Friday night in 1984, outside the puce-painted front door of his renter at Abbotsford. I believe that the season was autumn. It was Roland who answered my knock. He looked very pleased with himself, his delicate features contorted artlessly into the broad grin that he bore, as though it were a tic that afflicted him, whenever he believed he had done something impressive.

"Hi!" he said. "We've just got back."

"Success?"

"Yeah."

He led me down his hallway to the living area at the rear of his house. Waiting for us on Debbie's sturdy steel-framed dining chairs were Steve Hurtley and, I was surprised to see, Bob. Also seated at the white Formica-topped dining table was Stanley Jones, a former schoolmate of Roland's who lived nearby in Collingwood. Like Bob, Stanley was still at Melbourne University. I was not impressed by his candidature for a doctoral degree so much as by his securing of a grant to exploit it, which paid him more than I earned from my part-time job then with the Totalisator Agency Board—a call-centre role that had seemed to me lucrative.

"Have a look at *this*!" Bob, eyes wide, turning to engage me from his seat at the hall end of the table. He held open for my inspection a small plastic bag that I remember for its resealable mouth—an innovation I had not seen before.

I took the vacant chair next to Bob and accepted the bag. It was obvious what had got Bob so excited. The bag was full of big cannabis heads, spiky bushes shaped like short, fat, cigars. Some were tinted a poisonous purple. How did they smell? Perhaps expecting the hay-like, sour flavour of dried grass to dominate, I met instead the sweet reek of hashish.

"Smells pretty good!"

"Just look at them!" Bob exhorted me.

Roland and Steve had shared liberally in recent weeks a big haul from our source for this bag, a woman named Jodi who shared a house with Bob's sister. We had appreciated its components as potent, but this batch looked venomous.

"Well," Roland said, having resumed his place to my right. "Will we have a bong?"

Bob, looking alarmed, declared: "We need to weigh it!"

"We won't smoke this," Roland said. "I've got some of the last deal left."

"I think it would be better if we weighed this out before you guys lose control of your mental capacities," Bob said.

"It won't be a problem," Steve, gruff and dismissive, assured him from the opposite end of the table.

"I think we should weigh it out first," Bob said.

Roland looked at Bob and shook his head.

"It won't make any difference." He looked in turn at his other guests. "Who wants first bong?"

IT IS A VERY long time since I last composed dialogue. Have I recorded accurately the remarks that each of us made, and that we made such a long time ago? Of course I have not. I remember almost nothing of the evening. Bob had been doing a placement at St Vincent's Hospital, and was nearing the end of his training—I am sure about that. He had resided for a few months in nearby Fitzroy, having relocated from his mother's place at ritzy South Yarra, occupying a well-kept terrace house leased by two women who had advertised their best room. It had been the front room upstairs, with access via French-style double doors to a full-length balcony from which you could look out over Grieve Street. In theory, it was a score—and I assumed that Bob had convinced his mother, rebutting forcefully her every objection, that it would be good for her if she stumped up his rent. In practice, I do not think Bob had found the house very warm. The Churchmouse and the Feminazi, as he nicknamed his co-residents almost immediately, did not seem to be Bob's sort of people. The Churchmouse was a practising Catholic, he soon revealed to me sneeringly, complaining also that she rarely emerged from her bedroom. The Nazi I had met briefly, and while she was slim and quite beautiful—a major attraction for Bob, I assumed—it seemed plain from her Doc Martens boots and the direct way in which she met my appreciative stare that she was mistress of the house, and much less manipulable than Bob's mum. Bob would have wanted to show her that he had powerful friends on his side. Or at least that he had friends. I had visited him only once since he had taken up residence there. I wondered whether he had received other guests, or had found society mainly elsewhere—just as he had done when he had lived with his mother.

He did not respond immediately, on that Friday at Abbotsford, to the dismissing of his demand that we allocate the alluring contents of the bag I still held. I like to think of Bob as shrinking from Roland's rebuff, withdrawing in spirit from his place at the table. He grabbed the bag back from me and lowered his face to its open mouth, as I had just done, perhaps immersing himself for the first time in its pungency. He straightened himself and withdrew a large and richly coloured bud, holding it before his face and inspecting it. It was as though he were revering a relic whose value only he recognised.

"I'll have it," Steve said, taking up Roland's invitation that someone have a bong.

Roland passed Steve the pipe, and Steve smoked it.

Bob replaced in its bag the bud he had been admiring, and made a resolute return to the fray. "Come on," he demanded. "let's get this stuff weighed out before you guys get too stoned and decide you can't be bothered. Where are the scales?"

With a sigh, Roland directed Bob to a cupboard in the kitchen. He also repacked the bong, and passed it to me. I had brought beers, which I had offered around.

Bob returned to the table, depositing on it an elaborate mechanical balance. He assessed it with his usual intensity.

"Okay," he said, "How much did you all want?"

"I want as much as I can get," Steve said, indicating reverence in his own way. His audacity drew my attention as I began to accommodate the effects of my draught. I can almost see Steve as he sat there, even if I am compiling a montage from the many occasions when he had commanded the table from his favourite end, near the back door. I see his crinkly hair, coloured a dog-like dirty brown, and shorn now to earlobe length, above a wiry full beard, contrasting crisply with the blue wall in the stark light from Roland's overhead fluorescent tube. Was Steve wearing an earring? He had started his job at the bank: I am certain of that. A cheeky smile had begun to form on his face, and he had sought to hide its formation from Bob, turning his head and looking over his right shoulder towards the door out to the rear veranda and yard.

"How much did you order?" Bob asked, headmaster-stern all of a sudden.

"I ordered forty bucks," Steve said, composing himself. "But if I can get more, I'll have it."

"We just got as much as everybody ordered," Bob said.

Steve shrugged: "I'll have my forty bucks, then. How much did *you* order?" he asked me.

"Ten bucks." At that time I was supplied freely by Zoom, who had sown cannabis with tomatoes behind our big shed at Queen Street.

"Ten bucks!" Steve gave a laugh. "Who's got all the rest?" He looked at Stanley, alone on the window side of the table, opposite Roland.

"Not me," Stanley said, his broad face guileless behind gold-rimmed spectacles. "Twenty bucks."

Bob had withdrawn again, focusing narrowly on the scales.

Roland passed Stanley the bong. He said to Steve: "Bob's getting two hundred dollars' worth."

From the silence that followed, Roland extended his explanation, addressing Stanley and me also: "It was his idea really. I just came in to make up the ounce. But I really only wanted to get fifty bucks' worth, so I asked you guys whether you wanted any."

Bob, making fine adjustments to how much material he had on the scales, said without looking up: "If you want more, why don't you go in for an ounce on your own?"

Stanley attended carefully to his bong.

Steve exclaimed finally: "Two hundred bucks!" He released a chuckle. "Whoa! What are you going to do with it?"

"What do you reckon I'm going to do with it?" Bob retorted. "I'm going to smoke it!"

"Speaking of which..." Roland said. He looked at Bob. "Do you want a bong?"

"No," Bob said.

"Do you want half a bong?"

"No. Fuck you. Let's weigh this up." He looked again down the table at Steve. "You want forty bucks' worth."

WHAT WORK DID YOU *do before you did this newspaper work? What led you into this work? Did you do a cadetship? Did you prefer to work as a reporter?* No, Ms Felicity, I never was a cadet, or a reporter. At one time I reported my friends' observations, but that was hardly reporting. It was inventing as much as reporting. What I did, Ms Felicity, if you must know, amounted mainly to my composing imaginary conversations, conversations that purportedly I had remembered.

2

IF SOME'S GOOD, MORE'S BETTER

Sometimes it helps to get away. And so I have rented a room with a view, in Khancoban. This is the first time I have stayed here in winter. In spring and autumn it has been a handy stopover at the northwest foot of the forbidding Snowy Mountains, a town near enough to Melbourne to be reached in a day. This time, however, I have taken two days, staying the first night near the east coast at Bruthen, at the southern end of the Omeo Highway, where entrancement begins for a motorcyclist who likes lots of bends. From Bruthen you can skirt the Victorian Alps on small roads that are mostly sealed, meandering north through tiny Mitta Mitta, before turning east again, near Tallangatta. The stop at Bruthen has given me time, allowing me to substitute a much more pleasant route east alongside the Murray River for the droning Murray Valley Highway. I will hole up here for a few nights, and then turn and head home.

It is all but impossible to describe how soothing has been the steady pulsing of my Ducati as it draws me past moist stock in paddocks and battened-down rural towns. The road takes your mind off your troubles, especially when the air is cold. It has been cold but I have been warm, under cosy clothing in multiple layers. It is as though my soul traverses the world in a bath.

It comes to me that I might have arrived at this place with Bob Cottleman, if Bob had learned to ride better. Bob did not like to ride his motorbike on roads that were wet. He used to worry that its wheels would slip out from beneath him. I liked to look at that hazard as part of the mystery, something to work on. Bob would lecture me on the mechanics of the rubber-bitumen interface, as he labelled the place where your tyre met the road. If the bitumen were wet, the coefficient of friction fell sharply as you started to skid, denying you every hope of recovery. Bob would spell this out for me in painstaking detail, apparently exasperated that I privileged my experience over his analysis. It made no sense to take such a risk, he would claim, when you would also be cold and uncomfortable.

As you age, friends you rode with mostly become mere friends, or past friends. My first road companion, Jamie Danielson, ceased to ride in his twenties, when he moved overseas. Jamie had met Bob through the university motorcycle club, and about the same time I met Bob through the club. In his motorcycling Bob was a dilettante, if a well-mounted dilettante—which made things worse in a way. I might easily have shunned him. When he rolled into the car park off Tin Alley for his first run with us, his bike, a big and costly BMW that looked new or near-new, attracted attention as much for its bright yellow learner plates. The tall black figure of Bob added context, his leather riding suit having been tailored in the inconvenient one-piece style favoured by racers. It had been impossible to guess, even after Bob had removed his helmet and revealed his youth and black plaits, whether this was indeed a racer, newly licensed for public roads, or an unwisely ambitious novice who was exceptionally solicitous of his skin. Bob, confirming most of the latter characterisation, defended his choices: BMWs very rarely broke down, and one-piece leathers were best if you crashed. No one argued. Within twelve months Bob had sold that bike, and he never replaced it.

It was good to see Jamie in November, at the cremation for Bob, and better that he repaired afterwards to Roland's, where he partook in a smoke. For an hour or two, that was just like old times. We even had bongs. We spoke then of Bob's riding. Jamie was typically straight in his assessment for Roland, who had known Bob well but not at all as a motorcyclist. "Having purchased the bike he had worked out was best—as in the most expensive, with the least maintenance—Bob had so much invested that he couldn't risk learning to ride it. But I think he rode mainly for show. He was too frightened of falling off it to really enjoy it. He was like that a lot, as I see it."

"He was into his drugs, though," Roland revealed, defending, by emphasising Bob's sense of adventure, his one-time partner in the dissection of frogs. "In a way that I don't think you guys realised. At least in the early days. He was sneaky about it, but he was definitely interested. More than you were," he said, nodding to me in that meaning way of his that left no one in doubt that I in particular was the object of his remark. "In a different way from how any of us were. Not that we were all the same anyway. I'm not talking about now. I don't know about now. Well, not now, but recently, obviously."

"You don't know people, do you," Jamie said, in a musing but subtly patronising tone that reminded me of how direct he had been even in his twenties. And that I understood I had missed, while wondering whether he too was referring to me. To this acquaintance whom he had seen about every five years, on his trips back from England. He might have pondered upon what had become of me. Sub-editing on my suburbans. Living resignedly with Marge. Jamie liked Marge. But he had liked all my women. Or more precisely, both of my women. Or more precisely still, I suspect now, he liked Marge.

"Bob was weird on the bike." And Jamie smiled to himself. "I just couldn't believe how slow he was. And he never really got any more competent. It wasn't that he didn't want to ride fast. And he wasn't that slow—there would have been people slower, and there would be today. But he had those road-racing leathers—which just looked so out of place, on a big bike, at the pace that he rode—and I'm sure he wanted to ride in an impressive way. He just couldn't do it. He would have needed to start on a 350, probably even something smaller. And probably riding on dirt, but not necessarily. He just needed to relax, that was the main thing. To relax, and to take some more chances. Which I will admit, could have meant crashing. And really, that was the problem." Jamie had been a racer, on dirt tracks, in his teens, his father having been sympathetic, and so he knew about crashing. A crash rarely threatens your life or your limbs. The part of your body that a crash threatens most is your skin. But chiefly, a crash threatens your bike. Although the skin damage does hurt a lot, even in leathers. I do not like to talk about crashing. I do not like to write about crashing. The table here that I am typing on has been constructed from wood, and—there—my naked finger just touched it.

I REMEMBER, IN GENERAL, how my smoking with Roland and Steve would get started at Keppel Street. The two of them would have started already. They may have had a bong each but felt bored, perhaps wondering why their smoking together seemed less entertaining than it had been when they met. I think they saw me as fresh clay, an unshaped object that could be moulded. It would engage them even to attempt to draw me into having a bong. I did not like Keppel Street much while I lived there. I had hoped for more there. I had not seen Roland's sessions with Steve as exciting. I had joined those sessions, but I had not joined them always. It was so common as to have become a cliche among us that I resisted entreaties that I join in their smoking. Unlike Roland, I had a job. Like Steve, I was studying. I was passing, in fact. For a time it delighted me that at last I was passing, in some subjects in which I enrolled.

Things hide unnoticed in your mind, and then emerge as though from behind a curtain when you had forgotten even that there might be a curtain. I am thinking about a period after I started sub-editing—this would have been a few years in, and long after Keppel Street. I would wake from a dream. I would have fallen asleep in the lounge room, on the green fabric sofa that Marge and I bought after we moved into Haig Street. We had a gas heater—wonderfully bigger and warmer than the tiny unit at Keppel Street—and this dream would have drawn itself to my attention in a cold part of the year. Marge would have closed all the doors, to keep in the heat, and the rising level of carbon dioxide in the room would have made me drowsy. Perhaps Marge had abandoned me for bed after we had smoked a joint, leaving me to half-watch the television and drink a little more wine. On at least two occasions I awoke with a start, believing that my hallucination had been recollection and expecting to see my father standing scowling before me. I had been telling him things. "I've got a great job now," I had been saying, or something like that. "I really like it. And I am quite well paid. I think I am one of the better subs on the desk, now that I have had a fair bit of practice. I like my headlines, and I think the reporters quite like what I do. I think they know that I improve what they write. And I pick up some errors too." And then as I said that, chirruping winningly to my father in the dream, it would occur to me that I had failed to register an error. I could not recall just what was the error, but my failing to fix it had been a grievous mistake. Perhaps I had neglected to notice that a prominent person's name had been misspelled, and I had followed the reporter's spelling when reproducing the name in the headline. And perhaps the misspelling had slipped past the check sub-editor and had appeared in the paper. Perhaps it was on the front page, in big, bold print above a photo on the glossy white cover. Perhaps the error had been yet more serious. My dream focused not on the nature of the error but on my feeling in connection with the error. It was as though I deserved every censure. I could not show my face at the office. Since I had learned of the error, at first from the glances of other subs and then verbally from the chief sub, someone curt and insulting, I had taken leave, inadvertently, by discovering myself to be so ill that I could no longer pass my front door at the appropriate time in the morning. I had not returned to work. It was not clear that I would return to work. And in chattering to my father about how good my job was, I had overlooked this very relevant fact.

Each time when I awoke from the dream it would be as though I had been surprised by a sudden and powerful onset of nausea. I did not have a good job at all. Things were not going well. Things had turned out just as my father had said they would: badly. The success that I invited him to share in had been an illusion that I had attached to myself. Upon awakening I would be disoriented, wondering where I was and why there. I would seek to reacquaint myself with the details of my career-ending error. And as I did so, reflecting upon my most recent day at work, finding no memory of a damaging mistake, realising that the mistake must have preceded that day, and then noting that after all I must have returned to work, it would become plain to me that I had made no such error. I still had my job. An error of that kind would not be, in any case, a career blocker. I could boast to my father after all, if an occasion arose when I thought he might hear that boast from me.

IT IS AN ADVANTAGE of my staying here that I would be embarrassed to begin drinking early. I could of course concoct and consume a drink in my room, but then I would be embarrassed to step out of my room. I drink and smoke in the afternoon.

Almost everybody else is here for a day on the slopes. They all get up in the dark, breakfast in the dining room, and make their way noisily to the early bus, which gets them out to Thredbo or Perisher in time to maximise the value of a day-pass on the tows.

So my hostess tells me. "You were lucky we had that room. Don't you want to go out? You can hire skis." I would rather sit here by a window and drink the cups of chocolate that she brings me hot from the bar. "Another? Let me know when you want breakfast." It lifts me that she is solicitous of me. I am enjoying sitting here before my computer, which is new and small enough to carry on the bike. Why bring a computer? Because I have found this exercise to be soothing. I will admit that I even find it engaging. I can acknowledge that as I contemplated taking this trip, I imagined myself lingering at this very table, most guests having gone out for the day, and composing my notes to myself. As I told Ms Felicity, there was a previous period, deep in the past, when I did something daily that was rather like this.

Over much of that period, which began when I first came down to Queen Street, I would daydream that I had rolled up a joint for my father. Every now and again, Gordon and I would drink beers together, as we still do at Christmas. He has never been much of a drinker, but his pouring us beers before lunch at Christmas and sitting with me as we drink them still warms me. I never see him drink like that with Charles. Of course Tessa, like my mother, does not enjoy beer. I used to imagine my proposing to Gordon that he smoke a joint, perhaps as we partook of a second beer after lunch. I would imagine that he might have been curious. I would imagine that we had discussed this before. I knew that when he was young he had smoked cigarettes, and so he would know how to smoke. I could imagine him saying: "This doesn't seem to be doing much." In the conciliatory and curious tone that rarely but sometimes he would adopt when I sat alongside him. And then I could imagine his getting voluble. Telling me about something he had done with my mum. Or that he had wanted to do with my mum. Or that he had wanted to do on his own. Perhaps even something that he had wanted to do with me. We might have, for example, gone riding together. But he would never climb on to a bike that I rode. "Do you know," he might have said to me, "your mum and I always thought you were someone who would be very special. We really don't mind that you've done what you've done. We don't mind that you're doing what you are doing. You seem to have some good friends. It's good that you keep your head above water, that you can find funds to live on, and at the bottom of it, we don't care much how you do it. You could come and work for me if you wanted to, but I can see you don't want to. It can be slow at the factory. I like it, and I think it has brought us good fortune. I never knew where I wanted to go. I just needed some money. I think all of us, in those days, needed money. Except perhaps for the toffs. We'll come into a bit of money when your mum's mother and father pass on. And I've got a bit saved. You'll be okay, when we go. You don't need to worry much. You should do what you want to do. We thought you might like the engineering. We thought you had a great brain for numbers. But if it wasn't that way, we don't care. You do what pleases you. You can do what you want. Just relax, and everything will work out. You know what, I am saying a lot. Loose lips sink ships. Is that what this stuff does? I think it's begun to wear off."

HAD BOB COTTLEMAN LOOKED forward to showing me, one day, the creative non-fiction that he wrote about me? A little bomb there with which he could punish me, should the chance arise for him. He would have been conflicted because of his vanity. He would have been saving himself for something more devastating. Something more successful—maybe something that I would see only after it were published widely. And perhaps I would have deserved nothing less. Did Bob nurse his wounds from me over the course of his life, exposing himself to me and feeling pain from my deflating arrows? Even if I loosed those arrows reflexively more than deliberately.

When I was at Queen Street, it would be late in the week, and well after dinner, when Bob rang the bicycle bell affixed beside our front door. Only sometimes would he phone in advance, preferring simply to assume that as usual I would be celebrating the day's end at home, and would put him up. He would defer respectfully to Zoom, would flirt mildly with Jessica, and would adopt a confiding tone when engaging with Sandy. I suspect he saw none of my housemates as a competitor for him when we conversed, and about this he was right, as the talents of each were rooted less in logic than in intuition, and none viewed rational argument as an appealing field of combat. Much of what they saw as obvious, Bob would have denied was discernible. His disputations with me they would watch with amusement, in Jessica's case accompanied by discreet rolls of the eye. Bob would see that his assertions were alienating his hosts and would retreat from making them, relying on jokes or punning turns of phrase, or asking one or the other to expand on elements of their artistic practices. He would soften us up by supplying reliably two bottles of red wine, and always more expensive wine than we allowed ourselves. It was only after the others had retired to bed that Bob would renew our affray over whatever claim of his I had been so presumptuous as to contest.

This would have been about the time when he bought his big dope deal. My participating then in our hazing of him had not affected his interest in seeking me out. On one night he brought a bud down to Mornington, a bud that must have come from that deal, where he added parts of it sparingly but effectually to our joints, declining offers that he smoke some himself. I recall my showing to him the first of my attempts to capture Roland in prose, which I had titled *The Ethics of Roland*. My co-residents had retired, but as usual we lingered. Bob's first comment on that composition echoes still, and he delivered it before he had got to the end. "There's a character here who is obviously me. Why do you say that I'm anxious?"

It had been late, and we had been in the lounge room at Queen Street—a square box between my writing room and the kitchen.

Pale blue walls, and grey carpet. An ancient, flowers-on-khaki fabric sofa that Zoom had found at a garage sale. Two coffee-coloured beanbags that Jessica and Sandy had contributed, which commonly we supplemented with director's chairs from the dining room. Again a gas radiant heater, big and fan-forced but not very hot. A bolted-together pine bookshelf, unpainted, that I had put there, about my only piece of furniture apart from what I had in my bedroom. Zoom's valve-modulated stereo amplifier and a high-end turntable he had brought back from London, both perched on maroon plastic milk crates. We would have cut the volume to a hoarse hiss so as not to wake anybody. Likely I had my eye on the last of Bob's wine.

I had forgotten that Bob played a peripheral but decisive role in my account of Roland and his behaviour at Keppel Street.

"'You know what he's like ... couldn't do it at his mother's place—*because of the smell*—so he brought it here!'" The first-person narrator, the I of the story, had quoted Roland as reporting this about Bob. "Thanks for the compliments. What *am* I like?"

"I'm sorry about that stuff. I forgot it was in there."

"'Dumpy and motherly, studying teaching,'" Bob quoted, having flicked back through the typewritten pages. "Debbie's going to love you for that one. At least you changed her job."

"She doesn't have to see it."

"What's the point of this, then?"

"I think of it as a kind of history," I told him. As I did think of it. "A study that preserves something, maybe something small, but something that was true of that time and that place. There are bits of that house that I miss. Not that I don't like it here—it's great down here. And it's not as though that house was that special—as you well remember. And yet there was something special about it. Which I wanted to capture. Although I don't think I've succeeded that well. Do you think Roland will ever write a hit song?"

"How would I know," Bob said. He had lost faith in Roland the would-be rock hero, just as I had begun to lose faith in Roland.

He read silently through the rest of the manuscript, before delivering judgment.

"The stuff about sealing the guitar, which is at the core of events here, is impossibly obscure. Nobody tries to lacquer the inside of an acoustic guitar. Especially nobody who's got a Maton or anything nice like that. You can't think I'm that anal and stupid. As for Roland putting cigarette butts in one ... he's got to get them past the strings for starters. Or had I taken the strings off? In which case he would have known the guitar was mine. And even then, would a smouldering butt have set it on fire, even if the lacquer was wet? Roland says Greg locked a cat in his room when he was over with Debbie. But three days isn't that long. A cat can go without a piss for three days. And then I steal Greg's guitar. However you want to muddy it up with competing insurance claims or whatever, that's effectively what I have done. That's libel. I would never do that. I don't even think Roland would, no matter how much he thought Greg was a hypocrite and therefore deserved it. He would talk about it, but I don't think he'd do it. And I can't believe you think he'd do it. And this is hardly a history. It's mainly all bull.

"Basically all that happened was, Roland was a bit messy around the house, as you know, and Greg didn't like that. And so Roland didn't like Greg. And so when you went away on that big trip with Jamie, Roland stayed over at Debbie's. And then he and Debbie took that house together at Abbotsford. Say what you want about Debbie, but I think he feels better off living with her than when he was living in squalor with you."

Or something like that. Bob in his typically critical style. It is not as though I remember all of his words. What I remember most is how incensed he became. And also, that he had encouraged me strenuously to move in with Roland to that very house. Which was not squalid. It was just a bit old.

I know I made other attempts at Queen Street to preserve in prose my previous household. At one time I elaborated upon an account, extracted from Bob, of how Roland had become friendly with Steve Hurtley. I left that manuscript with Roland, who liked it and told Steve about it, and who allowed Steve to abscond with it. Steve and Roland had been much more drawn to its portrait of their companionship than I had expected. Steve in particular seemed fascinated to have experienced himself as arising in facsimile from the typewritten page. He was much more accepting than Bob had been of his image as I had constructed it.

The manuscript returned eventually. And it was transmitted to me in a memorable way. Good times. Was the repatriating of the Steve story one of the best times? I have thought so. And yet when I review the events of those hours in which it reappeared, it is as though I am attempting to restore a delusion.

IT HAS RAINED ALL day and so I have stopped at Bright, at the base of the Victorian Alps. A town that feels small and pretty and moody. Wet roads are still scenic but they are not as much fun on a bike. The turns today have been mainly sweeping, which makes it easier to relax in the rain than when they are slower. The Murray River Road from Jingellic almost to Granya was majestic. But I tiptoed over the fabulous Granya Gap road, for much of it following a white hatchback that I did not attempt to overtake. And then the Kiewa Valley Highway was as beautiful in the winter drizzle as it is in every other season but high summer, when the paddocks alongside it turn grey. I do not want to go home, and there is no good reason why I am going home. Except perhaps that my house is abandoned. Except perhaps that I was tired of eating alone publicly in the dining room, notwithstanding the flow of kindly remarks from my plump hostess. Except that my next meeting with Ms Felicity is approaching on Tuesday. Except that I have remembered some things.

It has seemed implausible that on the evening of his big buy at Abbotsford, Bob had not foreseen how uncomfortable he would become with the posture that he had adopted. It is only now that I have focused more attentively on the course of events that I can see how he had wandered into this trap. Bob had not expected that the dope he had purchased would be as good as it was. He had thought it would be much like past deals that Steve and Roland had purchased from Jodi. It might still have looked odd that Bob wanted a half-ounce or more, given that we had seen him smoke only in tiny increments. But Steve easily could have let those facts pass. Bob's proposal to Steve, that if he wanted more he could assemble orders himself for an ounce, would have looked much more straightforward. Steve could have his fill as soon as he could do what Bob had just done, which was to build a consortium of buyers with Roland. Steve had done that before. What had aggravated Steve's interest, and had led to his impertinent proposal that he get more than he ordered, was Steve's assessment of the power in those buds. None of us said so, because none of us needed to say so, but it seemed improbable that dope so enticing would be available endlessly, and at a price no higher than had secured lesser fare.

It may be that Jodi had wanted to help Bob, and had supplied him her best. Perhaps he had confessed to her the project that he had conceived of. She would not have been slow to see the advantages socially of possessing a hoard of good dope. Did Bob even reveal to her that he had wanted mainly to attract Roland, and therefore Steve? Had Bob thought that he could reform Steve—that he could lead Steve to finding more pleasure from the proceeds of a single bong than he could find in the prospect of inhaling a second? Might Bob have thought he could tease Steve, if Steve were to visit him in his big room at Grieve Street? "No! You can't have another one yet. Make this one last!"

Bob, even stoned himself, might have addressed Steve at Grieve Street in his most lordly manner. "Steve, tell me something surprising. Tell me about your life. What is your work really like? I have no idea what you actually do. Where is the interest for you? Do you feel like you are helping people, or are you just helping your employer exploit the defenceless? Does that matter to you? For me, I think one of the things about being a doctor, even just a GP, is that as a doctor you are making money but also you are helping people, and you have security and a good income as well. There really aren't many jobs that are like that. Is that something that you have ever thought to look for? Does contributing to people feature for you, or do you see a job as just a way to make money?" That could have been Bob with Steve, or with Steve and Roland, in his room with the French doors open to their balcony over the street, bongs safely hidden inside where they could not be seen from the footpath, and bong smoke drifting out into the atmosphere but untraceable from below. I could imagine Bob taking it upon himself to instruct Steve, pointing out to Steve something that he had assumed Steve would not see without coaching.

A discussion arose at the table about whether we should take up Bob's proposal and order some more. Everyone but Bob had consumed a bong.

"I could probably have a bit more," Roland said. "Who wants more?"

I believe I told him I was good for twenty bucks.

"That would help."

"I've probably got enough," Stanley said. "Well, maybe another twenty."

"I could probably go a hundred," said Steve.

"Bob?" Roland asked.

"I'm fine. Are you kidding?" Bob was still measuring out Steve's forty dollars' worth from the bag full of head.

"Just thought I'd ask," Roland said. "So we've got, maybe, twenty and twenty and a hundred, a hundred and forty. We're one-eighty short of an ounce. I've got fifty and I could probably go another seventy but I can't do one-eighty. We're over a hundred short. Anybody else? Stanley?"

If Some's Good, More's Better

Stanley declined, saying forty was plenty.

Bob handed Steve a bag that held a few good-sized buds and some bits and pieces.

"Right," he said, "Who's next?"

"I'll have mine," Stanley said.

"Whose bong is it?" Roland asked.

"It's yours!" Stanley told him. "You haven't had one yet."

Roland smoked the bong. He packed another and passed it to me.

"I think you did already have one," I remarked.

Roland thought for a moment. "It's funny," he said, "I'm having trouble working out whether this is my first bong or my second bong."

"It is your second!" Stanley yipped. "You had one after Seamus; before me. I remember now. Got you!" He laughed and looked at us with delight. "I can't remember the last time that happened!" Much more often it had been Stanley who displayed confusion when he was stoned. Usually Roland had acted to entangle him further.

"I think you're right," Roland said. He reflected for a few moments. "Just shows you how good this is." He nodded at Bob and the dope on the scale. "Imagine what *that* will be like!" He pondered again. "So it's Shamo's bong now. If he'd had his, it'd be mine now. But since I've had mine, now it's his. It's Shamo's bong."

"You're getting it!" said Stanley, still delighted with his misdirection.

I smoked the bong, and returned it.

"Stanley?" Roland asked.

"I guess so, though I have to drive."

"You'll be fine," Roland said. He passed Stanley his second bong. "You could walk from here."

"Twenty bucks, was that right?" Bob asked Stanley. "For fuck's sake, you guys, get it together! Twenty bucks … Stanley!"

Stanley exhaled a stream of smoke. "Yep, that's me. Twenty bucks." He burped up more smoke. Tonight not even Stanley was coughing, evidence that in recent weeks he had been a frequent guest.

Bob bagged a sixteenth of an ounce and handed it to Stanley.

"Your turn, Bob," Roland said.

"I don't want one," Bob said. "Who's next? Shamo. Ten bucks, was it? That's about one bud, if I can find one small enough. Or would you like bits and pieces?"

"Just get on with it," Steve urged, on my behalf.

"Well, I can see you're contributing," Bob retorted. "Do you want to weigh all this out yourself then?"

"Nah," Steve said. "I've got mine." He took the bong from Stanley. "We need more mull."

Roland pushed down the table his bag from the previous deal. Its contents looked meagre. Steve glanced instead at the small bag he had just got from Bob. "What about if we have some of this," he said.

Bob looked sharply down the table at Steve.

"Can you at least wait until I've weighed out the rest?"

"Why?" said Steve. "I've paid. This is mine. Are you worried you won't get to have any?"

"I don't want any," Bob said. "Not while I'm weighing."

"We might smoke all this while you're weighing," Steve pointed out. "At the rate you're going. And then you'd have to smoke some of your own, if you wanted some. Whoa! You can't smoke it *and* look at it."

"You can't smoke it and look at it," Roland told Bob.

"I like that!" Stanley said. "You can't smoke it and look at it. I do like that. You can't smoke it and look at it, Bob."

"That's a good point!" I expect I chimed in.

"It's a very good point," Roland said, affirming his own observation. He returned to Steve's proposal that he mull up from his fresh deal. "I'd have a bit," he said approvingly to Steve, "And then when I've got mine I'll throw some in for the next round."

"The next round!" Bob expostulated. "Are you going to just sit here and smoke all this up? Your whole share of this deal. This is almost certainly the best deal that you'll see for a while. Just look at it! And you're going to waste it."

"You can't smoke it and look at it, Bob," Stanley said, drawing chuckles from Roland and me. "You can put a bit of mine in," Stanley told Steve, sliding his bag down the table.

IT'S MY LAST NIGHT at Flemington—*come round for a steal*. Steve wrote that on a piece of paper that he pushed through the letter slot of our front door at Keppel Street. Greg Morrison found it, and expressed to me his disgust. But we left it on the living room table, so that when Roland woke up he would see it. From the raid, Roland brought back chocolate and chocolate biscuits, which he stacked in our fridge against moments of greed. I deplored Steve's breach of trust but enjoyed the biscuits. This would have been in the last months of my fifteen at Keppel Street. I do not recall why Steve was looking forward that night to his final shift, at the 7-Eleven grocery store he had operated. It is tempting to suggest that he was about to complete his degree and had accepted his bank job, and so he was preparing himself for a life of crime. But that would be to dilute the facts.

Steve had met Roland the year before, soon after both commenced three-year programs. Roland had been ejected from his Bachelor of Medicine, and had enrolled in business studies, at RMIT, in the hope of arresting his fall from grace. That hope had lasted until the mid-year exams, when Roland abandoned the course, and for the same reason that medicine had ejected him. Unable to study. Today I suspect he could have been diagnosed with attention deficit hyperactivity disorder, a susceptibility to distraction for which the cure is a pill. I too might have merited that diagnosis, even if no one accused Roland or me of hyperactivity.

What distinguished Roland and me then from Bob was mainly this: Bob was distracted from his explicit aims much less easily. But neither Roland nor I had seen things this simply at the time.

It had seemed for each of us, I believe, that very little connected our studies with the lives that we wanted to live. Perhaps the only connection was a wish to be wealthy. Our shared difficulty was to find motivation. Neither of us had known where to look for it.

When you discover yourself to be deficient in motivation, you encounter yourself as deficient in your humanity. It is as though everything that everybody had assumed about you, and that you had assumed also about yourself, had been true only partially. If we could have worked at our studies like Bob worked at his studies, we would have done so. Even Steve must have worked better than we did, during those times when he was not debauching himself at our house, for away from Keppel Street he made steady progress.

"If some is good …" he would say, as he sought to corrupt my resolve on some evening when he had visited Roland. He would refrain from completing the sentence, trailing off and squinting at me over a grin that I recollect as rendering his face cherub-like: as casting the often gruff and sometimes hectoring Steve in the image of an innocent. If Roland did not chime in immediately, Steve would suspend his grin briefly so as to turn upon his partner in excess a prompting gaze.

"… More's better!" Roland, prompted, would exclaim, completing the duo's ironic mantra and immediately reiterating it in full: "If some's good, more's better—remember that! If some's good, more's better."

The two would invoke earnestly this dubious premise as they encouraged me to draw down a second bong or perhaps a third. I might have returned from an evening shift at my TAB job, and might have made myself a bedtime cup of tea. I might even have opened a stubby of beer. On my mind might have been a class the next day, for which I had planned to prepare in the morning. An early start would have been the plan's key component. Steve and Roland would have been seated in front of the heater, on the chrome and crimson lounge chairs Steve had stolen for us from RMIT. The question was often whether to sleep or to settle down on a third chair with that pair, reeled in by their imploring of me to have just one bong.

"Just have one," Roland would propose, his tone inviting and fatherly, as though he were encouraging me to taste a novel but ugly confection.

"You could have at least *one*," Steve would tell me, as though he were inviting me to purchase a discounted sweet from a charity.

"You'll feel better after one," Roland would add, as though my resistance were a sign of recalcitrance rather than prudence.

"This one's yours," Steve would tell me, proceeding to pack the cone with the mull of the moment.

"Have this one, and then if you decide you don't want another one you will know that you really don't," Roland would advise me. "You'll be in a better place to make a decision."

"You have probably had a big day," Steve might say in his gravelly voice, his concern all the warmer for its contrast with his usual scepticism. "You deserve this."

"Yes!" Roland would exclaim. "You have *earned* this!"

"It's yours," Steve would say. "I've packed this just for you."

"You should have it," Roland would enjoin me. "It would be rude to refuse."

"Not *rude*," Steve might say. "More like foolish."

"You would be *foolish* to refuse," Roland would correct himself. "You would be missing out on a great opportunity."

And so it would go. It was never easy to resist the conclusion that they were right.

If Bob too had visited Roland that day, he would have gone home by this point—or he would be about to go home.

It would be very unusual that Bob had a bong, even if I did once see him have one, sipping away at it as though he were tasting for the first time, through a straw, an exotic and expensive cocktail that he feared was too potent. Should the others begin to smoke when he stayed late on a weekend, Bob liked to petition Roland for a pinch of mull and a smaller pinch of tobacco, which he would roll into an unattractively slender one-paper joint that he reserved for himself, and which he would consume while exhibiting an archive of frowns and grimaces. If Steve or Roland had purchased hashish, which they seemed to find every couple of months, Bob would badger them to sell him a portion, and then would smoke tiny specs of it neat in a short brass pipe that he would secrete at our house. I used to find that method uncomfortably hot on the throat, but Bob saw it as efficient and clean. He observed to me that almost none of the resin was wasted.

AND I AM HOME again, after a dry day and the excruciating run south from Mansfield at the speed limit. I would have preferred rain, as a slippery highway would have been more entertaining. Squeezing back into the traffic at Healesville—formerly a country town and now almost a suburb. As is my own town. Of course I celebrated my return with a glass of wine and a smoke. And of course, with more wine and more smokes. Glorying dreamily in my having survived another wild ride. Perhaps happiness is simpler than I had thought. Perhaps one is happiest when remembering happiness. I was happy last night. I woke late this morning.

I have been thinking about Bob's sister, Julia, whom I saw again at Bob's funeral, and who had seemed to be so much that Bob was not. She was Bob's elder by a couple of years, and I had met her when I visited Bob at South Yarra. I had noticed she was carrying a copy of Lawrence Durrell's *Justine*, and had opened a conversation about it—not because I had read it, but because I had wanted to say something to Julia. She seemed far too sophisticated to be taking an interest in me, and I suppose that was why I could engage her.

"If you're out that way, feel free to knock on the door for a cup of tea and a conversation about books," was how I remember her invitation. And so I had made sure that I was out Camberwell way, on a Saturday afternoon. Which was how I had met Jodi—and before Roland and Steve had started buying from Jodi. Julia, who had a no-nonsense straight nose and was skinny, had offered me a cup of tea. Jodi, tall, blond and robust, had offered a beer and a joint. The three of us had chatted about books and their authors, and Julia had advised me against studying literature. It was the kind of impromptu and easy social afternoon that I believe Bob had aspired to hosting at Grieve Street, had anyone but me ever knocked on his door.

There was a successful attempt at Abbotsford to have Bob phone Jodi and ask her whether she would sell us a further half-ounce, given that we could not muster the funds for an ounce. We hoped she might have done so to please Bob, who had hinted that he knew Jodi better than we might have assumed. Our attempt was successful in so far as Bob made the call, but a failure more broadly. Bob returned from the hallway, where Roland's telephone line had been terminated, to report not only that Jodi would sell no less than an ounce, but also that she had reserved the remainder of this outstanding consignment for her personal use.

WHERE AM I WITH all of this? And where is everyone else? Bob has gone. Steve is long gone. Greg Morrison? No idea. Jessica is famous, almost. I suppose I could have expected that, but I did not expect it. However upbeat we may have been at Queen Street after a good day and a drink and a smoke, in my more sober moments it always seemed vanishingly unlikely that Jessica would make a living from painting her pictures. Zoom running a gallery. Yes, that would have seemed plausible. Roland a mid-level market researcher, if no longer at his father's firm. And still stuck with Debbie. And from time to time jamming with someone or other in his foetid basement in well-to-do Hawthorn—even now decorated with amps and guitars, grim reminders of his youthful enthusiasm. Or non-enthusiasm—you could argue that also.

I have wondered whether Keppel Street allowed Roland briefly to live as a rock star, in so far as he aspired honestly to so doing. Bringing in some bucks from playing. But mainly sleeping in as late as he chose, and attempting to test every stripe of intoxicant. The Keith Richards model, as he understood it. Roland had brought a big poster of Keith to his Keppel Street bedroom, but it was never from his admiration of Richards' playing that he accounted for his having displayed this image, almost life-sized. I believe now that it was the Rolling Stone linchpin's feted way of life that he had dreamed of, and in particular Richards' getting out of it in all sorts of ways. "Imagine what he has put into his body," Roland had urged me once in a reverent whisper, when he caught me contemplating the portrait. "And he's still doing *that*," a clear reference to Richards' pose, in which he focused intently on the guitar in his hands.

3

THE GENEROSITY OF STEVE

BOB COTTLEMAN ATTENDED QUITE HUNGRILY TO THE reports I composed about the lives we had lived with our friends. I had sought out that attention and had found it affirming. But I wonder now whether his hunger was of a kind with his hunger for improvising leads on guitar over Roland's accompaniments.

As well as his locally made Maton acoustic, Bob had a new Fender Stratocaster, an American guitar that he claimed was identical functionally to instruments played by several rock legends. He did not have a guitar amplifier, but on an occasion when I visited him at South Yarra he had displayed his prowess on the Strat, as he called it, by playing it through his stereo system, wailing away over a recording from the rock band Santana.

Roland had apportioned his musical expenditure differently, purchasing, as he explained to me, a cheaper guitar made in Japan that was nearly as good, and an English-made Marshall amplifier. Given how much he could spend, Roland confided, he had got a better sound from the Marshall and the cheaper guitar than he would have got from a Strat and a less costly amp. When Bob visited Roland, he would play his Strat through the Marshall, attempting to improvise leads while Roland tested new riffs. I believe that Roland profited from Bob's participation in the same way that I profited from Bob's attention: it encouraged him that Bob wanted to join him, and that Bob engaged with his fitful inventing.

Roland was critical privately of Bob as a musician: Bob had too much sense, Roland would say, in a tone that condemned him, and not enough rhythm. But in playing with Roland, Bob was doing more than extending his Strat in a place where its being a Strat made a difference, just as in commenting on my productions Bob was not merely rendering judgment. In each setting, he was sharing in our activities but from a safe distance. He was exercising his interest in the possibility that our efforts would reward us materially, while restraining that interest on a very short leash.

Just as he enjoyed toying with solos but never played on a stage, so Bob secreted his literary output behind closed doors at his house. I might never have learned of this buried life. Given that I have learned of it, I would prefer that Bob had written a lot less about me. I do not believe that as a protagonist I was very intriguing. My innocence with women was not as complete as Bob may have assumed, and Bob's laughing at me from a position of competence merely made him look grasping—as though in presenting the defining features of an acquaintance, indeed of someone who had been all but an intimate, he was determined to focus on the one deficiency against which he could appear worldly by contrast. And yet, however much I can credit Bob with a wish to make me look silly, I cannot unsee the portrait that he painted of me. You inhale an image of yourself from the page, and although you know the person described there is not you, it is tempting to think that this is how not only Bob but all others must see you. You become aware of the distance that the author has kept from you, and you wonder whether your other associates maintain such a gulf also. The author encodes assessments of you that in your conversations with him he had withheld. He reveals details about others around you, about their circumstances and their motivations, that you had not been privy to, and that he had not thought to pass on to you. You understand that things he could have said or done might have helped you. And you understand that he has refrained from saying or doing these things, and likely because he has valued his relations with another of his drawn-from-life characters more than he valued his relations with you.

"THERE'S A WHOLE BAG here that's Steve's." Roland said that at Abbotsford a long time ago, after he had risen from the table to retrieve some more dope. Not long before he said it I would have had a bong, and so my memory for how Roland expressed himself cannot be accurate. Did he add: "We went halves in an ounce"? Did he really tell me, about the same time: "He was going to come by today"? Or was it "tonight"? Or perhaps: "He was going to pick up his share today." In a voice that seemed perfectly even and matter-of-fact.

Roland's delivery of these remarks I admired as straightforward, in circumstances that made it difficult to be so straightforward. Roland made them less than a year after Steve had challenged Bob to account for his dope buy, and as he stood before making them, he relinquished the very seat in which Steve had sat at that time. Roland knew as he made the remarks that Steve was still living, and so in principle could lay claim to the bag. But Steve was alive only technically, or so Roland believed. And Steve would have wanted no one but Roland to inherit that bag, which held heads that were not much inferior to those Bob had so marvelled at.

In observing that he was in command of Steve's stash, Roland would have been telling me why I did not need to advance the tiny quantity of contraband that I had brought with me, and had just proposed that we smoke. But I think he was seeking also to bring home to himself, and to me, the suddenly altered nature of our reality, where recently important distinctions between what was Steve's and what was Roland's no longer counted for much. I admired Roland for his willingness, and perhaps I saw it even as eagerness, to embrace the practical implications of this change, where an alternative would have been a hopeful denial that anything had changed: "We won't smoke this yet, just in case," and so on.

AND I FIND MYSELF here. Resisting over three days my return to this exercise. Turning away first by rolling a cigarette, and then by mixing some brandy with dry ginger ale, and then by smoking the cigarette and drinking the brandy. Drinking the brandy while considering how soon I will need to replenish my stock of it, and whether that need will precede my rendering myself unfit to drive or even to walk in a public place. This while nominally attempting to recall only good times. And yet, I am aware that in its own way this time was a good time. I think more fondly of this time than I think of that time in the previous autumn when, at the same table at Abbotsford, we had thought that we might pry open Bob's chamber of secrets.

I THINK SOMEWHERE IN this mess I am telling myself that this more recent of my memories of Abbotsford does not matter—the afternoon when I celebrated Steve's departure, which was imminent, and in a way that I have told myself celebrated also his life. I would like to deny that this was an afternoon that stands out from others as a time when I felt unusually buoyant. I would like to assert that I have no reason to take steps that might help me to recall it more vividly. And yet what I have retained of it winks at me, much as Roland in those days used to settle upon me his significant glance. Yes, there were parallels between my enjoyment of this latter afternoon and my enjoyment of the evening when Steve, large as life with his wiry hair and pointed retorts, had led the rest of us in diminishing Bob.

Bob too was present at Roland's on the latter occasion, when we spoke resignedly of Steve and his foibles, and I know that again Bob did not smoke at all. Bob had not brought over the dregs of his deal, or if he had brought some he made no attempt to proffer them. An attempt might have been very poignant. "I've brought over some of those super-heads that we all got from Jodi. I don't know what got into me then. But aren't you glad that I kept them and I've still got some left! I'm just regretful that Steve can't share this with us." No such thing. Bob was present, but he was present for me only peripherally. It was as though Bob had wanted to wash his hands of Steve's tragedy. Steve had been unlucky, Bob would have accepted, but he had also been foolish, Bob would have insisted. I do believe that, in contrast, I wanted to honour Steve and his behaviour. Even though I was relieved, mainly, that our connection with Steve would continue only as history.

STEVE'S CALLING OUT OF Bob at Roland's, his persistent invitations to Bob that he come clean with us, I think I had found compelling as a spectacle. Bob had never been an easy man to pin down. If he began to fear that an argument you were making was sound, he would mount a distracting attack on one premise, and before you had advanced your conclusion. Steve on that night would not be diverted.

"Have you weighed your bag?" he asked Bob, having given Bob time to think that he had weathered our probing.

"I've weighed out everyone's bag. Mine's what's left."

"Which is interesting."

Each of us but Bob would have had another bong from the new batch of dope, Steve having mixed a pinch from Stanley's buy with his own. I think I had smoked only half of my bong, deflecting Steve's demands that I finish it. We had all become very merry, however. Bob had made no move to offer us a smoke from his own haul, which looked monstrous.

"It's not interesting; it's just a fact," Bob snapped back. "You've all got what you paid for. I've got what's left, which is what I paid for. It's a zero-sum game: yours plus mine equals one ounce."

Steve, looking dubious, turned to Roland for an interpretation. "What the fuck does that mean?"

"There's nothing over," Bob said. "You wanted forty, Seamus has ten, Stan has twenty, Roland has fifty. That's forty plus ten plus twenty plus fifty is a hundred and twenty; the deal was three-twenty, so I've got what's left. QED!"

"Yes, but ...!" Roland said, always ready to support Steve if he could.

"But what? There's no buts."

"But!" Roland said. He exchanged a glance with Steve. "There is something I've remembered." A subtle grin that prepared me for mischief. "Jodi's generous. She's usually over." Roland swivelled to regard Bob accusingly. "She's almost certainly over, in this case!"

"So, you've probably got more!" An accusatory yelp from Steve—almost a snarl. "We need to know how much more! It is funny that *you* were the one weighing this."

"I was the one weighing it because you guys wouldn't. All you wanted to do was smoke. Why am I not surprised. Your bags will be accurate to within a tenth of a gram—maybe a hundredth. There won't be any over. And if there is," Bob said, taking a stand, "I deserve it."

"You don't deserve it!" Roland feigned indignation as only he could. "You deserve less, because we've got no idea why you want it!"

"And we're suspicious!" Steve emphasised.

"We've got reasons for being suspicious!" Roland declared.

"We want to make sure that *you* got what *you* paid for," Steve said.

"And not a speck more," Roland said. "Just like us!"

"Exactly," Stanley chipped in. "We just want to be fair."

The Generosity of Steve

"You've got exactly what you paid for!" Bob reiterated. "There is nothing you could have to complain about. And," he said, "for all we know, this deal was under!"

"Jodi's never under," Roland asserted. "We've had ... what?" He looked briefly at Steve. "Three deals from Jodi. We've got three ounces from Jodi and she's never been under. She has always been over. And sometimes quite a bit over."

"She was quite a bit over, once," Steve said. He lifted his own bag and dangled it before him from one corner, looking from Bob to the bag and back and scowling in distaste. It was as though he were suspending a rat so that we could examine it. "This is all I've got," he observed to us, his delivery emphatic but mournful. "And look at what you've got!" he invited Bob. "What are you going to do with it? Are you going to tell all your doctor mates that you're gonna blow all their minds?"

"Does Bob have doctor mates?" I said, feeling uncensored from the half bong alone. "I don't think Bob has doctor mates."

"You'd have mates if you let them smoke some of that!" Roland assured Bob. "You would have heaps of mates."

"You'd be popular!" Stanley said.

"You'd have visitors, Bob," I predicted. "People would come around and want to smoke bongs with you."

"You'd be the most popular doctor at the hospital," Roland said.

"Maybe the most popular in Melbourne," I said. "And we'd visit too."

"You'd have a queue!" Stanley said.

"And you could start right now!" Roland said.

"You could give us the little bit that you're over," Steve said. "That would be a good start."

"I'm not over!" Bob made an attempt to dig in.

"But how do we know?" Stanley asked.

"And more to the point," Roland said, "If you aren't over, why wouldn't you want us to know?"

57

"That's what makes me suspicious," said Steve. "And I think we should be suspicious."

"We're suspicious for a reason," Roland said. "And it's for a good reason. And Bob should just throw some in anyway, since he does have so much. Or sell us some. If he doesn't want even to sell us some, then that's probably for a very good reason. A very good reason that he has," Roland finished.

"It is suspicious," Stanley said, "that Bob was so keen to weigh everything. He could have just weighed his own. And then let us divide up the rest."

"We would have all the rest," Roland said, wrapping up Stanley's point. "We would have everything we paid for, *and* we'd have whatever was over," he summarised. "Which is exactly what Bob has now. We could have smoked the extra instead of smoking Steve's."

"And mine," Stanley said.

"And yours. Bob, it's the only fair thing to do. Give us your bag. We'll take out what's over, and we'll smoke that. You could even have some. And then you could still look at what you had left."

"I don't want a bong!" Bob declared.

"All the more reason why you should give us what's over," Roland said.

"You need to give us that bag, Bob," Steve said. "You need to be fair. We've been fair, and now it's your turn to be fair."

And yet not one of us was fair, after Bob had thrown Roland his bag. And Roland had weighed it and found it was under. And more under, as Bob howled at us after he had absorbed this result, if the weight of the bag itself were subtracted. Almost a gram under, Bob calculated. "All your deals had no bag on them, when I weighed them!" he exclaimed, blending indignation with pride in his probity. As every one of us but Bob cackled crazily, unwilling but also unable to rein in our satisfaction with having inflicted on Bob this reverse. We had not thought he deserved a margin. We did think that he deserved richly our laughing at him, a group giggle that seemed to go on for minutes. Even Steve gave himself up to this reflex, adding his tenor convulsions to our alto rejoicing.

"I deserve what I've paid for," Bob said, having waited until he thought we might hear him. "Hand over your bags!"

Roland, struggling, managed: "I don't think that's necessary." And lapsed into more giggles.

"It's not," Steve confirmed.

"I'm happy with what I've got," I said.

And as I recall it, the talk passed to other things. Bob knew better than to pursue his claim further. Steve had won. All of us but Bob had won. It had felt wonderful, liberating, legitimising, to be with the winning team as a member. I doubt that any of us thought then about what we had won. It was a victory for profligacy, our side united behind Steve's unflinching sallies, over logic and parsimony, Bob's indentured attendants.

GO TO SCHOOL AND *do well. Come home and study. Go to school and do well.* It had seemed so straightforward. But it had come tumbling down in my senior years at school, where I had ceased to do well. At least by previous standards. It had become clear that I would not be studying medicine. Or law. Engineering, Gordon would tell me, was real. I could get into something constructive. Get my teeth into something. Get into a solid job with a proper company and establish for myself a position that was secure. Build up a deposit. Purchase a house. Find a girlfriend. Get married.

Since I had never given either parent a sign that I might find a girlfriend, to me this had seemed like a long shot. If I were to find a girlfriend, it would not be from my having made myself more eligible through my purchasing of a place where, if all went well, we could live. And yet that was the way my father thought, I believe, in so far as he thought about these things at all. My fantasies about smoking with my father contained no trace of fact. He would have been disappointed to have learned that I had ever smoked anything. He would have been horrified had he learned that I knew a person like Steve, who bought illegal drugs from criminals and who stole this and that. He had despaired of me when I bounced from engineering to studying in the humanities, an effort for which he could not foresee an end: there was no ticket for which it could qualify me. My mother would not have felt happy about the sort of girl whom she thought I might meet in arts. Not that she said so. And not that, in her sense, I met girls. No one whom I met in arts was as keen on partaking in a relieving smoke as I became over my time at Keppel Street.

"STEVE WAS AN IDIOT." Another line I remember from Steve's last night alive. And so simple a line. I am certain that this quote is accurate. Especially as I am quoting myself. "Steve was an idiot," I told Roland, after we had made inroads into Steve's bag. We sat facing one another, smoking and drinking and talking, across a corner of Roland's table at Abbotsford, the kitchen-side corner nearest the blue rear-side wall against which Steve on that prior occasion had stood out so sharply. I imagine that we had both been thinking quietly about what it might mean to have lost Steve. When I thought about Steve, it was common for me to reconstruct a journey we had taken, on one chilly night in the Keppel Street era, the three of us together, to a pinball parlour in North Carlton—Matt's Blue Room, or for us simply Matt's. Roland asleep in the back of Steve's Kingswood wagon, on the foam rubber slab that Steve kept there permanently, the rear seat folded down to accept it. Steve at the wheel. We had downed a few bongs, perhaps several, and it had been quite late—perhaps between one and two, wee hours with which we had become very familiar.

Was it true, as I believed, that we had been lucky we survived this short trip, or had Steve been on a sure bet? Roland, afterwards, had been firmly in the sure-bet camp. Indeed, he had never acknowledged to me that Steve made that bet. "That could have been a disaster," I said to Roland across our corner at Abbotsford, possibly on my second bong from Steve's bag. "A complete fucking disaster. And you would have known nothing about it. Unless you had lived for a few seconds. Or worse, for a minute. With your neck broken, and bones sticking out of your skin. Or worse: what if you were just shaken up, and we had killed some poor cyclist? Or a motorbike rider? Or a pedestrian? You know what, I reckon if we'd hit a pedestrian, Steve would have just gone on driving. He'd have looked across at me and said: 'He had it coming.' He'd have been daring me to deny it. And then he probably would have laughed. He'd have probably dropped us off somewhere and then tried to get rid of the car. Or he might have driven home to his mum and dad's place and snuck in the back door. 'I've been here all along. I got home around midnight.' We'd have been asked to back him up, if the cops ever came. Which would have been another disaster. It would have been in the papers. What if it was a woman? What if there were two people walking, and he'd only got one?" That is a summary. A reconstruction perhaps of what I think I said—or perhaps it is just what I hope I said. Letting Roland know where I stood. Now that we had gotten to a place where he was disposed to hear what I really thought about Steve. Roland had always turned aside my forebodings, telling me that I panicked. That my imagination was too fertile. The worst case never happened—that had been how Roland looked at life at that time. Perhaps here was the source of his fascination with Steve. It was amazing what you could get away with, and Steve had always gotten away. Because he was lucky? Or because he only bet on sure things? Now we knew.

"I had wondered whether you would bring that up again," Roland told me. "I think I was asleep. What was it you think happened?"

"He drove through three Stop signs," I said. "At high speed. Foot planted."

In fact there had been only one Stop sign: if there had been three then my screaming before the third would have roused Roland from his dope-infused slumber. The other two signs had been Give Way signs only. On smallish roads. It had been late, as I have said, and we had been motoring down a residential North Carlton street, as I recall it walled-in and narrow, which had crossed bigger streets. There had seemed to be no one about. High speed was probably only a hundred kilometres per hour. There had been a point as we ran up on the Stop sign when Steve had needed to brake, if he were indeed to stop for it, and as we neared that point he had looked left at me, and I had looked right at him. My memory now of his state cannot, of course, be trusted, but I recollect his inspection of me as expressing silently the sort of merriment I had long ago attributed to the devil from the demonology of my schooling, a devil experiencing ecstatically the core element of his reason for being. But doubtless I exaggerate. Fear makes foes look worse. Certainly, Steve had seemed very absorbed. More precisely: abandoned. He had probably wanted to see how I looked. I suppose it was street lighting penetrating the windscreen that had allowed me to see him. I think of wild, wiry hair and red eyes, even though his eyes could not have looked red when the light was so poor. And a leer, his lower lip curling. A leer that I interpreted as at once offering me a challenge and supplying a taunt. And then the car, rather than slowing, surged ahead, as I thrust my feet against the firewall, in part reflexively trying to press into it an absent brake pedal, and in part pressing myself into my seat as though I were preparing myself, uselessly, for a calamitous impact. We accelerated murderously through the double white Stop bars and across the near and far lanes and then we were back between tall brick walls, racing towards a small roundabout with its Give Way sign, for which Steve slowed, disinclined to risk mounting the tall gutter that bounded it.

When I thought about this episode afterwards, I concluded that it had represented for Steve a version of Russian roulette, except that in typically thoughtless Steve fashion, Roland and I and anybody dreamily making their way home late with the right of way would have suffered with Steve had that chamber been loaded. And yet it occurs to me now that this may have been Steve's way of baiting me over my caution, of showing me how even sensible social rules could be flouted without consequence if you picked your time and place well. Our chances of avoiding a dolorous fate would have been much better than five in six. Had he done this sort of thing on his own?

"Across *Rathdowne Street*?" Bob had exclaimed, incredulous, when I told him, likely that week. Until then I had not thought about which street it had been, focused much more on its breadth and the Stop sign. Roland, asleep in the back, had accused me, when he woke up, of embellishing. He had never wanted to think Steve was dangerous. Steve had been all about fun. Perhaps Roland thought I had been hallucinating. A hypothesis that was plausible.

DOES THAT SATURDAY SOJOURN at Roland's Abbotsford house, while Steve lay in what Debbie had described as a coma, amount for me to another highlight, a bright spot that illuminates a grey backdrop? I believe I had spent the remains of Friday night watching TV at Myrtle Street, with my mother and father, and I suppose necessarily Tessa, my sister, after completing a shift at the TAB. My mother may have kept a roast dinner hot for me, just as she had kept a bed for me. Or perhaps I had arrived in time to eat with them, and had thought that I would spend the rest of the evening there quietly but would catch up with Roland, or someone, the next day, before heading back out to Queen Street and Zoom, Sandy and Jessica. On Saturday I had phoned Roland's house, I think about lunchtime, and had got Debbie, which at first seemed sub-optimal. Things went better if Roland picked up, when, I have always assumed, he could assent to my visiting, fix an hour, and alert

Debbie only shortly before I was due, having deflected her prior suggestions that they keep the night to themselves. He might take an opportunity—perhaps when Debbie went shopping, or to walk her dog around Abbotsford's bluestone-trimmed footpaths—to make further arrangements, which traditionally might have involved, for example, a quick call to Steve. But Debbie had shocked me by saying: "You should come over." That Debbie had prefaced this invitation with an announcement that something had happened to Steve had done nothing to diminish the delight with which I received it.

My mother then was acutely interested in what I would do on a Saturday, and it had pleased me to demonstrate that while I might not have a girlfriend, I did have friends who would host me. For the next three or four hours I had thought that Steve might wake up. People awakened from comas. It had seemed reasonable to assume that our Steve would be one of them. And then things would go on much as they had. Steve would have had a close shave. He might have grown more circumspect. I had been there myself, almost, two or three times, on the bike, each time walking away. Did I ruminate upon this as I rode down Heidelberg Road towards Roland's, having augmented the remains of my dope with a six-pack of light beers and a half-sized bottle of Jim Beam bourbon whiskey? I doubt I thought about it, and yet I suspect I carried also a sense of myself as fit for comforting Roland on this occasion. Roland and Steve had enjoyed tasty drugs, but these, like motorcycles, notoriously, had their hazards, and not just those connected with discovery and its institutional penalties. Was it my admiration for Roland that had led me to assume he had not risked those hazards blindly, and therefore had accepted in advance all dire outcomes? Or was I simply naive?

"You never really liked Steve, did you?" Roland, in the depths of the evening. Perhaps wanting to re-engage with his loss, now that he had allowed himself some relief. By then I knew that it would be a permanent loss. I do not think I had recognised any loss to myself. If the bell that was about to toll for Steve would be

The Generosity of Steve

tolling also for me, then I was a long way short of acknowledging that. Perhaps Roland had apprehended in me something of this. He may have noticed, possibly with surprise, that I had been having a fabulous time downing bongs. As though I had not been affected by my discovery that Steve lay where he lay. His lungs, as I see now quite clearly, inflated regularly with an electro-mechanical pump. Roland may have wanted to challenge me.

"I did like Steve!"

"You liked it that he had lots of dope."

"No, it wasn't just that. I did like Steve. Sort of. I liked it that he was always trying to get me to have more dope."

"You did not like that!"

"I did. It was, really ... it was the start of all this, really. Here we are—and I know Steve's not here with us—but I am, kind of, loving this. I am loving it. Having bongs here with you. Without Steve—if it hadn't been for Steve, that's what I am trying to say—if it hadn't been for Steve, I would never have had this many bongs with you. Because I wouldn't have wanted this many bongs. Even with you. I would have said: 'That's enough.' I would have had one bong and that would have been lots. Maybe two bongs. I would have thought it was stupid to have more bongs than that. I would have been like Bob. I wouldn't have seen the point. I would never have got as ridiculous. I would never even have known you liked it when I did get ridiculous. I would never have known you liked it—or didn't mind it at least—when I raved on about all sorts of stuff. Just like I am probably raving on now. Steve, Steve, idiot Steve. But he was good. I did like Steve. Sort of. I would never have smoked nearly as many bongs if it wasn't for Steve."

"Because without Steve, you just wouldn't have had enough dope."

"No, it wasn't just the dope. You are making me into a dope. I liked Steve. I liked the bongs he made me have."

"He didn't make you have any bongs!"

"He did in a way. He was very encouraging."

"He was generous. He liked you."

"He didn't like me. That night he just about killed me."

"He didn't kill you. And what about the time you attacked him? That could have been just as nasty. Or more nasty. I heard about that a lot."

We had heard about that mere hours earlier. It had astonished me that anybody but I had remembered it. It had been a very brief incident. We had been very ripped, and it had not been an attack.

I HAVE BEEN THINKING about this a bit more, and I get it now, or I imagine I get it, why Roland would have wanted to bring up the knife thing at that point. I think he may have been wanting not only to challenge my indifference to Steve's plight, as he inferred it from my behaviour, but also—and relatedly—he may have wanted to challenge my very understanding of Steve. I had never ceased to think of Steve as a nuisance. The Stop-sign incident, which had arisen perhaps twelve months after I met Steve, had put the finishing touch on my framing of him: he was a dangerous idiot, if an idiot who must be tolerated—for just as long as he was tolerated by Roland. Roland, understandably, never had wanted to see Steve so narrowly. Very possibly, he thought I had taken for granted, always, Steve's gifts—and upon seeing how little I had been moved by our loss of Steve, he had been wanting to show me that Steve had been no mere instrument of my desire to get whacked for free. It is possible that Roland had wanted to explain Steve for me as, after all, human: to make it plain that Steve was an ingénue who had met tragically with bad luck. Roland had always wanted to assess Steve's behaviour as, on balance, well judged. He had found in Steve's acts evidence that much more fun could be had innocently than was widely promoted, simply by breaching a range of taboos that were rooted in history much more than in science.

The Generosity of Steve

STEVE'S FRIEND SHOOKA HAD been at Roland's house midafternoon when I got there, drinking tonic water with gin from a bottle standing tall on the table. "Rhymes with hooker," Steve had said maliciously at Keppel Street years before, introducing her. This was, I am certain, a nickname, and her surname I never inquired about. I remember the bottle as rectangular and reflecting blue from the label, and so I suppose it was Vickers. Shooka had not drunk much of it. It was not as though she had been slurring her words at 3pm, or whenever it was when Roland brought me inside.

Shooka had made much of my alleged attack on Steve, and gleefully, after a bong, even though she had not been a witness. It had never been an attack. I had merely removed a boning knife from a drawer in the kitchen, had grasped its handle in my fist, and had returned to accost Steve with it, but from a distance that allowed error. This had been at Keppel Street, and again late at night. I remember still that Steve, noticing me in the gloom as I advanced towards where he sat by the little gas heater, had exhibited a tremor, as though for an instant he had thought I really was about to attack him with the knife. I was aware of course that as intoxicated as we had become, advancing on anybody with a sharply pointed knife held in one's fist could generate consequences that no one would welcome. Even when removing the knife from the drawer I had pondered, although only briefly, as I imagine this now, on the wisdom of my doing so. I can imagine easily that I would have observed my doing so, aware of a gap that existed, under the influence of a good bong or three, between impulse and impulse control, as it were: I knew that withdrawing the knife from the drawer would not be the most prudent thing I could do at that time, and yet I knew also that I would withdraw the knife. It had felt much the same when I advanced upon Steve. And then there was the question whether I would stab Steve. Of course I would not stab Steve—and I did not—but I was conscious of the possibility that I would stab Steve: that I would understand it was a bad idea to stab Steve, but that I would stab him anyway. I think it was possibly that sort of thought running through Steve's mind—he would have been surprised that, in the circumstances, I was advancing across the room with that knife in my fist, and he would have wondered instinctively what else might take place—that had led Steve to betray momentarily a jolt of some kind. And he would have been affected by his multiple bongs. He had not enjoyed the vision of my advancing upon him when armed. He had found me, momentarily, weird and frightening, as much more frequently I had found him. That involuntary recoiling that I observed in Steve was probably all I had looked for, and an unrecognised wish to provoke such a reaction might have been precisely what had driven me to fetch the knife. I can recall nothing of the conversation that had surrounded this incident. There is every possibility that I acknowledged almost immediately I observed Steve's reaction that the knife might fall into Steve's hands, and that I would feel much less comfortable if the knife were in his hands than I felt with its handle gripped securely in mine. Nor would I have welcomed a tussle over its possession. I returned the knife to the drawer, and for some time afterwards attended to the possibility that Steve might retrieve it. But he made no sign of doing so.

    I had thought nothing more of the event until that very afternoon, when Shooka had introduced me as "the guy with the knife". She had been addressing Joey, until that day Steve's flatmate, one of five of us sitting then at the dining table in the rear room of Roland's house, and the only one of us with whom I had never previously sat smoking. The fifth was not Debbie, but Bob. Debbie had, mainly, left us to get on with our mourning, once the bong had come out, from time to time I think offering tea. That Debbie, perhaps alone of us, had shed tears over Steve had been obvious when I arrived. Steve, she told me, had been settling down. And she had wept. He had been settling down with Patience, she said, recalling to my mind Patience Moore. I had met Patience once, at a party, and her pairing with Steve had seemed to me so unlikely that I had forgotten her the next day. Had Steve found me as weird as I had found him? I do not think so. Nevertheless, Shooka must have known of the knife myth only because Steve had told her about it, and the same must have been true for Joey. "*You* know," Shooka had said, prompting Joey, "the knife." Joey had called for a re-enactment. To have acquiesced might have enlivened the gathering. Four of us had enjoyed a bong, Bob and Debbie declining, and we had been reflecting sombrely on the Steve we had known, having heard from Roland—twice, because Bob had arrived after me—on the circumstances to which Steve had succumbed. With detail added by Shooka, who had been at Steve's small flat at the time, the two of them having attended a concert, and subsequently having scored—at a pub—a narcotic that proved tastier than Steve had expected. "I told him that was way too much," Shooka insisted.

Roland had responded to Joey's knife suggestion immediately, looking nervously, I thought, towards the kitchen. "I don't think that is a good idea," he told Joey. "I don't think you would like it." On receipt of the suggestion from Joey, I had made a movement towards getting up. "The knife?" Bob had asked. "You were there," Roland said, his intonation just as dry as it usually was. "Weren't you?" "Maybe I was," Bob said. "Maybe I was there. No, I think we should let sleeping dogs lie." And I imagine Bob gave a Bob snigger: Seamus was in his cups, when he could behave—and often did—like an imbecile. Better not to encourage him further.

Bob's presence there at the time I did not remark upon publicly, even if privately I was surprised again to have seen him. Only a little surprised, because Bob at that time was more assiduous than I was in seeking out Roland's company. Or so I believed. I had come to prefer my time with Roland when Bob was not there to intrude. Just as I preferred it, or so I had thought, when Steve was not there to intrude. But Bob clearly knew more about Steve's recent doings than I knew. It was clear that he had gotten to know Shooka well too. I made little of that at the time, but it seems plausible enough now that he had joined Steve and Roland in foraying excitedly into ingesting something tastier than mere dope, and less offensive to his sense of what was unhealthy.

THE MEMORIAL FOR STEVE was anticlimactic for me, given that we had conducted Steve's wake before he had died. There was a service at a church of some kind somewhere near Footscray, and then Steve's parents had put on drinks at their home, which was not far away. I have only the merest of inklings that their address was in Seddon. It was about putting on a show for Steve's mum and dad, really. They had been told the cause of death. Roland, who had met Steve's parents when Steve was in excellent health, had said that he had no idea why Steve would have taken this risk. He said he believed Steve had never done so before. Or so he revealed to me some time later, expressing relief that Steve's father had swallowed this, and that he had not been asked pointed questions about how Steve had dosed himself. Steve's mum and dad had reminded me of my mum and dad. Delighted Steve had done well. Shocked that something so bad had happened so soon—it was as though they had stepped into a movie. And then that opportunity to define themselves as the nurturers of their brilliant younger son had gone. They seemed to me bewildered. We stayed only a short time. I spoke to Patience again, and remembered she was called Pash by most people. She remembered me more than I remembered her, but she remembered me by reputation. Steve had presented proudly to her my report that had featured him, and had proposed that she read it. "It was a great story," Pash said softly, which was not true but which I accepted, given where we were, and given how much I had been enjoying standing there and talking to Pash. It was the best story that Steve would ever see himself in. I had proposed to Roland that we return to Abbotsford afterwards, but he said that he and Debbie had a few things to do.

The Generosity of Steve

SHOOKA HAD LEFT ROLAND'S house long before it got dark, on that Saturday when Steve's spirit still lingered. Citing a family engagement, or so I seem to remember. And taking Joey away with her. I did not think much about this at the time, but I can imagine now that they had been there at the table in Roland's living room since breakfast, having come to recognise at the hospital the futility of keeping watch over Steve. As I write that, I see for the first time how misplaced I may have been at that gathering. It is not that I should not have been there. But I see how my motives, and my mood, might have been incongruous with the moods I encountered. Was I trying to jolly Roland along? I can recall how good it had felt to me when Roland suggested a bong. Before then I had felt some apprehension. Which I had interpreted as a problem for me, and not for the others there. Was it my exuberance, after a bong, that had persuaded Shooka that she did need to leave? The guy with the knife, returning to threaten even their opportunity to reflect, in the company of those others who had last seen Steve intact, on Steve's fine qualities, and on how much they would miss Steve and what he had brought to them. Perhaps even on how unlucky Steve had been. And relatedly, perhaps on how lucky they had been. Shooka had discovered Steve immobile, on his beanbag chair, after waking from a long sleep of her own. At a loss, she had phoned Roland. None of them had thought this event had been likely: that much should have been obvious to me. Was I simply relieved it had happened, having, as I thought, foreseen it as a possibility, and having assumed that the others had foreseen it as well? Had I assumed we were celebrating together our survival of Steve? If I had, then that was not an assumption of which I was conscious. Had Bob seen that in me, and departed in disgust—and not disgust over bongs—to join Debbie in the lounge that adjoined us? A spare bedroom that she had converted, with its still-working fireplace, and with the grey and unaccommodating couch and chair suite she had imported, or so I had speculated, from her parents' garage, stacked there after they had upgraded to leather.

"I've got to go," Shooka had said. "Another bong?" Roland had offered. "No, I've got to go. I think I'm late already." Roland had risen to see them down the hall to the door. There was some murmuring as they farewelled Bob and Debbie, which I could hear from my seat at the table. Was it later than I have remembered? I am certain it was not yet properly dark. Might it have been polite if I had set out for home then myself? Perhaps that thought had occurred to me. But if so, I dismissed it. I imagine I was feeling quite cheerful. Bob too had not taken his leave. We had turned a corner, and the evening looked promising. Even if it was not clear yet how it would go. I heard the snap of metal striking metal as Roland closed the front door, and possibly footfalls and creaks as he returned down the hallway. I do not think he did more than look in at Debbie and Bob. Would he invite me to join them, in the lounge? Perhaps start up the fire—even though the temperature inside was still, as I remember it, comfortable. It is likely I was drinking a beer. Roland may have left on the table a part-consumed Jim Beam and Coke. I did not want to join Bob and Debbie. Surely Roland would return at least for his drink. But what then? I cannot claim accuracy in recollecting the material detail of what happened next. I can recall only mild apprehension about what might happen next. And, overwhelmingly, my corresponding relief, the infusion of comfort, of peace, and yes even of joy, but a quiet joy, which I did not need to advertise, as I saw what would happen next. Roland returning to his seat at the end of the table. Probably sipping his drink. Perhaps lighting a cigarette. Looking across at me. I saw no hint in his behaviour that I should have departed. "Well," he said. "Shall we have another bong?" The effect from my first had attenuated considerably, and so nothing motivated me to rebuff that invitation. It may have been then that I offered my dope. "Don't worry," Roland would have said, "I'll get mine." And my worrying ceased. It was almost as though I had stepped myself into a dream, but of a kind from which I would awake feeling lighter.

"I've just remembered," Roland said. "There's a whole bag here that's Steve's." Or something very like that.

SPRING

4

ANOTHER SATURDAY NIGHT

S O I HAVE DUG INTO A FILE THAT I HAVE NOT OPENED in at least twenty years. Why now? Because I do not know what else I can write, and I need to write something. Because I want to be refreshed in my sense of the life that I have found myself to be recalling. Because it is true that, for all its unpleasant surprises, and for all that I was pleased at the time that I had put it behind me, I was fond of that life, or I was fond of some elements of it. And having unearthed this manuscript, typed up on paper and amended in biro, dismissed at the time as comprising mere trivia, I am reassessing the record it makes of my friend. He had seemed different then, and he was. He has since made much more peace with Debbie. And yet his spirit endures. I am reminded of something that I know I have missed. Would I describe that something as contentment? Perhaps.

"ROLAND," Debbie stormed, "You are a pig.

"You are, Roland. And you were a mess again last night, after you promised you wouldn't be. You promised, Roland. And now look at all this—get up, Roland, it's 12 o'clock and look at all this mess. Get up and help me clean it up. Well? You always say you'll do it later. You do, Roland.

"Well at least I'm glad to see you're getting up; it's only a quarter past 12. Well are you going to help me or not? Roland, you couldn't be mean enough not to help me. Well, hurry up then, I've nearly finished.

"Don't get that out, Roland, I've just put it away. You're not going to have another bong are you? You're not going to have another bong after I've just finished cleaning up all this mess. Roland? Oh Roland, how mean of you!"

Roland's bony body shook. He coughed. And coughed again, expelling clouds of grey smoke.

* * *

"You're late for lunch anyway." Roland lay on the yellow folding lounge in his back garden, eyes closed against the bright afternoon. "Look, I've said I'll do it, okay?"

"Well ... Get up then."

"I'll do it in a minute. I'm a bit stoned."

"You'll have to do it soon, Roland, or it won't get dry."

"All right, I'll do it soon."

"There, Roland, it's stopped. Now are you going to put it on the line or will I have to do it and be late?"

"Look, I've said I'll do it."

"Could you please do it now, Roland. There are things in the washing that I want to wear tonight."

Roland rolled onto his back.

"Why do you have to wear those things tonight?" he asked.

"Because they are the things I want to wear tonight, Roland. Roland, it's one o'clock. Will you put the washing out?"

"Okay, I'll put it out."

"When? When will you put it out?"

"Soon."

"It needs to go out now, Roland. Roland it needs to go out now. Roland, get up!"

Roland stood with an effort. He walked unsteadily to the back door.

"Are you going to do it, Roland?"

He moved through to the living room, sat at the table and loaded mull into the bowl of his bong. He lit the bong and sucked, long and hard.

"Roland, are you going to ... Roland!"

Roland coughed, a wet cough from deep in his chest. Smoke erupted from between his lips.

* * *

"Goodbye," Roland called after Debbie's retreating figure. "Have a good lunch."

Debbie did not acknowledge the farewell.

Roland shut the front door, trod lightly down the hallway, sat at the table, drew the bong to him and filled it. He lit the bong and sucked at it, watching the flame-front retreat down the bowl as his lungs filled. He knew that the glowing red disc would consume the whole bowl before his lungs filled, and when this happened he was pleased. He sat, the smoke in his lungs, satisfied. He blew the smoke out. It rasped across his throat and he coughed.

A cup of coffee, he thought. He rose, walked into the kitchen and filled the kettle, realising as he did so that he was hungry. He opened the door of the fridge.

Occupying the entire middle shelf of the fridge was a pavlova, baked marshmallow topped with meringue. Its uncut crust struggled to support an inch of whipped cream and grated peppermint chocolate.

* * *

Roland thought about a baked-beans and cheese jaffle.

There were tins of baked beans in the cupboard. The bread lay on the bench, pre-sliced, in its plastic wrapper.

The cheese, he knew, was in the fridge.

In the fridge with the pavlova.

He made his cup of coffee, carried it carefully back to the table and sat. The mull beckoned. He reached out, tamped some mull into the bowl of the bong, lit it, sucked. His lungs raced the flame front. They won.

* * *

Roland considered the baked-beans and cheese jaffle. First, he thought, he would go to the cupboard, take out the baked beans, get a can-opener and open them. Then, the bread, spread on the outside with margarine and placed in the jaffle-maker. Then, last of all, the cheese.

To get the cheese he would have to open the fridge.

He drank his coffee. It tasted sweet and familiar, soothing him but failing to satisfy.

* * *

It occurred to Roland that perhaps the cheese was not in the fridge.

Or, he thought, perhaps it was there, but he had not seen it, because of what was before him. Or perhaps it was hidden.

He lit a cigarette, made another cup of coffee and was half way through drinking it when the phone rang.

"Is Debbie there? Oh, Roland.

"Listen mate, we can't come over tonight, Amy's not well. She's been in bed all day. Sorry about dinner and all that. Tell Debbie, will you. Thanks mate. We'll have to have you over to our place soon. Okay, thanks mate."

*   *   *

Roland took a knife from the cutlery drawer and opened the door of the fridge.

He reached inside the fridge and cut deeply into the pavlova, exhaling as the blade bit through the crisp meringue and into chewy marshmallow. He cut the other side of the slice. He slid the knife under the slice, stuck a finger into the whipped-cream topping to steady it, lifted out the slice and kicked the door to.

*   *   *

The pavlova, Roland thought to himself, was not sweet enough to make him sick, no matter how much he ate of it. The taste delighted him and its substance satisfied him like no cheese and baked-beans jaffle could ever have done.

He cut another slice, separated it from the rest of the pavlova, transferred it from knife to fingers, ate it quickly. He cut another.

He rinsed his hands in the sink, took the pavlova from the fridge, laid it on the kitchen bench, re-opened the cutlery drawer and found a spoon.

*   *   *

Roland sat in front of the bong and the bowl of mull. There was only one thing to do, and he did it, racing the flame-front to the bottom of the bowl with his lungs. He coughed, emitting smoke and smelling sweet whipped cream.

There was more than one third of the pavlova left but he no longer desired it.

Lucky, Debbie's ageing cocker spaniel, lay on the carpet and eyed him balefully.

He could say, he thought, that somehow Lucky had eaten it all.

But Debbie would never believe him, plausible though the story could be when the animal's appetite for sweet treats was considered.

Or he could say he noticed it had gone off. Yes, the fridge had been turned off accidentally and the cream had gone off and he had fed the pavlova to Lucky.

The plan seemed, briefly, feasible, as he doubted Lucky would take long to dispose of the outstanding evidence.

But he remembered Debbie's anxious vigil the last time Lucky had gorged herself on the ingredients of a dessert, cooking chocolate that Debbie kept to make mousse with. Roland had raided her hoard with a friend late one night, neglectfully leaving what remained, a packet or two, on their coffee table in the lounge. He remembered, too, painfully paying the bill at the vet clinic where Debbie had insisted on having Lucky examined.

Lucky yawned, stretched and stood up. She padded over to Roland and looked up at him, her tongue hanging out, drops of drool collecting on the hair fringing her lower jaw.

"Lucky!" Roland yelled. "Go away!"

* * *

"I'm sorry," Roland said.

"How much did you eat?"

"There's nearly half left."

"You ate half of it!"

Debbie went to the fridge and threw open the door. Cream, marshmallow and meringue lay scattered over the platter, rubble from the intricate edifice she had constructed that morning. Only a forlorn wedge still stood.

"Roland! You've hardly left any! You know that was for when Amelia and Brett come for dinner!"

"You didn't tell me that!"

"I did, Roland. Why would you have eaten it?"

"I don't know. I was hungry."

"I suppose you've been having bongs again."

"I've had a few bongs."

"Well I can't make another one. You'll just have to go out and buy something for dessert."

"Amelia's sick," Roland said. "They're not coming."

* * *

"I don't really feel like a movie."

"What do you want to do then?"

"I don't know." Roland added, tentatively: "I thought maybe someone might drop around and we could have a few bongs."

"Roland. You've been having bongs all day. The least you can do is go out, after eating all my pavlova."

"That's true." Roland sighed. "I'm sorry. Where will we go?"

"Have we got a paper?"

"Yesterday's is around somewhere."

"Let's take Lucky for a walk and get today's."

"Won't yesterday's do?"

"No. Things change. Anyway, Lucky needs a walk."

"Okay."

"Are you coming?"

"No."

"Come on. Come with me."

"Why can't you go by yourself?"

"I want you to come."

"I don't want to go for a walk."

"Come on. It will do you good."

"No."

"Roland..."

"I'll stay and make dinner. Have you made dinner? I'll make some jaffles for dinner."

"You can make them when we get back."

"I'll stay and make the jaffles," Roland insisted.

"No, Roland."

"Yes. Why do you want me to come?"

"It will be good for you."

"I don't want it to be good for me."

"Oh, Roland."

"You go, I'll stay and make the jaffles."

Debbie knelt and clipped Lucky's lead to her collar. Still kneeling, she twisted to look up at Roland.

"Promise me you won't have any bongs," she said.

"Just one..."

"No, Roland!" Debbie stood up, red-faced.

"All right," Roland said.

WAS THIS SKETCH THE last that I ever composed? It may well have been. I have not disinterred another more recent. In its spotlight is Roland, having bongs on a Saturday. At the fringe of the spotlight is Debbie, responding as Roland manipulates her—as he manufactures her assent to his smoking more bongs, assent that turns out to be effective if far from explicit. I got the impression that Roland was having a lot of bongs in the first year or two after Steve. But then again, he had been having a lot of bongs with Steve. I did not think to myself that Roland was hitting the bongs a bit hard. I was just happy that he continued to make bongs available.

There is more here than I have quoted. The very next line reports that Roland phoned Jamie, a friend. Implicitly, he offers Jamie an invitation, and Jamie accepts. When Jamie arrives, it is not obvious to Debbie that Roland has orchestrated his appearing. Again implicitly, Debbie accepts Roland's welcoming of Jamie because she was accustomed to receiving visitors for Roland unannounced, during the afternoon or evening of a Saturday.

How frequently guests not expected by Roland or Debbie had

punctuated the couple's weekends in Abbotsford, I do not know. Certainly every now and again Bob dropped by, as he would have described his arrivals, in the days after Steve's visits ceased. And from time to time I would arrive speculatively on a Saturday, commonly after a shift at the TAB. Perhaps I would have convinced myself, as I headed in to work, that when the shift ended I would want simply to ride down Queens Road towards home—and hence that I had no reason for warning Roland that I might take instead the road to his front veranda. I may have predicted that I would find it burdensome to cross town and carouse at Abbotsford, with the question open whether I would embark upon the long journey to Mornington later that night, while affected by bongs, or would request a blanket from Debbie before she retired, so that I could crash uncomfortably on her couch. Or perhaps I had doubted that my visiting would appeal to Roland, in prospect. Perhaps, as I might have proposed to myself, he would think that having a drink or two and smoking a bong or two with me at his living room table would not count for much as a plan for a Saturday night. Whereas, if it had gotten to evening and no plan had materialised, and I arrived unexpectedly, he would count my arrival as an upgrade on a night with just Debbie. There remained the possibility for me that Roland would not be home, but even if he were not home I would avoid an explicit rebuff. If Roland were not at home, I could turn around and go home; if he were at home, it did not seem likely that he would turn me away from his door.

I think I may have cultivated unconsciously the belief that Roland preferred for another reason to receive guests unexpectedly. If the arrival of someone had not been premeditated, then Roland's piloting of that someone to his table was easier. Roland could present himself as a victim of circumstance. Debbie's objections could not fairly be directed at him. And the uninvited guest, once inside, could either court or assume Debbie's approval. Perhaps Roland's engaging responses to past unadvertised visits had encouraged me to incubate that belief. I imagined that others had formed similar views. *Maybe I'll drop in on Roland and we'll have a few bongs*—that might have been the triggering thought for many a foray, from someone pondering upon what might complete his Saturday.

The sketch too seems to expand upon my recalling of Roland as a generous host. I am thinking not so much of his material generosity—his ready supplying of bong ingredients—as of his generous outlook. After he had moved in with Debbie, and once you had got yourself inside his front door, you always felt as though Roland wanted nothing better than to host you and share a few bongs. Your aim too was only to share a few bongs and go nowhere. Once you had settled in at his table, you never got the impression from Roland that your weak appetite for further excursions made you a second-rate guest.

* * *

Roland made the jaffles, put them in the jaffle-maker and phoned Jamie.

* * *

Roland attended to a knock at the front door.

"Jamie!" he exclaimed. "I'd been thinking of phoning you!"

"Roland! How are you going?"

The duo joined Debbie, who was inspecting the movie guide, at the living room table.

"Would you like a bong?" Roland asked.

"I'd love a bong."

"Don't you have one Roland, you won't be able to drive." Debbie turned to Jamie. "We're going out tonight," she apologised.

Roland packed the bowl of the bong with mull and passed the instrument to Jamie, who had sat down.

"If I have one," Jamie said, fingering the bong thoughtfully, "then Roland will have to have one to keep me company."

"That's right," Roland said brightly, as though he had not thought of this until then. "Jamie's the guest."

I SUSPECT THAT WHEN I composed this sketch, I had loosely in mind as the third point of the triangle Jamie Danielson, who had graduated about the time I decamped down to Queen Street and had found work immediately, even in those meagre days. Within a few years he had departed for England, having secured an offer from none other than Jaguar cars, a firm that may have been failing but was still very famous. While I was at Keppel Street, we had hosted Jamie every now and again. He had got to know Roland slightly, and he had got into conversations with Bob, which I believe he found less exhausting than I found them. Ambitious claims that I might have sought at length to refute, Jamie would dismiss, and with incisive ripostes that left Bob with little ground to defend. I have seen it happen, but I cannot reproduce those dismissals.

After I came down to Mornington, and Jamie started in Broadmeadows with Ford, I saw him less often, although I knew he had kept up relationships with Roland and Bob. There was an occasion in the year after the expiry of Steve when I experienced myself as mildly affronted by how comfortable Jamie had become with Roland. I had arrived at Abbotsford one night unannounced, and had found Jamie there. It had disconcerted me to see how secure Jamie looked, behind a bong at Roland's dining table.

* * *

"Jamie! Is that your second?"

"It is," Jamie said. He nodded sagely. "I've had two bongs."

"I'll just have to keep you company with another one," Roland said.

"Roland! You won't be able to drive...!"

"How do you feel?" Roland asked Jamie.

"I feel pretty good."

"Could you drive?"

"I think I could," Jamie said, emphasising could.

"Roland! If you have another one and can't drive I'll be very annoyed."

"I'll be able to drive."

"What time is it?" Debbie asked.

Jamie looked at his watch. "It's just after seven."

"We'll have to go soon."

"See what's on later," Roland suggested. "A lot don't start until nine thirty." He filled the bong with mull, lit it and smoked it, extinguishing the match with a flick of his hand. He blew out the smoke, shook his head, and frowned in satisfaction.

I NEVER TOLD MY father about how the end had come for Steve. I never told him about Steve at all. He would not have been sympathetic. And my feelings in connection with Steve's death were complex. I thought I ought to have felt grief, but I never discovered myself to be grieving. I was sad for Steve, but I was glad he had gone—glad for me. Gordon, doubtless, would have told me I was lucky that I had not gone with him. My father's instincts, and those of my mother, would have been restraining, as though by retiring behind the boundaries of your parish you could shut out all of the world's evils. Perhaps my attraction to attending Roland's table on a Saturday, in the years following immediately upon Steve's departure, was founded partly on my desire to connect with those evils, through connecting with the event of Steve's passing away. My awareness of my jubilation on that mournful afternoon has nagged at me since. I might have liked Gordon to help me make sense of how good I felt then.

We had brought to those circumstances no guide from our elders. We had constructed a ritual for our mourning, or so it seemed to me afterwards. The service for Steve that his parents held had felt trivial. No one else there but Pash had known Steve like we knew him. It had been as though I were at a memorial for somebody else. I think that Steve would have characterised his memorial as a bit of a gyp. He would have laughed, and passed on. Or so I imagine, now that I am thinking about what Steve might have thought.

If I had invited my mother and father to the service, as warm participants in this acknowledging of loss, and if they had attended, they would have lectured me afterwards in a way that made them sound clever. Neither had been silly enough to know someone like Steve. You chose your company carefully.

I recall an occasion on which I acted on advice of this kind, and my regretting soon afterwards that I had done so. Very likely, I formed then an intention to forestall further regrets, and by refraining from offering occasions for further advice. I had begun at university. A member of the motorcycle club had invited me, with every other member, to a party. It had been made plain that I could stay overnight at the venue, and under admonishment from my father, on the likelihood of my drinking, I had revealed this possibility as a mark of my forethought. I can capture the flavour of his response. "You're proposing to stay out all night, and drink. With people you have met once or twice. And heaven knows who else. Will you sleep on the floor? On the floor, drunk. Where you don't know the owners." His tone, a mutter as much as an outburst, had not invited a defensive reply. My mother had deeper concerns. "They might throw in their keys," Mary-Therese warned me, having been advised by my father of the sleepover offer. "If you don't know what that means, you're too young to be going." All of this in a mere day and a half. But I had felt bound to forewarn them.

On the Saturday morning, my mother breakfasted in her bedroom. My father sat me down for a chat. "Your mother is very, very worried about you going along to this booze-up," he said. Or something like that. Said softly, perhaps wearily, as though I had inquired at an opportune moment whether he were well, having observed over days a persistent frown and bleak smile, and he had accepted the opportunity to confide in me. "You could skip this one, surely. There will be other chances. Settle into the year. You know we are very proud of you. We don't mind you having the motorbike—we know that you're sensible. We just think you should wait." Something like that. The venue was on the other side of town, in a suburb with which I was not familiar. It was not very difficult for me to share dinner with my family and announce over the course of it that I would be staying in. Do I recall a mocking look across the table from my brother, two years younger and less successful at school? Whether I recall it or not, I assume it. I do recall a breezy thank-you from my mother, after dinner while I dried dishes for her. She added a coda that I have dwelt upon since. "Your father really had been very anxious about you."

I am noticing now, and perhaps for the first time, that I had been surprised by these expressions of concern for my welfare. I had not thought even of my mother as an unusually anxious person: rather, my parents were cautious but competent. I had attended to such expressions not as disclosures of their inner states but as attempts to share wisdom.

My father had expressed to me, on one occasion joining in this with my mother, some concern that I had shown little enthusiasm for excursions with girls. Perhaps I had been surprised because a girl I knew had shown some enthusiasm for me, I think earlier in that same year. I had not imagined that my parents might have preferred me to exploit this interest publicly rather than privately. Certainly, I never thought that if I had revealed to them our activities, Mary-Therese or even Gordon would have celebrated those activities. I may have assumed this was something they preferred not to think about. But evidently, it was something they did think about. I can all but imagine their consulting one another over whether they should act to correct what they may have apprehended as my tardiness in approaching a milestone, when in infancy, as they reported it, I had whizzed past all milestones. And I imagine also that they had little idea what they could do to advantage, apart from poking me with their pointed inquiries. I am certain that if I had taken to stepping out every Friday and Saturday with one girl or another, I would have been reproved for failing to prioritise study. There had been no girls at school.

I do not think that my mother had wrung much interest from men before she met my father, when well into her twenties. Perhaps in part because of her damaged leg—or more obviously, because of how she had felt about that. No one ever described to me in detail the incident in which she came to merit her prosthesis. I believe that she had been very young, and that the instrument of her misfortune had been a tractor, and I believe that my grandfather, an orchardist, and always extravagantly solicitous of my mother, had been the only other witness to this event. As far as I know, my father had never been attracted to amputees as a class. It was accepted that he had admired my mother for her spirit in the face of adversity, and she had admired him for his never retreating from the prospect of taking her on. I can see that as you grow up among such accommodations, you accept them as facts. I have imagined since that my mother made an unusually stationary target at a suburban dance she had attended with my patient aunt, and that my father, new to the parish, had persuaded himself that she might be waiting for him. I have wondered how he felt in the moment when he discerned her disfigurement.

* * *

"What's Debbie like as a driver?" Jamie asked Roland, assuming a dramatically serious, big-question tone.

"Who votes we should drive in Debbie's car?" Roland asked, loudly enough that Debbie, washing dishes nearby, could not fail to hear him.

"I have to admit," Jamie said, persisting with his grave intonation, "I don't really think I'd feel comfortable driving at all."

Roland giggled.

"What about you?" Jamie asked.

Roland shook his head. "I really don't feel like driving."

"I'll drive," Debbie announced.

"I think Roland means he doesn't feel up to driving in a car at all," Jamie explained. "Even if you were driving."

"Especially if you were driving," Roland said, giggling. He giggled again. "No," he said, "I didn't mean that."

"Roland, you are a giggling mess. You both are. You've both turned into giggling messes. Roland, I'm sick of it, we never go anywhere."

"Is there anything you desperately wanted to see?"

"I was waiting to see what you wanted to see."

"I don't mind. Is there anything you desperately wanted to see?"

"No. I just want to go out."

"Does it have to be tonight?"

"Roland, I want to go out somewhere. I'm sick of sitting around here."

Roland said solemnly: "I'm a bit too stoned to go anywhere. I could make the effort, but ..." he looked at Jamie, "we'd prefer not to."

"Roland. Come on, make an effort."

"Is there anything you desperately wanted to see?"

"I don't mind. I just want to go somewhere."

"What time is it?" Roland asked.

Jamie consulted his watch. "Nine twenty-five," he announced.

"Is it nine twenty-five?"

"Looks like it," Roland said.

"Is it really nine twenty-five?"

Jamie showed Debbie his watch.

"Oh well," Roland said. "I guess we'll just have to have another bong."

HOW I GOT IT into my head that Roland might like to read this sketch, I do not know. It is possible that I had believed my place to have been usurped by Jamie, and I had wanted to punish Roland, but I do not think that was the case. By the time it was written, a year or more after the time in which it was set, Jamie would have been overseas. I think it was more a matter of my having assumed that Roland when he stymied Debbie understood himself better than he did. There had been times when I had smoked bongs at Roland's with Jamie and had observed the sort of parrying dialogue reported in the sketch. Possibly I had been impressed by how effectively it had shielded us, and had wanted to see whether I could capture it and present it in prose. I would have been proud of my effort, and may have wanted Roland to admire it, as he had admired previously the vignette that he had handed on to Steve. Perhaps I had also thought it might prod Roland towards disentangling himself from Debbie's clutches, which I had come increasingly to view as smothering. I would have written it long after I had begun to see this sort of deflecting as commonplace.

I cannot say whether the descriptions of the late rising and of the lying about in the backyard while stonewalling Debbie's entreaties that he participate in household chores had been drawn from observations I had made, or had been invented—although I do believe I observed Roland reclining lazily one afternoon on their plastic folding outdoor lounge. Possibly I had been sitting next to him at the time, on a chair dragged into the sun from the living room, and ruminating upon the suggestion that another bong might be helpful. Possibly Debbie had come out then and had implored Roland to do something that she had thought would be helpful. The pavlova was a construction, along with Roland's interior processes, but my constructing it would have been founded on a tale I had heard from Debbie, about how Roland had interfered greedily with her plans for a dessert. I have the faintest of recollections that the two of them had developed a custom for when Debbie was baking and Roland was stoned: if she had mixed something sweet, she would present Roland with the mixer blades so that he could lick them clean. Perhaps she had offered him this private thrill in my presence.

It is not difficult for me to see now why Roland was much less appreciative of this story than I had hoped. He read it in front of me, one night at his house after not many bongs, occasionally looking up at me, but not laughing as I had expected, and then he had handed it back. Debbie had been out somewhere, probably working. When I asked him what he thought of it, Roland told me simply: "I don't think we're like that." I explained to him that the character Roland was not intended to represent, directly, him. "I suppose we are a bit like that sometimes," he admitted.

I would have been drawn by Roland's unease into pigeonholing the piece as an extended speculation on the conflict that seemed so often to simmer, if usually quietly, under the hospitality that Roland extended at Abbotsford. But as I transcribe it now, what strikes me much more is the attempt to paint in the cosiness together of Roland and Jamie. Jamie, as presented, was not much more than I plus a couple of undermining remarks—remarks I might even have made myself in effect, although less directly.

I think it is that comfort that I have enjoyed as I have reinhabited that period through pursuing the prose. And perhaps also, I have enjoyed the commonality expressed in my conspiring with Roland to frustrate Debbie's interfering desires. Desires for something other than what Roland and I desired, which was to sit together and have a chat and a drink, and to down a few bongs. At the time, I was able to believe that this was what we both desired—I suspect my high degree of confidence in that belief is why I have returned to a theme that I have reflected on previously. In a way—I suppose in every way—Roland's stonewalling of Debbie's entreaties provided me constantly with evidence that Roland did indeed want what I wanted: to continue with what we were doing until we were soothed, or until one of us needed to sleep. I do not know what we talked about. My engaging with Debbie on Roland's behalf I would have undertaken warily—more warily than I represented Jamie to have engaged with Debbie—but then that overt engagement had been something I had noticed, and had rejoiced in, about Jamie in those circumstances. I would have feared that in engaging as directly with Debbie I would have taken a step too far, and would have manoeuvred Roland into colluding with her to repel me. I would not have wanted to risk that.

I suppose I should ask myself what else I feel as I re-encounter this piece. I cannot answer that question easily. My first thought is simply that I find reading it to be pacifying. That I experience a sense of calmness and also a sense of belonging, neither of which I think of as feelings at all. Rather, I apprehend them as absences of feeling, or at least as absences of distress. There I was at Roland's, on another Saturday night, and everything was in its place.

As I meditate upon that easy mutuality, I remember again that there was coexisting with it some tension: the possibility that all of it would be swept away in an instant and that Debbie would have her victory. And so, over the entire evening I would have been working to support Roland in his keeping Debbie at bay. Such cosiness as I experienced was the sort of cosiness you might feel in a tiny but sturdy tent pitched in the lee of a natural windbreak while enduring a storm. You were protected from furious Nature by an artfully constructed device, but that protection depended on your being alert for any instability in the device that might betray an incipient failure.

And then eventually, if you were vigilant, the storm would abate and the tent would still be comfortable. You could relax in your outpost and enjoy the profits of your attentiveness and good fortune.

* * *

"Would you like a bong?" Jamie asked Debbie kindly.

"No, thank you."

"Have a bong!" Roland said.

"No! I'm annoyed."

"You will feel good," Jamie told her helpfully.

"You'll feel as good as us," Roland said.

"NO! I don't feel well. I've got a headache. And I'm very annoyed. Roland you promised we were going out and you promised you wouldn't be a giggling mess. And look at you. Look at both of you."

Roland looked at Jamie.

"Do I look like a giggling mess?" he asked, giggling.

* * *

"I'm tired," Debbie said. "I really am very tired. I was up quite early this morning. I'm not used to being up this early on a Saturday. Oh," (she shuddered) "only one more day and then I have to go to work."

Roland, who had been eating a chocolate and marshmallow biscuit, stopped chewing.

"Ooer!" he exclaimed, as though he had stepped waist-deep into a sewer. "Work. Oh well, there's still tomorrow."

"Now you won't leave too much of a mess tonight, will you," Debbie implored him. "Put some things away before you go to bed, Roland. Please!"

"I'll help you clean it up in the morning," Roland said.

"And don't make too much noise. I don't want to be woken up."

* * *

"Can I have another one of those chocolate biscuits?" Jamie asked, when Debbie had gone.

"Yeah," Roland said. "Oh," he continued, "No."

"What's the matter?"

"You can have one if you want one. But I've just remembered. There's something much better…"

He stood up, stepped lightly to the fridge, opened it, removed Debbie's cake platter, returned to the table and placed the platter before Jamie, repeating the return journey to the kitchen for spoons.

"I saved some for you," he said.

"Is it pavlova?"

"Yeah. I'm sorry it's a bit of a mess. Have some."

Their spoons scraped on the platter. "Quiet," Roland said.

"Mmm," Jamie said. "This is great."

"It's pretty good."

"Good dope, too," Jamie said.

"Thanks."

"In fact, this has been a really pleasant evening. It was really worthwhile coming over. But then," Jamie smiled at Roland appreciatively, "It usually is with you."

"Thanks." Roland gave a small laugh, blowing frothy marshmallow from his lips.

"Sorry," he said. He wiped his mouth.

"Well," he said, "I guess it's time for another bong."

5

GENUINE FILTER COFFEE

I HAD MET PATIENCE MOORE ONCE PRIOR TO STEVE'S funeral. It had been at a party for Shooka, in a South Yarra bar. I had felt diminished by the flamboyance evident in the outfits I had been glimpsing as people moved in and out of their groups. Most guests were industry friends, Shooka had told me. Roland had pointed out a few rock identities—local players whom he recognised and thought I may have heard of, or whose bands I may have heard of. I had not known previously where Shooka worked, and I had been impressed to learn she was with a promoter. She had welcomed me, and had seemed very happy to see me, but I had not felt very comfortable there, and had recognised no one else but Steve, Roland and Debbie. The four of us had kept to ourselves. Bob had arrived, had joined us for a single drink, and had departed after a brief exchange with Pash. Pash had been all over the room. I have an image of her silhouetted against a lamp over the bar, her head thrown back, drinking from a bottle. Debbie had introduced her to me as Patience. Patience had extended her hand to be shaken. "Everybody calls me Pash," she had told me, leaning close so that I would hear her over the music. I understood that this was a familiar setting for her, but I had been astonished to discover that this was Steve's girlfriend. I had been astonished again, when Steve lay in his coma, to hear Debbie say that at last he had been settling down. I had forgotten about Pash. I had assumed that such a mismatch could not endure.

I WAS NOT GOING to write about Pash. And now I am writing about Pash. A chapter in my life that went nowhere. But perhaps it went somewhere. Pash changed me, and simply by choosing me. And Pash changed me, I need to admit, for the better. Where would I have been without her. That is not a question, for I know where I may well have been. I may well have been sidestepping inquiries still from one parent or both, about when I was going to meet a nice girl. I had got good at that, and it had helped that I saw those two less and less often. Pash was impossible, and yet Pash materialised. And then ... but I am writing about happy times. Of course my time with Pash was a happy time.

I feel less agitated today about where Bob was in this. What had motivated him? Had he thought he was helping me, or had he thought only that he was helping Pash? Or had he mainly been helping himself? It is difficult for me to think of Bob's motivations as selfless. Possibly Bob was there mainly for the show: he had thought he might find it entertaining to observe our encounter. And then again, Bob knew more about Pash than I knew, and perhaps more than I ever knew. He foresaw the whole thing. Or at a minimum, if I can believe what he claimed of himself after the fact, he had speculated accurately. But then again, when he recorded his speculation the facts had long been established. That would have been just like Bob, representing himself in narration as a soothsayer when his prescience relied on hindsight. Was there no end to Bob's pride?

ZAMYR ZHUZHUMI, AND JESSICA Faithfull. One name a source of delight for bike club members quizzed about Zoom. The other, in hindsight, ironic but apt. Jessica had faith in herself.

Nor was Zoom in the habit of second-guessing himself. He was proud of his past. Left school early, got a job and went motorbike racing. Did as well as he could on the means that he had, and then ditched that for travelling. Backpacked his way through three continents, and resolved that painting would be his new thing. "There's nothing else I want to do," he would say, with a half-grin, explaining himself. "I've done everything I used to want."

We enjoyed Zoom's resourcefulness. Our galley-style kitchen had a sink at one end that lay under a window. A U-bracket had pulled free from the sink's rotting backboard, so that it no longer supported our cold-water tap. Zoom had undone a wire coathanger, had looped an end around the tap, had led the other end over the window sill, and had suspended from it, balancing the tap, a house-brick. A groove carved into the sill let the window close snugly. "Fuck nails!" he exclaimed, when he had satisfied himself that the fix would endure. "And the board's rooted anyway."

When Sandy teamed up with Jessica, both had been teenagers. Perhaps this was three years before I had met them. Did I know that feeling where you just wanted to be with someone *all the time*, Sandy had asked me rhetorically, recalling the intensity of his youthful obsession.

On one warm afternoon my composing was interrupted by a smirking Jessica, trailed by a reticent but high-spirited Sandy.

"We wanted to ask you ..." Jessica said, turning to her spouse for affirmation.

"Yes?"

"If we made a spa bath, would old vacuum cleaners make enough bubbles? And," glancing again at Sandy, her expression telling me she knew just how silly she sounded, "would you be electrocuted?"

WHEN I WAS STILL at Carlton I had read Thoreau, alerted to the existence of *Walden* by a passage in *Zen and the Art of Motorcycle Maintenance*, which I had purchased on the strength of a favourable review in the magazine *Two Wheels*. There was a time when magazines were thick and contained articles that I found enlightening. *Zen* I enjoyed, if partly for the bike trip it recounted, but reading *Walden* was like eating a dahl that concealed tiny chillies. "The mass of men live lives of quiet desperation," Thoreau had written, and that had resonated—indeed, it still resonates. I thought immediately at the time of my father. This was the kind of line I might have quoted in conversation with Bob, in the hope that I might impress him with a titbit he had not tasted already. But I doubt I did quote it. What I quoted to Bob, more than once, was an injunction from Thoreau on commitment: "As long as possible live free and uncommitted. It makes but little difference whether you are committed to a farm or the county jail." I had been very taken with Thoreau's opening qualifier, *as long as possible*. As I enjoyed reminding Bob, and especially as he became less available to me, and more needful of preserving himself for his work: Thoreau knew that commitment crept up on you.

WAS IT MY FATHER'S relations with my mother that had most exercised me as an example of a wholly voluntary and avoidable constraint that nevertheless, once volunteered for, became a constraint? I am sure that I never discussed this example with Bob. I had formed the belief, even before I had settled upon an account of their meeting, that my father would have done much better had he moved to another city after he confirmed that my mother's lower leg was prosthetic. And that, had he not waited for confirmation but had simply moved on as soon as he had intuited that there was something amiss, he could have done so with his honour intact, or very nearly, and so would not even have had to move suburbs. But drawn into an awkward embrace, perhaps wondering at first why she danced so badly, perhaps even ensnared almost immediately by a confession from her of just why, he must have felt himself bound to dance on, I had concluded. I can see now that matters beyond my callow understanding may have influenced him. I believe he has long overvalued the bird in the hand.

My mother had learned to walk well enough, and I have seen her dance slowly. Long ago I saw her run, contriving a loping hobble. I have seen her balance on a bicycle, also very long ago. She has never been drawn to strenuous exercise.

Have I ever seen Gordon grin unreservedly? Perhaps once or twice. Once after he had pulled off a fluke shot at pool. He used to play sometimes with the husband of a friend of my mother, whose property we would visit as children. It was as though a fragment of fun had slipped into his body, and had animated him briefly before he collared it and expelled it. It would have helped that he had been drinking a whisky, a form of release that I never saw him partake of at home. He may have told himself that he was being polite.

Satisfaction came from achievement, my father would explain to me in a grave tone at moments he thought opportune. Mainly in the years immediately following my abandonment of my studies in engineering. It was as though he were pointing out for me a truth that he thought I had missed. He had swallowed his disappointment over my failing to qualify for a profession, but he seemed determined that I replace my lost prospects. I needed to obtain for myself, he would tell me, a ticket. By which I believe he meant, if metaphorically, a licence to trade, such as the boilermaker's licence that he had secured and that had qualified him for a maintenance job at the food factory he went on to manage. A ticket that could entrench me in a role from which the drifters whom he hired seasonally as grunt labour were barred. Possibly I addicted myself to receiving this speech, in the way that a gambler might addict himself to the discovery that, once again, he had lost. Did I envy my father his steady empayment, as I may as well call it? I did not. I will admit that he never said so, but I inferred that satisfaction described for my father all that was good about life. I could never see enough goodness in it.

It was at Queen Street that I named for the first time what ingredient I thought my father's simple formula for good living lacked. It was pleasure. It was as though he had swallowed whole the Catholic principle that it was wise to refrain from pursuing pleasure before you had died, so that you could be more certain of finding it afterwards.

When I looked at Zoom, Jessica and Sandy at Queen Street, I think it seemed to me, although I could not have said this then, that they had achieved contentment through their pursuit of pleasure. Even if they found pleasure in activities that were, in the broad sense, productive. That such a heady chase carried risks was not beneath my notice, but things seemed to be going well. The price of my adopting their priorities was most apparent to me late at night, when I would wake and worry about being overtaken by Bob and by Jamie, and by other acquaintances who had entered professions. Jamie's starting income had staggered me for its generosity. It was not that I envied people their money. Rather, I wondered whether their wealthier lives were more pleasant, on balance. On any sunny morning, subsisting at Queen Street seemed overwhelmingly preferable to doing anything else, but at other times I could admire others' choices.

I do not know whether it was Steve's death that led me to withdraw from my job at the TAB. At the time I did not think it was; rather, entering I think my fourth year there, I had begun to fear I would do something that would get me a dishonourable discharge. I had been nodding off while on duty, and more and more often. I would wake to a chirp in my headphones, and a supervisor's two-word demand that I rouse myself. A break from the job might preserve the possibility that I could return, which looked smarter than staying until I was sacked. The dole office did not put up much of a fuss: it was not as though I had left something permanent.

Not needing to get to the city on even three days each week for work meant I got there less to see friends. It became much more difficult to justify simply dropping in on someone, a consequence of my quitting that I had not foreseen.

I think it was about February of '85 when I left the TAB, and for a while the winnowing of short-notice sessions with Roland and others was made up for by the usual throng of warm-weather visitors to Queen Street. Our fortunes suggested that my fortnightly reports to the dole office were whimsical. Jessica had picked up regular evening shifts as a part-time telephonist at the Frankston exchange. I had thought she would prefer pub or restaurant work—she would have made an alluring barmaid—but the job had come to her through a family friend who was about to retire. Sandy had won a weekday morning shift running the desk at the biggest local fuel stop, a pioneering self-serve on the highway just out of town. He was not happy about getting up early but he enjoyed the free afternoons and it brought in the bucks. Zoom had exhibited in a couple of group shows organised by his teacher and had sold a few pictures, at prices that barely covered his costs for the canvases but he felt he had taken big steps. He still had better paid activity behind the parts counter at the big multi-franchise bike dealer at Frankston—just helping to catch up with ordering Mondays and Tuesdays and to cope with traffic Saturday mornings, or so he had told me when I asked. It did not sound demanding. I had long been the wealthiest, not counting the capital injections Jessica got sometimes from her parents, but quitting dropped me to poorest, with Sandy taking the lead on the strength of his five days—at a lowly rate but the hours added up.

I wrote a piece for a bike magazine. We had a stack of these in the lounge room, donated by visitors, and they included some biker-lifestyle titles—stories about hot Harley-Davidsons and silly things that girls did for blokes. My story was an embellished rendition of a tale that had amused me on an evening years before at a pub with the bike club. The editors placed it in a section they held open for readers' tall and true yarns, and sent me $65. I had spent many days piecing together those 500-odd words, returning to them half a dozen times over almost as many months and producing as many versions. When I told my father of my victory, he asked me how much my occupation would have earned me per hour. A fair question, I had thought at the time.

Over the next few months I did two more bikie stories, both accepted, and sent off a fourth. That was not going to keep me in comfort, but $90—they had got a bit longer—covered a month's rent at Queen Street while leaving plenty for bills, and after receiving two such cheques in the mail, and having been assured of one more, and having seen no reason why I would report my small windfalls to the federal government, I was feeling quite prosperous by the beginning of June, not missing my city friends nor our dwindling drop-in guests a great deal, and settling in for a solidly productive winter.

IT WAS WHILE BENEFITING from a relatively optimistic outlook, then, that I sat sharing a quiet joint with Zoom about eight one Thursday evening, watching Sandy's back retreat down the dim hallway as he responded to a surprise jingling from the bicycle bell. We had all thought it might be Jessica, for some reason returning a few hours early from work. But it was not Jessica; it was Bob, accompanied, I could see more clearly as Sandy led them down the hall, by Pash. I can still get a sense of my successive responses as I recognised Pash's dark hair and diminutive, compared with Bob's, figure, and excitable voice, a metre or two before the trio reached the brighter light of our dining space. They had the contrasting themes you might encounter when sipping on a gin and tonic: excitement and anticipation as the cold, acidic, slightly sweet liquid hits your tongue, followed almost immediately by a resistance to the bitterness of the quinine. It was not Pash herself whom I resisted; rather it was my own leap of interest in accommodating the visit. I appreciated before that leap was complete that Pash had attended with Bob, and that this could mean all sorts of things, most implying that she had not expressed a strong desire to see me.

"Bob and ... Pash," Sandy announced to Zoom with the gleeful inflection he used when he thought something was funny.

"Pash," Zoom said. "I suppose you get a few giggles with that."

"Not especially. Not from anyone who knows me, anyway."

"That's *worse*!" said Sandy, his voice rising, slightly stoned and perhaps somewhat relieved that our visitor had been neither a distressed Jessica nor an official of some kind with a nose for the smoke in the hall. "Don't people keep coming up to you and going: *Pash?*" He presented his lips.

Pash kissed him, a soft-looking, but evidently saliva-laden, smack. Sandy sprang back, wiping his mouth.

"Ooer!"

"No," said Pash. "I do that."

"Do it to me," Zoom said. "I won't go anywhere."

"Yuk!" said Pash. "I've heard about you!"

"What? That I've got AIDS?"

"No! Just that you might have. Anyway I don't like kissing gay men." Pash looked vulnerable, but rebounded with: "And you've been warned; you'll probably do something disgusting back."

"What you did wasn't *that* disgusting," said Sandy.

"You're married," said Pash. "You're honour-bound to find it disgusting."

"Well, I'm not *really* married. I could still change my mind."

"Yuk!" said Pash.

"Come here and give me a juicy one," said Zoom. "Otherwise I'll be offended."

"You won't be offended!"

"I will! I'll tell everybody *Pash won't pash poofters!*"

"Shamo!" said Bob. "Are you happy to be presiding over all this fun and merriment?"

"I don't know that I'm presiding over it but I'm happy to see you both."

"Seamus," Pash said. "Hi ..."

"Where's *my* pash," I recall myself asking, infected by the mood and the dope and the wine that I had been sharing with Sandy. And then, collecting myself, "Sorry, that was a bit silly."

"Later, maybe," Pash said, with a quick glance at Bob, generating in me that quinine jolt again.

We offered them seats at the table. Zoom began rolling another joint; Bob opened a bottle of red wine; Sandy found glasses. I felt peculiar about Pash being there: in hindsight, enormously excited, but also frightened that I would say the wrong thing, something sillier than had popped out already. That I would make a fool of myself, and by betraying my excitement.

"How is your work going?" Pash said.

"Okay. Sort of. I am getting stuff done. Doing pieces for a bikie magazine."

"Bob said you had written a few other things."

"I have. Just things about me and my friends."

"So ...?"

"I've realised that the friends might not like them. Don't really know why I did them."

"Well, I liked your story about Roland and Steve."

"I was really grateful, at Steve's funeral, that you told me you liked that. And I'm a bit embarrassed it was you offering me stuff, rather than me offering something to you, who really had lost somebody. Well, I had too, but—I'm sorry, I knew this would happen. I was sorry about Steve, but not as much as you. Of course. Still am. Of course I still am. But not as much as you. Damn," I said. "How's that joint going, Zoom?"

"Roland has told me how you felt about Steve," Pash said, giving me a wry but accepting smile. "You don't need to apologise."

"But I am sorry. I can be so insensitive..."

A laugh from Pash. "Well, I *had* heard that."

Bob said: "Insensitive, Shamo? Who'd have thought such a thing."

"Only those who know him," Sandy said.

"When he's had a smoke, or two," Zoom contributed.

"And a drink," Sandy said.

"Or two," Bob added, drawing sniggers from Sandy and Zoom, the latter having to suspend moistening the sticky edge of his joint but soon returning to the task and handing the finished article to me.

"Just what the doctor ordered," Bob said.

"Ha ha," I said. "I'll smoke this and then you'll all laugh at me."

"I promise not to laugh," Pash said, attempting a flat expression, but I could see she was repressing a grin.

"Laugh?" Zoom said. "If you laugh, we'll parade your poofter-shy pucker down the main street in a pram, yelling PASH, PASH, IT'S PASH THE GAY BASHER!"

"We never laugh at Seamus," Sandy said.

"Unless he laughs at us," Zoom said. "Or makes fun of us. Or insults us. Or tells us we're idiots. Or that my pictures are piss-poor..."

"...Or that he's in love with Jessica, and is only pretending to write things so that he can stay down here and fuck her," Sandy said.

"But you'd never do that, would you Mr O," Bob said. Bob had taken to calling me Mr O, short for Mr O'Hare, because I had begun to show signs of early-onset baldness, or so he diagnosed, claiming he had got to know an expert through his doctoring contacts.

"He'll start doing something like that in about ten seconds," Sandy said, glee rising again in his tone, as I inhaled a toke from the long three-paper joint Zoom had rolled, privileged to be beginning it so that my draught was well cooled by unburnt head and tobacco before it entered my windpipe. It went down smoothly, without triggering coughing.

"He could have handed it to Pash," Zoom said. "Let *her* start it."

"I'll be fine," said Pash. "I can see you have your own rituals. And I'm not laughing."

"Not yet," Zoom said. "I give you about forty-five seconds."

"There's nothing to laugh about," I said. "You didn't put anything in this. It's a trick, a placebo. If I laugh, then you'll laugh because I'm laughing, because it's funny that I'm laughing, because there's nothing for me to be laughing about, because you've given me a placebo. Which you probably think already is funny," I finished, admitting to myself that I sounded lame.

"You wouldn't know a placebo if you smoked it," Bob said. "You're just hoping that's a placebo, because if it's not then things will go the way they usually do and Pash will start laughing at you."

"Pash wouldn't laugh at me," I said. "She knows I know this is a placebo, and so if I do anything funny she'll know I'm putting it on because I know this is a placebo."

Or so I imagine. The conversation went something like that. All excitement and general merriment. I took my second toke on the joint and handed it on to Pash, next in line to my left at the end of the table.

"I might laugh after I've had this," Pash told me.

"Well who cares," Zoom said, "We're all friends here. Even if you won't pash me."

"Yuk!" Pash said, mirthful but unwavering. "It's your moustache!"

"You're worried it will get tangled with yours."

"I don't have a moustache!"

"All dark-haired women have moustaches," Zoom said. "It's a scientific fact. You'd know," he told Bob. "Tell us it's not true."

"Well, technically speaking, all Caucasian women have moustaches," said Bob. "It's a defect of the race …"

"*I am not defective!*" Pash retorted.

"No, normal," said Zoom. "Moustache."

"Do I have a moustache?" Pash turned more side-on to me, so that I could have examined freely, if less agitated, her cute nose, slightly soft, rounded chin with, I realised suddenly, a scar under it reaching around towards her cheek.

"Not that I can see," I said.

"Are you sure you can see mine?" Zoom said.

"You're disgusting," said Pash.

"At least I'm not a poofter basher."

"Lady and gentlemen," Bob said. "I think the talk should pass to more weighty matters. Who would like some more wine? And where is Jessica? And would you mind if we stayed over? We can sleep in the lounge. We've brought sleeping bags. Could use the beanbags and couch cushions, if you were okay with that. We have serious business to discuss with Mr O here, if we can conclude this orgy in time to say something serious. But there's no rush. We can let him get a bit weirder, and wait until he straightens out. And if he doesn't straighten out, we can get him tomorrow. We're here for tonight and tomorrow, if nobody minds and we can get a little privacy for shut-eye when we need it. I'm not back at work until Sunday; Pash is okay till Monday. We're here to keep you entertained, distract you from your usual unproductive stress-free lives, absorb some of that into us; have a holiday from the real world."

"Bob!" Pash said. "No wonder I've never seen you smoke! We can drive home tonight," she said. "If that's easier."

"Yeah, we'll kick you out!" Zoom said. "No poofter non-pashers allowed."

"Stay as long as you want," Sandy said. "But I'll be crashing soon. Five o'clock start. Just don't be too noisy, please. Better not get him started," with a nod at me, as the joint, having bypassed Bob, reached me. "That should be his last toke."

"I've a big day tomorrow too," I said. "Lots to do."

"When do you start?" Pash asked me.

"Ten," I said, thinking already that I might take the day off.

"A likely story," Bob said. "We've only just started."

IT WAS AFTER JESSICA had returned from her shift, drunk a glass of wine with us, and retired, and after Zoom had declined to roll me another joint, had reminded us to keep his stereo low, and had retired also, that Pash said brightly:

"Well, we've brought something down for you!"

The three of us remaining had moved into the gas-heated lounge, from where our voices were less likely to carry. It was the room where Bob had dismantled a year or two earlier my recording of Roland's departure from Keppel Street. Zoom's amp and turntable were still mounted on milk crates. Pash and Bob had sunk into beanbags on either side of the fire, and I had seated myself between them, nearer Pash, on a director's chair I had brought from the dining room. Pash had looked across at Bob, and had reached into a small black shoulder bag.

"What?" I asked.

"Something you mislaid," said Bob, picking up Pash's cue.

"And I rescued," said Pash. "Tell me you like me."

"What...?"

"Tell me you like me. Go on. Is that such a struggle? You don't like me? I thought maybe you did like me. But if you don't..." She began to withdraw from her search of the bag.

"Wait! I have to tell you I like you or you won't show me whatever it is you've brought down for me..."

"... Which you've sorely missed," Bob said. "Or maybe not so sorely."

"Well of course I like you," I told Pash. I believe I remember this scene accurately, and I do not find the memory wholly pleasant.

"Of course...?"

"Look, I think I like you. You know what? I'm feeling nervous. I'm nervous around you. I've no idea what you're driving at. You come down here with Bob ... well anyway, I'm sure I like you, if it matters, and whether or not it matters. But I don't think it does. But yes." I looked Pash full in the face. "I like you."

"*Really* like me?"

"Come on you two," said Bob. "Pash, this is Shamo, I've told you already. Maybe take it a bit easy."

"A bit easy?" I said. "Yeah, maybe a bit easy. Or maybe a lot easy. No wonder I'm nervous. What have you two got planned for me?"

"Well, *ta-da!*" exclaimed Pash, producing from her bag a sheaf of papers that I recognised as a typescript, and a familiar one.

"You want it?" she said.

"What is it?" But I knew what it was.

"Your story. Your *Steve* story."

"Oh." I felt discomfited, and mainly by the extent to which I also felt gratified. I felt much as I had felt when Pash walked in from the hall, but I felt it more powerfully: delight mixed with terror. I am thinking of a man with his head through the open lunette of a guillotine, lapping up crème brûlée.

"It's been eight months," Pash said. "I was fine with you at the funeral. I had to go through Steve's stuff for mine, and stuff he'd have wanted me to have. There wasn't much competition for any of it. And I found this. I've read it a couple of times. It is a bit of a ... beating ... to read it but I like the pain. I think you have caught something about Steve in a way that's kind of special. And Roland. I like that too."

"It's different from the guitars thing," Bob said.

"Well, that doesn't have Steve in it."

"I've got something else for you," Pash said. She reached back into her bag, withdrawing a miniature bottle. She looked again at Bob and threw the bottle across to me.

"Dex," Bob said.

"Dex?"

"Dexamphetamine. Speed, or close enough. Way better, actually, given what passes for speed the way it usually comes."

"Want some?" Pash said.

"You *are* a bundle of surprises. Will it be good for me? What will it do?"

"It'll chill you out. Just have a couple of drops."

"How do I take it?"

"Down the hatch. On a spoon."

"Nothing to it," said Bob. "It's fine. I'll even have some. It's a gift horse and not to be looked in the mouth. Better you don't know where she got it from but it's completely pure. Medicinal quality, let's say—but don't read anything into that."

"Will it keep us up?"

"Probably." Pash started chuckling. "Definitely," Bob said, "And you'll be clenching your jaw. It's a bit sad coming down. But that's about it, really. It's fine on a special occasion."

"And," said Pash, "I think this is a special occasion." She took a small spoon from her bag, retrieved the bottle, and shook some drops of a clear liquid onto the spoon, handing the spoon to me. "Down the hatch. Then I want you to read to me."

"Read to you?"

Pash picked up the typescript and waved it with her free hand. "Down the hatch!"

Obediently, I swallowed the liquid, mentally consigning the next day to recovery.

Pash prepared similar doses for Bob and for herself, afterwards licking her lips and slipping down to recline on the beanbag. She proffered my typescript with an outstretched arm. I noticed for the first time her long auburn cardigan, more of a jacket. Or rather, noticed it as a carefully chosen item of apparel, rather than merely a hue inhabiting someone I found fascinating and alarming in equal measure.

"That cardigan is a beautiful colour," I said.

"I told you he liked me," Pash said to Bob. And to me: "It's a jacket."

"Thank you," I said. "This doesn't seem to be doing much."

"It's working," Bob said. "There's no rush."

"It is working," Pash said. "You look cute. Now read."

"Do you want to lie back and think of Steve?" I said.

"You are horrible. It's just as well I like you. But yes, I do actually. The music's stopped. Put some music on, quietly. What would be suitable?"

"Chick Corea," Bob said. "Have you still got *The Leprechaun*?" He told Pash: "Roland made a tape of *him*—" indicating me "—stoned and carrying on one night when he was there with the two of them. He was really excelling himself. In Carlton. Then he chopped up bits of it and set it to *The Leprechaun*. It's hilarious. I've got a copy at home, I'll play it to you some time."

"Sounds perfect," said Pash. "Put it on." She pointed a finger regally at me: "Now read!"

"I'm not even sure I can see in this light."

"There's a reading lamp there," Bob said, setting up the LP. "I'll bring it over."

In the bright light from the lamp I examined the typescript, having forgotten even what I had given it as a title. I know that under influence from the dex I felt deeply thankful for Pash's command, as though a fairy godmother had insisted it was my birthday and had decreed that I should realise any fantasy. I leaned back in my director's chair, glanced over the top of the typescript at the others, each eyeing me in expectation, and read the title I had handwritten barely eighteen months earlier: "The Student, the Dropout, and the Unemployed Man with a Degree". Steve had completed his business course, but had not yet found his job with the bank.

IT WAS an ideal autumn afternoon [I began, determined to edit freely as I went from the many handwritten corrections]. The sun's rays struck the earth at exactly the right angle to produce in the lunchtime habitués of Carlton a pleasant half-baked glow, and the wind blew litter up and down dead-end Keppel Street with satisfying gusto. Outside the bluff and uniformly forgettable single frontages of numbers 86, 88 and 90, a young man altercated with a traffic officer.

"But I live here!"

"I don't care. You haven't got a sticker on your car."

"What if I've only just moved in?"

"You'll have to take that up at the town hall."

"But that's ridiculous. You can see that I live here. I wouldn't be standing here if I didn't live here."

"It doesn't matter whether you live here or not. What matters is whether you've got a sticker on your car. You haven't. That means I can book you."

"Beautiful," said Pash, looking relaxedly at the ceiling. "I really like the way that starts. Parking guys. They are like that, aren't they. There's a spider up there I think. *No*, not a big one! Keep going!"

The parking officer got into his Mini Moke with his partner from the other side of the street, and moved off slowly down the line of cars. Leaning languidly over the side of the Moke, he began marking tyres with a yellow crayon he had fixed to the end of some water pipe for just such a purpose.

"What a wonderful person you are," shouted the youth after him. "You're probably dying to get home so that you can beat your wife!"

They ignored him. He entered his unwelcoming terrace house and slammed the door.

The closure of that heavy portal reduced by half the level

of illumination in the living room; what remained fell from the laundry skylight, passed through the interior window, and was all but absorbed by the often cursed, hashish-brown coloured carpet. As Greg moved down the hallway, past the stairs which led up to Roland's room, his eyes acclimatised slowly to the gloom. It was not necessary nor desirable to turn on a light, for he knew what he would see: the remains of Roland's nightly orgy.

He had thrown out a saucepan of boiled datura lilies, from the tree in their tiny backyard, before he had left for lectures early that morning, and had also put away or binned what food had been left out on the kitchen bench. Now, when he turned his attention to the layers of coffee cups, half-eaten bowls of cereal, bongs, ashtrays, cigarette packets, airsickness tablets, lumps of hash and silver foil which seemed to occupy every surface in the room, his spirit failed him. "Fuck him!" he said to himself. He had a lecture in half an hour, had eaten no lunch, and had just got a parking ticket. Why, he wondered, should he spend any more of the bright day in this dungeon, cleaning up after his spineless housemate as he had day after day for more than a month? He picked up his bag to go, then on an explosive impulse took out some paper and scribbled an abusive note to Roland. Then he fled the house.

I paused, seeking to signal a change of scene, and looked again at my audience, Pash still examining the ceiling, Bob reclined in his beanbag chair and regarding me intently.

ROLAND rose late in the afternoon, groaned, and staggered stiff-legged down the stairs as though he had defecated in his pants...

Pash snorted. "I do find that image funny," she said. "Even though I don't quite know what it means. Is there a certain way you walk when you've pooed your pants?"

"There was another thing I wrote earlier. I was trying to get the way Roland used to come down the stairs. He was kind of stiff-legged and he always put the same foot first, down to the next stair, then brought the other foot down to the same stair, leaning on the banister. It was like he was too sleepy and woozy and wobbly to trust himself on the stairs, so he had to take them carefully and one at a time so he wouldn't stumble and break his neck. Anyway I didn't really get it with the other story and so I had another go with this one. I was sort of thinking of the way you see little kids sometimes walk and you know they've pooed their pants. I know it doesn't really work but I'm glad you get an image out of it."

"I don't know why you think it matters so much," Bob said. "Go on..."

... He had horribly thin limbs, curly black hair and a translucent body...

Pash snorted again. "He doesn't! He's not emaciated. Was he then? I doubt it. What do you mean translucent? I suppose he is a bit fair. I don't know that he is particularly fair, not much fairer than you. But then he has dark hair."

"You used translucent in that other sketch," Bob said. "I remember finding it odd at the time."

"I wasn't trying to report," I said. "I was just thinking of a way Roland's skin can look, sometimes, when his veins stand out. It is like you can see through it. Anyway, that just must have occurred to me. Let me get on with it, if you really want this and aren't bored already. Haven't you both recently read it?"

"This is different," Pash said. "Go!"

... He burped on the way down and tasted hamburger and instant coffee. Clad only in tattered black footy shorts, he looked dazedly around him, then settled in the gloom of that littered, sunless living room like an albino fly.

Over the typescript, I detected a grimace from Bob.

"You really can be quite insulting," said Pash. "Was Roland really that untidy, to live with? Did he really read this, and still talk to you?"

"He gets that it's not *him*," I said.

"But it *is* him. Sort of. Well, in a way. A good way, mainly. A funny way. Oh God! Maybe one day you'll write about me. Visiting in the middle of the night, dragging out dex..."

"I'm sure it would be a sympathetic portrait," I told her, feeling more comfortable with her than I had to that point. "Do you two really want the rest of this?"

"Yes. There's no hurry. I'm really enjoying this."

"Bob?"

"I'm not bothered. I'm taking it easy. It's fine. We've got all night if we need it—depending on what *you* want to do, and you don't look like you're miserable."

"Okay, I'll relax."

"Do," said Pash.

> He was used to rising to a clean house; this mess annoyed him even though he had caused it. Worse, he knew that he should clean it up—but this task, unused as he was to it, seemed so monumental that he could not bring himself to begin. Yet he could hardly ignore it—he had seen the note. If the mess was still there when Greg returned from uni, his situation would become extremely uncomfortable. Roland's tolerance for such situations was low; in fact he hated them. He would rather slink off somewhere and come back when, hopefully, the mess had disappeared. He began to resent Greg for leaving it there.
>
> The percussion of the great brass doorknocker echoed down the musty hallway. When he opened the door, Roland discovered

a grinning, wiry haired youth who in some indefinable way seemed scarred—he looked like a lad who sat around in divey pubs, hoping for a fight. It was Steve, Roland's best friend. He breezed in with a "Hi there!"

"Steve," said Pash. "Steve-o-Steve. Why were you such a dumbarse? I know that is a terrible thing to say, but I feel it sometimes. He *was* a dumb-arse!" She slapped a forearm onto the beanbag, which responded with a gentle *thwok*. "I just can't help thinking of him sometimes. So cold..."

"Are you sure you want this?"

"Yes! I'm *loving* it! You know," Pash said, "I'm not sure Steve was all that good in a fight. I don't really know because I never saw him in one. I suppose he'd seen a few, growing up around Footscray. His brother was a bit rough. His family was pretty straight, though. He was kind of confident. And curious. I suppose he would have enjoyed watching fights; he'd probably have sat there and cheered them on."

"I don't know either," I said. "I was never very happy with that bit."

"Steve was. He *loved* it. Thought it was *really* funny. He read this to me quite early, when I was first getting to know him. He got to that bit and his voice went funny. He was trying not to laugh. Then he said: 'No way do I do that!'... It is sad..."

I took the opportunity to continue.

> Roland feebly hi-there'd him back.
> Steve said: "I see Greg's got a ticket," and laughed.

Pash chuckled: "I can just imagine that..."

> "A parking ticket?"
> "Yeah. Sitting on his car—hey, what's this?" He picked up Greg's note, and read: "Dear Roland, meet your filthy residue.

Wherever you go, filth follows you. Disgusting, greasy filth!"

"*Oi!*" he exclaimed. "That's a bit rude!"

Like a scythe through a stand of dry grass, this sympathy cut a swath through Roland's finer feelings.

"Yeah," he agreed, "He's a cunt."

Chuckles from Pash, and a snigger from Bob.

The two were silent for a moment.

"You've got to live with him, though," Steve reminded.

"Yeah, that's true."

"You are a bit slack, you know."

Giggling from Pash.

"That's true too."

"Still, we can't let him get away with it."

"No."

"Get me a cup of coffee," Steve commanded, "and I'll think about it. And make it with our machine."

"The coffee machine," Bob said. "I've always wondered why you didn't call this 'The Filter Coffee Machine'. Way better than that abomination you've actually called it."

"I might. The title is provisional. I just did this, and thought Roland might like to read it and took it with me to town. Then probably forgot to take it home with me and then hadn't seen it since. Until tonight. I hadn't really even thought about a title."

"The coffee machine," Pash said. "That's right. Steve said there really was a coffee machine."

"There was."

"Okay, go on."

BOTH Roland and Steve were so used to drinking instant coffee that they preferred it to the real thing, but "their" filter coffee machine had brought them together. When they were both first-year students in business statistics, the lecturer used to boast, at each of his morning lectures, about the recently improved standard of the staff-room coffee.

"I look up at you sleep-stunned undergraduates," he would say, "and I thank the Lord that I am not like you. Here I have—" (he would indicate the cup in his hand) "—a magnificent cup of genuine drip-brewed coffee, made with the new drip-filter coffee maker, use of which is exclusively the preserve of the staff. I can see that you would enjoy a cup of this extraordinarily aromatic beverage, with its wonderful recuperative properties, but I am afraid that you will have to wait until you have passed through the purifying flames of undergraduacy and into that exalted state in which I myself ... etc. etc."

Both Roland and Steve, who did not know each other then, would have been on time at the lecture only at the expense of their morning cup of coffee. And each, independently, determined to resolve the situation.

And so, after two weeks of the above speeches, Roland, having waited around until 7pm to get a reasonable chance of avoiding detection, was leaving the department staff room with the coffee maker stuffed in the most nonchalant possible manner under one arm when he was confronted by Steve. Steve recognised him as a fellow student.

"Where are you going with that?" he demanded.

"I'm just borrowing it for a party."

"Did you get any coffee for it?"

"No, I was going to buy some."

"It's too late, it's after 7 o'clock."

At a loss, Roland looked at his watch.

"So it is," he said weakly.

"Look," Steve said, taking command, "You've got that; I'll get the coffee." He went into the staff room and returned with the entire stock of four 500-gram bags, finely ground.

"Now," he said, "which one of us lives closest."

Roland did, so they went there for a cup of genuine filter coffee, which neither particularly enjoyed. But it happened that Roland had a small block of hash, and they enjoyed that thoroughly. Each was delighted to find someone with the same positive ideas about dealing with someone who was a problem.

With a cup of this genuinely thought-provoking coffee in their respective hands, they turned their attention to the problem of Greg.

HAVING AGAIN REACHED A change of scene, I paused and again looked at my audience, prepared for discovering that one member or both had dozed off. But while obviously relaxed, neither seemed drowsy.

"This didn't really happen, did it?" Pash asked.

"I'm sure it didn't happen quite like this. What did Steve tell you?"

"I don't really remember. I'm not sure I want to remember. In a funny way, this character was better than Steve. I wonder whether that's why he liked it. Steve wasn't really so masterful. There was more of a kid in him. You've got Roland more like a kid, and Steve's masterful, but really I think Steve was more like a kid, dreaming up various outrageous schemes, and he would be kind of delighted that Roland thought they were possible, or worthwhile, and not just really dumb. Roland really brought him out, I think. You know, he'd have been still living with his parents when he met him, met Roland. I don't even know he'd thought of moving out. He didn't really think far ahead. But I got the impression it was visiting Roland and having so much freedom in that house where you lived with him to stay up late and get stoned, play loud music and all that stuff, that got him wanting to move out. Well, I don't know but he did talk about it, about how much he enjoyed that house. I don't think he liked things so much when Roland was living with Debbie. Which is fair, of course; they're a couple. But I think he really liked that house. In a way I think his whole life after that was trying to recapture that house. Oh, that makes me sad too."

Pash continued to stare at the ceiling. Bob and I let her be. She had given me plenty to think about. After a short time, she fished again in her bag and withdrew a tissue, applying it to her cheeks. She turned her head and glanced across at me.

"I really am enjoying this," she said. "In a way I've never really done this. I was sad when it happened but then I think everybody wants to take your mind off it. They don't get it that you just want to talk about him, and talk about him. I thought Roland would want to talk about him but I tried and I don't think he really wanted to. I don't know Roland all that well. I don't think he liked my crying, either. And then I suppose I wanted to *have* something with Roland and do it, and Debbie didn't really like that or want to have some herself."

"What about Shooka?" I asked. "Did you know other people who knew Steve? How did you get to know Steve, anyway?"

"Don't you know that?" said Pash, turning her head again to look at me, this time with a smile. "I'll tell you. But I think that's another story. Finish this one, then we'll go there. I can't quite remember the rest but I do remember I liked it."

"I remember it," said Bob. "It's okay. Go on, get it over with. This is good space. I don't think any of us is going to fall asleep. Just read it through."

"Read it through," said Pash. "I just want to sink into it. Don't mind me if I cry. If I do, I'll be happy."

"Can I have that in writing?" I said. "No, I believe you. Well, I don't really, but here goes. To the end." I held the typescript under the light.

UNABLE to face a return to his embattled domicile, Greg had eaten out with a friend, then gone to the pub. Suitably fortified, he re-entered number 86 soon after pub closing and found the place spick and span. The only evident piece of dirt was Roland, lounging in a corner of the living room, who looked, Greg thought, as though someone had picked him out of their nose and flicked him onto a chair ...

A ripple of giggling from Pash, a soft "Eew" from Bob.

... He moved past the hall door and noticed Steve, muscled and swarthy in contrast to Roland's pale concavity, engaged in lighting the bowl of the household bong. Steve looked up as Greg moved in his peripheral vision.

"Greg!" he exclaimed. "Have a bong!"

It had been a cold walk from the pub—the autumn night was typically moist—and the ambience of the room, the two young men sitting around the little gas fire sharing the bong in a clean, snug house, affected Greg most agreeably. Never one to knock back such an offer in normal circumstances, he accepted with dignity. He took a long pull on the pipe, then sat back, blew out the smoke through a smile which had begun to kindle on his frank face.

He drew a chair closer to the heater and passed the bong to Roland, who was looking more like a human being with each passing moment.

"Thanks for cleaning the place up," he said. "It's great."

Roland paused in the act of relighting the bong to mumble: "That's okay."

Greg, never one to feed a grudge, decided to go further.

"I'm sorry about the note, too," he apologised. "Oh fuck! I've just remembered that I've got another fucking parking ticket."

Roland said: "Why don't you get a sticker?"

"Who knows. I guess I just haven't got around to it. Why should I have to go down to those arseholes and get a sticker?"

Steve said: "We've got you one."

"What do you mean?"

"We went and got you a sticker."

"They took back the fines, too," Roland added.

Steve said: "Your bong."

Greg said: "I don't believe it."

"It's true," Steve averred. "We felt sorry for you."

Greg took his second bong, leaned back, blew out the smoke. He looked around.

"So I don't have to worry?"

"Nope."

Greg was beginning to feel really good. He had a low tolerance for dope, and enjoyed the fact. There was nothing, he thought to himself, half so good as being really stoned.

"Whose bong is it?" Roland asked.

"Greg. It's Greg's bong."

Greg was feeling more and more ripped.

"No!" he dissented. "When you're in so disgusting a state as mine, the last thing you want is another bong..."

"Greg's bong! Greg's bong!" the other two chorused.

"No really, you have it. I think it's time for Roland's bong."

"But I've just had one!" (Roland.)

"It's your bong Greg." (Steve.)

"Come on Greg," Steve said, "I've had a bong, and Roland's just had a bong. Now it's your bong, that's fair."

"You can't get much fairer than that, Greg," Roland reminded him, shaking the stinking pipe under Greg's nose.

"Do you want bong water all over your hair!"

"Ohh, heavy vibes, HEAVY vibes..." Steve and Roland chorused.

"Greg," Steve said, "that was heavy vibes."

"I'll say!" Roland agreed.

"Roland's only doing it for your own good Greg. Roland's always doing things for you."

"I'm so honourable."

"Yeah, Roland's so honourable. He's got your best interests at heart, Greg."

"Yeah … it's your bong Greg."

I BREATHED DEEPLY WHILE Pash's giggles subsided. There had been no more tears as far as I could see, just laughter. Bob was grinning.

"And no needles," Bob said. "Those were innocent days."

"But they didn't feel that innocent," I said. "All this felt quite risky and exciting. I mean, for me, it probably still would: having another bong when you're already completely whacked would feel scary. That's why Greg resists. Most of the people I knew would have a couple of bongs or joints and then just enjoy it. Maybe topping up every now and again. That's what *we* used to do, you and me. Maybe not even topping up. You didn't get their thing but their thing was, in a way, just that risk-taking. It might not seem like much of a risk now but it was a risk, or felt like one."

Bob, looking thoughtful, said: "It was kind of a safe risk. Like watching a boxing match. Or a horror movie."

"It was their thing," Pash said. "Sounds like fun to me. Wish I'd been there. Who was Greg?"

"Someone we used to live with. Well, inspiration came from there, anyway."

"I've enjoyed this. Thank you. And for writing it. Is there more? I seem to remember there's something."

"Well, there's the rest." I offered her the most subtle of leers. I must have been feeling very pleased with myself. "You want it now?"

Pash looked straight back at me: "You are even weirder than they said." She leaned back again in the beanbag. "But I do like you," she said, more quietly, as though interrogating herself. "Okay, let's have it."

GREG succumbed eventually [I read, my voice less steady than I would have preferred], smoked the bong, and became, as Roland liked to put it, a quivering mess. His most ingrained inhibitions were dissolved by sufficient quantities of dope, and things he would normally think about before saying would be pouring in a blather from his lips before he was conscious of formulating them. He would take on a different character, pour forth diatribes against friends, sing, tell stories, or insult whoever was present.

Roland looked at Steve, and Steve grinned back at him. Their hearts felt warm in the security of ritual. And what fun! It was hard to think of anything more entertaining than filling Greg up with enough dope to make of him an utter idiot, and then smoking enough themselves to feel sick.

It was, Roland thought, a bit of an anticlimax. But this way there would be many more nights like this. Besides, he knew that Greg would feel such gratitude for their parking efforts that he would unflinchingly do all the housework for a month.

The two filled bongs, led Greg on, laughed themselves silly at him, and provided him with numerous cups of genuine drip-brewed filter coffee. Roland, although not generally meditative, found himself ruminating dreamily upon the real pleasures in life. He knew well the incomparable satisfactions of revenge, but it was part of growing up, he thought, to realise that such joys must occasionally be forgone in favour of the long-term benefits which may accrue from the doing of a noble deed.

6

PROGNOSTICATING WITH PASH

THERE WAS SILENCE AFTER I HAD COMPLETED THE read, but for the barely audible pop, pop, of Zoom's stereo as its stylus rode the innermost track. Bob had closed his eyes, but I suspected that the dex had prevented his sleeping. Pash was still lying back on her beanbag, staring as far as I could see at the ceiling. I stepped to the turntable and turned over *The Leprechaun*, connecting from its earliest notes with my disappointment in Roland at Carlton. I also felt nervous. I was not sure what Pash had thought I meant when I asked her whether she wanted the rest of the story now. I was aware that I had intended a double entendre, but I had felt at once abandoned and confident. Confident because I doubted she would recognise the allusion I had intended. And abandoned because the allusion was to a common feature of my erotic fantasies, in which I would bring myself off while imagining myself to be partnered with a highly engaged creature who, for a reason I did not need to fathom, was desperately excited to be with me. Usually she was naked but sometimes she was clothed, and in a way that affected me more than mere nakedness. Having imagined the circumstances of our encounter in relevant detail, usually settling, for a model, on someone I had met briefly or perhaps even had got to know—a former classmate from university, or a friend of a friend—I would find myself approaching the climax of the story, and commonly would ask my fantasy partner somewhat rhetorically whether she wanted "it" now. It was a flattering aspect of every such tale that she would answer, urgently and breathlessly, in the affirmative. Why I chose to offer the same line to Pash in that setting I do not know. Perhaps, feeling triumphant, I had wanted to say something witty, and had been emboldened by the likelihood that it would seem witty only to me.

"That was beautiful," Pash said at last. And then, turning her gaze to me, "What did you mean when you asked me whether I wanted it *now*?"

I was silent for a good few moments. "What did you think I meant?" I responded, finally.

"Well, I wasn't sure what you meant, or whether you meant anything. But I was reminded of something."

"Which was?"

Pash sat upright, leaning against the wall, and reprised her wry but accepting smile.

"Which was, well, there has been the odd guy, let us say, that I have known, who would say that at certain, times when he was, umm," her eyes rolled upwards and her smile widened a little, "distracted. Distracted by me, let us say." She looked back at me: "I wonder whether you know what I am talking about."

"I think we all know," Bob said.

"I think I do know," I said. "It is possible that is what I was getting at."

"And so why would you say that to me just then?"

And there I was, transfixed. And extraordinarily apprehensive. I am sure I recall that exchange accurately. It was a very direct thing for Pash to be saying, in her excitable and yet curiously soothing mezzo-soprano, and I felt invited to be direct in return, while fearing powerfully a trap of some kind, or embarrassment even if untrapped. The potential for embarrassment was enhanced by

Bob's being there. Partly because I still did not know where Bob was in this. I had not heard that Pash was his girlfriend, but you never knew with Bob. And even if she was not his girlfriend, you still never knew what could be—or even could *have* been—between them. The thought occurred to me that Pash was alluding right then to Bob. And therefore that the two of them were setting me up to make fun of me. Not that I had got any sense of that from Bob: he had seemed to deplore Pash's remark as inappropriate, even given our cosy circumstances.

"I'm sure it's *your* fault," I said, possibly imagining this would offend Pash, and so save me. "Look, I want to say that I am extremely enjoying your visit tonight. Was extremely excited that you visited, whether or not you came with Bob. And then the three of us here, you wanting me to read my story... being so appreciative. You can understand, I expect, that I am feeling extremely nervous. I already told you that. I was probably trying to defuse things, somehow. Maybe test something out. I don't know. You probably have got it right and I was probably hoping and thinking you wouldn't notice."

"But I did notice."

"You did notice, and I suppose I now feel rather dumb."

"You're not dumb," Pash said.

"I did tell you," Bob said to Pash.

"Shoosh!" Pash said. And then: "Seamus, have you ever been with anyone?"

"*Been* with anyone?"

"Why do I imagine you know what I mean?"

"Why would I tell you," I said. I heard Bob chuckle. "Not telling you says something," I said to Pash. "Do you really want to know?"

"I think I do know," Pash said.

"You might not know," I said. "Anyway, you haven't really answered my question."

"Okay. Yes, I'm quite interested."

"Well," I said. "Yes."

Pash stared at me for a moment.

"Yes what?"

"*Yes*. Yes I have been with someone, if you really want to know. Has Bob put you up to this, or what? What's all this about?"

"It's not really about anything," Pash said. "You know what?" She reached into her bag again. "Let's have one more each."

"Not for me," Bob said. "I don't want to get too much out of cycle."

"Seamus?"

"I think so," I said. "Tomorrow's done for anyway. I have enjoyed this. I have to say, I can't believe how much I am enjoying all this. I might be nervous, but I'm probably nervous as much as anything that it will soon end. I can't believe, really, that all this is happening."

"Down the hatch," Pash said, offering me the same small spoon.

I sucked the liquid off the spoon, returning it to Pash and feeling a tremor this time from her declining to wipe or rinse it before applying her own dose. Which she consumed with concentration, licking her lips and then wiping the spoon with a tissue before returning it to her bag with the bottle.

"Come down here," Pash said, patting her beanbag.

"Why?" I said. I stole a glance at Bob.

"Do what you want," Bob said. "I don't mind what you do."

"Why?" Pash said. "I like you. Here we all are. You're up there on the chair, responding to my impertinent questions. It's like you're facing the Inquisition. I want you to be cosy. Don't you like me?"

"I do like you," I said. "I like you a ridiculous amount. But ..."

"Down here!" Pash commanded, patting the beanbag. She squirmed nearer one side of it.

"You want me to sit next to you."

"Um, *yeah*. Why not?"

"No reason, I suppose. All right, I will."

I abandoned my chair and slumped down onto the beanbag, leaning up against the wall beside Pash. The truth was, there had been several occasions when I had felt like doing something like that, with somebody whom I had liked, but I had never been able to get to suggesting it. I was careful not to touch Pash. I turned my head to look at her, and was confronted immediately by her smiling face looking at mine, which felt too intimate. An excess abetted, I can guess, by the enhanced prominence of her scent. I looked away.

"You don't look comfortable," Pash said. "I want you to be comfortable."

"Are you comfortable?"

"Not especially," Pash said. "How about we settle down a bit. In the chair." She squirmed again and slid forward on the beanbag, turning to look up at me. "Is that better? I feel like I'm sliding off." She slid further, until her head rested on the beanbag next to my hip. "Try this. Come down here."

I obeyed, slipping down the beanbag beside her. Now my head was again beside hers. It felt like the beanbag was not big enough for the two of us like this, allowing room between us to prevent our touching inadvertently. I was in danger of slipping onto the floor.

"You two look like gingerbread men in a box," said Bob, who had been observing our manoeuvring keenly.

Pash giggled. I remember thinking, over my agitation, that her laugh sounded musical.

She turned her head. I resisted turning to meet her.

"Why don't I lie across you," she said. "Would you mind?"

I said, again summoning effort to keep my voice steady, that I would not.

Pash rolled off the beanbag and knelt facing me, alongside the heater, which was working but as usual not very effectively. "Move your legs over this way," she commanded. "Get comfortable. Make sure you can talk to Bob. Get your head comfortable. Then I'll go back where I was."

Obedient, I adjusted my posture.

"Are you comfortable?"

"Yes. Well ..." I laughed briefly. "Sort of."

"Good. Now I'll come down here."

Pash turned and rolled back onto the beanbag, lying across me, carefully smoothing her knitted jacket and pulling it around her. Now her head was not so close to mine and I felt better, noticing tacitly the developing tension where her thigh was compressing my lap.

"Now, put your arm around me," Pash said. "If you want to."

"Umm, yes I want to."

She snuggled towards me, raising her head so that I could slip my arm around her shoulders and sliding forward a little. I gripped her upper arm, aware immediately of how close my fingers were to her shirt as it enclosed her breast on that side. She wriggled closer again, nestling her shoulder onto my chest and rotating me toward her slightly.

"How's that?" she asked, glancing over at me.

"Feels good, actually. Are you happy?"

"I am happy," Pash said, music in her tone—or perhaps I imagined it. My observing that my contact with her felt good had understated the case: I was aware, now that she seemed secure in my grasp, that I felt wonderfully, magnificently, exhilarated. I squeezed her: a squeeze that was almost involuntary, a reflexive attempt to quell agitation so intense it had become painful. Pash patted my squeezing forearm.

"Where were we?" she asked Bob. "I feel very good. You should have one."

"I don't need one." Bob said. "I'm not sure you two do either."

"I'm good," Pash said.

"They are good," I said, risking speech.

"I'll *bet* you think they're good," said Bob, and I was suddenly aware again that his status with Pash was still, for me, unresolved. Not that it mattered much, really, I told myself.

"So what really brought you two down here?" I asked, beginning to experience as pleasant the sensations that had overwhelmed me. My delivery was not steady, but they let me get away with that.

"We wanted to see you," Bob said.

"We?" I said, emboldened by my happy positioning.

"I wanted to come down," Pash said, her voice small even though it was alongside my left ear. "I asked Bob to bring me."

"Well," Bob said, "I made an offer."

"Which I had solicited, if implicitly," Pash replied. Again softly, as though she were mouthing a reflection intended for her own ears rather than ours. "I wanted to see you," she said, to nobody in particular, and so not making it obvious which of us she had wanted to see. Even though logic told me the *you* was not Bob, given that she could see Bob without making the journey to me.

"To see *me*?" I risked.

"Well ... yes." The inflection of the *well* extended flatly to the *yes*, expressing agreement and no more.

"I liked you," Pash said, this time adjusting her head a few degrees towards me, so that I could not doubt it was me whom she liked. "At the funeral. I liked you." She spoke as though she believed nothing more on the subject needed saying. But then, as though realising this might not be the case for me, elaborated: "I liked you, and I thought you liked me. Then after a while it didn't seem like you were around. I talked to Bob about it. He said he doubted you would come looking for me, whether you liked me or not. And I'd found your story. It was nice to read it again. Think of Steve. I told Bob. He said you'd probably like the story back. So I thought, when I was ready, why not bring it down. And then I was ready. I suppose I could have called you or something. Or given the story to Bob. That wasn't what I wanted. I just had in mind a surprise visit. Which Bob will do anyway ... I like that about him." A shift of the head and, I guessed, a grin in Bob's direction, intended to reassure: "*Even if I am embarrassed, sometimes, by the way he goes about it.*

"I don't really know what I would have done," Pash continued, "If you'd been away, or caught up in something. It didn't really matter. We could have left the story behind. Or made inquiries and brought it back later. But you were here, and it's been really good," Pash said, the music back in her voice. "I think I probably had something like this in mind. Maybe even something like *this*." She wriggled, a mere flicker, settling into my sprawling embrace to a degree that would have been barely perceptible were it not for the sensitivity, given the circumstances, of my sensors, which recorded her settling as earth-shaking. "This is *good*," she said. "I really don't think I've done this, with someone I really liked, since Steve. *Eight months* ago. It is very good," Pash said, settling—barely perceptibly—deeper. "Do *you* think it's good?" Twisting her head again towards mine.

"I think it is very good," I said, wondering how I had stepped into this parallel universe but beginning to accept that I had.

"You do look cosy," Bob said.

"We *are* cosy," Pash said, music again.

"Mmm," I said.

I was not quite sure what to do or say next, and so I just lay still, feeling Pash breathing steadily in and out, breathing even a little myself, although it felt almost as if I needed to hold my breath or this illusion would fade, dissolve into cold reality and everything that went with that. It occurred to me that if I just lay there and held my breath, or at least breathed fairly shallowly, then I would not be doing anything that contributed to that dissolution, and therefore that the illusion would sustain itself for as long as it could. From the speakers sounded lightly the *Leprechaun's Dream*, with its flute and piano leads and wordless feminine vocal, and even Bob did not seem to feel a need for speech until it ended, and with it the record.

"That's it," Bob said finally. "You two look cosy. What are we going to do? I probably should try and sleep. It's late. Not that I think I'll have much success. We could go for a walk. The beach is not far away. Or the cliff-tops."

"I'm happy here," I said.

"I'll bet you are," said Bob. "But I'm not sure that's compatible with everybody's welfare. I should sleep, and if I'm going to sleep I probably should sleep here. The only alternative is the car, and I don't like that idea much at all. But I can't sleep here if you two are going to be talking here, and you won't be sleeping here if you've just had another dose of dex. You can lie there for a while, but then you'll probably wake me up, and if I do get to sleep, I won't be happy if I'm woken up straight away. So we've got to work out what to do."

"Bob!" said Pash. "You're lucky they've let us sleep here at all. Why are you giving orders?"

"I am not giving orders, I'm just letting you know how it is. It seems ludicrous for me to sleep in your car. There's space here. But you're here." He indicated us both.

"Well," I said, "There is my bed."

Pash gave me a corner-of-the-eye glance.

"Could you sleep there?" she asked Bob, a question obviously as much for me.

"You *could* sleep there," I said, fearing to move and relieved by this unseen solution. "You might need your sleeping bag."

"I'll get it," Bob said. "I might go for a walk."

"Take the needle off," I said. "Please."

"Or play it again," Pash said. "Maybe."

"Or something else," I said.

"What?" Bob said, removing *The Leprechaun*.

"Well," I said, "*Kind of Blue*, I suppose. My favourite," I said, mainly for Pash. "I can't believe they did this. Nineteen fifty-nine, of all times. Twenty-five years ago. Sounds like yesterday."

"To you, maybe," Bob said. He located the sleeve among our collection, which belonged mainly to Zoom. "I get tired of it."

"I don't think I've heard it," Pash said.

"You have," Bob told her. "On the way down."

"Seduction music," I said, and then felt very silly.

"I'll leave you to your seduction," Bob said, not letting me get away with that one.

"I hope not," said Pash, as Bob departed. We heard the outer screen door at the front of the house shut with a bit of a bang, left to its closing spring. I hoped it had not woken anyone.

"Seduction music?" Pash asked.

"Well..." I said. I was not sure where that had come from, but did not want to tell Pash that, even if I had told her just about everything else that she had wanted to know. Again, looking back I have a possible explanation. Lying there with Pash lying over me, feeling tension, knowing it was late—and knowing that Pash had made every move, and feeling a little ashamed of that, now that I had her here in my lap—I wonder whether I had been worried by the possible implications of having her there, and had wanted to determine those possibilities, and quickly, one way or another. Her forwardness had not frightened me as much as it might have. Why not? Again, hard to say. But I think I may have received it as illusory. Given how much I was learning I liked Pash, her advances had seemed too direct to be real.

"Well, I thought it was about time I seduced you," I said.

"About time? A few hours after you met me for the second time in your life?"

"Well, you've been seducing *me*."

"I have *not*."

"Well..." I was feeling the illusion dissolve, and it did not feel good. A leaden ball had lodged itself behind my navel and was swelling, quite big already. It was compressing my lungs, affecting my power to speak. I remembered encountering Pash at the party for Shooka. It seemed so long ago.

"Third time," I said. Without much conviction. "What was all this about then?"

"All what?"

"You know. This..." I gave Pash's shoulder a squeeze again. The leaden ball had shrunk, but not much.

"Don't you like it?"

"Of course I like it."

"Well then. Why stuff it up? Isn't this *enough* for you? Do you think you deserve more of me?"

"No," I said, the leaden ball shrinking further but cooling. "I don't think I deserve you at all. I thought you wanted *me*."

"So if I want you, you want me. Is that it?"

"No! Well, usually it's the other way around."

"If I don't want you, you want me."

"Probably. Most of the time. Just about all the time, really."

"And if I do want you, usually you don't want me."

"Yes. Except not you. I imagine, because I *don't* think you want me."

"You don't."

"I don't think so."

"But you just said you did."

"I know. But I don't really think you do. You can't possibly. I feel like a complete idiot even saying this stuff."

"And what if I said I did want you?"

"I don't know. I'd say that's what I thought."

"That I did want you? But then you wouldn't want me."

"No, probably not."

Pash seemed to think this was very funny. She started to laugh, and so richly that, entranced though I was, I shook my head and put a finger to my lips. If she was to attend to me, that involved my sitting up a bit and relinquishing my grip on her shoulder, which I had accomplished before noticing what I was doing. Pash slid down the beanbag, quieter but still shaking, putting an elbow on the floor to steady herself and then rolling off me. She turned to face me, rising to her knees.

"Good seduction music," she said.

"Doesn't always work."

"Has it ever worked?"

I pondered that one for a moment. "No."

"So your successful seduction…?"

"Well… I think she seduced *me*."

"Ah! And only one."

"Yes," I admitted, discovering I had given away the game.

"And how old are you?"

"Twenty-five. Hey, what's this about?" A suspicion seized me. "Are you and Bob having bets or something?"

"*No!*" Pash laughed again, again drawing my warning finger. "Bob said some stuff about you. I probably am being rude."

"*Probably*. Well, I knew it couldn't last."

"What couldn't last."

"You cuddling me."

"Oh. Did you like that? Actually, I think *you* were cuddling *me*."

"Perhaps. Yes, I did like it. Actually," I leered at her, "I *loved* it."

Yet another rich laugh from Pash, again muted at my command.

"Do you think you'll get around me that way?"

"No," I said. "I don't think so. I don't think I'll get around you at all. That is, even assuming getting around you is what I was trying to do. Which I don't think it is."

"The idea was that *I* get around *you*, wasn't it?"

"Pash," I said, all of a sudden feeling very, very relieved. "That's very naughty."

"Well? Wasn't it? No," Pash said, "I won't push you. Not fair, you poor thing. One seduction. Not that I'm surprised. Well, actually, I am surprised there was one. Bob told me some things about you. Not that I am going to say what that was. You are not very comfortable with girls, are you?"

"Not really," I said. "Well, you know, sort of. But not, you know, *as women*."

"What bothers you?"

"I don't know," I said.

"Are you scared I'll eat you?"

I laughed, suspecting again a double entendre. But I knew I did not sound as though I had found her question funny.

"I'm probably just scared that I'll make an idiot of myself."

"Which is not altogether unreasonable," Pash said, but she was smiling in her accepting way again. "What are we going to do now?" she asked.

"Well," I said, "I could take you to bed. And Bob could sleep in the lounge... Or we could go for a walk, maybe meet up with Bob. It's cold out there but not raining."

"Why don't you take me to bed," Pash said. "I liked that cuddle, didn't you? *But no promises I'll be getting around you.*"

IT TURNED OUT PASH was wearing lacy peach-coloured knickers and a teasing, lace-trimmed cream bra that cupped opaquely breasts which I guessed were sized attractively on the small side of medium—attractively for me, anyway: my mother was large-breasted, and big boobs had not adorned any of my fantasy partners. Certain details of this experience remain firmly lodged in my memory—I suppose from repeated reviewing. Pash had requested, successfully, a hanger for her jacket, had turned on my bedside lamp and demanded I turn off the overhead light, and then had stripped down and climbed between sheets that suddenly seemed to me grubby, pulling my race-car themed double quilt cover up to her neck and looking openly across it, backlit by the lamp, as I followed her swift example and removed my shoes and socks, jumper, shirt and jeans. It was cold in the bedroom. My physique had never impressed me, but Pash seemed to approve. "Looks like you do like me, after all," she said, in what I assumed was an allusion to the bulging of my briefs, or to a shadow around the bulge that told a tale of sustained titillation. "Come on!" I slid under the covers beside her. "Now," she said, "We're not going to do anything with *that*," reaching under the quilt to place a hand briefly over my bulge, "for quite some time, if at all. So relax." Her touch had not contributed to my relaxation, and I told her so.

"You have very high expectations," I said, "lying here with me like this, thinking I am just going to be able to ignore you. And I have to tell you, you touching me then was just about enough to do everything that would be needed."

Pash laughed her musical laugh again, and this time I did not caution her, more confident that our location behind a door in my bedroom would prevent her from disturbing the others.

"For you, maybe," she said. "Which is a good reason why you need to relax. I haven't said we'd become lovers, remember. I just thought you'd enjoy this. When was the last time this happened for you?"

"Well," I said, "I suppose really *this* has never happened for me. It is all so unexpected. One minute I've met you a couple of times and quite like you; the next you're down here and in my bed—in *those* clothes," I said, pointing at her silhouette under the quilt cover. "If you want me to relax, then I'd better not touch *you*. Or anything you are wearing. No cuddling. This is a bit different from how I imagined it. *Not that I've imagined anything before with you.* That's part of the mystery, really. I still can't believe this is happening—and," I said, looking now at her face, "I can't believe that before, you were with Steve. What did he do to deserve you, that's what I want to know. It is what I have always wanted to know. How did he even find you? And once he did find you, what was he doing taking shots of street heroin? I'm sorry," I said, "I know this is crass. Maybe I want to be crass. We were cuddling before; now we're here and can't cuddle. Why are we *here* again? Why did you take your clothes off? If you'd left them on, we probably could have cuddled here, and I'd have liked that."

"And you'd probably be trying to get them off me," Pash said. "I've saved you the trouble. And it's cold. Now just enjoy being with me. Anyway, if I did anything else, you'd have to think I quite liked you.

And you've already told me, you probably wouldn't like me then. But I want you to like me. So you need discipline. So just lie there, and talk to me. I'll turn the light off."

She did so, having chosen the side of the bed that I usually slept on. I gazed into the gloom, assuming she was doing the same. It was certainly easier to relax when I could not see her.

"It *is* dark," she said.

"Usually you can see by the streetlight, eventually," I told her. "I think I am relaxing. Not that I really want to relax."

"Discipline," Pash said. "What shall we talk about?"

"Well, let's talk about Steve," I said. "That would certainly be relaxing."

"Maybe less for me. But I know I have wanted to talk about him. That's probably why I came down here, partly anyway. I did want to see you. Why, I'm not quite sure now. But you don't always know why, do you?"

"Well, I'm extremely glad you wanted to see me." I was beginning to relax, and could see Pash, a ghost on the next pillow, in the illumination from the window, which was becoming effective. "I *am* relaxing. It is actually quite amazing, knowing you're there, not doing anything, knowing you could disappear at any moment, and in a way, I've just realised, *not caring*. Well, I do care, but I mean, it's not really in my control. You're there; I'm here. I didn't bring you here, and I didn't really bring you in here, and I don't think it was anything I did that made you take your clothes off. So I may as well just lie here and enjoy your presence. It's not really relaxing, but in so far as it's not relaxing, it is *really* pleasant. And you're probably right about the liking–not-liking thing. Anyway, Steve. How you met Steve, what you liked about him ... any of that stuff, really. I can feel myself relaxing already."

"Steve," Pash said. She moved in the bed, and looking across at her I could tell she had begun to stare again at the ceiling. "Steve-o-Steve. Oh well, I guess I did ask for it."

"Now!" I said.

"Yes. Well, where to start."

"IT WAS AT ROLAND'S," said Pash. "that I first saw him. I'd gone over with Shooka. She was picking up a deal. Roland used to get her things to smoke. Well, Steve and Roland. She'd get them other things, sometimes, I think. We went over in the afternoon, and Roland sat us down at a table and offered us coffee. Steve was sitting at the other end. They had a scale out on the table. I didn't pay much attention to him. Roland introduced him. Shooka said she wanted coffee, so we sat there. I think I just asked for water. I was looking at him and he looked over at me and said: 'Do you want a beer?'

"He had this funny, schoolboyish look about him. I thought, anyway. He's got that crinkly hair—wiry, you said in your story—and he sort of looked young, to me. I don't know. There was this *young* thing about him. And at the same time he was old, or seemed old. Do you know what I mean?"

I said I did, sort of. The bed had warmed up a bit, and I had relaxed a bit more. I still did not dare touch Pash, although I had started to think about touching her. I could see her fairly clearly now, if I looked towards her. I realised I could not work out whether her hair was black or just a very dark brown. She had folded her pillow in half so that it lifted her head more, and her hair cascaded onto it. I took the pillow from under my head, folded it and replaced it, following her example.

"You can touch me," she said. "If you want to." I reached towards her, and found her hand. That felt very good, but at the same time I felt silly.

"Here we are in bed, holding hands," I said.

"Yes," said Pash. "Is that okay?"

"It is very okay. Okay with you?"

"Very okay. Where was I?"

"Steve seemed old. And young. I do know what you mean. Although to me he seemed mainly old. I knew he was young, but he seemed old. I remember it being a bit of a shock when I was at Roland's on, you know, that night, and I remembered how young he must have been. Joey was there, and he seemed like a kid. But Steve couldn't have been all that much older than Joey."

"When he died, twenty-three," Pash said. "Just. It really isn't very old, is it."

"How old are you?"

"Wouldn't you like to know! Didn't your mother tell you never to ask a woman her age?"

"If she had, I probably would just have assumed that was stupid," I said.

"You don't trust your mother?"

"Not at all. Not with that sort of stuff. Not with much, actually."

"What's your mother like?"

"Okay, I suppose. She's got a bad leg," I said, as though that explained everything. And I suppose at that time I thought it just about did. "You asked me *my* age. And I told you. Unflattering though that may have been, given what else I was telling you."

"Twenty-six," said Pash. "Do you believe me?"

"Of course not," I said.

"Well then, your mother must have taught you something," said Pash. "Anyway, Steve. Yes, twenty-three. When I met him, he was twenty-two. He looked young, and old. I liked that. He offered me a beer. I hadn't thought of having a beer. It was the middle of the afternoon. Shooka said, 'Yeah, why not, if you want.' I think she was mothering me. I'd had kind of a bad time."

"A bad time?" I was interested.

"Yeah. Later, maybe. But I had had a bad time, or felt I had. Okay, it was a medical thing. But I'm okay. Enough! I took the beer. Steve said we should have a bong. That seems so funny now, after getting to know him, and having just read your story. He sort of said it to Roland: 'We should have a bong.' And Roland looked at Shooka and me and said: 'Would you like a bong?' And I said I didn't want a bong but if they really wanted to smoke I would probably enjoy a few drags on a joint. And Steve asked Roland if he had papers, and Roland said he'd get some and then came back and rolled a joint. It was very good, too. It smoked a bit like Zoom's tonight, but it was much stronger. I had a couple of sucks and then suddenly, everything looked different. Steve asked me would I like another beer—I hadn't even finished the first one. I said yes. Shooka was saying things to Roland—she never seems all that high, though. I don't know where Debbie was. I've got the impression he has people pick up stuff when she's out, mainly. Oh, no—she came back later, said she'd been shopping. Came in with a handful of bags. Asked Roland to get the rest from the car. I felt sorry for him as by then I could hardly do anything. I'd had another couple of draws, which wasn't smart, and then I was just hoping to straighten out. Then Roland told me I was looking ill, or pale I think, which was not very nice of him. And Steve said I probably needed another smoke. So he had Roland roll another joint, even though I said I was not at all interested. And of course I had some, to show them I wasn't ill. Which was stupid. Roland had already weighed Shooka's deal. Then she said she had to go. I thought I should have gone with her but I just didn't feel like doing anything, let alone a car journey. I asked would it be okay if I stayed and Steve said he could drive me home later. Shooka said it was fine, so I knew I'd be okay, but I thought I'd get a taxi or maybe catch a tram when I straightened out. But then Debbie came home and I could tell it was pretty much party over. I wasn't ready to face a walk and a tram, so I went with Steve. I have to say, given the reputation I know he did have for driving, he was always very good with me. Even though I was a bit worried because he'd smoked more than I had."

"Steve was shocking," I said. "In the car. I've heard stories. And I know they are probably true. There was a night when we went out to play pinball and I still can't believe I let myself get in a car with somebody who was going to do what he did. Straight through a Stop sign at an intersection with walls on each side where you couldn't see what was coming. There was no reason at all why we survived it: just luck. And he was just trusting to luck. Had no plan. And of course I was ripped, as he was. Which made it worse. After that I never drove with him. That was part of my issue with him. Not the car; the stupidity. Well, as I saw it. If we'd hit anybody it would have been a complete disaster. Steve, Roland and me, all paraplegic or quadriplegic or dead, probably dead, and whoever we hit as well. Last healthy moments, stoned terror. And for what? So you could say you'd done it? No upside. Or hardly any. And it wasn't as though he had asked me if I wanted to."

"Yeah, but something about that *is* attractive," Pash said.

"What? What is attractive about it! I've heard about this stuff with women and I just don't get it."

"Well, I don't know. It is kind of masculine. Women tend to be more calculating. We have to be. And you just want to throw caution to the winds, sometimes. You just want to give in to whatever happens. Without *making* it happen. Or if you have made it happen, you'd rather, sometimes, feel like you can't necessarily control it. I don't mean all the time. But there is something about men, some men. I mean, nobody can be calculating about everything, or you end up where *you* are. One seduction—and not yours. I'm sorry, I don't mean to harp on it; unfair of me but it's an example.

"But I know you've taken other chances," Pash continued, before I had finished evaluating my impulse to protest. "Motorbikes. Coming down here. I'm not trying to say *you're* not a risk-taker. You are. I'm sure that's one reason why I liked you. But I just mean, well you can't calculate any of *that*, can you? Anyway, Steve probably did take too many. Obviously, I suppose, in a way. But there was something about him, an edge he had. Not that I really noticed it, at first. He wasn't particularly forward, if that's what you're thinking."

Having considered, briefly, another impulse, I withdrew my hand from Pash's and moved it towards her chest, finding flesh and then the object of my searching, her bra. Its fine material felt smooth under my fingers.

"Hey!" Pash said, grabbing my wrist and restoring it to its former position on the sheet beside her. "That is not what I'm talking about. You can't be half in charge: doesn't work. Tonight, I'm in charge. Get it? Completely in charge. The way things have turned out. It's just the way things have turned out. Just lie here. What else did you want to know?"

"Did Steve have you on that first day?" I said, chastened and wanting to intrude.

"No! He drove me back to my flat and I gave him orange juice. Didn't even make a move. And why would he—all we'd done was share a joint. Anyway, he was quite tentative. A bit like you, actually. That was *young* Steve. He asked Shooka about me. I suppose she thought we'd be good for each other. And we were, really. He certainly helped me feel better."

"For a while, anyway."

"Not just for a while. It was good. I still feel good. Okay, what happened, I was sad, but I still feel good. Better than I was feeling back then, by a long way. I really did like Steve. I don't know that I was in love with him, but I really did like him. But what happened, happened. That was Steve. I can't wish I hadn't been with him, and I can't really wish he was different. I just wish he'd *behaved* differently, *that time*. But there'd have been another time, probably. He really wasn't very happy. But I did hope he'd have got happy. I'm not sure if *we'd* have been happy. I don't know that I wanted to settle down with him..."

I took it that Pash wanted to reflect on that thought, and I did also. I lay quietly beside her.

"But I still think it's sad, what happened," Pash continued. "You know, he did kind of ask for something like that, but he didn't *deserve* it. Didn't deserve to be where he is, and us where we are. Even me with you. Here we are, and whatever happens I've liked tonight. Hope you have. But Steve's had all this, every part of it that he's going to get, which believe me, wasn't all that much. He really did deserve more. Much, much more. That's when I get teary. Have you got any tissues?"

"Next to the lamp."

I could see Pash sitting up in the bed, reaching for the tissues, rearranging her pillow so that she could lean against the wall behind her. That gave me a view of her bra again, and I gazed at it with some hunger, but not comfortably, not sure whether she could gauge the direction of my look precisely in this light. It turned out that she could.

"Stare at my tits all you want; I don't mind."

"How do you know that is what I was doing?"

"It's not rocket science, believe me."

"That's the sort of thing Bob would say."

"So? It's the sort of thing plenty of people say."

"But you're not plenty of people."

"No. Just one person. But plenty!"

"Ha ha," I said. "I'm sure. In fact I'm becoming very sure. But you're different."

"How so?"

"Well, coming in here. Being here with me, like this. You pash people. You come here with dex—"

"—like plenty of people."

"Well, not here they don't. But plenty of people don't have dex like you have it. Where did you get that from, anyway?"

"None of your business!"

"Sorry! Anyway, you're different. I think you're different. You're like no one I've ever met. And I still can't believe I'm here with you," I finished, admitting to myself I sounded lame once again. I sat up, adjusted my pillow, and leaned like Pash against the wall behind the bed. The bed slipped forward. Pash squeaked and sat up. "Damn," I said. I got out of bed, walked to its foot and pushed it back into place. "Castors," I said, climbing back under the quilt. "Can't do that. Brr, it is cold." I snuggled back under the cover, retrieving my pillow. "Come down here and give me a hug."

"No way! I think I'll get up."

"No!"

"Yes, I think I'll get up. What time is it?"

"I don't know. About three, I'm guessing."

"Do you have a clock?"

"A watch. I'm still wearing it. Two-thirty. Well, forty."

"I'm getting up."

"What are you going to do?"

"I don't know. Make a cup of tea maybe. Maybe go for a walk."

"You'll wake people up."

"No, I won't. I'll be careful."

"You'll wake people up if you make tea."

"Well, I'll go for a walk then."

"Don't slam the door."

"I won't slam the door. Aren't you coming?"

"Do you want me to come?"

"Why? Won't you come if I want you to?"

"No! I mean, yes of course. It's not like that. Of course I'll come if you want me to."

"Well then, get dressed." Pash had pulled on her white button-up shirt. She turned to face me, grabbed the shirt at each side and drew the two sides apart, exposing her bra again. "Last look. Now get up." She fastened the shirt swiftly, sat on the bed to pull on socks, her back to me, and then jeans. Worried suddenly that I would be left behind, I got out into the cold and fumbled for my clothes.

Prognosticating with Pash

BOB WAS NOT IN the lounge room, I saw as I stuck my head in the door. I had directed Pash to wait in the kitchen. The stereo was still running, popping away metronomically. I replaced the tone arm on its rest, aware of relief that Zoom had not discovered my neglect of it, and switched off the amp and the heater, returning to the kitchen and opening the back door for Pash. At this hour, it had seemed more considerate to leave via our backyard. It was quite cold outside. Pash took my hand as we walked up the drive, past the kitchen window and Zoom's brick, still suspended. I did not say anything, fearful of beginning a conversation within earshot of the house. I directed Pash down our street, away from town, my favourite route to the rudimentary cliff-top path that ran alongside the bay.

"I didn't think you'd do this," I said, when I thought us safely out of range.

"Do what?"

"This!" I said, giving Pash's hand a squeeze and swinging our conjoined arms.

"Oh. Didn't really think about it. Don't you like it?"

"Of course I like it."

"Whoops. Danger, Will Robinson! Soon, you won't like me then."

"I don't think that will happen."

"Does that mean anything? Do you usually think that will happen?"

"No," I admitted. "In so far as I can say anything *usually* happens in this sort of situation, which for me isn't usual. Isn't at all usual."

"Where are we going?" Pash asked. We could see quite well, from the streetlights, but had turned towards the bay, invisible beyond the broad and well-lit esplanade that carried traffic from beach to beach. There was no traffic at this hour but the carriageway seemed very bright, dyed orange under its sodium lamps.

"To the cliff-top," I said. "There's a path, and a spot we could sit at and look out to sea."

"Sounds a bit scary," said Pash. "But I'm up for it. Don't imagine we'll see much. Not much of a moon, is there."

I had not thought to look, but did now. "No. None that I can see." I looked further. "Not many stars either. Must be cloudy."

"I'm warming up," said Pash, "From the walking." Still with her hand in mine.

"I like it that you're still holding my hand," I said.

"Enjoy it while you can," Pash said, and I felt that leaden ball once more.

"Pash," I said, "I don't even know you. What do you do for a living?"

"Is that knowing me?"

"It's a start."

"I think, somehow, we've started."

"Well let's continue. What *do* you do?"

"Hospitality," Pash said. "I work with Shooka."

"Hospitality? Doing what?"

"Looking after bands. You know, our acts. People we promote. I look after them. Or help. Get them stuff they need. Try and help them relax. Keep them happy. You know."

I didn't, really. But didn't say so.

"Do you like it?"

"It's okay. It's fun, usually."

"Well paid?"

"Not too bad. Not great, but not too bad. It's not your average job. Sometimes I think I should be paid megabucks, for what I do. Other times I think I should pay them."

"Sounds good."

"It is good, really," Pash said. "Although sometimes I wonder whether they just want a pretty face."

"You're not *that* pretty." I never know why I say some things.

"Thanks. You're no oil painting yourself."

"Well, I'm not claiming to be."

Prognosticating with Pash

"And I am?"

"Well ... hey, look, I don't want to go this way."

"Do you just want to go home then?"

"No! I mean ... Do I have to tell you I'm sorry? For saying you're not that pretty? I meant not *that* pretty. For me, I think you're incredibly pretty. I really can't believe how nice-looking you are. That's part of what I can't believe about this whole evening, which seems more like a dream, that I'm scared I'll wake up from. You're so beautiful, and here you are at three in the morning walking along holding my hand."

"For *you*, I'm incredibly pretty. For *you*. Is that supposed to be a compliment? Do you think I haven't, kind of, worked that out?"

"Look, I just mean, you're not so pretty as to be brainless." I could tell I was getting in deeper, the harder I tried to dig myself out. "As in just a pretty face. So pretty they'd hire you even though you were useless at your job. That's all I was trying to say, that I think you are probably good at your job—and not just because you're pretty," I finished, suddenly feeling like I had got my head back above ground level. "Of course I think you're pretty. I think you're astonishing. And not just because I think you're pretty."

Pash laughed, the first I had heard outside the house. Her laugh sounded much smaller, but no less musical. We had crossed the esplanade, and I had turned us towards town, seeking the path to the cliff-top.

"Enough!" she said. "I'm okay at my job. And I'm probably okay to look at. But what about you? To look at?" She released my hand and moved a little aside, regarding me in the light from the street lamps, more yellow now that we were under them. "Okay, I guess. Not your strong suit, though. What do you think is your strong suit?"

This was not something that I had thought about.

"I don't know. My strong suit. Do I need a strong suit?"

"Well, most people have something. They look good, or they're strong, or they're good at sport, or they stick with things, or they're clever. What about you? Are you just hiding yourself away? What's your plan?"

"Do I need a plan?"

"Well, how are you going to make money?"

And there it was. A fair question. Just like my father's fair question.

"I've made money from bikie stuff," I told Pash.

"Okay."

"Magazines. Sold a couple of stories. Could sell more. Not that I don't know what you're talking about."

"Will you go somewhere with that?"

"Not far," I admitted. "They might take one a month. If I could do one a month. I just do what I do." Was I hoping that Pash would abandon me? "Plans haven't worked for me. Here's the path."

WE TURNED LEFT, OFF the paved footpath onto a well-trodden track that disappeared into darkness, dimly vegetated.

"Hey!" Pash said. "Where are you taking me?"

"To the cliff-tops. It's this way. Good spot to sit. There are rocks and you can look out to sea."

"I must be crazy," Pash said.

"What do you think? That I'm going to push you off, or something?"

"Maybe." Pash had paused where the path disappeared between bushes that we would have to push our way through. "It's a bit spooky. Do we go through here?"

"Follow me," I said, keeping hold of her hand, leading her forward. The way opened again and, out of reach from the streetlights, we could see faintly the cliff-top path. I turned left on to it, still leading Pash. After a few dozen steps the remaining shrubbery on the cliff-side cleared and I could see my way down onto the familiar outcrop of rock. A hazard sign, decipherable even in the poor

Prognosticating with Pash

light, warned of its instability. I stepped over the path's knee-height seaward fence—stubby pine posts and horizontal poles.

"Wait!" Pash demanded. "What's that sign say?"

"It says the rocks might slip. They won't. Not tonight. Very solid. I've been out here heaps of times. It's not even an overhang."

"You're not completely unlike Steve, are you," Pash said. "Is it worth it?"

"Great spot to sit."

"Big upside," Pash said. "Not much downside ..." She sighed. "Okay then. Lead on."

I led her seaward on to the big grey slab, looking carefully at my footing. Secure there, I looked outwards. At the end of the slab, I realised, on the darker rock that formed a broad seat looking over the bay, sat a figure. I turned back to face Pash, placing a hand over her mouth. She twisted away.

"Hey!" she cried.

"Sorry," I said. I gestured.

"Oh," Pash said. The figure had not moved.

I was not sure what to do. I had wanted privacy, and had assumed it. This was not a place to be avoiding a menacing stranger, or even to be moving quickly if there was confusion.

"Looks like Bob," Pash said. She took a step past me.

I looked again and admitted to myself that it did look like Bob. Mainly because it was about the right build, although perhaps a bit broad, and seemed to have on the Irish flat cap that I knew Bob sometimes affected in winter. A cap that he may even have carried with him when he had entered our dining room.

I followed Pash down the slab. Within a few steps it became obvious this was Bob. He was sitting with his back to us, legs presumably hanging over the edge of the rock, which looked dangerous but which I knew was quite safe, there being a ledge on the far side sufficient to save him if he slipped. Pash, having reached the motionless figure, sat down beside him, immediately to his right.

There was no room for me next to her, so I sat to Bob's left, away a little where the rock surface was smoother. The rock felt cold.

"Hello," Bob said, to neither of us in particular. Or rather, to both of us. A warm greeting, on this very cool night. There was little breeze. He remained gazing out to sea.

"Did you hear us?" Pash asked.

"From about ten minutes back," Bob said. "I wasn't that surprised. I'd thought I might see you."

He was wearing, I noticed, a quilted vest, of the sort that might be insulated with duck down, again the sort of thing he typically carried, protection against the extremes of the season. It occurred to me that he had bought this one recently and the whole walk idea when he had suggested it was Bob wanting to try out his vest, which I guessed he had left in the car with his sleeping bag.

"Have you been down here all this time?" I asked.

"No. A little while. I walked out towards Mt Eliza. And down on to the jetty. It's very quiet. Relaxing. And I'm not very sleepy. Not surprisingly. You two must be wired."

"I don't know about that," Pash said. "We've had kind of a nice time."

"Kind of?"

"Yeah! It was good, wasn't it," Pash said, leaning forward to look across Bob at me.

I felt very cold, and it was not just from the icy surface beneath me or the occasional stiffening of the breeze. The leaden ball was swelling, suddenly just about at my throat. I swallowed, knowing that no one could notice, and looked out to sea. Did not say anything. Could not. Well, without giving everything away, and in front of Bob.

"Wasn't it?" Pash said.

"Mr O?" Bob said.

But there was nothing I felt I could say. I can easily imagine, looking back, that I had felt I might cry, and did not want to do that, because it would have been completely ridiculous. I looked out to sea and tried to stop the leaden ball popping out of my mouth. I willed the ball to slide down, to slip down my throat and back into my stomach. To shrink, and to warm up a bit. I realised I was clenching my jaw.

"Seamus...?" Pash said across Bob, sounding tentative, somehow so much less definite than she had sounded at every point until then. "Was it okay?"

"Was what okay?" I said, my throat finally suppressing its leaden obstruction. "Yeah, it was great. We had fun, didn't we?"

"*I* thought so," Pash said quietly.

"What did you get up to?" Bob said. "Or maybe I shouldn't ask."

"Nothing much," I said. "Really. Did we, Pash?"

"Not *really*," Pash said. "It was fun though. *I* had fun. I hope you had fun."

"Of course I had fun," I said. And I had had fun. I imagine I had had about as much fun as I could have withstood, at that time. I remember wanting somehow to *claim* Pash, to demand we have more fun, and go on having fun. To ask her whether, after all, she still liked me. To admire again the colour of her jacket, tell her how cute her nose was, ask her about her scar, say she looked great in jeans, admit that the mere contact of her bejeaned thigh across my lap as we lay on the beanbag had thrilled me. To tell her I thought a thrill like that would satisfy me, if I had occasional access to it, for an awfully long time, and to ask her whether she had felt thrilled like that.

Instead I said: "We had a lovely time." The three of us looked out to sea, until Pash said she was feeling chilly. We walked home together, Pash taking a position between Bob and me, holding each of us by the hand. No one seemed to have much to tell anybody.

"Don't forget your sleeping bags," I said, as we approached what I assumed was Pash's car, parked in isolation across the street from our door. A blue hatchback that I recognised with surprise, envy, and another taste of lead, as a Peugeot, and quite sporty-looking.

Pash gave me a glance, released my hand and felt for her bag.

"I've got them," Bob said, releasing Pash's other hand. I stood awkwardly beside Pash while Bob unlocked the car and retrieved the sleeping bags from the back seat.

"I never got my pash," I said to her finally.

"You did pretty well," Pash said. She nudged me with her hip.

"Will you sleep in the lounge?" I said.

"It's probably best," Pash said. "Don't want to start rumours."

I let them in through the back. It was after four, I saw from the kitchen clock-radio. Bob wanted water. I got Pash a glass, too. I was worried about noise. Sandy would be up in an hour or so, and would not appreciate being woken early. Jessica would not appreciate being woken at all. Luckily, the bathroom was behind the kitchen, a further wall and door away.

"I need a wee," Pash said.

"Be quiet," I said. "See you in the morning. Well, the afternoon."

I thought, once I had reached my own bedroom, of cleaning my teeth, but decided I could not be bothered. I assumed I would sleep, but I did not drift off. I thought about Pash in the lounge, and wondered what she was doing with Bob. Hoped they would not make noise. I heard a click, and noticed a bright strip under my door. Heard someone fumble around in the kitchen. Hoped it was not Sandy woken early and angry. Heard the familiar sounds of Sandy boiling the kettle for tea. Making whatever he typically had for breakfast. Cereal, if I remember rightly—Coco Pops, or something similarly childish and sweet. I heard someone, Pash, talking to Sandy, but could not work out what she was saying. She was being quiet. I hoped Bob was asleep. Pash murmured quietly to Sandy. I could not drop off to sleep. I heard again Pash's musical laugh, and decided that if anybody else had heard it earlier, it would not have bothered them to be disturbed. Excepting of course Jessica.

The sounds got briefly busier and I heard, or assumed I had heard, Sandy leave by the back door.

There came a gentle knock on my door. Well, I imagined a knock. I did not do anything. To have opened the door would have felt completely ridiculous. I would have stared in at Pash, likely as she was sitting at the dining table finishing her tea. She would probably be staring at the kitchen window. Sandy would have looked in at her as he passed by, perhaps pressing his nose to the window, and would have waved. She would have waved back, then gone on looking that way at the pane, darkly blank but reflecting the dining room, and behind that reflection possibly the faint silhouette of the fence and the top of the caravan in the front yard next door. She would have turned as I stared at her, said hello. I would have felt a complete fool.

The door handle turned and Pash peered in at me. I wish I could describe the look she had on, but I cannot. Even though I can remember it with perfect clarity; or more likely, dim as it was, and Pash backlit, I imagine I can. She looked curious, impish, daring, confident, timid, unassuming, calm, wise, determined, decisive, inquiring. All of those things. I have never seen it since, not that look precisely. I felt pinned. I think of myself, looking back, as entranced by the glittering glance of a long-feared snake as it rose to strike. Except that I had no intimation of evil; I relate the metaphor only for its co-persisting with the memory, and for its rendering so accurately the style of my paralysis.

"Can't you sleep either," Pash said, that musical mezzo-soprano soft and so gently produced.

When I failed to answer, my trance disinclined to release me, she said, only slightly less effectively modulated: "It's cold. And not too comfy in there. Can I come in?"

And then: "Can I join you?"

"Won't people talk?" I said, released finally. I remember recognising that her hair indeed was not quite black; in the light from the kitchen, stray strands reflected a faint rust-red tint.

"Do you care?" Pash said.

"Leave your shirt on," I said. "Come and cuddle me. I don't think I could bear it if you didn't."

Pash favoured me with a smirk that I took to be saucy.

"It's been great tonight," she said gently. "I've brought us the dex."

Was I content? I was very content. I was happy for months.

SUMMER

7

A ROLL IN THE HAY

IT TOOK MORE THAN SIX MONTHS FOR ME TO GET TIRED of Pash. She was not like other girls whom I had known or had thought about. Not that I had known many. I had, however, thought about many. That moment in which it all comes together—well, I am being a bit assuming here, but from time to time Pash and I did seem to manage that. With a bit of practice. Well, a lot, when I think about it. Pash would sigh gently, and—I preferred to assume—gratefully. "You're okay, Shame," she would say, using a pet name I had agreed to. "You really are okay." She would relax away from me and look past me with another reprise, I can see looking back, of her wry but accepting smile. "That was pretty damn good."

It did not help that she kept sneaking off to see Bob. She denied it was sneaking. I said it was. She said she was just keeping up the friendship—and that if she had something to hide, she would hide it. This always sounded convincing when she was saying it. But it lost its ring of assurance when she was not around. I used to ask her what it was about Bob. I almost asked her—resisting using precisely these terms—what Bob had that I did not have. I never got anything much out of her in response. All she would say was that she found Bob interesting, just as she found me interesting. "Very interesting," she would elaborate, and I would never know whether she was talking about me or about Bob, and I would never quite be up to asking. I hoped it was me. She did seem to want me, and quite a lot, but I probably wanted her more. It was not all that easy to see. But she did not come down from the city desperate to throw me onto the mattress. I tended to be keen to get her clothes off quickly, whereas she tended to say that she wanted a drink or two and a smoke. We would crash after Zoom or whoever else was awake had had enough, and would make love, most of the time, in the morning.

Nevertheless it was a different life, in many, many ways, for me. I did not see at the time just how different. For years I had wanted a girlfriend. But it had never seemed probable that I would have one soon. Women, as I can admit more easily now, had bothered me. They had never seemed safe, from up close. My seduction? The daughter of family friends, and mostly connected, I had thought at the time, with her having got bored after one of our visits for dinner. Pun not intended. And, thinking about it, not very apt either. Perhaps she had wanted to try something out, and had noticed that I was nearby.

IT IS FUNNY WHERE these musings go. Perhaps, as Ms Felicity insists, that is part of the point. Eventually, I related to Pash the salient facts of this juvenile episode. Which was the first time, thinking about it now, I had disclosed them to anyone. I had been about sixteen, maybe nearer seventeen, and still living with my mother and father, and Charles and Tessa. This came up about halfway through the time that Pash and I spent together. As you would expect—but of course, I had not—the first half of that year was the best half. To begin with, Pash would come down to Mornington whenever she had a couple of days free. But sometimes, and more often as I felt more comfortable, I would get a lift into Frankston with Jessica, ride the train to the city, and stay a night or two with Pash in Richmond. She had a small townhouse, two bedrooms, fairly new, living downstairs and sleeping up, a black iron spiral staircase. She had a rule with her flatmate that two nights in succession was it, for a boyfriend. Otherwise, she said, "It's like they've moved in."

The family friends lived on a horse stud near Warrandyte, only about an hour by car from Heidelberg but in those days unmistakably rural. Riverside beauty, for just a few lucky people. Jean and Tony were not wealthy but they were doing better than we were doing. Their family mirrored ours: two girls, each a little younger than Charles and I, respectively, and their baby brother. Tessa would chase that kid around when we visited. I found the elder girl, Joanne, a bit odd, but she seemed to like me. Of course, she liked to ride. When I was about fourteen they bought a motorbike, a scooter-like Honda, for doing jobs on the property: much less hassle than horses, as Tony told my father when he demonstrated it to us. They sent me off for a ride. It had an automatic clutch and was easy. I loved it. We would sometimes arrive mid-afternoon on a Saturday, so that the parents could get together for a drink and a game of pool before dinner. I was excited by the pool table, as was Charles, but we were invited to play only rarely. I would go out on the bike, and quite often Joanne would saddle her horse and ride with me. It was not a big property, but there were fun places to go. Charles was considered too young to ride by himself and would whinge. Later he got revenge, after his way, by refusing to learn. I know I was very happy, even proud, that Charles had been denied the opportunity to demand that I share the bike. But as I was to discover, left to himself he found his way to plenty of fun with Joanne's sister, Pamela.

It was Joanne who told me about that. Many months, it appeared, after it had started. I had gone out to retrieve the bike from its shed, and Joanne was hanging around. She was blond, or rather, sandy, a bit taller than I, slim but long-boned. She had freckles. "Do you really want to go riding today?" was what she probably asked me. I would have said: "Of course—don't you want to?" And she must have said something like: "Pam said she was doing something with Charles."

"So? They always do something."

"Well, I thought it might be fun to see what they were up to."

"What would they be up to?"

"Well, Pamela said it was fun. Not that I really care."

"What *are* they up to?"

"Well I don't really know." I can imagine Joanne, looking evasive. "We could see them. Find out."

"See them?"

"Well, I told Pam we might meet them. They've made a sort of cubby at the top of the hayshed."

"A cubby?"

"Sort of a cubby. I said we might have a look."

"We could ride there."

"We could," Joanne said. "I won't take Black Boy. I could ride on the back."

"You couldn't," I said, pointing to the large metal rack that sat starkly behind the rider's seat. "Not very comfy."

"I'll throw a blanket on," said Joanne, and she did. "I'll ride sidesaddle." And she managed that, too. It was not far to the hayshed, after all. "Park on the other side," Joanne said.

I have guessed at the name of Joanne's horse: cannot remember. Cannot remember the time of year, either. It was probably summer. There was plenty of hay, but also plenty of grass, so that the hayshed was not getting much use. Where we parked the bike, the haybales screened us from the house—something I did not immediately see as significant. The hayshed was open on all sides and a couple of storeys high, stacked with bales pretty much to the roof. There was a step arrangement of the bales that let you climb to the top, from where they would throw down bales when hay was needed. Joanne climbed off the bike and led me up the giant stairs. Under the iron roof, someone had arranged the bales into walls, I discovered, which enclosed a space about the size of a bedroom. Bales were lined up along each wall for seating. A couple of slits, where gaps had been left between bales, allowed a view of the house, perhaps 400 metres away. There was a protected doorway, around the corner of one wall from the stairway: it would not be obvious immediately to a climber that the room existed. Not that it would have mattered: the hayshed had long been available as a playground, although I had always been frightened I might find spiders, rats or a snake as the weather heated and the bale level fell.

Pamela and Charles were sitting together on a bale opposite us, as we stepped through the doorway.

"You made it," Pamela said.

"Hi Seamus," said Charles. "Having fun?"

"I was," I said. I was a bit annoyed.

"Well?" Joanne said. I do remember her seeming awkward.

"Well, what?" Pamela said.

"Well, here we are."

"Well, that's good."

"I hope it's good," said Charles.

"It will be good."

"Well, it was your idea."

"And? It'll be fun. Maybe. Worth a try."

"I suppose so," Charles said.

"We're doing strip-teases," Pamela told me brightly.

Joanne threw a look at me, and blushed. I could feel myself flushing also.

"Oh," I said. "Really?"

"Yeah. But you don't have to. Sit down. It's fun. It's cute in here, isn't it?"

I had to admit to myself that it was cute—or rather, that I was finding the hayshed cubby, all of a sudden, much more intriguing than I had expected, notwithstanding the prickly atmosphere and furnishings. What went with that was an overturning of my interest in the bike, parked outside by the stairway. All of a sudden I saw it as utilitarian: crude and built for productivity, not entertainment, with that big chromed luggage rack Joanne had sat on. It seemed astonishing that I had been so set on riding it. I cannot remember quite how old we all were. I suppose Pamela was about twelve by then. Maybe thirteen. She had dark brown hair, a kind of squared-off jaw, and was skinny like her sister but more petite. No freckles and a darker complexion. She opened a small pouch by her side and said: "I'm going to put on lipstick." And then to Joanne: "Do you want some?"

"Maybe," said Joanne.

"This will look good," Pamela told her, proffering a second stick. "There's a mirror; it goes there." Charles, who it appeared had carried a bag also, removed from it a small rectangular mirror, which Pamela propped up on a head-high shelf she had constructed near the top of the wall to our right.

Joanne joined Pamela by the mirror. I sat by the wall opposite, a good distance from Charles, and watched Pamela apply make-up. The bale I sat on was not terribly accommodating, and I was not sure what all this was about. I was not comfortable with Charles's seeming to have done this before, or something like it: certainly he seemed very complicit. Perhaps he was embarrassed, too. Or maybe just embarrassed that I had not seen this opportunity before he had: my younger brother stripping off with a girl while I fluttered about on the motorbike. It is possible I consoled myself with the thought that he might have believed I had done something with Joanne—not that I ever had. It had not occurred to me. I was just happy that she came on rides with me sometimes, and seemed to find me congenial.

I looked at Pamela. What was she wearing? I think of a black, narrow, calf-length skirt and a pink button-up top. But it could have been anything. I realised she had secreted an overnight bag among the bales, packed with clothing that she had wanted to try. The trouble was, watching Pamela and Joanne from behind as they applied make-up and peered into the mirror, I could feel myself getting interested. And I was far from certain that this was allowed. Or at least, that it was quite what the girls wanted to see, if I did strip, which I thought I probably should, if *they* did. I was not sure whether Joanne would, but I was not so stupid as to fail to notice that she had drawn me out here, and it seemed plain she found the situation appealing. I did not want to be the only one not to strip. Not that I could quite believe anyone would strip. Not completely, anyway.

"Did you fuck a twelve-year-old?" Pash asked, sounding indignant, when I exposed this unadvertised piece of my history.

"No, of course not! This was earlier. I'm just filling you in on the background."

"I thought this was about your seduction."

"It is about the seduction. But you need to know how it happened. *Who* it happened with."

"I'm not sure I needed that much detail."

"Well, you weren't going to get all that. But it seemed important."

"I might have known," Pash said. "I'll roll you another smoke."

We had begun this occasional ritual, on weekday mornings in Richmond, where we would wake up, have a smoke and have sex. It felt like, in its way, the ultimate in self-indulgence. Better, really, than dex, which took so long to come down from. Pash got days off because she often worked weekends, and while she still used those days sometimes to pop out to Mornington, more and more I would find means to head her way. I would meet her after work at a pub or cheap restaurant, and we would have a nibble and a drink and head home together. Pash was never interested, on those nights, in doing anything that was more broadly social. It was part of her job to be sociable, and she preferred to leave all that behind when a day off approached—or so I assumed, and I did not need a lot of convincing. So we would have a couple of drinks, head home, maybe watch a video or get stoned or have dex and then sit around listening to music, and sometimes get sexy. But not that often, really. Usually, sexy was reserved for the next day. Pash would wake and pour us a drink—mainly a gin and tonic—which she would serve on a tray with a glass each of water and a carefully rolled joint, preserved from the night before. I would wake properly as I sipped on the drink, accepting Pash's passing of the joint—a joint she always started: I insisted on that. Before she made the drinks, Pash usually would put her bra back on, whatever she had worn before bed, because she knew that I liked that. She would lie there next to me with her bra drawing her tits up, sipping on the gin and tonic, which she could just manage with her head on a doubled-up pillow, and smiling at me from time to time as I watched her while I smoked. Then she would take the joint and I would sip, watching her while *she* smoked. Eventually, after she had taken her last toke, she would pass me what remained of the joint and then place a finger on my hip. Usually I would be well turned on by then anyway, but that was her signal—that from there on in it was anything goes. Well, anything she was happy with that I could think of—which was never very different from what I had thought of the last time. Sex was indeed pretty good when we were ripped, or even a little bit ripped, almost always. We would lie around afterwards. Often Pash would make us another drink. And sometimes, another smoke.

"Anyway," I said, after she began on the smoke, "I haven't got to the interesting bit. There was something I wanted to tell you. I don't know why, but it seemed important."

"Sure. Tell me."

"Well, we did strip, you know—"

"I thought you might have."

"—we did, but that wasn't the bit I wanted to tell you. Not that particularly."

"No?"

"We did strip. Where was I? Looking at Pam. Black skirt and pink top. She was very precocious."

"You *did* fuck her!"

"I told you not. Of course I didn't. If you think I did, then you must have missed something. It didn't even occur to me to fuck her. And even if it had occurred to me it wouldn't have occurred to me that I was actually going to." The dope would have been kicking in.

"Okay then. *Fuck! Fuck!*" A cameo from my memories of Pash, damaged I suppose by how often I have thought of it. "Sometimes I love saying that."

"I sure wouldn't have then. I'm not sure I even knew what it meant. I probably still thought sex before marriage was illegal."

"You thought that?"

"Yeah. I think so."

"Why would you have thought that?"

"I don't know. Mum and Dad. Another time. Not this story."

"Get on with it. Your stories take ages."

"Yeah well, it's hard when you get interruptions. Lots of interruptions. You know what? I really like you with that bra on."

"You've always liked me with any bra on."

"Well, any that you wear. I'm not sure I'd like just any."

"Bet you would. If you could. Now get on with it. The story."

"Okay. I was looking at Pam. Precocious. Black skirt. Why do I always think of that black skirt?"

"You're a boy. A very peculiar boy, but a boy. Black skirts aren't rocket science. Girls have been wearing them for a very long time. And usually for effect."

"I suppose so. But I'm not even sure Pam was wearing one. She was twelve. Well, maybe thirteen I suppose. Where would she have got it from?"

"An op shop. Did she sew? If you want something and have time, you can usually get it. What was her mum like?"

"Okay. Bit of a looker, I could say. That's the sort of thing he would say, Tony. Her husband. Not about her, though. He would say it about horses, but he'd have said it about women too—that was the point, really. Better than Mum. Much better."

"But she liked your mum." One of those statements that was intended to question.

"I think she did. They seemed to get on. They were at school together."

"Did they get on at school?"

"How would I know. I don't think they were great pals. I think they became better pals. And then Dad became pals with Tony."

"Are they still pals?"

"Dad and Tony are. Sort of. They get together for a beer every now and again, or as far as I know they still do. Tony's divorced from Jean, which Mum doesn't approve of."

"I'll bet she doesn't. Plain, dud leg. Must be scary out there."

"I don't know that she's *that* plain. I think it's more, these days, that she's overweight. It takes away sharpness of features. Sharpness of feature. Features. Did I just say that?"

"Sharpness of feature. I know what you mean. Anyway, back at the hayshed..."

"Back at the hayshed. Hmm. I was looking at Pamela. She was cute, really quite sexy..."

"She was twelve!"

"She was twelve but she was cute! You know what I mean. She wasn't hot but I *thought* she was. And she wanted to be, sort of, or to look like someone who was."

"She probably wanted that when she was six!"

"Okay, in my *memory* of her she was. I can still remember. Cute little arse, black skirt." I would have felt a shot of pride when I used with Pash a word like *arse*, would have thought I was becoming more sophisticated with women. "Well, I think she had a black skirt. And it was not just her, there was Joanne too, standing next to her putting on lipstick. And *she* was probably fourteen. You know, it wasn't just that one of them was that interesting. They weren't. But the two of them, standing there putting on lipstick and make-up in the mirror, and there we were, in this cosy room they had created, or Pam had but Joanne was definitely into this. Might even have helped. We weren't there much, remember. Anyway, it suddenly seemed very exciting. I was just sitting watching them and they'd been talking about stripping and it seemed very exciting and I wondered if they would be able to tell, if they turned around and saw me. I was glad I was sitting down."

"And?"

"Well the stripping was a bit funny, really. It was still pretty surreal. I can't remember *exactly*. I think Pam asked Joanne how she was going. Joanne must have said she was okay. Pam told her to sit down and then turned around facing us. And she said to Charles: 'Okay,' and kind of beckoned him. And Charles started making this chanting sort of music. I'm sure you know the sort of thing. 'Dah dah *dah* dah dah DAH, da da, da da,' you know. Stripper music, I suppose. People used to do it at school, some of the kids, not me. Not Charles, as far as I knew. Do you know it?"

"I think so. There was a hit called 'The Stripper' in the sixties, and I think you are talking about a bastardised version of that; it is kind of a burlesque cliché, but go on."

"So Charles is going: 'Dah dah *dah* dah dah DAH, da da, da da,' a few times and we all knew how it went, that bit anyway, and Pam started waving her hands like she was conducting us and said, 'Come on,' and Joanne looked at me and started going 'Dah dah *dah* dah dah DAH,' with Charles, and I didn't really want to be part of it but I started putting in the *da da*s at the end. It sounded pretty good, really. And Pam started swinging her hips in front of us, kind of jerking them when we got to the *da da*s, and then her chest, what there was of it, I suppose, but I was pretty entranced seeing her move like that, jerking sideways a bit to the *da da*s, and she started unbuttoning her blouse, a bit at the bottom, so we could see her belly button, and when she got there she stopped for a bit and on the *da da*s she'd jerk her belly button a bit forward at us, and we're keeping doing this—I was starting to have a bit of a good time—and she swirls her hips a bit and then kind of looks upwards at the ceiling as though she doesn't care and undoes the top button on her blouse and shakes her tits at us—well, that area, I mean—and then undoes the next button … anyway, I'm sure you get it. She did a bloody good job. She got down far enough that we could see she was wearing a bra underneath, a white one I remember—funny that, isn't it. So she left it at that for a bit, and then worked on the rest of the buttons and then finally when she had them all undone she just briefly pulled her blouse open and stuck her tits out at us, in the bra, for a couple of *da da*s, and then wrapped up again and spun around and put a hand up in a sort of halt sign and Charles stopped. Joanne and I did too, pretty soon. Joanne clapped and we joined in. Pam did up part of the blouse and came and sat down beside Charles and said: 'Who's next?' She really was pretty good. I remember I was pretty impressed, though nervous. I was sort of soothed that we didn't get past the bra, which was a bit silly anyway—it wouldn't have been that many years ago she'd have been running around topless under a sprinkler in the summer and there wasn't much under it. But it was still exciting. Soothing and silly but exciting. And I was nervous at the same time, I suppose because she'd put on such a good *performance*. And I suppose because I thought *I* had to do something."

"And did you?"

"Well, I don't know if I had to. I suppose I didn't really have to. But I thought I had to. Would have felt a bit wimpy if Charles had and I didn't."

"And …?"

"You're into this, aren't you."

"Not especially. But I am wondering why you are telling me so much about it. Your stories do take ages. I've heard your friends say that of you and I never minded but I am starting to get what they are talking about. Only when you've had a smoke or two."

"Or three. Well, what's it matter. At least I get there eventually."

"Eventually. If you're lucky. Or they are. Get where, anyway?"

"To the point, of course. I always remember the point. Or sometimes I do."

"Sometimes you do. That's my recollection. Sometimes you do. If we're lucky. And already, now I am thinking about that, you've got two points." She glanced across her pillow at me. "Both connected, as far as I can work out, with *your* point." A finger-tap on my groin. "So, the point and the point. *Hurry up!*"

Pash was probably right about my stories taking a long time, when I had had a few smokes. Roland used to tease me about it every now and again, and Zoom too. And Jessica. And really, now I think about it, Steve too, although he used to do it in a way that invited me to keep embroidering. Of course I used to like telling tales, when intoxicated anyway, when I would be relaxed about my performance and just enjoying the moment, holding the floor, I suppose getting off on the sound of my voice spinning a yarn and putting a spell on my listeners, whom I always tended in that state to assume were spellbound and not merely polite or resigned. Even the complaints were not unsettling, as they tended to comprise exhortations that I get to the point—reinforcing my belief that my listeners were so fascinated that they were desperate to know what was the point. And usually I got to the point, I believe—unlike Bob, whose dissertations would diverge endlessly from whatever point we could have imagined they had at the beginning. Pash seemed to put up with Bob, and so I could not see why she would not put up with me.

"I was getting to the point. Pam did that dance. She sat down. The question was, who was next. To tell you the truth, I wasn't desperate to see Charles perform. Especially if he did something like that. It was fun when Pam did it, and I was pretty interested to see what Joanne would do, but I couldn't imagine what Charles would do and I was kind of embarrassed for him, in a way. I mean, I didn't think there was a lot of point in him taking his shirt off. We'd both have done that whenever we all went for a swim in the river. So what else was he going to take off?

"Anyway, it looked like he was going up next. I suppose Pam looked at Charles and Charles looked at Joanne, who'd sat down next to me. I don't think I really wanted Joanne to go up either—that would have been the two girls, and then just me and Charles. And I suppose I didn't want to go last..."

"Why do I think I can imagine what's coming," Pash said.

"What do you think is coming?"

"I am guessing you did something stupid."

"Why would you guess that? Of course I didn't do something stupid. Do I ever do something stupid?"

A long chuckle from Pash. "You are telling me this story *because* you did something stupid. You did something stupid, and you are hoping that if you tell me while we are stoned, I'll forgive you."

"No, it's because I'm stoned that it occurred to me I might tell you."

"And that hasn't occurred before?"

"Well... it has occurred before. Quite a few times, actually. But it hasn't occurred before that I thought I would actually tell you."

"And I am wondering whether it is occurring to you now that you will actually tell me, or whether you have no intention of telling me and every intention of just teasing me. And remember, *this* story isn't even the story I thought you were going to tell me."

"No, that's true. I'm not sure I do want to tell you."

"Well, now you have to tell me. Or I'll hound you till I get it out. Publicly. I'll ask Bob about it."

"Bob doesn't know about it."

"Well then, I'll tell him something went on and I'll ask him to help get it out of you. We'll surround you and force you to tell us."

"I'm gratified you're that interested."

"Well, it is kind of relevant. Your first sexual experience before me. Well, proper one. Or so you've told me. Lots of girls would be curious. How about this: I'll roll you something else to smoke. Then you tell me. How about if I put on some music?"

Pash rolled out of bed and pressed go on her tape player, on a chair near her dressing table. She had another stereo downstairs; this was her small bedroom model, which I remember as sounding surprisingly clear. What did she play? Probably Dexys Midnight Runners, whose album *Searching for the Young Soul Rebels* had become a favourite for both of us. Even if I had resisted it sneeringly at first, renaming it *midnight drivel*, too new and not bluesy or classy enough. Pash would have made us another drink each, as I did not much like to smoke without drinking. She would have returned to bed with the makings of another smoke, and would have rolled it thoughtfully and carefully before handing it to me for approval, whereupon I would have handed it back for her starting it, and she would have lit up with her lighter, an imitation antique, token thanks from a muso whose band she had looked after. She would have taken an equally thoughtful toke or two, passed the number to me, and said something like: "Okay, I've done my bit, your turn. Who went next?" And in that so warmly musical tone of hers, which probably I was past noticing but still miss when I think of it: "And I'm not so sure I'd call what young Pam did stripping. But I am guessing it went further than that pretty fast. Am I right? Or wrong, maybe?"

"Well, right and wrong." It seemed time for a plunge. "Look, the thing is, I showed them my cock."

"I thought so." Warm, musical. Ironic? Maybe. "And were they excited?"

"Oh, I don't know. I suppose they were. They certainly made enough noise about it."

Pash giggled. "Well? Tell me ..."

"Oh, it was very weird. I can't imagine why I did it. I suppose I needed to beat Charles. Or to have a win, somehow. I was kind of pissed off to be sitting there, you know, finding it all quite exciting whereas he seemed to be taking it in his stride, so to speak. He had obviously done this before. I started to wonder whether Joanne might even have been there. Anyway, I can remember I'm sitting there, and Pam looks past Joanne to me. It's still in my head, that look I got. Kind of cheeky but daring me. Kind of. Well I must have thought it was. Anyway I sort of looked back at her, then looked away. I was a bit uncomfortable with that look. So I am looking ahead, about to where Pam did her dance. And I suppose I thought to myself: *It can't be that hard*. Pun not intended! I wasn't really even thinking then about being hard. I think I'd probably gone down. So I heard myself saying: 'Okay, *I'll* do it,' and I'm walking out towards the far wall."

"And thinking: *What the hell am I going to do*," Pash supplied.

"Well I suppose so. I don't know. I remember turning around, and they are all looking at me kind of expectantly. Charles had a bit of a scowl on his face. I liked that. Pam had a grin; Joanne looked a bit guarded, but happy. She was probably wondering what she would do if she had to go next. Pam calls out: 'Do you need any props?' I couldn't imagine what I'd use that she had, so I shook my head. It was way afterwards that I realised Charles probably had some. I had a pair of jeans on and a short-sleeved shirt. I didn't think there was anything I could do with the shirt. Pam looks at the others and goes: 'Dah dah *dah* dah dah DAH!' and then conducts them, and then they all go: 'Dah dah *dah* dah dah DAH, da da, da da,' and get into the swing of it and I'm not really sure what to do, so I start jerking my hips to the *da da*s and unbuttoning my shirt from the bottom, which felt *really* stupid—wow, I can only start to remember just now just how stupid it felt. Anyway they kept going and I kept going, and I got to undoing the last button and started dancing around with my shirt hanging open, and Pam yells: 'Get

A Roll in the Hay

ya gear off!' She really was a bit of a character. She had this slightly baritone, just slightly, deep but not deep voice for a girl. Kind of brassy but with that feminine softness. I can't imagine where she'd have heard that. Well, I suppose on TV. Plausible, anyway."

"Or at school," said Pash. "Girls get the other side of all that. *You* don't see it. 'Get your gear off' is all about us: a girl getting her gear off is a big thing for a boy, and we know it. But then there's also, once you've done that, what if they're not happy. It is a power thing to play with, but you can lose your power too. So it's an exciting thing to say or to hear, but not for the same reason as it is for a boy."

"Okay, thanks for the lesson. At school. I hadn't thought about that. Anyway, there was this funny sort of edge, or lilt I suppose, to her voice that I think must have triggered something, so I am looking out at her, and Joanne's got a bit of a smile on, and I start to get a bit of a tingle and I am suddenly more comfortable, so I keep jerking my hips around but start touching the top button of my jeans. Sort of touching it and not touching it. You know, they're still doing the *da da*s and grinning at me, and I'm feeling like I haven't really done anything yet, so I'm touching the top button of my jeans and then I flip it open and keep jerking around with the top button undone and Pam gives a whistle—you know, a real one with her fingers, like country people sometimes do. I've never done one. Don't know how. But it was pretty loud. So I start undoing the zip on my jeans ... You must be bored with this."

"Get on with it. What happened?"

"Look the thing is, I sort of let the jeans slip down my hips, and then started slipping my jocks down, and then Pam yells 'More!', so I slip them down a bit more and Joanne screams: 'SHAMO'S SHOWING HIS DICK!'—*really* loud—and then almost straight away I hear their mum yelling: 'Pamela! Pamela!' And everybody shuts up. Pam goes to one of the little windows and obviously their mum's just out there somewhere but Pam can't see anything. So she goes out of the room to see where her mum is. Of course I'm buttoning everything up pretty quick. We hear Pam talking to her mum just outside. I can't even remember what they talked about. Her mum must have gone around the hayshed, seen the bike and come up the stairs. I suppose she had a good idea where Pam was, if she wasn't at the house. After a bit, Pam says goodbye to her mum and comes back in. We're all just sitting there looking at one another on bales. Pam puts her finger to her lips and goes and looks out the window slit. After a bit she says: 'She's going back to the house.' Then she looks at me and says: 'Well!' Joanne says: 'Maybe that'll do.' Or something. Charles says: 'That's a hard act to follow,' or something like that. He probably didn't say that—I've just realised that's another pun, which he certainly wouldn't have noticed, even if he did say it. I could see he was a bit admiring though. But I didn't feel admirable. I felt—I don't know. I felt caught out. I felt, actually, really bad. Guilty, in a funny sort of way. I was embarrassed. It was like I had missed something. Like I had taken up their game and missed the point. Gone way over the top. I really don't know whether I had. Whether that's what they usually did, or whether that was just Joanne's first time, maybe. But I felt stupid. Like, maybe, a grade-sixer showing off, you know, maybe to the first-graders. Or something. And then realising that's what he's doing because a few other grade-sixers show up. Anyway, that's what I think about it now. I can almost remember how it felt: I felt quite sick."

"And what happened?"

"Well, not much. That's about it. I felt sick, probably went red, now I think about it. Things got a bit tense. Pam said: 'What will we do?' or something like that. And then: 'Does anybody want a go?' No one rushed to take her up on it. I wanted to get out of there. I told them I was going for a ride, and walked out. It felt weird going down those big stairs. I know I was hoping no one could see me. From outside, I mean. I got to the bike, chucked

Joanne's blanket—it's funny, I can still remember that, feeling sort of disloyal—and rode off, trying to keep the hayshed between me and the house. You probably can't make sense of all this."

"No, not really." We had finished the joint. Pash reached over, took my hand and laid it on her breast, over the bra. "Does that feel good? You're *allowed* …"

"It does feel good." I probably started to shiver, or something. I still do that, sometimes, in big moments. Not that I had much more idea than Pash, maybe less, why this was a big moment. "Why did I want to tell you all that? I don't even know why I *didn't* want to tell you. I suppose it was embarrassing. But it doesn't feel so embarrassing now, talking about it."

"Why was it so embarrassing? I don't quite get it. But I get that it was. I'm glad you told me. It was an okay story. An okay Shamo story. Quite fun, really. You really are full of surprises."

"And," I said, "I finally got to the point. I did get to the point. You waited and I got to the point. Didn't I!"

"Well maybe. I'm not sure I got the point. *Did* you get to it?"

"I think so. At least I got to the end of the story."

"Is that the end?" I can imagine Pash saying this, probably because she said it often. "What happened next? Something must have happened. When you met them again. Weren't you there for dinner? How was it at dinner?"

"It was a bit weird. For me, anyway. Maybe not for anybody else. I kept thinking everyone must know what we'd been doing. I was pretty quiet. The other kids pretty much ignored me but I got kind of a wink from Joanne. I think that's when it all started, really. Although at the time I thought she was probably pissed off about having to carry the blanket."

"With Joanne?"

"Sort of with Joanne. She got a lot more friendly after that. She was around more, if you know what I mean. When we visited."

"So, your seduction. Pam or Joanne?"

"Well, Joanne of course. I told you, not Pam. A few years later.

"Okay. We'd started kissing and stuff. Well, she wanted to. I liked it, of course. We'd go out there and after dinner we'd find somewhere and kiss. That went on for about a year I suppose. Just when we visited. And not every time. I don't think *they* visited *us* much. We did other things. It was funny. It was like I had a girlfriend, but I didn't really. It was more like a game, I suppose. But it didn't worry me when other guys got girlfriends, because I had sort of a girlfriend that nobody knew about."

"Didn't you get bored, just kissing?"

"No of course not. Anyway it wasn't just kissing. I told you. We would do other stuff. I'd touch her in places. It was actually pretty good fun. I used to look forward to going out there."

"But you know, didn't you talk and stuff?"

"A bit, I suppose. Not a lot. It wasn't that sort of thing. We did talk about some stuff. I would always wonder, when we went out there, whether she'd still want to do anything. But she always did, for a while, if we could get away somewhere. She was quite into it."

"And your seduction?"

"Do you need to hear about that as well? Haven't you had enough for one morning?"

"Well, I did think that was the point."

"It wasn't the point. You know what? I've forgotten what the point was."

"I knew it!"

"I can't remember what the point was."

"Did she ever talk about that day? The stripping?"

"Who?"

"Joanne. Did it ever come up? Okay, pun, you know what I mean." Prolonged mutual chuckling.

"Not really. Why?"

"Well, you were embarrassed about it. Then you got to know her. In that sort of way. I just wondered whether you ever talked about it with her. Whether you found out from her what she thought, at the time. What she thought of you. Out in the hayshed. Whether you had anything to be embarrassed about. I don't see it all as embarrassing, necessarily. Did you ever go back there?"

IT IS FUNNY: I can recreate these conversations easily until I come to here, when suddenly it occurs to me just how sketchy my recollection of all this is. Did Pash have white sheets on her bed or cream, or some other colour I have forgotten about? Was there carpet on the floor of her bedroom, or floorboards and rugs? What was in the room, apart from her second stereo? Where did the smoke go, when we smoked: did she open a window? Were we lying there with a curtain drawn open, or closed? Did I have a bedside table on which I could rest my gin and tonic? What was on her dressing table—necklaces and perfume, or was all that hidden away in boxes and drawers? Did she use incense? Almost certainly, but I cannot recall how her room smelled. Cannot even smell her. She did wear perfume, but which perfume I cannot tell you, nor whether she dabbed some on before sex in the morning. What colour did her hair turn out to be? I got that. It was a very dark brown, almost black, and she used to henna it sometimes, in fact quite a lot, when I think about it. Pash. I suppose I was lucky. Well, I know I was. I learned so much from her. Most of which I would have tried to pretend that I did not need to learn, that I knew already. So she would have missed out on my acknowledgement, a fair bit of the time. I suppose she got kicks from knowing I had not known, noticing tacitly my pretending, however much I tried to seem knowledgeable. At least I had not tried to pretend about how many women I had had—well, not technically, anyway.

Sex with Joanne had been—how can I describe it? Perfunctory is the cliché. Maybe not for her. I do not know. It was as though the point was merely to have done that. Which I was not actually that interested in.

"Did she bleed?" Pash asked me.

"No."

"Might not have been her first time, then. Well, unless it was the horses." She giggled, a little unkindly I thought.

"I thought you wanted to hear about this."

"I thought I did. But maybe I don't. It is starting to sound not so exciting. You didn't really like it, did you?"

"Well, not really. It wasn't that I didn't like it, it was just... I don't know. I suppose I was scared of it. It was her idea. We hadn't even kissed that much lately. I hadn't been around there much. I mean, it's a big thing—sex, I mean. It's not something you just do for fun. I mean, not just for fun. There's more to it, or should be more to it. Anyway it didn't last long."

"I can imagine."

I did not find this comment unkind. I took it to be less about me than about Pash's experience of men in general, and her ability to speculate about teenagers in general. After all, now that I had had a bit of practice, I was doing okay in that department. Or so she had assured me.

"It was the end of the kissing," I would have told her. No, I did not ever go back to that little room in the hayshed. Charles probably did, maybe Joanne too, even. But it was not for me. It was as though I had caught myself out, somehow; had caught a glimpse of myself in a mirror at a time when I felt debonair, and had seen something ugly. I know what I did was not that bad—was not, from anybody else's perspective, among those who knew about it, bad at all, as far as I could determine. But it felt bad to me, that was the thing. *I* was embarrassed, even if nobody else was. Or something. I had seen something ugly in myself, and I had not liked it.

"I just realised..." Pash said. "When you told me, that first night, at your place, that you had been with someone, you were talking about something when you were sixteen with Joanne. Who you had just about given up kissing. And that was so unappealing you

A Roll in the Hay

stopped kissing afterwards. Did you even see her? Wasn't that really uncomfortable? It sounds like it would have been."

"It wasn't too bad. By that time, my family wasn't seeing hers all that much, and I didn't always go with them when they did."

I had begun my next-to-last year of secondary school, and could say that I needed to stay home and study. I did not really want to see Joanne. In fact, I did not want to see her at all. Well, I did in a way. I suppose I would have wanted to see her to talk about what we had done together, and what that meant. But we never had talked much. I had been terrified she was pregnant. For most of the next year, on the few occasions the rest of the family went around there for dinner, I was fearful that they would come back with that news. I had not been sure that Joanne would say it was me. It did occur to me that if she was, it might not have been me. But it could have been me, if she was, unless she said it was someone else, and even then it could have been me in any case, depending on the timing, which I suppose I drew out in my fantasies, imagining she might not announce the pregnancy until it was obvious, and imagining anxiously that obvious could be three months later or six months, so that there was a three-month window, at least, for when it could have been me or else anyone. I spent some time at the big library near us at Ivanhoe reading gestation articles in encyclopaedias, doubtless anxiously looking around for observers. I did not assume Joanne had been available to anybody but me, but there had been a matter-of-factness about her, a detachedness, a persistent implication that she simply wanted to try something rather than being in love or infatuated or even properly cosy with me at the time; as I say, we had not been kissing that much before then. And then, well, the truth was I did not even get properly inside her, just made a mess all over her just about as soon as I touched her in that place. Which she may not have expected. Probably did not expect, although she said it was fine. So she might not even have been prepared to cope with all that; might have been thinking she would offer me a contraceptive or something but not yet, or that she could be penetrated innocuously if briefly and I would come somewhere else. I don't know. It was all very weird. We kissed afterwards but I was not really into it. We were sort of polite to one another. I suppose she might have been as confused as I was, but it had seemed to me that she was in charge. She had latched the door in her bedroom, had suggested we lie on her bed, had turned the light off, had unbuttoned my jeans and stuck her hand down the front, and had whispered: "Pull my pants off." A memorable moment, perhaps, but it is not one that I have ever dwelt on.

"I am not even sure why I went along with all this," I told Pash, forgetting that she had not been admitted to my reverie.

"All what?"

"All that stuff. What happened." I remembered that I had drifted off. "I was scared she was pregnant."

"Oh. Weren't you careful? No, I don't suppose you were. Was she? You'd have told me. Well, I hope you would have. Hey," she went on, and I remember I was surprised that she went this way so keenly, "is this what I needed to know about? Is this the point of your story, that even Bob hasn't heard? That you weren't, necessarily, going to tell me? You *are* weird. But not that weird. Surely, not that weird. That would be crazy. But you're not crazy. I am, sometimes, but not you. Not that crazy. *Are* you."

"Not that crazy," I said. "She wasn't, as far as I know. Well, I suppose she may have been, but there's no Seamus Two running around out there, anyway. I'd have known about it. I couldn't avoid knowing. They'd have talked with my parents. Would have had to. I mean, they would have wanted to. Or would have avoided seeing them altogether. They had dinner together, several times, afterwards. Charles would have seen Pam. No, there's no Seamus Two."

"I'm pregnant," Pash said. "So that's probably good."

I have not reviewed that moment all that much either. Perhaps it has resonated profoundly in some psychological cavern. I do not know. I suppose if you have sex with women, at least when they are young enough to be fertile, such a moment is bound to come up sooner or later. I assumed Pash was joking, or wanted to assume that, except that there was something in her tone that unsettled me. Or maybe it was just an unsettling statement. I cannot remember how I responded. Probably something inane such as: "Are you really?" or "Oh. Are you? You're not."

"I am."

"And ..." I suppose I was hoping she would tell me it was Bob's. Or someone else's. Or that she did not want children, and so she would not be pregnant for long. Or, doubtless my fondest wish, at some deeper level that I did not have immediate access to, that she would tell me this was a joke after all. It seems funny to say this when you are talking about an announcement that is presumptively joyful, and that in some circumstances, perhaps many, is indeed joyful. But the feeling of hollowness, the sense of this-can't-be-happening, that I recall from that episode I associate, however accurately or inaccurately, with the response of someone to the sudden loss of a limb, in some sort of industrial or recreational accident. There was that sense of life altering irrevocably and dramatically, and, from my perspective at that time, unavoidably for the worse. It was not that I never wanted to have children with Pash, or that my experience of sexual relations with Pash paralleled in any relevant way my prior experience of sex with Joanne. It was not even that I did not feel ready to be somebody's dad, or that my sexual adventures had been so intangible until so recently that it felt crushingly disappointing that they had become so tangibly significant so soon. It was, I think, that I had not expected this or looked for it, or made any decision about it. Sure, I liked being with Pash, and felt lucky to be with her, and wanted to drag her clothes off, and loved lying around with her drinking and smoking joints. But already I had started to wonder whether Pash was all I wanted—and perhaps more to the point, whether I was all she wanted, or whether I was just a curiosity she had wished to investigate for a time. And so there was that limb-cut-off feeling, something lost, something very important lost, and lost so sharply and irreplaceably that, like the accidental amputee, as I imagine him, I struggled to accept that it had indeed been lost—that I had not, somehow, failed to see that what I thought I had lost was still there all along, after all. And there was, I realised, still a chance of that. Which I was hoping Pash would elaborate upon, without my asking her straight.

"If you are wondering whether it would be your child," Pash said, "it is. No one else whose it could be. I know you think I fuck around, but I don't. Since we started, anyway. Well, almost." She grinned across her pillow at me. "I had a few debts to pay. But no, I've been yours. I don't quite know how this happened, but it has. Well, I do know *how* it happened," she grinned at me again, "but I am not sure why it happened. But I am not upset it has happened, even though you might be, I realise. It is quick, isn't it. I am sorry about that. It is not what I would have planned."

"It's certainly not what *I* would have planned," I told Pash, understanding as I spoke that this was not what she wanted to hear, even if it was obviously the case, and recognising also that my comment implied more than it stated explicitly. I felt this more than I understood it, but nevertheless I could not help noticing that I did not feel delight at the prospect of being linked to Pash for a lifetime in this all but indelible way. It was too soon, I did not know her well enough, we had not spent enough time together, I was not sure how much she really liked me, I would probably have to get a job—all this stuff was relevant but none of it, I could see, was conclusive. The conclusive bit, or so it seemed at the time, was just that I had felt my heart sink rather than jump.

"You're not happy, are you," Pash said.

"Did you think I would be?"

"I thought you might be."

"Well I am sorry to disappoint you. Oh my god, that sounds so callous. Look, I suppose I am just nervous again. It's just so unexpected, that's all."

"Unexpected? You've been having unprotected sex with a girl for seven months, and her pregnancy is unexpected? So it's all about me then, is it? I'm supposed to make sure I'm safe, without asking you about it, and then present myself to you like I'm a figure in one of your fantasies, all fun and then afterwards you forget about them and no consequences." I had told Pash something of these. "Am I just a Joanne? Available but not consequential? Do you really give a damn about me, or are you just happy I give a damn about you, until I become too much trouble or you get scared and piss off?"

It is not pleasant remembering this. It was something like that.

"But you told me not to worry," I said. And that was true. Because I had been worried, at first. Pash had been very soothing, and I had found her strikingly credible.

"Sorry," Pash said. We were, briefly, silent together. "I don't know where that came from."

Quiet.

"Anyway, you're okay. I'm not pregnant."

I looked hard at her. Doubtless I looked pretty fearful. "You're not."

"No, I'm not."

"Oh," I said. "Bloody hell. You're a marvel. You really did have me going there. I'm sorry if I wasn't all that supportive. It was, you know, a shock. I was—"

"Which is just as well," Pash said. "Because I do fuck around."

That is a moment I have dwelt on. I suppose because of what it followed. But I suppose also because I spent such a long time wondering quite what it meant. I never did work that out. My suspicion now is that it did not mean much. That it was just something Pash said. Just a bit of Pash weirdness. I suppose, having gone through this whole thing again—I am amazed that I have, and it has not been easy—what I think of is how you never really know how weird someone else is. You think that you are weird, and you think that some of your friends are weird, but then you meet someone you admire and you think they are not weird. Except for the fact that they like you, and with Pash somehow we skipped past that obstacle. And then all of a sudden—as I am recognising—she was weird, but I did not think she was weird. And so I just thought she had made a joke. And then the other thing I have puzzled over was why I was not desperately unhappy about the admission that followed. I was unhappy, but I was not desperately unhappy. Not really all that concerned. There are times still when I wonder about that. And I suppose I should have been very concerned. But I was not concerned. I really was not all that worried.

8

BELLYACHING ABOUT BOB

SOMETIMES BOB REALLY USED TO PISS ME OFF. I HAVE said that before, and possibly I should not dwell on it. Nevertheless it is a fact, and I am finding that it is good to face facts. Bob had this know-it-all attitude, and what made it especially irritating was that some of the time he really did know it all. So it was dangerous to challenge his claims—say, that every cigarette did you damage, or that women all wanted to dominate men.

I still saw Bob sometimes when I was seeing Pash. It annoyed me that I could no longer drop in on him unannounced, even though I had rarely explored this option when it had been available. Bob had bought a small house in Collingwood, not at all far from Roland, on Easey Street. It was in very good condition, by our standards, having been renovated from front to back only a few years before. He lived in it by himself. There were two bedrooms down the right side as you stepped into the big living room from the street. Above the bedrooms, in what previously would have been wasted roof space, was a mezzanine lounging area that could be reached via a ladder-like stairway. The living room held the dinner table and had lounge furniture too, but that mezzanine area was where you could lie about a bit, and without making a mess that would be obvious to anybody who looked in at the front door. We would have smoked there if Bob had been smoking. It was a great little place and it could have made an occasional base for me overnight near the city, except that I never knew whether Pash would be there and I did not want to find out.

Pash had become tougher to get time with, and that was bothering me. There would be periods when I believed from our rhythms that she would have days off, or was due for them, and I would be expecting a call or a surprise knock on the door any day, and there would be nothing. Eventually I would call her and would find her home, and would suggest we meet up, and she would say that we could if I wanted to. I would tell her that of course I wanted to, and she would make a time and it would work out all right. Usually we would binge on dex, dope or alcohol, almost always at her place. But at times she would seem remote. She had taken to borrowing movie videos. I would suggest a joint, and she would say: Help yourself. I still loved touching her, holding her. In fact, I can remember this time as awakening me to the effects of persistent intimacy on one's appreciation for the benefits of being intimate. We had begun at Pash's flat by getting stoned and lying around the lounge room on her couches. Always when her flatmate was out or at work, which seemed to be most of the time when I was there. We would just lie there together, usually listening to something, with Pash having arranged herself alongside me and on me, and I would be soaked in that same marvellous feeling of exhilaration mixed with wonder that I had become acquainted with during that memorable first visit she had made, with Bob, to Queen Street. As the first months went by, we did that less often, and would disport ourselves on separate couches or would keep more to our own sides of Pash's bed—she had preferred the right side, near her window, I suppose because that is where she had tended to sleep when alone. I had seen this separation as a sign of maturity, an indication that I could sustain our closeness without support from frequent tactile tests. Now that she seemed a bit busier, I was finding that inner sustenance less available, and was experiencing renewed interest in grabbing and clasping her. Interest that I recall her as inviting, up to a point.

With the fucking around, as she had put it, now acknowledged, I also wanted her to see that I could handle that. Pash was not the just-one-man kind of girl: this seemed obvious. I had developed hopes that things might go that way—my reservations about Pash had receded with the occasions for them—but I knew she would come to me only if I gave her plenty of rope. I know that was how I analysed it. I recognised that our getting together at all had been a product of risk-taking mainly on her side. The only risks I had taken were subsidiary: I had risked responding to her open invitations, exposed only to the fear that I was being set up, made a fool of. She had exercised her confidence more comprehensively, and while her confidence obviously was very much greater than mine, nevertheless she was a long way from being invulnerable to the sting of a diminishing remark—this had become clearer as I got to know her. I thought she was easy on the eye, as Bob might have put it, but even I could see she was far from perfect, given more time to examine her. I loved that scar under her chin—the product of a schoolyard fall, she had told me—but it troubled her a bit, distinguishing her from others whom she took to be flawless. I recognised also that her overtly inviting presentation at Mornington had been in part bravado, carried along on the dex, and in part predicated on her careful quizzing of Bob. Not that he would have been slow to offer her what he thought he knew of me. So Pash had taken an interest in me, had made an opportunity to explore that interest, and had researched me so as to develop some freedom in taking up that opportunity. Whereas I had just sat there: perhaps my contribution had consisted in my refraining from running away. I was aware of this, and had felt myself very fortunate. And so I was determined not to push that luck, and willing to give Pash whatever freedom she needed while I could manage to do so.

Not seeing Pash as much meant I had more time to do other things. The biker fiction developed into a series, and I took pride in the cheque each instalment brought in. The cheques were not large—they might have ended up $100 each—but the time and energy required to earn them had contracted, so that I had been able to meet what had become a monthly deadline while spending several days of the typical month in the city, seeing Pash and, usually, someone else there—most commonly Roland or Jamie. If I had come in on the bike, I would pop in on one or another on the evening when I was due to head home. Jamie in particular was impressed that I had got pally with Pash, as he put it, having met her one night when she called in to see Roland. That was after Steve had met his end, but before Pash had visited me. Roland, understandably, seemed a bit doubtful about our connection at first. But soon he endorsed it. I do remember that I felt very smug. I did not envy Roland his connection with Debbie. I used never to mention Pash first, but Roland, having learned about us from Bob or perhaps even from Shooka, never failed to ask me how Pash was going. He would pull out the bong, offer me a cigarette, refuse one of the light beers I would have brought, pour himself a bourbon and Coke, and would say, his voice rising a tone or two on her name, each time making me wonder whether he had inquired from duty or was enjoying a private joke: "And how's *Pash*?" I would tell him she was fine, or busy, or weary, or (if I had leant towards the joke interpretation more than usually) that she really was a lot of fun. "I love it that she smokes," I would elaborate. "And drinks. And likes to get into other stuff." Roland would take a drag on his cigarette, and would smile and nod. At about this point I would start to feel guilty and would remember about Steve. "Does she remind you of Steve?" I would ask, or something similar. This happened on several occasions, and Roland answered patiently on each that it did not bother him to be reminded of Steve. "Have you done any more stories?" Roland would say, sometimes offering a suggestion about whom

I might cover. "I am working on stuff," was my stock answer about that time. "And the bike stuff's still selling." "It's great that you're getting cheques for that," Roland would tell me. "Yes," I would say, "Cheques in the mail. And literally, they are in the mail!" Roland would grin at me, would cough from his cigarette and would hand me the bong. He was delighted I was getting cheques in the mail, and he understood as well as anybody I knew just how good it felt to be getting them: that I had taken a step into one of our dream worlds from Keppel Street. "Have you heard about …?"

Usually that question from Roland would be completed with somebody's name, and it would always be somebody whom I was interested in knowing about, or at least would find it entertaining to hear about. Roland knew who would interest me, from among his big circle of friends and acquaintances, and he knew also that he could balance my interest in the person against the likelihood of the tale itself proving entertaining. Indeed, at this point he was probably seeing most of my city associates more than I was. Stanley, Jodi, Shooka, even Jamie and Bob, were obvious candidates, but there were several others whom I had met through Roland and with whom he spent time or did things, and yet others with whom we had both been acquainted at Keppel Street and of whom he would receive news, either from a more frequent visitor or from Debbie.

"Have you heard about Bob? Oh I suppose you would have … Have you? You might have seen him since I did."

"Actually it's been a little while since I saw Bob. I've not been getting down as much."

I knew that in saying that, I was dissembling. I was far from convinced that I wanted to receive news of Bob. But I remembered that Roland would not have wanted to confront me just like that with anything very unsettling and so I relaxed a little. "What about Bob?"

"Well, I've suddenly realised you probably know about it. Anyway, have your bong."

"Is it strong?"

"Not particularly." Roland offered me the gleeful grin he seemed unable to detach from such assessments. "I guarantee you'll enjoy it."

"That's got me worried already."

"It's not that great. Things have been a bit... of a pain. But I have got onto something and I want to see what you think."

I knew well that Roland would not have ranked highly my ability to judge the quality of a dope deal. But I was flattered enough by the question to take up his lighter and bend my lips to the pipe. It is surprising how effective flattery can be, even with a person who knows that it is flattery.

"So," I said, having passed back the pipe and taken another sip on my beer. "Bob."

"It doesn't really matter," Roland said. "My bong."

I could have received this backward step as a warning. But Roland's having taken it convinced me that he had been about to reveal a detail about Pash. I knew perfectly well that I was not likely to enjoy hearing whatever it was. And yet... when you are giving somebody rope in the way that I was attempting to give Pash rope, you experience a kind of ache, an interior hollowing that intrudes and recedes like an itch, and you want to caress the aching bit, to fill the empty place, to scratch the metaphorical itch. But the only thing that can do the caressing, infilling or scratching is information, and information is precisely what you cannot have, because ignoring opportunities to seek information is exactly what it is to give somebody rope in these circumstances. If I had known just what Pash was getting up to, I would have been in a much better position to draw conclusions about whether the licence I was allowing her was freeing her to gravitate towards me—or instead, was freeing her to draw ever closer to somebody else. But to have made inquiries about Pash with Pash or with others would have been to obsess about her, to dog her footsteps, one way or another to hassle her. To turn myself into the sort of deranged admirer who on daytime TV would end up performing a kidnapping, or getting carted off by the cops after emerging from a stake-out in her front garden to confront a rival. And I had no doubt I would be a former lover very quickly if I took a single step down that path. I was proud that I had resisted doing so. Roland's reference to Bob, therefore, offered the possibility that I might scratch my itch while remaining resolutely on the straight and narrow road to uncomfortably accommodating Pash's experiments. My fear was that I might hear something unpleasant; but then, even hearing that would be pleasant.

"This is pretty good," I would have told Roland.

Roland would have given the nod he usually managed in such circumstances, holding in his inhalation of smoke and grimacing before releasing it, possibly with a cough or two and a shake of his head at the finish. "I think it is. It will get you soon."

"I'm not sure that I am desperate to be got."

"You will like it."

"I thought half the point was to find out whether I liked it or not."

"You will like it but I don't know how much," Roland said, looking, I thought, alarmingly complacent.

"You know, I already think I am liking it. In fact, I am already starting to think this is as good as I have ever had—or if not, then as good as I can remember having or am ever likely to remember."

"It's working," Roland said. "Have another."

"There is no way I am going to have another. You are hopeless with your 'Have another.' All you seem to want to do is to get me hopelessly ripped on some new lot of giggle-weed you have gotten hold of and then watch me do silly stuff. I've worked you out. I've told Pash about you, and she thinks so too. Sorry, I wasn't going to talk about Pash. And I wasn't going to tell you that I wasn't going to talk about Pash. Well I don't mind talking about Pash really, but

I was going to let you talk about her. I wasn't going to ask anything about her but I don't mind talking about her. If you want to know about her. Which I am sure that you don't. So let's forget I even said anything about her. I do like her though. I still can't believe I've spent so much time with her. I have had *such* a great time with her. An unbelievably great time with her. Sorry, I wasn't going to talk about her. I'm not going to talk about her. And I am sure you don't want to know about her. Let's pretend I haven't talked about her. I've just remembered about Steve. I don't mean just remembered, I mean just now I remembered him. How he was with Pash, I mean. I'm not sure that you want me to say that. Oh, Roland, I'm sorry that I said that. I didn't mean it the way it sounded. You know what I really think about Steve. And you know I wouldn't mention him unless I thought you really did want to hear about him. Which of course I probably do—*and*, I am probably reminded of him exactly by the way you are carrying on, trying to get me to have another bong when very obviously I am completely zonked by this one and can't even work out what I'm saying. You are a very nasty man, Roland, a very, very nasty man. I can see you grinning that very sneaky, very devilish-looking grin and just waiting until I say something *really* stupid that you can remind me of later. You *are* looking like a devil. You are looking really like a devil. You are looking *evil*. You are probably jealous and just hoping I will make an even bigger fool of myself than usual so that you can laugh and laugh and laugh at me. Oh my god, I am sorry I said that. I'm very sorry that I said that. What an ungrateful guest. I have complete trust in you, Roland, complete trust. You are my favourite host. My favourite host of all time. I can't believe I have just walked in here and this has happened. And it is all your fault! Oh my god, I can't believe this stuff. It is *really* good."

"I thought you'd like it."

"I do like it. Oh my god. There is no way I could have another one."

"It will relax you," Roland said.

"It won't relax me. It will make a blithering idiot of me. Even more so than it has already. It is funny there are waves and waves. I feel straight now."

"So it is definitely time for another one."

"No! Why don't you have another one!"

"I couldn't have another one. Because then I wouldn't be a great host. I would be acting out of turn. If I had another one now, I would be getting ahead. And that wouldn't be good for you, because then you would need to have two in a row to catch up."

"It is amazing how considerate you can be of my welfare. Especially when you've just had one of these yourself."

"I've probably had a bit more of this lately than you have. So it's not affecting me as much."

"Aha! So you *should* have another one."

"No, that would be rewarding me for being greedy. It wouldn't be fair on you. I would be a bad host."

"Let's just let this one settle down a bit. Then I'll have another one."

"*Steve* would have had another one," Roland said.

"I can't believe you just said that."

"Well he would have. And he wouldn't be sitting here saying one was enough. And he wouldn't be letting *you* get away with saying one was enough. He would be saying that you need to have one, that it's for your own good, and that you'll feel better afterwards."

"Do you ever think that Steve is looking down on us? Looking at us and grinning that we are having such a good time."

"I don't, but it's a nice thought," Roland said. "Have your bong. Here." He pushed the bong, its bowl carefully repacked, across the table towards me. And slid the lighter after it.

I suppose I had been flattered by Roland's bringing Steve into things. By his telling me what Steve would have said. It was another readmission into Roland's private world; recognition of my relevance for his pleasure there; acknowledgement that much of what had been fun about Steve had been fun *with me*. Well, I would have seen it that way, distorted as that picture was. I had wanted to see it that way. And the picture was not wholly inaccurate. Roland did want to share this, for some reason and at some depth.

The bong tasted delicious and I am sure I did not cough this time. I would have taken another swig on my beer.

"How does that feel?" Roland said.

"Nothing. Nothing. I feel nothing."

"You feel nothing."

"Nothing. Nothing at all. I feel nothing. I feel very weird and silly but I feel nothing."

"It'll come on soon."

"I don't think it will. I think I've got used to it."

"You probably have. So you can just relax and enjoy it. And then you can have another one."

"You are not going to get me like that, Roland. You are definitely not going to get me like that. When Steve was here, you might have got me like that. But Steve isn't here, so you won't be getting me like that. Probably ever again. You might never get me again like that ever again, Roland. But Steve might have got me like that. Probably would have done. He probably would have done, Roland. Or you would have done, with his help. You were quite a pair, Roland. Quite a pair. A horrible pair. You were a horrible pair, Roland. A horrible pair."

"We were a horrible pair."

"You *were* a horrible pair. No, I can't believe I just said that. Of course you weren't a horrible pair. You were a great pair. A fabulous pair. There was nothing like the pair you were. Oh no. It is bad, Roland..."

"It's bad that we were a fabulous pair."

"No. It's bad that you aren't a fabulous pair any more. That you aren't a pair. Any more. I do say terrible stuff sometimes, don't I."

"You do say terrible stuff sometimes."

"But it doesn't matter, does it. It doesn't matter. It really doesn't matter. Does it?"

"It doesn't matter," Roland said. "Well, it does, but there's not much we can do about it. I'll have this bong and then you have one and then not all that much will matter, after all."

"It's a bong *you* need to have."

"I'll have this bong, and then you'll have a bong. That's what we need. That's what this is about. I'll have this bong, and then it's your turn for a bong."

"I think *you* need that bong."

"I do need this bong."

"But *I* don't need another bong."

"That's where you're wrong. You do need another bong."

"I don't think I need another bong."

"Well, that's where you're wrong. But that's all right. I'll have this bong ..."

"... You have that bong! Good idea! It's a bong YOU need to have."

"And then you'll have a bong. But we will talk about that later."

"I don't need a bong."

"I don't know that you're in a good position to say."

"No, I'm not. And if I had another bong then I'd be worse."

"But *you* don't know that!" Roland's tone was indignant. I would have suspected that he was feigning that tone but I would not have been certain. "That's what you *think*, but as you've said, you're not in a good position to say! You think you don't want another bong, but that's because you haven't had enough bongs recently to remember how you will feel if you *have* had another bong. And if you could remember how that would feel, then you would *know* that it was good for you to have another bong. And the only way to remember that, since it's been so long, is to have another bong. So that's what you need. It will sort out all your problems. You'll look on the bright side. Life will feel much better, and you'll be happier." Roland had been leaning forward over the table, dark-browed and glaring at me. But now he sat back, having delivered himself.

"I think I'm happy enough now."

"I don't think you are. Look at you. You're moaning. You're moaning and gloomy and there's only one reason," Roland said, now leaning back in his chair. And jabbing an outstretched finger in my direction. "One reason, and I think you know what it is. And," he said, fixing me sharply with that acute gaze he had, "if *Steve* was here, he definitely would have told you it was your bong. In fact he probably would have told you it was your bong *now*. But I won't do that. I've got this bong here, and I'm going to have it. I'll have this bong, and then I'll make another bong and that will be your bong. And it will be good if you have it. Good for you and—" Roland's gaze again transfixed me "—good for the universe. Good for you and good for the universe."

"I understand what you're saying."

"Of course you understand what I'm saying. You're an intelligent person. Very logical. Your logic is impeccable. That's what Steve would be saying. Impeccable logic. And the impeccable logic of your brain tells you that the best thing you can possibly do over the next five or six minutes is to have one more bong. That I will pack for you as soon as I've had this one. Which I suppose I had better have."

It is of course impossible for me to remember the conversation this accurately, and so I cannot say whether it was precisely at this point that we were interrupted, but it was about here that we heard a knock. I am pretty sure I had had a couple of bongs, and Roland had smoked only one but was about to embark on another. We were at his Abbotsford dining table, that Formica-topped landmark that might have been stolen from a department store cafeteria, that site where Steve and Roland had so wound up Bob, and where Shooka had recalled me for Joey as the knife-wielding menace of legend. There would have been the bong on the table, the bowl of mull, a disposable cigarette lighter, my stubby of beer, Roland's mostly consumed Coke and bourbon in a tallish beer glass, perhaps a cup from which Roland had consumed coffee before I arrived, Roland's cigarettes, an ashtray with butts in it, perhaps a vase in the centre to which Debbie had contributed flowers from the front garden—I have no idea what colour, but I imagine something stalky, short and grey. I suspect it was about nine at night, and that I had arrived about dinner time, knowing that Roland and Debbie were not likely to have been sitting down to anything grand, believing that they might well make space for me, and hoping that after dinner Debbie might retire to the lounge and let the two of us get on with it, given that my visits were more rare these days, and that Roland during these still-dark times needed company—surely Debbie could see that. As it turned out, Debbie was not there, having gone out to a dinner with girlfriends, or to a book-club evening ... something like that. Whether Roland and I had dined together that night I do not know: it is possible that, assuming I had arrived early enough, he had made us jaffles, his staple, from tinned beans and cheese. The knock would have bothered me: after two bongs I would have been suddenly aware of how silly I felt, and aware also of how comfortable I had got with just Roland and how little I wanted to have that comfort disturbed. And I would have wondered who it was: Debbie returning, perhaps, or some Steve substitute Roland had picked up since I had last seen him.

Roland answered the door while I sat at his table. As I imagine that evening—and yes, I have been enjoying reliving it—I think of myself as seated at the end of the table nearest the hallway, looking at the blue kitchen wall and the redundant breakfast bench to the right of the table. But Roland would have taken his now customary place at the other end of the table, immediately in front of the wall, the place where Steve used to sit, and I would never have seated myself so far from him. Perhaps after he got up I had moved to the end opposite him, so that I could negotiate more easily any entering guests. Certainly, I felt agitated. The hall was long enough and dim enough that even a direct glance would not show me who had knocked. But before long I recognised from the exchange of greetings with Roland and some post-greeting mumbles that it had been Bob—and that, in what I registered at the time as a parallel with his appearance at Mornington the previous winter—Bob was accompanied by someone whose voice sounded feminine. The parallel did not end there. At Queen Street we had been expecting Jessica but got Pash. This time, having understood that this was a visit from Bob and that he was accompanied by somebody female, I spent a brief second or two assuming that again he was with Pash. But as Roland led Bob and his companion into the light of the dining room, I understood with a jolt that the companion was Jessica.

"Mr O!" Bob said, sounding I thought a little tight. But perhaps I felt tight.

"Seamus," said Jessica. "Hello. I didn't expect to see you here."

"Well, I didn't expect to see you here. Certainly didn't expect it. Very definitely didn't expect it, although I don't mind that you're here. Well I do mind, actually, but I don't really, if you know what I mean. Which I realise you probably don't. I thought you'd be Pash." I recollected myself. "I am sorry. As you can probably gather, I am a bit bent."

"You've been indulging in Roland's bounty, I see," Bob confirmed for me.

"Have a seat," Roland said, gesturing at Jessica. "Would you like anything? Cup of coffee? Juice? Jim Beam? Coke?"

"I'd like a juice," said Bob, sitting down. "Orange juice if you've got it."

"Do you have beer?" asked Jessica, seating herself near me and noticing mine.

"I've got lights," I said. "Have one. Roland, they're in the fridge ... would you like me to get one?"

Roland was returning already with the stubby and a glass. He noticed mine was low. "Do you want one too? No, I'll get it." He got me another stubby, got Bob his juice, mixed himself another Coke and bourbon. Sat back down at his favourite end of the table, next to Bob. Withdrew a cigarette and slid the pack down to me. "Help yourself!" His glance took in Jessica.

"Thanks," said Jessica. "I might." We lit up.

"Are you into those cancer sticks?" Bob asked Jessica.

"Only sometimes. But this feels like a pretty good sometime."

"So, Mr O," Bob said, turning to me. "What brings you in here? It's not often I see you here, these days."

"Just thought I'd pop in," I said. I was feeling straight again, all of a sudden, but wondering how long I would stay that way.

"Are you in town for long?"

"Not really. Probably head back tonight."

"So you've just popped in to get a head full of hallucinogen before heading out on the Honda."

"It's not a Honda. As you very well know. I popped in to say hello to Roland. It's not like you're often available."

"Me? Unavailable? I'm available. When did you want to meet up?"

"No time in particular. Just ignore me. I'm wanting to just settle down a bit. I'm probably home tonight. I really need to get some work done."

"So you've been in town for a bit?"

"Just a day or two."

"Would anybody like a bong?" Roland asked.

"I wouldn't mind one," Jessica said.

"Maybe not," Bob said.

"Oh," Roland said. "Here." He slid down the table a small plastic bag that was filled with, I could see as Jessica reached for it, khaki-green head.

"Thank you," cooed Jessica. "That's so nice of you. Was it ... seventy?"

"Seventy bucks," Roland said. Jessica took a purse from her handbag and passed Roland, via Bob, the notes.

"Thought it might be handy," she confided to me.

"Bong?" Roland said. "It's the same stuff."

"Yeah!" said Jessica, receiving a pained look, I thought, from Bob. "Well, if *you* don't mind."

"I wasn't thinking we'd stay," said Bob. "But why not."

I was still taking in all this, cogitating in that peculiar way in which you cogitate when ripped on something fairly tasty but not sure how much you need to be paying attention. Having Jessica sitting near me was distracting, much more so than I had assumed it would be, I think partly because she was there without Sandy. It was not just that Sandy was absent, however, because I had spent at least several hours sitting with Jessica while waiting for Sandy, if you added all those minutes up, and she had not then been as distracting. For some reason it was her blondness that I focused on: she was very blond, her hair flowing down onto her diminutive shoulders in big, healthy-looking waves, waves that I had conceived of, on several intoxicated occasions, as having been sculpted from a pale wood and varnished. I was wondering what the hell she was doing there. As far as I knew, she did not even like Bob much. Where was Sandy? Obviously she had dropped in to pick up a dope deal, but why with Bob and why would I not know about it? Why not ask me to pick up dope for her from Roland, if she wanted dope picked up from Roland? But why would she want dope to be picked up from Roland? How would she even know Roland might have dope that she could pick up? It is not as though I would have raved to everybody about where I got dope from, and nor did I ever get much dope anyway—at home now, mainly I just smoked Zoom's, given he had it in plenty, or bits and pieces I used sometimes to bring back from Pash's.

This sort of stuff was whizzing around inside my mind but on the other hand, I was just about relishing what I saw as a new kind of social opportunity. I had been stoned before with Bob and with Jessica, although not so often lately, but I had never been stoned with Roland and Jessica, as Roland had never visited Mornington and I had never visited anyone with just Jessica. So while I was wondering what the hell Jessica was doing there, at the same time I was assuming there would be a good reason and that it was probably obvious what was that reason, and I was also anticipating that far from wrecking my tete-a-tete with Roland and the spirit of Steve, Jessica's arrival had brought to the evening a fascinating new perspective. It had long been my hope that Jessica and Sandy would meet Roland, and would get to appreciate him when he was in a mood that made it possible to appreciate him. But those moods rarely arrived when Roland was not at home, and almost never arrived when he was out with Debbie. And he seemed reluctant to venture far from home without Debbie. I had developed little reason or excuse for inviting Jessica and Sandy to Roland's house for a couple of bongs and a drink. And so I had accepted that Roland, Jessica, Sandy and I getting together for a smoke was very likely to remain an exclusively imaginary event. And yet here it was, or half of it, handed to me on a platter.

"Where's Sandy?" I asked Jessica.

"Asleep, probably. He'll be working tomorrow."

"I didn't think you liked Bob."

"Well, I don't, really. But he is kind of useful, don't you think?"

She threw Bob a look, got an irritated, I thought, look in return, and turned her attention to the bong Roland was passing to her.

"Didn't think she liked me?" Bob protested, startling me. "That would be just typical of you, wouldn't it, having to say something like that. Why wouldn't she like me?"

"Well, no reason. But I just didn't think she did like you, that's all."

"So you thought you'd take the first opportunity to air your assessment in someone else's house where you've got the same status we have: we're guests. You don't think that's a bit rude?"

"It probably is a bit rude. I'm sorry if I was rude. It just occurred to me, that's all."

"And it would be typical of you to say the first thing that occurred to you, when you're on the bongs, wouldn't it."

"Probably. That's part of the point, isn't it?"

"It might be for you, but it's not terribly comfortable for other people who have to put up with the way you behave. Anyway, why wouldn't she like me."

"Bob, it's okay," said Jessica. "I do like you." She had examined the bong and tested the lighter. "It's a while since I've done this."

"About three weeks," said Roland.

"Well, that doesn't mean I am used to it." Jessica bent her head to the pipe and manipulated the lighter, the flame remaining obstinately upturned as she attempted to apply it to the mix in the bong's small brass bowl. She withdrew her mouth from the pipe and took a breath.

"Give me the lighter," said Bob. "Thanks. Now when you're ready. Here."

Bob lit the bong for Jessica, and we watched while she drew in the smoke. Explosively she withdrew for a fit of coughs.

"Oh my god," she said, "I hate that."

"You need more practice," Roland said. "Have the rest."

"Do I want the rest? Well I suppose so."

"Wait and see what that does," Bob said. "You're not that used to this."

"No, I'll be right. I'll have the rest."

"It's strong. Usually. Is it strong?" Bob asked Roland.

"It's not too bad."

"It's appalling," I offered. "Although I think I've straightened out from it. Not that you helped me by accusing me of being an idiot," I accused Bob.

"I didn't accuse you, and when you have this stuff in bongs you are an idiot."

"Not as idiotic as you."

"I rest my case. When have I been an idiot? I don't even smoke this stuff."

"You used to. And that just shows what an idiot you have become."

"So you sit here like an idiot, banging on about how I'm an idiot— completely socially gauche, not to mention rude and abusive, which is how you often get when you've had this stuff, and you don't even realise what sort of aggressive boor it makes you look like—and the reason I'm an idiot, according to you, is that I *don't* do that. Because I want to retain control of my faculties and take part in polite conversation with intelligent people. About things that have some meaning, and not just about how many bongs you've had and whether or not you should have another one when you've already had enough to reduce your IQ to about fifty. Or less." Bob gave a giggle. "Probably less." And to Jessica: "You can see what this stuff does. It looks pretty effective to me. Unless you think Mr O is already like this, most of the time. You've probably had enough for now, don't you think?"

"No, I don't think. I think I should have the rest of it. It looks like fun. Why are you so negative about it? This is why we came here, isn't it?"

"I thought we came here so that you could pick something up. I didn't think we came here to join in the sort of bong-bloated abuse-fest this pair indulge in when they fill themselves up on this heavy stuff. But if that's what you want to do, don't let me hold you back. I'll sit here and watch while you all tell yourselves how many more bongs you need. Are you getting that yet?" The question clearly enough an inquiry about whether Jessica felt she had been much affected by her draught of smoke.

"I don't know. I do feel a bit weird."

"It takes a bit to come on," Roland said. "And it will take more if you don't smoke all that much. And you might not have got much, because you were coughing. Have the rest. You probably won't cough again if you know what to expect."

"Don't take in too much at once," I advised. "Just have what is comfortable and then have a bit more. There's no rush."

"Well, I suppose I can hang around here all night," Bob said. "Take your time."

"I will," Jessica said. I found myself admiring her for that. It was hard to withstand Bob's sneering sometimes. Without being confronting or abusive. Of course he would deny that he had been sneering. But Jessica had just been calm, solid, no-nonsense. Solid.

"You'll like it," I said. "I am liking it."

"Thanks. I'll have the other half." She looked at Bob.

Bob slid the lighter to her. "Hold it yourself," he said.

"I'll light it," I said, and did, holding the flame over the bowl as Jessica sucked down the smoke. This time she stopped early as advised, giving just a tiny splutter, and then held down the draught before expelling it in a transparent grey stream.

"Nice," said Roland.

"Thanks," said Jessica. "That felt a lot better."

"You'll feel really good soon," said Roland. "You'll feel as good as Seamus, maybe better."

"She'll feel a lot better than I do," I said. I grasped her bicep. "She feels great. I wish I felt that good."

"You could keep your hands to yourself," said Bob.

"I do feel good, though, don't I," said Jessica, with a grin towards Bob.

"How would I know?"

"Well, you know. I just thought you could guess."

"Who have you seen lately?" Bob asked Roland. "How's Jamie? Do you see him much?"

"Occasionally. He's okay. Whose bong is it?"

"It's yours," I said. "You were going to have one."

"That's true. Do you want the rest?" Roland asked Jessica. "Or did you get it all?"

"I think there's a bit left."

"You may as well have it."

"I'll have it now, then."

I held the lighter for her. There was not much left.

"Good girl," said Roland.

"You're a corrupter of the young," I told Roland. "You really are a very naughty man."

"*I'm* a naughty man ..."

"Well, I'm not *that* naughty. I was just helping her light it."

"Sure. Anyway, it's mine."

Jessica passed the bong to Roland, via Bob.

"Thanks. How do you feel?"

"Pretty good. A bit funny. Is it strong? It doesn't seem to be doing that much."

"It's stronger than the last one," Roland said.

"Oh. I *like* it."

"As long as you're not feeling sick," Roland said.

"Roland!" I admonished.

"Because you are looking a bit pale, I think. Would you like some water, something like that? Maybe a cup of tea?"

"Maybe a beer," I said. "She's not looking pale at all."

"I think she's looking pale. What do you think, Bob? Do you think Jessica's looking pale?"

"She always looks a bit pale," Bob said. "I don't think she's looking paler than usual."

"Are you feeling pale," Roland asked, still packing his bong. "As long as you're not feeling pale, you'll be fine." He snapped his fingers for the lighter, and after I slid it down the table to him he devoured the bong in a single long draught. "That was great!"

"I think I do feel a bit pale," Jessica said.

"You look fine," Bob said. "You're not pale. Maybe you're just deprived of a bit of oxygen. Need some fresh air, which will probably fix you."

"I don't feel like moving," Jessica said.

"You *are* looking pale," Roland said.

"Hey!" said Bob. "Get off her back. She's fine. Or would be if you idiots didn't keep telling her she was feeling sick." He turned to Jessica: "It's suggestion. You'll have heard of suggestion. Suggest to someone that something is a certain way, and there is a high chance they will start to see it that way. It's well documented. Research coming out your bum. In fact it is behind the whole concept of a placebo. Which is directly related to this. Here, I'll get you an orange juice. That will cure you. I'll get you an orange juice and you'll drink it and feel better. Do you get that?" Bob pushed his chair back and strode around the bench to the kitchen. I could see him investigating the fridge.

"You are looking pale," said Roland. "How do you feel?"

"I'm not feeling that well," said Jessica.

"You're not really used to bongs, are you?"

"Not really. I have had them before." Jessica's voice, less melodic and pitched lower than Pash's, with a peculiar inflection that had led me to assume that her parents were recent immigrants from somewhere in Great Britain, had softened, as though she were seeing herself suddenly as a smaller and less significant person. She laid her head on the table.

I put a hand on her shoulder, thinking she might find the contact consoling. Bob came back with the orange juice.

"What's the matter? Jessica! Snap out of it! You're fine. Here is some juice. I've brought you some juice. It will cure you, remember. Drink this and you'll feel fine. You'll even feel great. And we can get out of here. Get you some fresh air. Away from bongs and crap and idiots."

"It's your bong," Roland said to me. He slid the lighter down the table to me and passed the bong towards Bob. "You'll enjoy this one."

Bob, still standing, picked up the bong and plonked it roughly in front of me.

"Jessica," he said. He placed a hand on her shoulder and shook her gently. I withdrew mine. "You're fine," Bob told her. "Have some juice."

"She was looking very pale," Roland told Bob.

"Fuck off with your 'looking pale,'" Bob said. "Just fuck off with it. She was fine, she's smoked before, she will be fine. If you idiots would just leave her to it. What's this on about, anyway? What do you want to make her feel worse for? She should never have had that bong."

"I wanted the bong," Jessica said. She sounded pale.

"Should we get a bucket?" I asked.

"Maybe," Jessica said. She still had her head on the table.

"Lift your head up," Bob told her. "Head up, look around. Get yourself onto an even keel. Take a deep breath. There is nothing wrong with you; it is just these two doing their best to make you feel ill. Why, I don't know. Just their bizarre—and very inhospitable—way of entertaining themselves. Which is not very entertaining and makes me wonder why we went out of our way to turn up here. Have your orange juice."

"Would you like another bong?" Roland asked Jessica. "Or would you like me to get a bucket?"

"Maybe another bong," Jessica said. "I think I'm starting to feel better." She still had her head on the table.

"You don't want another bong," Bob said.

"I'll have mine and let you know how it feels," I told Jessica.

"I bet it feels *great!*" Roland said.

"It will feel good," I said. "I know it will feel good." I took up the lighter and despatched most of the bong in a single, long slurp, holding in the smoke before exhaling it in a steamy looking stream. I felt very proud of myself. That feeling, rare as it was at the time, felt even better than usual.

Bob had sat down.

"Why don't you have one?" Roland asked Bob.

"Go and fuck yourself," Bob said. "This isn't very funny."

"Feels funny to me," I said. "Feels very funny. In fact I can't believe really just how funny this is. Jessica, is this funny? Don't you think this is funny? I think this is great. I haven't had bongs with you before, Jessica. Don't you think this is great? Don't you think this is great, Jessica? I've wanted to have bongs with you. I've wanted to have bongs with you for quite a while. I've always enjoyed you. I'm not sure whether you know it but I love living with you in that house. With Sandy. And Zoom. It's special. It's amazing what we do down there. Just getting on, having a good time, having a drink, having a smoke. But I've always wanted to smoke bongs with you. I've really wanted to smoke bongs with you. And with Roland. I've always thought it would be great to get Roland down there and smoke bongs with you. But Roland wouldn't come down there, would you, Roland. You wouldn't come down there. You wouldn't come down there and so we had to come down here. We had to come down here. But I couldn't get you down here. I really couldn't get you down here. I couldn't think of a way to get you down here. It didn't seem fair to invite you down here. And now you're down here. Having bongs down here with us. And I really like it. I really like it that you're down here with us. It's great having bongs down here. I am really glad that you're here, and it's really great having bongs down here with you and with Roland," I finished. And then remembered I had failed to acknowledge Bob. "And Bob, of course. It's great having bongs down here with you and Roland and Bob. How did Bob get you down here? How did Bob get you down here, that's what I want to know. I was surprised to see you down here with Bob. But I'm glad you're down here. I'm very glad you're down here. Don't worry," I said, again patting her shoulder, "I'm very glad you're down here."

"So, that felt good," Roland said to me.

"I'm glad Jessica's down here," I told Roland. "I'm sorry if it's an imposition on you, but I'm glad Jessica's down here. Have you enjoyed meeting her? I was pretty sure you would enjoy meeting her. Jessica is one of my favourites. One of my all-time favourites." I took in Jessica, acutely aware of her beauty, so different from Pash's. That long, rich blond hair, which she could also wear up in a way that made her look very sophisticated. Her boyish figure; a narrow face but satisfyingly, I thought, proportioned; her sharp nose and chin, that chin perhaps, I found myself thinking, a little too sharp but everyone needs a flaw. An ironic smirk, quirky and, I can see looking back, very unusual, but at the time very familiar. Her voice so often floating subtly on mirth—or so it seemed to me, but perhaps not to everybody.

"I am feeling better," Jessica said. "Why don't you like Bob?"

"I do like Bob. Bob's great. Bob's fantastic. Bob is one of my favourite people. But he can also be extremely painful. Extremely painful. About as painful as you can get without being too painful..."

"... And sometimes more painful than that," Roland said.

"Never," I said, "Never more painful than that. You would never be more painful than that, would you Bob. There is no way you would be more painful than that. After all, if you were more painful than that, we wouldn't want to have anything to do with you. And we do want to have things to do with you, don't we Bob. We do want to have things to do with you. That's why you like us so much, isn't it Bob. That's why you like visiting us, and why we are always visiting you. Because you are not more painful than that, are you Bob. You are less painful than that, and that is why we keep visiting you. Whoops, I think I have gone over the top. You are not painful, Bob. We don't think you are painful. I don't think you are painful. I am sorry I said you were painful. If you were painful, we wouldn't be telling you you were painful. Just remember *that*, Bob—you can't be as painful as we are telling you, otherwise we wouldn't tell you. Can you remember that, Bob? You're not really that painful, Bob. And I'm sorry we said you were painful at all. Except that because we did, we really can't think you are all that painful. Do you get that, Bob?"

"Seamus," said Jessica. "That's really not very nice."

"I was nice to you, wasn't I?"

"You were. But you really should be nicer to Bob. He is quite a nice guy really. I like him. I think Bob's great. I think Bob's really pretty special," Jessica said, favouring Bob with a smile—a smile that from where I sat, seeing it only very obliquely, carried no irony whatsoever.

"Well, that's great," I said, "that you think Bob's great. How is Sandy?"

"Sandy's fine, and Bob's great."

"Sandy's fine and Bob's great," I repeated. "Sandy's fine and Bob's great."

"Sandy's fine," Jessica said. "He really is fine. I'm sure he's fine and you don't need to ask about him. And like I told you, Bob's great and you should be nicer to him. Much nicer, I think. I think you can be quite nasty. I've heard you being nasty before, but then I didn't really know who Bob was. Now I think he's okay. In fact I think Bob is great."

"Are you coming home tonight?" I asked, suddenly straighter. "I am. I'll be home tonight."

"I might not be," Jessica said. "I've got school tomorrow."

IT IS FUNNY WHEN you are ripped, or at least in the days when I used to get ripped, properly ripped, the way you can seem to think a dozen things at once without any of them, even the most obvious and affecting, jumping out at you starkly: rather they all line up side by side and you can examine each for relevance without getting particularly worried about any of them. What I remember most definitely from that evening was that line from Jessica: "I've got school tomorrow." But I can also remember something of how it struck me, and that my reactions were multiple. I am certain the first thing I thought was how reasonable it was of her not to pop home when she had the trip the next day to RMIT, in the city centre, where she was studying. Probably the next thing was to wonder where she would be staying. And the next to acknowledge that it could have been with any of several friends she had won from the course. And then there would have been the question of whether Sandy knew where she was staying. Given that he was asleep. And then the thought that she would have told him where, before he went to sleep. And then it probably occurred to me that 10pm or whatever time it was now might be a bit late to be dropping in on a friend who had offered a bed for the night, although not of course out of the question. And then that Jessica was not someone who would do that out of simple lack of consideration, as Bob might have. And then that she had just bought a bag of very good dope, and so might be welcome at many places just about any time.

But then I am sure I got around to thinking about Jessica and Bob, and of how Jessica had rolled her eyes over Bob during his visits, and of how now she wanted to defend him as great. Which of course he was, and of course I had been a bit nasty. And then something else I am sure I thought about at the time, and likely at the same time as all those other things, was that I had little choice but to straighten out a bit and head home myself eventually, as Debbie would not be keen for me to stay over, and I had only myself to blame for my intoxication, and anyway had not been drinking much and so as far as the cops were concerned would be fine to ride, provided I did not say anything too silly if they pulled me over, and anyway I would not be carrying any dope. And that therefore, the following afternoon I would be unlikely to avoid seeing Sandy. I am sure I would have wondered for a moment or two what to say to Sandy. But then it occurred to me—I know this, because this is what I did, as I remember quite well—that I did not need to say anything to Sandy. Because it was not completely obvious that anything needed saying.

"It's your bong," I told Jessica. "It's great having you down here." I cannot remember whether I said exactly that, exactly then. But it was something like that.

9

ARE YOU HAPPY NOW?

"I'VE HAD A BETTER OFFER," ZOOM SAID.

I know that he said that on a Tuesday evening, and that I would have spent the morning proofreading advertisements. In the afternoon I believe I had shopped, and in the evening I had cooked, and what I cooked I had shared with Zoom. He would have rolled a joint afterwards, and I would have taken a toke or two. I had begun to tell him something of my day. "Told your mate today that I wasn't taking that job." Something like that. I had expected a nod of appreciation, from someone devoted to pleasure, even if Zoom did think I should get together the cash to repair my Ducati. Either that, or dump it: Zoom had little respect for Ducatis, partly because their failures tended towards the catastrophic, and partly because even when running they were not, at that time, very fast.

"That might not have been such a good idea," Zoom said. I remember precisely his saying that. I can envisage Zoom's long face, framed gently by his undulating black locks, with its straight nose and Osama bin Laden beard and moustache, the deep tan of his skin tinted pleasingly golden in the light from our unshaded bulb overhead, standing sharply in focus against a blurry green and grey background: kitchen wall, window, sink, dish rack, and as I imagine it the wire-supported tap. A stern expression where I had expected a grin.

"I think it was."

"I don't know that you are going to keep on thinking that."

"I don't need to get more involved. Don't want to be. Doubt I'd be good at it. Don't have the interest."

"Sometimes you need to do stuff even if you're not all that fascinated."

"Zoom. I've done stuff. You know I've done stuff. And I am glad you got me this proofing work. But I'm happy the way things are, really. I can't fix the bike but I'll pick up something else. If I had a new series I'd be earning from that, and if I saved up I *could* fix the bike."

"Will you get a new series?"

"I hope so. Not sure when but I hope so. I got one; I can get two."

"You might need something sooner," Zoom said.

"I might. I might not."

"No, you might. You might need something sooner." Zoom handed me the joint, a hint that what I was about to receive would go down easier with a gentle draught of smoke, a draught that might cushion impacts. "I've had a better offer. I'm getting out of here."

"Oh."

And so Zoom was going, too.

Sandy had gone, months ago, having found a small flat. It was nearer his servo, and our house contained too many reminders, he had explained. Jessica had gone; she was living with Bob. Zoom had got an acquaintance from the bike club to move in, Lisa, and we were getting on but I missed my favourite couple. Things just were not as much fun. The rent was higher too, with just three of us paying it. I had been on unemployment relief for nearly two years, I think—looking back and trying to count the months, I think it must have been nearly that long. The bikie editors had got tired of my series, or perhaps I had got tired of it first: I had found a formula whose permutations turned out to be finite. The dole was okay to live on for a while—it might be still, if you can live somewhere cheap enough. Even if such opportunities are much harder to find. But, then just as now, you cannot cover big items.

There is something about the way that disaster piles up, I have noticed. Things get bad but you hang on. They get worse but you hope for the best. You get some relief, and conclude that everything will work out, eventually. It does not necessarily occur to you that you do not have eventually.

I had known that Zoom would move on. Eventually. But I had seen no pressing reason why eventually would be soon. While parts of the house had run down, it was wonderfully good given what we paid, with its big backyard that had room for a dope patch, and a shed that hid the plants from the street. A dry and roomy shed, built on a concrete slab and clad in galvanised steel, that Zoom could paint in to his heart's content, and without falling over my motorbike or Lisa's or his own. The property was far enough from Frankston to feel peaceful and secluded, but close enough that Zoom could get to work on his 100cc Kawasaki, a ride with no assets beyond its utility. You could walk from the house to Main Street and the Mornington shops. And we were close to the beach. For how much more could anybody reasonably ask, and why would any aspiring painter relinquish a set-up like that? Given the prevailing financial conditions I had thought it improbable it would be sold out from under us.

"Well, I am hoping it's better. Thought I'd take it up. I'll be here for six weeks or so. The rent's due in a fortnight and I'll give them a month from then. You could take the place on if you wanted. But you'd probably need a job, or at least half a job. You could have some of my furniture. I don't think I'll want this table, or the chairs. Or the fridge. There's a fair chance Lisa would stay. I haven't told her yet. It still might not happen. But I'm thinking it will. Thought you needed to know."

"Where are you going?"

A frown from Zoom as he took a long pull on the joint, exhaled reflectively, and then passed to me what remained.

"Not sure I am going. But I think I might. There's a bloke I know. Bloke I've got to know. You've not met him because he doesn't really fit into this scene. If you know what I mean. Or maybe I didn't think he would. Well, I don't think he would. Likes my pictures. Anyway, we get on. He's offered me a studio. Has a place down near here with a flat out the back that he doesn't get down to much. Not all that much. I've been there. A bit mad for my taste but I will say it's pretty speccy. The flat's on a couple of floors, looks out over the sea. I think it was flash guest quarters—you know, if you've got enough money, have folk down to stay and give them a place with a shower and a kitchen and garage. They can look after themselves so they're not in your face, and you get together when you feel like it. That would have been the idea."

As this was all news to me, and not news that soothed me, I concentrated lingeringly on the joint. Zoom took up where he had left off.

"The flat wasn't his idea—it was there when he got it, so he reckons—but there it is, and he doesn't need it that much. Hardly uses the flat at all, he reckons. Anyway I know what you're probably thinking and yes, you are probably on the right track. But who gives a fuck, if you know what I mean. I have a good time; he has a good time. Then I can do what I like. And look after the block. Not fixing it up, keeping an eye on things. You know, taking in mail and the papers. Cleaning up crap left by seagulls and bugs. Anyway, I am thinking I might. That's all I can tell you, I am thinking I might. In which case you will need something. And I can see what you've been doing and what you've been going through and to me it doesn't look all that flash. That Pash babe was good for you but what's happening? The bike's fucked; you've lost your cheques in the mail. I like some of your stuff that I've read but I get the idea that you're not doing anything great. Anyway I'm not saying you need a kick up the bum—this is all about me. But if you want a kick—or even if you don't want one—here's a chance. Make a change. Well, I'll make a change, and then you make one. This bloke knows someone who has half a gallery. Good gallery in the city. Says he likes my stuff. Says there's a chance I'll get into a show there. I dunno. It might all be a load of ... But it's something different, a bit of a window. You know. Sometimes you have to make something happen. And even if it doesn't happen, the fact that you've made *something* happen—or that you've done something to make something happen, even if it doesn't happen—that can be enough to make something else happen. I know this place is great, but I've been here six years nearly. It won't last forever. I'd rather jump before I'm pushed. The heater's falling to bits in the bathroom. The gutters are fucked. There's a stain in your bedroom that I'm dumbfucked you've not talked about. That's water inside the roof, running into the wall. When the hot water goes—when the tank springs a leak, and it can't be far off—will they get us a new heater? Anyway, they might, but you know what I mean. Five years is a long run. We might make it half a dozen, but then what? I like living with you. But you're sinking. Your bike's rooted; you don't see anybody except sometimes Sandy. You've started smoking; you drink by yourself. If I move, you'll struggle to get somewhere to live. When you came here, you were doing better than us. You had that job in the city, and it sounded really good; better than anything we had. Now you can do something different. You can work on the paper. It's not the end of the world. You might like it. Or it might turn into something else. You've got a real good boss, I reckon, and you get on with him. He rides but he doesn't own a fancy-pants Ducati, even though he could probably afford to fix one if it fucked up on him. You tell me you like working for him. You *love* these Tuesdays—come home here, go shopping, cook us something good—you do better on Tuesdays than any other day I can think of. Oh fuck, I'm full of bull. Must be getting whacked.

You know, I think I will take this studio. How bad can it be? You know, the thing is, I like it that this bloke likes my pictures. And really, I don't even care if it isn't my pictures he likes. I just like it that somebody's taking an interest, and I'm prepared to think it's because he likes my pictures, or partly, because it helps me feel like what I'm doing is smart. And if it all turns to crap, I'll do *something*. I am ready to go for a jump. And I think you are too. I really think you *need* to jump. Get over young Pash, if that's the way it is heading. Maybe she's not really your type. She just shimmy-shimmied into your life, and it looks like she's shimmied out of it. Fuck, I'm rude. But aren't you happy she shimmied into it? What are the chances? This is none of my business but what the fuck. We're friends here. She came down here with Doctor Bob, but Bob never comes down now. You need to make *something* happen. Fuck, I'm gabbling. I'll roll us another one. D'you want another one? I feel like another one. I think I will take this flat. It will get us somewhere. It will get us all somewhere. And you should take this job. I reckon. I think it's time to do something. Well, it is for me; and then you'll have to anyway. But I don't think it's bad that you do. And I can't stay here just to sort you out, anyway. Not that I *am*—don't get me wrong, I know you're up for whatever. I just mean, there's a chance, a good chance: why not grab it?"

THIS WAS AS LONG a speech as I could remember receiving from Zoom. I cannot claim that I have captured well the rhythms of his holding forth, nor even his favourite phrases of that time—although he was certainly fond of describing this or that dysfunctional item as *fucked*. I can peer through a window towards the place where he spoke, a seaward-stroll distant in space but a galaxy distant in time. What will this reinhabiting disinter, Ms Felicity?

I know that Zoom was expressing concern for me more directly than I can recall from prior conversations. This was not a matter of whether I was hungry, or had enough dope or booze, or money to pay the rent. He was saying something about choices, and about what came from making them and when to precipitate those results; and he was saying something about the results I had been getting, and the direction in which they, or the lack of them, had been leading me, in so far as he could recognise my direction. The concern about drinking alone I thought excessive, as I felt I was drinking substantially less than when Jessica and Sandy had been around. Perhaps it was my taking up smoking—for Zoom had exercised for as long as I had known him a level of discipline that I have never seen since with respect to tobacco, reserving a yellow pouch of Champion that he would mix with dope for his joints, but neither smoking it undiluted nor smoking joint after joint for the tobacco in each. I was able to forgive easily his minor intrusion over the drinking because I valued the gift of his insight into how good moves were made. And I valued that because I had understood, while he was talking, that my good fortune in living at that address had been attributable mainly to the efforts of Zoom, who had secured the place to serve his own ends and had ensured it was populated.

Zoom was now entertaining an offer he thought might be better, and rather than agonise over whether it really was better he was inclined to assume that it would be, and not because he took his intuitions to be infallible but because he felt it was time to act, even when acting meant the abandoning of a situation he had found very comfortable for one that appeared—and it had to be admitted that appearances were all he had to go on in either case—much less secure. I can all but remember concluding amid the haze of intoxication, as we partook in Zoom's second joint, that Zoom was in this way presenting a moving target to Fate: at some time his secure and commodious renter would be torn out from under him, and rather than wait for that inevitable moment to strike, he would vacate the site of its striking, at once rendering himself invulnerable to *that* misfortune and preparing himself to withstand more effectively other blows that he had not foreseen.

"So you think I should get in there and help that old cranky bloke," I said. "Remember, he's not the boss—who is good, as you say—but he would be my boss. And he smokes by the packet. And I don't know that he thinks much of my proofing already. It is only that he refuses to do it."

"It is not so much that I think you should as that I think you might have to, or you might have to do something and this wouldn't be all that bad. When I move you'll need a house, and for this house you'll probably need a lease, and to get the lease you'll probably need some sort of job. And you'll need all that for just about any house. Or move in with someone else if you want to. And that's if Lisa wants to stay anyway, or if you can fill this house up. Or live in it yourself—I suppose it's cheap enough, if you've got half a job. What else would you do? I'd love to sort this out for you but I want to take up this offer and I want to get on with things, and you do have an option, a big fat option sitting right there in front of you that you want to walk around—into... nothing. That's the way I see it. And I suppose the point is, if you don't want it, that's up to you. But it's not as if I've left you in the lurch somehow. I'll be packing up; you work out what you want."

I USED TO WONDER what prevented people from living as well as they knew they could. All right, *knew* is too much. But I wondered why some of my friends had not sought more avidly to live as well as they possibly could. I had wondered, for example, about Roland and Debbie. I had wondered why Roland had played with only two bands, and then rarely in public, and neither of them his band. Why he had not practised more attentively, and created more songs. For a brief time at Keppel Street I had believed he would win renown for his playing, and even Bob had not foreclosed easily on the possibility that Roland might win renown. But something got in the way.

Bob became a doctor, as we all knew he would. And I think he liked many things about being a doctor. But had it been his vocation to tend to the sick? It is difficult for me to accept of Bob that he had felt called to do this work by an inner voice that was worthy of his attention. And he could have done any work. Well, almost any. He would never have become an accomplished musician. That tightness in Bob; that need to control. It does not seem plausible that Bob could have transcended that—that he could have become less sensible, in Roland's memorable phrase, and more rhythmic. And yet, I wonder too whether that was what did for Bob. Whether he needed to relax his grip on the steering wheel if ever he were to feel that he had travelled through life in a direction that pleased him. Which is not to say Bob did not live well. Or do I delude myself here? I delude myself. Of course Bob was not content. His practice, his money, his house, and his Jessica, and still he was not content. Even Roland was happier. Had Jessica reminded Bob daily of how his life could have been, and yet never would be?

I HAD COMPLETED MY cameo about Roland and Debbie, and about their hosting of Jamie and their not going out. I had put together also a first-person tale in which the narrator, about my age, met a young woman. The woman was based on someone whom I had met in my job at the TAB, and whom I had found entrancing, but with whom I had never got beyond collegial conversation because I had not been capable of suggesting that we meet socially. Now I had some perspective on that incapacity, having spent my year with Pash. And so I turned out something that contrasted my head talk at the time with the sort of thing I would actually say. "'How was the tram today?' *You look so sexy in that black skirt; I don't know how I manage to stop myself squeezing you.*" Zoom had been accurate when he had said that my recording had lost impetus. Yes, of course I missed Sandy and Jessica. Lisa was good, as I have said, but she was not a pleasure seeker in the same way that they had been pleasure seekers—she was a waitress or something who had got a job managing the bar at a pub in Dromana, about twenty minutes further along the coast if you drove. She did not have Jessica's depth, and she did not have her beauty either—not that it mattered, but in that common male fashion I had attributed status to myself from Jessica's presence in our house. Wine-o'clock had not been the same. It probably just reminded me of what I was missing. I had discovered Hemingway's *A Moveable Feast* by then, that series of memoirs about the novelist's pre-fame days in Paris, and I can remember being struck by a comment Hemingway had made about loss, I think prompted by his having left his first wife and his having regretted that. "When you lose something," he wrote, "you miss it until you find something better." Or something like that—I cannot vouch for the quote, and I cannot be bothered looking it up and discovering that I have misremembered. It is the sentiment that counts here. That is how I remember it, and I assume I am close because I can certainly remember my connecting that remark with my loss of Sandy and Jessica, and my awareness that Lisa, fine as she was, made an unsatisfactory substitute. Mostly Lisa was at work around dinner time anyway. Zoom worked longer in his studio, but I rarely felt like working longer. Frequently I would get up from the typewriter about 3:30pm or four, pour myself a cheap red, and settle down to a book or the paper. With Zoom's joints not available so immediately, and in any case having no one to share them with, I had bought on a whim a pouch of rolling tobacco—I can remember I started with Bank, a mild and aromatic preparation that real smokers, I learned, tended to sniff at. And not every night but quite often when sitting there alone, I would roll myself a cigarette or several and would smoke them, developing a habit that had begun with OP's—other people's, as we used to describe them collectively.

Sitting at the dining table and reading and drinking, and from time to time smoking, I would feel again something that had not presented itself to my notice so insistently since the days following upon my abandonment of my studies in engineering, a tightening of the chest that I had associated then with a term new to me, *melancholy*, but which I am more inclined today, looking back, to connect more simply with fear and loneliness. Not that I experienced that feeling, at Queen Street, as wholly unpleasant. It seemed, rather, to be something intimately entwined with my social status as someone on the outside, financially precarious and disconnected from the workaday world, but free to get up from my typewriter just when I chose and settle to a drink and a smoke by myself with the paper, aware too that when I got bored with the paper I could move on to a book that had captured my interest. I attributed the keenness of the feeling to the absence of Sandy and Jessica: in my estrangement from the typical concerns of most others I had available less support than before. Sandy paid a visit less and less often, and without Jessica alongside him our conversational envelope was shallower and its contents less nourishing. Jessica did not appear, not by herself or with Bob. I supposed that my indiscretions had resonated. That was something I had enjoyed about Roland: it never seemed to matter later what I told him when ripped.

It is easy to see, from this distance, that more underlay my evening intimations of loss. In what seemed like little more than an instant, it had become months since I saw Pash. Her invitations that I visit had become less easy to elicit by phone, and her phone calls to me unprompted had become so infrequent as to be describable with the phrase *almost never*. And *almost*, only while I could still remember, if indistinctly, the last one. It was not as though she had made herself unavailable. It had remained possible for me to phone and arrange a time to meet, and we would do pretty much what we had become used to doing: meeting in the same places; retiring to her flat; watching a video; having a drink; perhaps—if I prompted her—having a smoke together; retiring to bed and—most times, anyway—getting sexy. Well, it might be more honest, now I think about it, to replace *most* times with many times. Or some times. But we still would get sexy. However, something seemed to have left our relating. I guessed Pash had become increasingly preoccupied with whomever it was she was seeing in addition to me—still careful to avoid prying, I did not know whether that was one person or several. I was happy she still saw me, grateful even, for I knew that if she ceased to see me then my strategy of waiting for her infatuations to wane would require modification, or even abandonment in favour of a fresh approach, and I had no idea what fresh approach I could muster. There was also the unspoken question whether I really wanted to be with Pash after all, in any long-term sense. I wanted to be with her because I could not imagine how I would replace her, and because it appeared she was attracted elsewhere and I resented her being attracted to someone else more than to me. But then when I was with her, and we would have sex and afterwards feel close, I would be reminded of that morning when I had told her my stripping story, and about what happened afterwards and how I had felt about that, and I would wonder whether I should just tell her there and then we should quit and be done with it. I would wonder, but I never did tell her. I think I reasoned, and again I am attempting to reconstruct my thinking rather than recall serial ruminations that must have been convoluted, that if she was happy to see others casually then there was no reason she should not see me. And as she never revealed to me so much as a whisper about her pursuit of those others, I relieved myself of any obligation to reveal my own traitorous subtext. As the frequency of our meetings diminished, I felt at times an almost agonising awareness of her withdrawal: an out-of-control, sickly apprehensive, big-dipper shock. Such moments would arise most intensely in response to certain promptings, such as when Sandy sought to explore with me his anger over the way in which he had lost touch with Jessica. But then my own irritation would rescue me, as I thought about how Pash had, in a sense, used me. I know that *used* is too strong a description, but while I had not assumed much during our early relating, I had taken it tacitly that I was at least her *main* interest. Following such occasions of stress, I suspect I would also seek the comfort of revisiting familiar pre-Pash fantasies, doubtless made all the more compelling for me by the recent expansion of my experience. And I do not doubt either that I contrasted these psychological adventures favourably with many sessions with Pash, observing their superior support for spontaneity and the satisfying of my wish for variety.

"HOW ABOUT ONE MORE joint?" I asked Zoom, as he butted out the remains of our second. "I'll think it over. Probably will take that job. Just want to think about it. Or don't want to think about it, tonight anyway. Shit, what a shock. You're a bastard! No, I know you're not a bastard, but it feels like you're a bastard. I *hate* this. You're a bastard and I really *don't* want to think about this right now. I *hate* bastards like you. No I don't really, but you know what I mean. Always pointing out the truth. Always pointing out the truth about somebody but not always so ready to hear the truth about yourself. *Are* you. Lulling me along like this because it suited you not to say anything and then springing it on me when I'm stoned. You're appalling. You really are appalling. No, you're not appalling. You really aren't appalling. I suppose I needed it. I needed it, but that doesn't mean I was *ready* for it. You could have waited till I was *ready* for it. Maybe you are a bastard. Didn't wait till I was ready."

That had generated a chuckle in Zoom. His chuckling after a puff or two would be almost giggling, involuntary and high-pitched but still dry. It seemed to come from someone much younger; it was as though dope and humour drew out momentarily from within Zoom an inner teenager of much lighter spirits. "Do you want another joint or not?" he asked. "If you are going to abuse me, I am not sure that I'll roll one. But why not, we might not do this too much more often. Probably won't. You know," he said, "I will miss you."

"Miss my being an idiot, that's what you'll miss. Because it makes *you* feel good. I'm the idiot and it makes you feel like you're not an idiot. But if you're living down here with me, then you *are* an idiot. Because I only live with idiots. Then I can be an idiot, and feel I'm in good company. That's why I'm here with you. I hope you realise that. And I do want that other joint."

"Yeah, yeah," said Zoom, reaching for his pouch of Champion. "It's coming. And then you'll be even more of an idiot. Well, I don't know whether I'm an idiot, but I *will* miss you. I will miss these sessions, occasional as they've gotten to be. I do notice that we haven't got Jessica, and of course Sandy. That was good, while it lasted. Which you stuffed up, really, bringing down Mister Fancypants Doctor. That's probably why I want to move. You're saying it's my fault, when really it's your fault. So really it's all your fault. We are having what might even be our last session here, and it's all your fault." But Zoom was grinning at me, embodying that inner teen. "I've invited you in and you've stuffed things up for me. You're a disaster." He succumbed to his near-giggle as he finished rolling the joint. "Here, suck on this. And I'll have some of your wine. Abuse me if you want. I don't care. I'm going. And it's *your* fault." Zoom handed me the joint and rose to pour himself wine.

Of course, this too is reconstructed. Again, I have sought to capture mainly the flavour. I had enjoyed Zoom, and liked him particularly when he relaxed. There was a sternness about him that I admired because it seemed to go hand in hand with a discipline that got him places. But it also bothered me, that sternness. He had chided me savagely a couple of times about minor household matters—things I was doing or not doing that he thought inconsiderate—and I had found him then formidable. On one such occasion he had made two trays of vanilla slices—crude imitations of the French *mille-feuille*—by sandwiching custard between unsalted savoury biscuits and icing the tops, describing them with typical deprecation as snot blocks and inviting us to partake as we wished. Jessica and Sandy had still been there, and the three of us had treated ourselves liberally. However, I had returned for fourth and fifth helpings the next day, and Zoom had brought it to my attention that I had presumed upon his generosity. I think I had decided that he must not have wanted any. After his lecture on my failings, I had felt like a dog might have felt who had been nipped into line. Obviously not the top dog. I did tiptoe around him for a day or two, probably longer, for the lecture had not stopped at the biscuits. And so I enjoyed it all the more when I could get Zoom to relax, and when I could have a go back at him, knowing from experience now that he would not take affront, that he would understand the spirit in which I attacked him and would push back in kind. It had been good to live with someone like that, and especially with someone like that who supplied all the joints. And now—soon, anyway—it would be over.

DID BOB KILL ALL my hopes? Or did he make my life liveable? My past would have felt thinner if it had not been for Bob. That I cannot deny. But Bob could have done so much more for me. And then again, could he have? And then again and again, even if he could have, why would he have? Bob was such fun to play with. When Roland was there to help, anyway. He was different when I had to negotiate him on my own. He was more in control. Bob had seen control as a good thing. And if some was good ... as Steve might have said. I do wonder how that all played out with Jessica. But she, I think, liked control more than I did, or needed it more. Perhaps she was happier with Bob in control. Maybe she had wanted more security, and she had felt as though Bob gave her that. In fact, it seems rather likely she did want more security. Why else swap Sandy for Bob. But then Bob had status, too. Until she took up with Bob, I would never have thought status important for Jessica, in a man she was with, but perhaps I was wrong about that. And then maybe status was not it—or not all of it—after all. Women had always liked Bob, even when he had been merely a student with prospects. Even Pash had liked Bob. Pash in many ways had liked Bob more than she had liked me. No, that is not fair. Pash had liked me, but I had never been sure just how much Pash had liked me. And then again, the thing is, if she had liked me more obviously then I would have retreated. I can see that now, much more starkly. Was that morning with Pash, when I told her about my high jinks in the hayshed, as we lay there with our G&Ts and a joint, feeling like we could say anything and it all would be fine, as good a morning as I have spent ever with anyone?

And then it all fell apart. The peak before the trough. The summit before the long trek downhill. The summit for me, anyway. Whether Pash was at a summit with me I am not so sure. Perhaps not. Obviously not, when I think about it. Had Pash been at base camp, looking up? Had I seemed like hard work? Or had it just been that close was too close? Had we really been seven months in? There is, I now understand, a turning point about that time in any romance. But had it been a romance? I had been excited, but was I in love? And was Pash as excited? It is not at all clear that she was as excited, to be with me, as I was excited to be with her. But if she had been excited, then certainly that would have scared me. Had I told Pash I loved her? No I had not, not once. Not a single time. Had Pash said she loved me? Never. Had it all been just too convenient? Had convenience, for Pash, been the point of her being with me—as I know now Bob had believed? Convenience and a weakness for lost causes, the lost cause being I. And of course, in a way Pash had been right. She had been just like a girl in a fantasy. In one of my fantasies. One of my erotic fantasies. Available almost at my whim, for a time, and certainly fun and arousing. Pash had been, as I knew even then, much too good to be true. And she was not true. How much of her had I known, and how much had I merely imagined?

I TOO HAVE NOT been very content. That has become plain, if it was not plain before. My life of pleasure seeking at Queen Street had felt pleasant indeed. When a fantasy has absorbed you, you do not seek out its seams. And Queen Street had absorbed me. I had been doing better than Jessica, in certain respects. At the time when she met Bob, Jessica had not sold a painting. Had I become too pleased with myself? Had I needed to fail, as I had failed in the past? Could I have sustained myself indefinitely on the dole, selling the Ducati for parts and picking up some spare cash here and there? Was it Jessica's absence that had damaged my confidence? Had I simply reached the end of my courage, and needed to bolster myself with a job and some money? Or was it just that the living and the recording had ceased to be enough fun, the balance of pleasure having swung towards wealth and consumption? You think the job will work out. Mine was, after all, in the field. I would have been a fool to have turned it down, obstinately looking past lush reality towards the darkening dreamscape spread out before me. I think that was how I had felt. If I had not grasped at this lifeline, would I have foundered by now, just like Bob has foundered—or worse than Bob? It is not straightforward how things could have been worse for me than for Bob. But Bob must have gone quietly, and peacefully. He had means; I did not. I could have gained access to similar means, but I doubt that I would have. My end would have been sadder, and a whole lot less pleasant in the way it played out. Bob had remained in control. I would have behaved more impulsively. But then, a caveat: my end would have come more spontaneously, if it had come at all. Had I been stronger than Bob had been? Fairly clearly, I had been. And yet, stronger for what?

WHAT I CANNOT DENY about the period that followed my taking up of Zoom's suggestion was how well everything seemed to pan out. The recognition of how much energy I drew from my change of tack strikes me almost forcibly, as I relive it in retrospect. Zoom's move was disconcerting, but I had got into a rut and I could agree with him that his move might jolt me out of the rut. Which it did, and into something very engaging. I had developed a fascination with language, and thanks to Zoom I would be working with language, and in a way that arguably was more disciplined, and indisputably was more remunerative, than any way in which I had worked with language before. All had turned out, then, for the best. And given that I am still performing, in a sense, the role I took up at that time, surely I can look back at this period of dislocation and realignment as setting me down finally on a sure path to prosperity. A path that satisfied, as effectively as they seem to be satisfied for almost anybody, my spiritual as well as my material needs.

I enjoyed the money. Indeed, I was amazed as much as gratified by how quickly my small weekly wage piled up in my bank account, after so many months of living frugally on one-third of its sum. Within about three months I was able to book in the Ducati with a mechanic whom Zoom recommended, with some confidence that I could cover his bill. Within six months I was riding to the city again, and dropping in to see Roland, and had persuaded Lisa that we could share the house together amicably if somewhat distantly for the foreseeable future. It was probably nine months before I dropped in on Bob, found him out, and left a note saying that I had called. And just a day or so later that I received a phone call from Jessica, inviting me to stop in the following Saturday at a small party she was giving to celebrate her engagement.

AUTUMN

10

WHAT BECOMES OF US

I HAD ALWAYS THOUGHT I WAS GOING TO LIKE PETE. I DO not know whether it was the way he looked and carried himself—tall and straight, with all his hair and worn longish, and full, crossbow-shaped lips, and a face that had been lucky with its lines in a don't-need-to-care sort of way. I have wondered since whom he reminded me of, and it occurs to me now that it was a character in a TV advertisement for Peter Stuyvesant cigarettes. A playboy type, but a very competent playboy. Except that Pete did not smoke—or rather, not cigarettes. Or not much. He would borrow a rollie from me from time to time. Which was how I first got to know him. I know too many cigarettes are not very good for you, and I had got to smoking too many this year and did need to stop, but at the same time I cannot help but think about how many good people I got to know over the years through smoking of one kind or another. Often tobacco. With the habit getting extinguished smoker by smoker and fewer children taking it up, it used to be almost—almost—a passport to the very caution-to-the-winds sort of club that several firms had sought to associate fraudulently with their brands. If someone asked you for a cigarette, without thinking about it you took them to be the sort of person who would risk emphysema, heart disease and lung cancer for a brief and bitter dose of pleasure. And particularly if he or she were an occasional smoker or a binger, as most botters were, rather than committed to downing a packet or three every day. I used to make a packet of Drum last a fortnight, which I thought was pretty good even if Marjorie insisted on telling me that I ought to give up—like she had done. It was one of those things, I think, that had bothered me about Marge, that she had needed to quit. Rather than cutting down. Or more to the point, rather than being able to quit but still have one or two every now and again. That was what I had liked about the way I was smoking: I did not have to smoke all the time. I did not always have a smoke in the morning, for example. Used to wait until lunchtime, when I would have one or two, and then a few more after work with a beer or some wines. And a joint, maybe, until Marge requested we stop that as well. Too hard, apparently, to smoke a joint but never tobacco. Well, I do get that. I much prefer tobacco in joints: it makes them smoke better. Which is why I have just about given up joints myself, recently. So I get it.

Anyway, Pete Ulverson. Liked tobacco in his joints, but never brought it to work. From a cigarette at work we had got to motorbikes, which he liked a bit, and then world championship bike racing, which he said he liked quite a bit, and then an invitation to head out to my place and watch a motorbike grand prix with me—Marge always said they bored her. Which was where he dragged out his little plastic bag stuffed with head and asked me whether I would enjoy a joint before the show started. I was a bit surprised because we both had work the next day and Monday was a big day for us, and the big bikes usually did not start to race until quite late, roughly 10pm or later our time, on TV. So we would be a bit sleep deprived anyway, in the morning, and it was just interesting—nothing more than that, really—that he wanted to add on a bit of dope hangover. Which of course I would have done sometimes by myself, but I had not assumed anybody else would want to do that just for a bike race. Especially if they faced a long drive to get home in the meantime. And most especially because he was my boss, and had a fair bit more on his plate for the next day than even I did.

I am realising as I write this that I am going to explore a more recent parallel with the nights when I used to get ripped with Roland, and I am not even going to speculate, Ms Felicity, about why that might be. By this time I was not getting ripped with Roland much. I would not say we had drifted apart. I still felt about him much as I had always felt. And I assumed that he still felt as good about me. But I did not get down to see him often, and things had not changed at all with respect to his getting down to see me. And so I had found myself hanging out for the sort of experience that I had enjoyed with Roland.

When I got together with Marge she had not liked Debbie greatly, which was I suppose part of it. And Debbie had not liked Marge. Perhaps because—in the earlier years anyway—Marge had preferred to join Roland and me for a smoke rather than to pair off with Debbie for a deep-and-caring about girl stuff and work. Which had forced Debbie to be a largely silent but sometimes nagging spectator ringside at our smoking sessions, or to withdraw and read or watch something by herself while the three of us got on with carousing. That had left Marge feeling uncomfortable, or so she had said. And not just because she was not that keen on getting cosy with Debbie, but also because the sessions did not grab her all that much either. Her view was not that much different from what Bob's had been. She complained that Roland never talked about anything interesting.

I explained to her that this was almost the point, but she never quite got it. It was also the case that the sessions were a little bit flat with her: it was not the same as when Roland and I had done that sort of thing by ourselves, or with another similarly minded individual such as Jamie. Or, back when that was still possible, with Steve. Which was the model that, when I think about it, had informed my most pleasant subsequent smoking occasions with

Roland. Maybe I should not have been surprised when Marjorie failed to get it. But I was. Well, not surprised; more disappointed. She also started hassling me about my behaving like an imbecile, as she put it, when I was stoned. It was funny that one of the main things I had liked about smoking with Roland, as I have said, was that I could behave like an idiot and no one would care. That too was almost the point, for me. But Marge said it was embarrassing, for her. Which I never quite got about her. What was there to be embarrassed about? It is not as though I became a different person. Surely I did not have to be careful about who I was all the time. Anyway, add it all up and a visit to Roland's with Marge was not as much fun as I was always expecting it to be, and so I suppose I did not get to see Roland as much, because with Marge home I did not spend as much time in the city nor stay over at somebody's place as much. Partly too because we were all getting older. Roland and Debbie had got kids and had bought a nice place at Hawthorn, a bit further out, which also made things a wee bit tense at times about getting stoned. I could be an idiot, but not necessarily a very noisy or messy idiot, which was inhibiting, even though I could see completely why I did need to be careful in those respects.

Anyway, Pete. I never used to come properly stoned to the office, and I imagine he did not either, although there were days, after that night watching the racing, when I wondered about that. A week or two later—for all I know it was more like six weeks—I got an invitation to his house after deadline on Monday. Monday was the big day on the chain at that time and we would finish the flagship papers then and also most of the small ones. It is still a huge day, actually. Some of the subs start about seven in the morning and we go until six or seven in the evening. Just processing pages. I had got pretty good at it, by then. I suppose I had been in the business a dozen years. Just subbing the pages. There were a couple of other subs who had been there longer than I had, but I was one of the longer serving by then. I never used to do layouts, or hardly ever, just copy editing. Which is how I ended up checking. I could not really see the point of layout, why you would want to do it. It is not as though you could do anything very exciting. Especially at the pace we were turning out pages. But anyway, exciting was not what anybody wanted, in layouts. It was more a matter of following a formula, and not upsetting anybody. Not disturbing the reader. Not that anybody ever laid that down, as a rule. But I think we all got it. I was not much good at layout, anyway. Well, I thought the pages I designed were okay but I was pretty slow at it. And did not really want to do it. I had never got why someone would end up there doing layout when they were there, I had assumed, because they liked language. But I suppose not everybody did like working with language, who was there. People do get into newspapers for all sorts of reasons. They all do like language, on the editorial side, but perhaps some find layout less stressful, or they do not like their language, or maybe they just find layout—designing the pages, placing the pics and story boxes and headline spaces—more satisfying. I have always liked the language best. And of course you get proud of the pace you can work at. The trick is to prevent the pace you are working at from getting in the way of your pride in the work. I think everybody struggles with that.

 So it was a Monday and we had knocked off the final pages and were sitting around having a couple of beers. It was a tradition that at the end of the shift on a Monday someone would go out for beers and would bring them back to the office, and usually people would start on the beers as they finished the last of their pages. Since it was often nearly dinner time when we knocked off, the beers session would last only an hour before most people had headed home, not wanting to be drinking more than a stubby or so before getting into a car, or maybe three for those who were heading off by train or taxi or walking. Journos are supposed to be piss-heads but most of the subs I worked with were not that bad—or if they were, did not want to show it at work. Sometimes people who did not have families to go home to would step out for a bite together. The office was in Moorabbin even then, which was at least on the right side of the city for me, and we did all our suburbans that covered that side. Usually though I just headed home. Anyway, Pete said he was living in St Kilda, which was straight down St Kilda Road, and did I feel like popping down there for a bite with him and we could retire to his flat afterwards and sink another beer or two. We always had Tuesdays off. I was pretty happy to do it, and would have put in a call to Marge. Not sure where we ended up going. Possibly Leo's for pasta.

"So, do you want to come up for a smoke?"

Why is it that I find myself recalling this night in particular? There were others like it. I suppose it is partly because this was the first one. But in a way, too, just my receiving that offer was memorable. I think, possibly, it was a bit like when Bob introduced me to Roland. I could tell then that Bob was proud to be demonstrating his connection with Roland, the insouciant dropout with the biting guitar and the bottomless stash. But Roland had seemed as curious about me as he had seemed pleased to see Bob, and I had encountered that curiosity as affirming. Similarly, I had felt excited to be heading to Pete's for a post-dinner yarn. None of the other subs was with us. And I had not thought it was just because Pete knew I smoked. Or was interested in motorbike racing—I had realised already that bike racing was not among his core enthusiasms. I was not the only sub who smoked, either. I had sucked on a joint at the occasional party over the years hosted by colleagues. That had been fun but I had not found it exciting enough to want to develop these relationships.

If I am honest, I was not all that impressed with any of the other subs, even then. I took them seriously, and especially when I was getting started, when they all knew so much more than I did about assembling newspapers. Or most of them did. But as I got more into the game, I was less daunted by the language they turned out. It was not bad, considering the time constraints. But it was not often it wowed me. Whereas Pete straight away had shown me that extra magic: had demonstrated that it was possible to put over a suburban story a headline that had something special.

There was a piece about a kid with achondroplasia—dwarfism, in layman's terms—that Danny, who at that time worked next to me, had got hold of. He had asked me whether I could think of anything for it. It was a difficult piece for a junior reporter, a human-interest yarn where it is hard not to ham it right up. The deal was that this dwarfish young kid had such an extroverted, friendly attitude that he had become a popular figure in his Year 1 class. Which his parents said fitted with how he was as a member of the family: not just a member, but an admired member. Which was great, except that it brushed past the elephant in the room: no one would have published a story about his being a popular kid in Year 1 if he had not looked like a toddler. So the piece in a way was insulting. It was saying: "Look, this kid is doing better than most kids even though he's a freak." And what is more, there was a page-dominating picture to go with the text, and the photographer had used a lens and an angle that had made the kid look quite big. He had not wanted to make him look small, I suppose. It is really hard when you get a story like this not to get sucked into the condescension so that you cannot think of anything that is not patronising when you do the headline. And in this case, because of the way the layout guy had wanted to use the picture big while not making this the leading story, there was only a narrow vertical slot for the headline, which turned out to be four decks of five or six characters each.

You get something like this as a sub and the pressure for speed does not help either. You are immediately scared that you will not do a good job no matter how long you take over it, and so you are also scared that you will take forever over it—and still will not get a good outcome. It is easy to resign yourself very soon after you pick it up to just turning out dross. I cannot remember quite what Danny turned out in the end but it was something like:

> **Little
> with
> big
> punch**

which made the subject, named Raymond, sound like an underweight prizefighter, and not only missed the point but managed to insult Raymond twice, once by emphasising his short stature and a second time by suggesting he had a chip on his shoulder about it. What I also remember is that even though I hated the headline, I had not been able to think of anything better in a hurry and so had told Danny it was not bad and tacitly congratulated myself on not having opened that page. What made it worse was that it was a front page: papers for other suburbs likely would use the story inside but the editor of the title that circulated in the area where the family lived had thought it a cute leading picture yarn. We did stuff like that every week so I was not bothered particularly, but I suppose because I had got involved in it I noticed later in the week that the cover with the kid on it carried the headline:

> **How
> Ray
> lives
> large**

and I knew straight away that Pete, overseeing the finished pages as chief sub, had been as bothered by the original headline as I had been, and unlike me had been able to do something about it, and something that not only avoided the insults but also worked with the picture and supplied an effective antidote for the implicit condescension. No one else would have done that. I was a bit worried about the shortening of the name until I looked closer at the story—intrigued to read it again now and assess just how well the new headline worked with it—and noticed that the reporter had alluded to Raymond as "Ray" in a quote from Raymond's sister, which was obviously something Pete had cottoned on to. And I could not help but be excited that we had someone leading us who took it to be important to do something like this if you could. I think all the sub-editors—certainly most of us—had been impressed by Pete's air of nonchalance when he had come onto the floor, but we had also wondered what that might have been hiding and whether it would survive his first couple of weeks. I think this headline came up about three weeks in and by then nobody doubted he had the talent and confidence to back up the swagger. And so being invited up to his flat for a smoke was a bit like being accepted by Roland as a prospective co-resident, on the grounds that we might support one another in spurning licensed professional practice.

"So, how long have you been here again? Subbing suburbans?"

"A dozen years. Probably more. I started in '87."

"Which would make it thirteen years. Or nearly. Twelve. And something."

"Does it matter?"

"Not really. Just wondered. Where did you come from?"

"Nowhere." I had always found it uncomfortable that my first job on newspapers was just about the job I still had. Most people seemed to have started somewhere, often with a cadetship of some kind, and then moved on and around. Before finding a certain level of competence somewhere else. Or incompetence. I had read *The Peter Principle*—Bob had suggested it. Of course it was the sort of thing that Bob loved. He used to quote it in explanation of all sorts of stuff-ups. I did not think I had simply found my level of incompetence straight away. I had decided that I was a creative incompetent, which meant—if you accepted the theory developed in the book—that I was competent in my job but had worked out a way in which I could appear incompetent so that I was not promoted out of my competence zone. Almost by default, since my background and how I had got into the job did not really fit me for being promoted. But there was also my declining to get into layout. "I started on a local independent, down at Mornington. It got bought by the group and I came with it."

"Were you a sub?"

"Yes. I started that way, or pretty much."

"Lucky bastard!"

"Really?" I had assumed Pete would chide me for not having been a reporter.

"I spent ages trying to get into subbing. In the end had to quit and work on suburbans. It's been a tough road but it's a much better gig. For me, anyway. After a while, it gets almost mechanical. Not that it isn't creative. It's not boring. But you can do it and go home happy and have a smoke and a drink and not be worried someone is going to phone you about some update they need to have on a story. And you get overtime. And night rates, if you get into that part of the industry."

"Dailies, you mean."

"Mainly. It's good work. I used to talk to those guys, and they'd do fewer stories in a shift than we do pages. Much fewer, often. Mind you, the stuff you do has to be good. Or pretty good. Actually I'm sure some people did next to nothing and badly and their check-subs would fix it. But I think most of them are pretty good. Mind you, they don't move around much. There aren't that many openings."

"Is that where you're going?"

"Maybe. What about you?"

"I'll probably just stay here. Don't really think I could hack it. Just don't have the background."

"I'm sure you could hack it. Question is whether you want to. There is a different sort of pressure. Bigger stories. You're supposed to be good—not like here, where being good is a bonus."

"I'm amused that you see it that way. I did wonder."

"Here it's banging them out all day. And putting up with it, and hanging in there. And weird obsessions. Have you noticed that thing they do where they always expand the type on the headline so that it fills ninety-nine point nine-nine per cent of the available space? Why would you? It's an extra step. You can see that the dailies don't bother, and they're trying to sell papers, not just give them away. Some negative space usually looks better. But here when I change a headline I rarely find one that has been set without a squeeze or a stretch on the type. You do that too, I've noticed. Why? ... Joint or a bong?"

"Do you have a preference?"

"Tonight I think I'd like a bong. Maybe two. It's been quite a day. I don't smoke bongs by myself, but I wouldn't mind if you'd like one. You can sleep on the couch if you need to. Have you got much on tomorrow? I've got to go in but I can get in latish, just have to check the advances, put out any bushfires. Beer?"

Pete's flat was upstairs in a cream block of four, one of those Art Deco-style places that had been built carefully, probably in the 1920s, and kind of looked after but never properly renovated, so that the kitchen was a bit basic and ancient but there were impressive glass-panelled French doors dividing the dining room from a lounge, and a balcony that looked reasonably private and protective. He seemed to have furnished the flat with antiques.

"My mum's stuff," he said, noticing my roving eyes and anticipating a comment. "She deals. Has a place down towards you a bit, out past Brighton."

"You bought this?"

"On loan. She always gets more stuff than she can fit in the shop. Keeps it in her garage—which drives my dad spare. So she was pretty happy to send some out here. Don't worry about making a mess on the seating. It's all items she will re-cover anyway. Not that I'm encouraging you to spill anything. Make yourself comfortable."

I sank into a deep, crimson-velvet chair whose squared-off arms ended in stubby platforms that could support drinks.

"Weren't you in Sydney? They said you were coming from Sydney."

"Sure, News suburbans. Before that, SMH."

"So to leave a big daily paper and then end up here...?"

"Wanted to be the boss. Felt like a change. Felt like a change of cities, too, for that matter." He sent me a glance—a Roland-like glance? Perhaps, but less weighty. "Someone I wasn't that keen to be hanging around with."

"Oh."

"I had a fling with the boss. Don't want to say too much about it. Not really my taste, but certainly fun at the time. Who do you like, in the office? But you're married, aren't you."

"Not married. Good as, I suppose. I don't cast a lustful eye at reporters, though. Not that we see many. One issue would be, Marjorie was part of the firm."

"Ah! So you used to cast lustful eyes!"

"Well, I'm not sure whether it was my eyes or hers. I had gone through a dry patch."

"It never works just one way. That's my motto and I'm sticking to it. Cross eyes with someone and they're thinking what you're thinking, whether or not they'll admit it. And of course they may not admit it, at first. But the thought's always there."

"Maybe it is for people you meet. You are kind of a looker. A friend of my Dad's used to say that: a looker. And you have that ring of confidence. I could call you the Colgate kid, if you remember that ad. But I can easily imagine that the responses you get to yourself back your theory. Not so sure it would work for me."

"You're not bad!"

"Don't have the confidence thing. Anyway, it's academic. I'm not going to go sneaking around and not telling Marjorie. We'd have to split up, and I'm not in a hurry. And we don't have an open relationship. I've been there, didn't work."

"You've been there?"

"Well, sort of. Not with Marjorie. Long time ago. More open for her than for me, I'll admit. Well, it was open for me too, but she took advantage of it. I didn't. More fool me, I suppose."

"Recipe for disaster. You have that sort of thing going, you've both got to use it. Not that I'm saying it would be easy, if you did."

"It wasn't easy. In fact, it was bloody terrible. I suppose in a way, it was meeting Marge got me over it. But I suppose it was over long before that, really. If I'm honest about it. Which I don't want to be. I don't have your confidence. I wish I did, in some ways, but I don't. Which is probably just as well. I'd just get myself into trouble. Stay out of trouble is my motto these days. Seems to work."

"It's not dull?"

"Not really. Well, I suppose it is, in a way. But not really. You know, you have these things you once wanted. All sorts of exciting stuff. But it can get too much for you. Maybe it all happens too fast, and you can't quite keep up with it. Like having five minutes to finish a page, and you knock out the three headlines but you're not really happy but you also know there's no point in agonising. You wouldn't necessarily do better anyway, if you did take more time. You'd just hold up the check-sub. Or you might do better once, but you couldn't keep it up. Well again, *you* might not have that problem. How's that bong going?"

"It sounds like you're needing it." Pete had handed me a stubby of something—I think he liked Coopers—but now he wandered off towards the kitchen, from which he returned with a bong and a bowl and an ashtray. "Would you like to contribute some tobacco? It'll be nicer than mine. Feel free to light up."

"I don't know. I admire what you've done. What you can do. I liked your headline on the dwarf kid. I liked it not only that you could do it, but that you thought it worth doing. But I'd looked at that headline—Danny asked me for thoughts when he wrote it—and I was just glad I hadn't had to deal with it. I don't know where your line came from. It was yours, wasn't it. I thought it was great, but it would never have occurred to me. Not under pressure, and probably not anyway. I get too hooked up in it. And then worry about taking too long. Whereas you seem able to take what time you need, and then do something with it. I don't know how you do that."

"Maybe I just got lucky. I was a bit apprehensive, actually, with that one. I do remember it. Wasn't quite sure what living large meant—sounded good. But you do it and move on, and sometimes you fuck up. I've seen plenty of good heads from you. You've certainly got some flair. Tell me, do you write the heads first, or last? Here, have this."

THE LINE OF DISCUSSION and indeed the whole situation had made me nervous, I am realising as I recall it. Quite nervous. I am wondering now what that was about. I think I should have been comfortable, settling into an armchair with a boss I admired but who was clearly younger than I, and who had chosen me, to get confiding with, from among the dozen or so subs on the floor—indeed, as was also obvious, he had had more options than only the subs. And he was being complimentary, and we were about to have a bong, which was something I had felt very comfortable doing in the past—indeed, it was about the only situation in which I had felt properly comfortable. And yet, I was feeling tension that expressed itself powerfully. As I reached across Pete's beautifully crafted, glass-inlaid coffee table for the bong, I know my hand shook.

"When did you last have one of these?" Pete asked me.

"A while ago now. I've had plenty of bongs, though."

"I'm not insisting you smoke the whole thing or anything."

"No, I know. I probably won't get through half of the first one. I usually cough my lungs out when it's been a while, the first time.

There's that point you get to when you think you can take some more, and then you realise you already should have stopped. But if you don't mind me coughing..."

"Cough all you like, but don't aim for it. Maybe just have a small one. Here, I'll hold the lighter." I assumed Pete had noticed the trembling of my wrist.

"Don't know why I'm nervous. Anyway, here goes."

But the draught was pure and clean. I remember being very impressed. And that I stopped in time.

"Great bong!" As I exhaled the smoke.

"Thanks. You did well. Sorry if that sounds patronising. You've obviously smoked a few."

"Yes, but not for a while. Phew, this isn't bad stuff. I'm impressed. Haven't had one of these for a while. Forgotten the way it comes on. No, it isn't. I'm imagining it. I probably should have some more. Or do you want the rest?"

"Have the rest of the bowl, if you want it. I think you've had about half."

"I will, then. I'm feeling better already. Beer first. No, I'll light it." I sucked down the rest, still no coughing. "Amazing. Best bong I've ever had." The bong was a glass contraption of multiple chambers.

"It works well. Double filtration."

"Wow. This is cool. Are you going to have one?"

"I'll have one. I just want to tell you, I get a bit loose sometimes when I have had a smoke."

"Loose? Isn't that part of the point? Or the whole point?"

"I'm just conscious of our work relationship."

"Well it's great that you're worrying about that now, when I've just had a bong!"

"Yes. No, I am going to have one. Just want you to know that the bullshit that goes down here goes no further, from me anyway. At least, not into the office."

"No, of course not. Hey, I'm sobering up."

"Well there's plenty more where that came from. Hold the lighter for me."

Pete demolished the bong at a draught, but coughed briefly—much as Roland would have done. I intuited that his most recent previous attempt had been more recent than mine.

"You've done that before."

"I have, once or twice. Another?"

"Maybe not just yet. I want to see what this does. You know something...?"

"What?"

"I'm just realising it's good to be saying that. 'Maybe not yet.' Good to be saying that. Usually when I smoke bongs—well, I suppose I mean in the situation where I was most used to bongs—I'd have been told that I *should* have another."

"I can do that if it would make you feel comfortable."

"How are you feeling? I'm feeling fairly comfortable. But a bit nervous, I am just realising. In fact, quite nervous. I'm just realising how weird all this is. What we are doing here. You're my boss, for God's sake. And I admire you. I do admire you. Can't help it. You seem to have all this confidence, and at the same time a sort of nonchalance with it. And you're good-looking. No, seriously, you're a good-looking guy. You *must* be aware of that. And you've had all this experience I haven't had. And you're good with the girls, where I'm not, or not really. I think I'm just delighted—no, I know this will sound like sucking up but I'm just saying how I feel in the moment—I'm delighted to be here. Delighted you wanted me here. And no one else. To get stoned with. It's so fun getting stoned. I can't believe how much fun it is. But are you having fun? Sorry, I am blithering on here. I do that a bit, people tell me. Or used to. Are you having fun?"

"Well, I'm having fun watching you. Not sure I'm quite as affected. Maybe we should have another."

"Should have another. Suddenly this is getting familiar. *Should* have another. Maybe you should have another, and then you might be somewhere near where I've got to. *You* should have another, and then I'll have another."

"Sure. I'll just get some more beers."

"So, you used to smoke a bit," Pete said, when he returned with the stubbies.

"Yeah, not really all that much. But you know. Just for fun. Of course. Used to like it. Well, mainly with a couple of people. Just one person, eventually. Well, other people with him, but him mainly. He was the mainstay, if you like. The person I most liked to smoke with. But really it was him and someone else, that got me started. On really enjoying it. Well, not enjoying it—I suppose I've just about always enjoyed it—but it became sort of a ritual. Well, not a ritual but... I don't know. Are you going to have that bong or not?"

"I'll have it. I'm just getting fascinated."

"Well, get into it then. I think I'll roll a cigarette."

"You were just telling me you were enjoying having no pressure. Now you're ordering me to have a second bong. I've told you I get a bit loose with it."

"I'm not ordering you, I just think it's your turn. Well, it's my turn but in the circumstances it's your turn. It's your turn because you're not as affected. And you want another. You said we should have another, so *you* should have another. And then I'll have another, if you like. Hey, I am enjoying this, and it's very nice of you to provide it. I haven't had a proper smoke for... I can't remember."

"It's pleasant to have someone to smoke with." Pete again downed his bong at a draught, with a minimum of coughing.

"That's a great bong," I told him.

"It's not bad. So, now it's your bong. Is that right?"

"Yes, when I've finished my smoke. Help yourself. How are you feeling, after two? As good as me?"

"I don't know if I feel as good as you," Pete replied with a chuckle. "But I will feel good soon. A couple of these and I usually feel pretty happy."

"Are you going to repack the cone?"

"Whoa! Hassle, hassle!"

"Well it's just that you did such a good job with the last one. Last one I had, I mean."

"Sure. Not much to it, really. There you go."

I got the second bong down in a single draught myself, a long, slow pull from which I expected at any moment to explode into coughs but which did not have that result.

"This is an amazing bong."

"Thirty-nine ninety-five at the bong shop. Bargain."

"How do you rate the other subs?"

"Rate them?"

"Yes. Sorry, don't know why I asked that. Curious, I suppose. You see, I've never worked anywhere else. You said you thought I could work elsewhere. Somewhere more demanding of class, or that's what I thought you meant. Could they? Could the rest of them? I know some of them have worked elsewhere. Are they good? Do you think they'd do well elsewhere? Are they here just because they prefer the low pressure, or are they here because they'd be forced out elsewhere? Oh shit, this is embarrassing. Forget that I asked. I am probably pretty competitive."

"Everybody's competitive, in this business. It's what keeps you in it. You want to earn it on merit. Want to be a star. That's why I'm surprised you've been stuck in there so long. The others? Don't know, really. Haven't really been here long enough. Well, except for Hermie. I think we all know about Hermie. But he knows his limitations, stays away from front pages. I will tell you something, though. You're the only one who's told me you like that dwarf headline. In fact, you're the only one who's told me they liked any headline that I'd done or anyone else has done. I think Danny was sour at me for a month over that headline. Sour. I believe it was about that: he'd been fine before. It's not that I was expecting him to be bloody grateful but I didn't expect him to be walking around me like I'd kicked his cat. Made me wonder for a while whether I'd stuffed up in some way with it that wasn't obvious to me and that he wouldn't tell me. That is something about working at this place: you don't get much appreciation. Except for the number of pages you can knock out in a shift. You look at Helvetica—why do you call her that, by the way?—in the real estate, and she can get through an enormous number of pages but every bloody headline is the same: X-street stunner; Floral beauty; Great entertainer. You could program them on a computer with a vocabulary of a hundred words. Somebody once did that, by the way. Well, not somebody—I am thinking of a novelist, Michael Frayn, guy that wrote *Copenhagen*, don't know whether you've seen it, amazing play, saw it in London, anyway the computers wrote the headlines. In his book. They just had nouns that could also be verbs that went together. Like shock and rush and strike and row. So you'd have: Strike row. And then the next day: Strike row shock. And so on. Anyway one day they'll do that. And Helvetica—what's her real name? Helga? Helvetica will be out of a job. But not you. I don't think you would. I think you'd be better than that. I don't think you are fazed by the pressure. Or not as much as you think. I think you do a good job. How did you get into this?"

"Force of history! You know, it feels good to hear you saying all this. No, I just lucked in, really. I suppose everybody does. Someone I lived with knew someone who needed someone like me. And I needed a job. Guy I was living with was moving. Who had the house, pretty much. Down at Mornington. Near where I'm living now. Funny bugger. Well, he was a bugger. No, sorry I said that. Irrelevant. Sort of. Anyway, he was moving, and he got me the job so that I could take on the house. Sounds a bit grand, and a bit instrumental, doesn't it. Wasn't really like that. Things just fell into place. One of those things. Small paper. Very small paper. I wasn't really hired as a sub, to start with just proofed the ads. Very part-time. But you know how things happen, on papers. And I did need the money. You know, this hasn't done all that much for me. Maybe you should have another one. And then I'll have one. Another beer?"

"Sure. What were you doing before? That they'd take you on?"

"Writing things about my friends. A few silly stories. Had a series going once with a bike mag. Was living off that—and the dole. It wasn't much. Started with a piece that was basically just telling a joke. Went on from there. Other jokes, silly things bikies might do. Probably got too silly. Maybe they got letters, I don't know. The last one they never ran, and I never asked why. Was doing other things. About people I used to know. Well, based on them. You know, life in a household I used to live in. Actually, my bong household. The house where I learnt to smoke bongs. Well, not really learnt to smoke them, but where the ritual stuff happened. You know, the bong ritual. Well, not a ritual. You probably don't know the bong ritual. Do you want to hear about the bong ritual? You probably don't want to hear about the bong ritual. Do you have a bong ritual? It's about the 'should smoke one' stuff I was just talking about. We were just talking about. Do you know what, it's great just relaxing and blabbing and bullshitting with someone. Haven't done this for ages. For an age. For years, really. Marge doesn't like it. Doesn't really like it. Says I'm an idiot. An imbecile. I think that was her word, an imbecile. But I'm not an imbecile, am I. No more than you're an imbecile. I think everybody who doesn't get into this stuff, in this way, is an imbecile really. But you're not an imbecile, or I don't think you are. It's very nice of you to be offering this, by the way. Very nice. I hope I'm not taking advantage. Do you think I'm an imbecile? Have you got any music? I think we should have music. I think you should put on some music. I think you've got a stereo. You have got a stereo, haven't you?"

"The music is on. Berlin Philharmonic. Do you want me to turn it up?"

"No, no, I can hear it now, just hadn't noticed. Probably didn't think of it as music. Sorry, no, I mean I'm enjoying it. Something different. I don't hear much classical. I hope I'm all right. Getting loose here, I mean. You said you got loose. But I haven't noticed much. When you say you get loose, what do you mean? Have you got there yet? Is this loose?"

"It's a bit loose. I probably wouldn't normally talk like I have. About people we work with, maybe. Not fully appropriate. From my position. I am relaxing. Maybe still not as relaxed as you. I'm not insulted about the music. Lots of people don't hear much classical. I like this, but I won't bore you with chapter and verse on it. What do you like? Another beer? No! I've got a better idea. Cognac. Would you like a good cognac? Bong and a cognac: great combination. I'll get a couple of glasses."

The glasses I remember with fondness. It was probably the first time I had been served a very good cognac, and it was served in an enormous fine glass that I guessed was no less ancient than most of the furniture.

"Do we have this with a bong?"

"You could. Two bongs is often enough for me, though."

"We used to have a lot of bongs … sometimes."

"You. In your bong household, you mean?"

"Yeah. There was this guy called Steve. He was always saying you should have more bongs."

"That's all right if he was bringing the hooch. Not that I mind, of course. Have another. I'm thinking more when I was younger. This stuff could be hard to get hold of in quantity. Depending on how you were placed, whom you knew."

"It was. And we wanted it more, I suppose. Than we do now, I mean. Or that I do. No, he did bring his own. Probably gave me half the dope I've ever smoked. Him and Roland."

"Roland? Sounds like someone from a Celtic myth."

"Steve and Roland. Steve … and … Roland. Steve and Roland. You know, I wrote a couple of cameos that featured that pair. Steve carked it. Had a heroin overdose. It was pretty sad. Well, I wasn't really that sad at the time. I've been thinking about it ever since. Why I wasn't. It was a funny thing. I'd been pissed off at him because he knew Roland. Well, he knew Roland more than me. Well, I didn't think he did. I know I'm not making much sense. Thanks for this brandy. I mean cognac. It's fabulous."

"Well, it ought to be. It's nice stuff. Do you want another bong?"

"Wouldn't mind one. Since I'm staying. Might as well make the most of it. They're nice, but they're not appallingly strong. Just nice. Nice of you to provide it."

"No problem at all. It's nice to kick back. In good company. Plenty more cognac where that came from too. Nice to drink it with someone who appreciates it. Same with the smoke."

"I do appreciate it. Both of them. You're very generous. You know, I never really used to think of Steve as generous. He was a bit of a crook, in a way. Used to steal things, which I was never that hot on. Used to do stupid things. He was a really bad driver. Just reckless. Idiotic. Used to get stoned and do stupid things in the car. Not that I gave him much of a chance."

"You gave him short shrift." I remember Pete laughing at that. I think he was a bit offended by my not having noticed his music.

"No, not short shrift. Just didn't often get in a car with him. I always used to feel guilty about smoking so much of his dope."

"You didn't offer him any?"

"No. Well I did, but at the time I didn't have much. I didn't have much money for it. I wasn't doing much work. Although Steve was a student as well, at the time. Actually I wasn't. I had quite a good job, taking bets for the TAB. Over the phone, at their headquarters. They run a phone betting service, or used to. Look, to tell you the truth, it was as though Steve smoked just for the sake of it. Just because he could. It was like a game for him. Whereas the point for me, at the time especially, was to maybe get a bit ripped but to do something with it. To have some sort of a conversation or play a game or do something interesting that looked different from the perspective of having had a smoke or two rather than simply to see how many you could have without keeling over. Which is funny to think about, given that now what I mainly want to do *is* have more. Or just to do whatever I feel like. Even if someone else is supplying the means. Thank you again!"

I drew down my third bong.

"Your turn. Are you going to have one?"

"Probably. No rush." Pete grinned at me. "So you're doing what you said you were glad I wasn't doing to you. Putting pressure on me. Telling me to have a bong."

"Yes, it's your bong. It's your bong, Pete. How does that feel? It's your bong, Pete. That's how Roland and Steve would go on. If Steve was here, he'd be saying: 'It's your bong, Pete.' And then Roland would say something like: 'That's only fair, Pete: Seamus has had a bong and I've had a bong and Steve's had a bong and so now it's your bong.' And then Steve would tell you it would be good for you: 'You'll feel a lot better when you've had that bong.' He had this sort of dry, gravelly voice and when he wanted to sound serious he could sound quite grave and like he had authority. And then Roland would say: 'You will feel better when you've had a bong, Pete. You'll feel as good as we do.' And then if you said something like you didn't want another bong, Steve would do this thing he did where he pretended to be astonished—well, not quite astonished, it was more a mixture of astonished and disgusted, somehow. Can't quite describe it. And he'd sort of throw his arms out—metaphorically I mean, I don't think he used to really do that—but it would be in his voice and he'd go something like: 'WHAAT? Here we are having bongs, and you asked me if I'd like another bong and I had one, and you asked Roland if he'd like a bong and he had one, and you asked Seamus if he'd like a bong and *he* had one, and now YOU WON'T HAVE ONE! So we've all had one, because you've asked us to, and you wait until after we've had one and you say you won't have one. I don't think that's a reasonable attitude. I think that's a bit of a gyp. I think you've been having a go at us. I think I'm offended. I don't think that's fair play.'

"He'd have picked it that you have a bit of a posh accent, a posh voice I mean, and that's why he'd be talking about fair play. He wasn't a posh guy. He came from the other side of the sticks. Of the tracks, I mean. Well, almost literally. He was from Williamstown, or somewhere near there. No, I mean Footscray. One of those western suburbs. He met Roland at business school. Ended up working for a bank, which I thought was really ironic. Still there when he died. I used to go out with his girlfriend. Actually, that sounds a bit bad. Or a bit sad even. Actually it was sad. She was the one I had an open relationship with. But it wasn't really open. I think she just got tired of me. You know, she was my first girlfriend. I probably shouldn't say that, to you I mean. Not that it matters. You can see I'm not very confident. Compared with you, anyway. It's not like I root everything in a skirt on two legs, like you probably do. No, I didn't mean that. Anyway, it's a compliment. I like you. I like you a lot. I don't mean to come down here and get stoned and insult you. You're not insulted, are you? You know I am really enjoying this. I am loose. I get like this when I'm loose. Roland understands it. Roland doesn't mind it. He's about the only one I know who doesn't mind it. Do you mind it? Am I boring you shitless, as they say? Do you wish you'd never invited me? I'm sorry if I become a bore.

"I'm just remembering Patience Moore. She was the girlfriend. Steve's girlfriend and my girlfriend. In a way, I still miss her. I never really got what she saw in Steve, but in a way now I do. You know, I've just realised that here I am, getting a bong or two on with you, and I want to talk about Steve. And Roland. Roland's still around. Still alive. Haven't seen him much lately. Not much for a couple of years, actually. Don't think he really likes Marjorie. Well I think he does, but she doesn't like him. Or doesn't like the way I am with him, that's what she says anyway. Probably wouldn't like it if she was here now, either. I hope you don't mind it. Oh God, it is good to get ripped and just forget all about it. Have your bong. I notice you've not had your bong yet. You are just sitting there watching me be an idiot. Have your bong. Have your bong or I'll tip this cognac over you. I will. I will tip it over you. No I won't, I'll just drink it. Oh my God this stuff is delicious. It's all delicious. My God, will I ever have any credibility. I notice you're keeping very cool. Very cool over there, Mr Cool. Am I putting on a display for you? I'm not normally like this, as you know. Even after a joint or two. It's just bongs, when I feel comfortable. You must have made me feel very comfortable.

"I think that's what I liked about Steve. He made me feel very comfortable. Even in my own house, he made me feel comfortable. Well, it was also Roland's house. I don't think I feel that comfortable in my own house. Marjorie doesn't like me getting like this. She really doesn't. And I never do with her. I really never do. If you came to my house, we wouldn't do this. Which you would probably think was just as well. Anyway I wouldn't have any dope. I don't get dope any more. I just don't bother to get any. I used to get some from Roland occasionally. Hardly see him these days. It's funny, I don't know whether you'd like him. He's not always that funny, just with anybody. Usually he's fairly reserved. He's pretty shy, really. I think it was Steve who brought him out. Steve was impressed with him. And he brought Steve out too. That's what Pash said—Patience I mean, that was her nickname. I got with Pash after Steve carked it. It wasn't what you think. She tracked *me* down. I'd always liked her. Well, I'd only met her twice, but I liked her. Never thought she'd track me down. She came down with Bob, who is someone else I don't see much these days. Haven't seen him for ages. Something went wrong there. Well, I know what went wrong, really. He was a doctor. Used to get some good drugs, sometimes. Got dex once for Pash. Well I think it was him. Mind you, it could have been anyone. That was good stuff. She was right into music. Had a scar. I must have bored you to death. Bet you're sorry you gave me a bong. Have your bong. HAVE YOUR BONG! HAVE YOUR BONG! Sorry to yell at you. I'm sorry to be yelling at you. Just trying to give you the experience. But it isn't really the experience. Nobody used to yell at me, unless I yelled at them. It was just about freedom, I think. Just about freedom. The freedom to blither on. That's what I always liked. And they used to laugh at me. I used to like it that they used to laugh at me. Steve used to. And Roland as well. Roland was a guitarist. I thought he might be a bit of a star. He was good enough. Just about. Do you know people like that? You admire them, and you are pretty sure they are good enough. But then they don't do what you thought they would do. Something doesn't happen, somehow. Or they don't seem to see it. Just go and do boring stuff. So things started exciting, and then they go and do boring stuff. And probably seem happier. But something is missing. There's a core or something missing. Roland's still with Debbie. I can barely believe that. They've got kids now. You're a bit of a loner, I've just realised. You don't have any kids, do you? I've never really wanted kids. I don't think Marge did either. I told her I didn't want any. I don't know if she believed me. She's good though, we haven't had any. Probably don't have sex enough these days to have any. Anyway it's about last-ditch for her now. Bloody hell, what I am talking about. Bullshit, bullshit, bullshit. Just as well this isn't getting back to the troops. Have that bong!"

DID I REALLY SAY all that? Of course, I do not know. I am pretty sure I rattled on for about that long or maybe longer, and said something like that. But most of it is probably stuff I wish I had said. Or might have wanted to say. I know I did want to introduce Pete to the idea of hassling one another about how many bongs we had had. And he had seemed resistant. And I had not wanted to push it. But he had seemed appreciative, and I suppose I had felt okay to reveal myself. I know I did say things about Roland and Steve, and about Pash for that matter, because that is part of what I find memorable about that evening.

I had a few more nights with Pete, and Marge and I went out to dinner with him a couple of times with a girl he hooked up with. I know I stayed a bit straighter for all the subsequent times. I think Pete was a bit blown away. But I think it did me good to talk about all that stuff. I was missing it. Life was sort of a bit of ho-hum even then. I did not think that at the time, but I can see it when I think back to then, and especially from where I am now. I think it is probably less than ho-hum now. Not that I really mind. I am in no rush to get another job.

It was fun for a while with Pete there. I suppose he was there for most of a year. He was very encouraging. Probably that is something else I have missed, Pete's encouragement. I know people thought we had a bit of a private club going, for a while. Pete would encourage me, and I would encourage him. I took on the check-sub role—well, it was informal back in those days, just looking over some of the page proofs that Pete would give me, mainly checking the big print, and trying to think up better headlines if he was not overly sold on the ones that were on there. It was a lot of responsibility, I suppose. Pete used to help me. We would run things by one another. The papers were better, and I think management noticed. Which you would not necessarily expect. I think they do get feedback, from unlikely places. Someone they see at dinner says a front page was good, or better than expected, or that the papers have been looking better, or they contrast how they are now with how they used to be—even though they used to say nothing *then*. Pete probably gave me credit. Which might have been why, when the check-sub we had had for ages, Griff, passed on—he died, not at work but pretty suddenly, just at home—they gave me the job. I did not necessarily want it, but it was hard not to take it, especially as I had been sort of sharing the job with Griff anyway ever since Pete left for Adelaide. I stayed in touch with Pete for a while, traded the occasional email.

Anyway I sort of had to take it on at least temporarily. And then ended up with it.

FEELINGS. HOW DID I feel about becoming a check-sub? I do not know. In a way I was proud of it. In a lot of ways, I suppose, really. And then in another, I almost knew it would be the end of the road. There is really nowhere to go after that. If they thought you would make a good chief, they would have done that already. No one had thought I should take over from Pete, I could see that. Which was not hard, as it was not a job I wanted. I have never wanted to be in charge. I just like to have a chance to add my bit of value and get some appreciation for it, even if the appreciation is institutional: expressed only in the position where they have placed me. Creative incompetence? I suppose I had choices. But in another sense it just happened. I do not know what else I could have done, that would have given me the same pay and benefits. I did not feel that secure, and did not really look forward to work. But it was okay. I suppose I was settled.

11

THE SOUL AND ITS APPETITES

As unlikely as it had seemed, I think my mood has improved. Whether these reveries have helped, I do not know. I could have written of simpler highs, which would have merited less exploration. Of my securing an outstandingly high mark at school. Of my first attempt to ride a bicycle, when I surprised its lender, a neighbouring playmate, with my ability to balance it easily. Of playing cowboys at Myrtle Street in the backyard with Charles, a sharp figure behind the blurry foresight of my revolver. And all of these times could have counted. My allying with Steve and Roland to badger Bob about his intemperate purchasing was not, in any straightforward way, an episode in which I had rejoiced subsequently. And yet it was at such tangled threads that my mind tugged immediately, when it was suggested that I write about happy experiences. These encounters were richer, or deeper. I was more content at such times than at other times, even if I was also intoxicated. Perhaps I have learned something that I might have recognised usefully a long time ago: happiness is not straightforward. Or at the least, mine is not.

At intervals as I recounted that session in which we tormented Bob I felt disloyal, as though I had betrayed Bob by allying myself with Steve and defending improvidence. I wondered what it was saying about me that this memory should have demanded that I rank it among the peaks of past gratification—rather than accepting silently a place in the lowlands among other times when I had profited guiltily from the distress of a friend. But again, perhaps that is the point. That my victory over Bob had demanded such prominence might not have supported an assessment of myself as someone wholly admirable. And yet it did demand prominence. I have been learning that it is better to accept such belligerent inner responses to questions I have been asked to reflect upon. Some choices that I discover have directed me more than the choices over which I have deliberated.

Not that the discovered choices necessarily promoted my wellbeing. That is something else I have learned. It could have been obvious to me all along, but I had never before seen things that way. I imagine the decision that I would buy a pouch of tobacco was more of a discovery than a choice that I had reasoned my way to. I wished to smoke, and if I were to smoke then I needed tobacco, and so I bought some tobacco. I cannot, with any assurance, remember what I was thinking and feeling at that moment when I purchased my first packet of Bank, but I imagine I felt the relief of surrender, of giving in. I understood that I had crossed a line, and a line that I had been warned not to cross and that I understood was difficult to cross in reverse, or to reinstate in one's life as not crossable. And yet coexistent with that understanding was a demand from within that I cross that line. The place beyond it was a place I had chosen already to dwell in. To have resiled from the purchase would have been merely to have delayed my realising of that choice.

Was my decision to have a drink before work a decision of that same kind? It is scarcely imaginable that it was not. It does not seem possible that I had developed a convincing argument for the conclusion that having that drink would do me good. And yet my decision to have it, given that I had smoked a cigarette, and given that I was not feeling terribly well, was a decision that seemed good to me at the time. And I believe I concluded as I swallowed the drink, Jim Beam mixed with Coke as I remember perfectly well, that the choice had been good. The level of liquid remaining in the glass fell intermittently, and I drew on my cigarette and thought about life. There was a sense of peace, as I recall the moment now; almost a sense of lightness. For a few minutes it had seemed as though I did not need to go in to work. Times spent smoking over a glass of wine and reading my book of the week while waiting for Zoom to appear from his shed arise now in my mind as a parallel, although I do not recall their having done so at that time. There arises also an inner tension, a grudging self-description of my behaviour as reckless, which probably was there at the time. And with it the recognition—perhaps more accurately a mock recognition—that nothing much mattered to me a very great deal. I understood that I could have another bourbon and Coke, and that my doing so would make very little difference to the progress of my day.

I can remember, if only in outline, the day I decided I could enjoy a fourth drink, and with it a fourth or fifth cigarette. That was the first day when I decided that on that day, I would not go in to work. Work could cope. I was not feeling well. I would phone in, and did. There came a day when I did not phone. I did not want to tell Danny or anyone else that I would not be coming in, and that was partly because I was not sure how I would sound on the phone. I can remember sitting and sipping at my little breakfast table in the nook opposite the kitchen, looking out over the yellow lawn of the backyard, observing that the few green bits needed mowing, and waiting for someone to phone me. Someone did phone. I did not answer the phone. It would not have been a call that I could have taken. Whoever was phoning, really. For all they knew, I reflected, I had been called away to a family emergency somewhere. Something urgent enough to have prevented my taking time to call in. Or I might have died.

My entertaining the latter possibility did not lead me to feel sad or fearful. There was, if anything, a connection again with relief. I would not have to explain the next day what I had been up to. Would not need to concoct the family emergency, or even to admit that I had suffered through a tough wake-up and had felt too flat to want to pick up the phone and let them know what was happening. That day's papers would go to print without me. They would carry more mistakes but likely no one would notice. Or if a reader did notice, it was not likely he would think much about it. Danny would make time to scan the pages, hoping to see any spellos that remained in the headlines. If the heads made less sense, he would not think that mattered. He might even welcome the quicker progress to print. Would not have me insisting pieces needed re-editing, perhaps even rewriting. The other subs would be relieved. They would not be offended by my changing their headlines. The minor—I knew they were minor—style errors that I had got into the habit of fixing quietly would go through unchanged, and readability would not suffer much.

There had been a time when I would draw attention to the style errors. A time when I would send a private message over the production system to whichever sub had offended and ask him to pop over to my workstation for a quiet chat about style. "We never use *according to* as an attribution unless we wish to signify scepticism. We re-write it, using *said* or some other impartial attributive clause. If you get it a lot, attend to which reporter has been doing it and have a quiet word. It is in the style book. They need to know this. Do you get what I am on about here? *Said* is always safest; that's in the stylebook too. It might not be what the source literally said, but of course that doesn't matter unless the paraphrase is wide of the mark, in which case *according to* doesn't help. Do you understand me? If you have doubts, phone the reporter and check. They need to be getting this right." At one time I would have written a bulletin if something like this started coming up frequently, and I would have distributed it by email to all reporters and subs. I knew that people made fun of these, but for several years it had seemed important to produce them. Made my job easier. Helped me maintain a certain standard. Every now and again I would see a phrase I had objected to in a certain context come up in a similar context in one of the dailies, and I would groan inwardly—doubtless, sometimes outwardly—because that made my job harder. But it did not matter that a daily might have accepted a certain ambiguous or inaccurate usage as good enough or reflective of popular usage. It was up to their editors to define their own styles and they could do what they liked. If we were more accurate than the dailies, notwithstanding our smarter pace and our dependence on junior reporters, then that just showed that the dailies were getting sloppy. Which they were. Perhaps their check-subs were not doing their jobs properly. It had seemed to me that once you had been appointed check-sub—and it was not a post I had coveted—then you needed to do the job properly or not at all. And properly meant keeping the other subs up to the mark, and following the style book. Simply fixing the other subs' errors silently would be a slow road to ruin. They would get sloppier, and you would have more and more work to do. You had to keep on top of them, or look at another job. Same went for the style book. It was a good style book, if a big one, and it had been developed over a long period. If you did not want to follow it, then change the style book. Simply ignoring the style book would get you in all sorts of trouble, because a gap would open between our formal authority on usage and our accepted daily usage. There would be no final arbiter to which you could appeal so as to demonstrate that, after all, you were right.

WHEN IT WAS SUGGESTED to me that I liked to be right, I agreed. It was as though someone had claimed that I liked to be fed. It was a claim about me that I could safely permit. I was happy to be wrong, I told Ms Felicity, provided that whoever claimed I was wrong could back up the claim with evidence that I found convincing. She accepted that, up to a point. She said she wondered whether there might be more to it. I asked what more there could be. She said it seemed to her that sometimes, who was right did not matter. How did I feel about that? I let her know that I did not have to pursue every argument; that if I was not convinced, then sometimes I would just say that and move on. Some people—most really, I said—were not worth arguing with. Often I would understand early in a conversation that I was not going to get a discussion that met the points I could make, and I would let things slide, just nod and say "Sure," allow any claims to slide past unanswered, however absurd they might be. But, I said, I could not do that at work. Well, by then of course I had been doing just that, but as I told her, it unsettled me. I would try to fix stuff myself, and if people complained I would point out that I was the check-sub. Not that I got many complaints. But it had got that there was too much to fix—what with our posting more stuff in a rush on the websites. I had found it demoralising, I said. I had felt that I was not doing my job properly; that things had gotten out of hand. It had seemed as though there was no way back.

Ms Felicity asked me whether I missed my wife. I said we had not been married. Partner, then, she said. "You said you had lived with her for about eighteen years. That sounds like a marriage. Or something very close. To me. Not to you?" I conceded it probably had been a marriage, in a common-law way, even if it had not been quite eighteen years. "I never asked her to marry me. I did think about it, from time to time. There were a few times when I was almost going to ask her. But it never seemed quite right. Anyway, they didn't last long. Most of the time, we were just getting along, really. We were companions, I suppose. It's probably true, in many ways, that she was my best friend. People say that about their wives. I've never quite got it." And I can remember laughing then. "I mean I've never quite got it before, but when people say that—I suppose mainly I've read of people saying it, in newspapers and things—I had always thought they meant there was something really special about their relationship. But suddenly I'm thinking it might just mean they don't have other friends. They have acquaintances, and might have known some of them for some time, maybe even a lot of years, but they are friends only in a good-time, shallow sort of way. Not that they wouldn't do things for you, and you'd ask them if you had to, but they don't really know you. I don't think Marge knew me either. But she knew me better than my friends did. Or should I say, my acquaintances. I suppose that's my fault really, about the acquaintances. When I got into this trouble at work I didn't want to tell anybody. I didn't feel like there was anybody who would really get it. Anybody who wouldn't want to lecture me, or something. Or tell me I had it coming. Or nod their head in that pitying sort of way that meant they could listen to me but thought I was probably bullshitting about all the problems and deserved what I'd got. Do you know what I mean?"

"What would you have wanted a friend to do?"

"Well, not that. I don't know. I don't really know. I suppose, maybe... just listen to me. Hear me moaning, I suppose. I suppose that's what most of my friends would have said, that I was moaning. I don't really think it is moaning. I suppose I think my friends would say something was wrong with me. Those I have left, anyway. Which isn't many now, I don't think. Although I imagine I could restart some friendships. Phone a few people up. They would answer. Probably they wonder what has become of me. But I didn't want to phone anybody when all this happened, and I still don't. I mean, part of it is, I still don't really know *what* has happened. I mean, what do you say? 'I've been drinking a bit and haven't got in to work.' I could imagine how that would have gone down. The pity thing. Sympathy, and a kind of washing of the hands. Glad it's not me. You know, that sort of thing. Don't want to get infected. Feeling lucky they're not like me. You know. 'They've told me to see a psychologist.' I mean, look, I probably do know people who've done that. In fact, there is someone I used to know who said he did that once. But no one I know has talked about it. Told me they have. I mean, told me why. I don't even know what this guy got out of it, if anything. I had no idea what would go on here."

"And what is going on?"

"Well you know, talking, talking about stuff. You ask questions, you listen to what I have to say. You are *interested*—or at least, you pretend to be. I suppose you are paid. I shouldn't take your interest too seriously. But I do, strangely enough. Either you are interested, or you are very good at pretending to be interested. I suspect you are good at pretending. Actually, I've just realised, you're a woman. I don't mean I've just noticed; I mean it's about the significance of it. Pretending. I am thinking now you are just pretending."

"Do you think women pretend ... to be interested in you?"

"Yes, I think so. Or some do. I am never sure whether they really are interested. There is always a sort of self-interest simmering away in the background that motivates them. They are interested because they think it will help *them*, to be interested. Or to seem interested. Perhaps."

"And do you think men are different?"

"Probably not. Probably not, now I think of it. Well, I suppose the difference is men don't appear to be interested."

"So nobody is really interested in you."

"No. Not really."

"How does that feel? For you?"

"Oh ... well ... normal, I suppose."

That was a surprise question, or at least I found it surprising. Certainly, I did not have a ready answer. How did it feel, she had asked. Thinking on my feet—well, on my arse, as at the time I was sitting in a high-backed swivel chair—I had answered honestly, or as honestly as I could under pressure and having thought about it for such a short time. *Normal. That nobody was interested in me.* It had come as a bit of a shock, sort of, to hear myself saying that. I knew as I said it that it was not a particularly happy thing to be saying. Part of me told the other parts it was not true. That I was bullshitting, just saying the first thing that came into my head. Moaning.

"I'm probably just moaning," I said.

"You're allowed to moan here." Do women therapists always have such soft, almost sexy-soft, voices?

"Well, it's not really moaning. People would say it was moaning. But it is what I feel. I don't think people are interested."

"How interested are *you*, in you?"

"How do you mean? I'm fascinated!" Probably I made a wry face.

"And yet you say you are moaning. I asked you how you felt about something, and you answered me. And your answer to me felt honest. But you say of it that it was merely you moaning. You think your friends would accuse you of moaning. But you go on to accuse yourself. Have I got that right?"

"Well, it's not that I really think I'm moaning. But, what I said. Well it sounds pretty sad, in a way. It's like I'm saying I think no one cares about me and that's normal. But that's all bull; people do care about me. A bit, anyway. I mean, my employer sent me here. Or sent me somewhere, and I ended up here. Which they're happy about. They're paying for this. They don't have to. It might be convenient for them, at some level, but they don't have to. So even they must care about me a bit. So if I think no one cares about me, I'm wrong, aren't I. Someone cares. Probably plenty of people care. So I'm moaning."

It was an argument and I had thought I was winning.

"I didn't ask you to consider, though, whether anybody really did care. That would be a different question. You told me that nobody—no woman, and no man either—was really interested in you. And I asked you how that felt. You said it felt normal. So the question was not whether you were right about nobody being interested, but how you felt about your own assessment: that no one was interested. Can you see the difference there?"

I admitted I could.

"So, do you want to deny now that you have that view, or do you want to look at the implications of your having that view?"

"Well, probably what I want to do is deny it."

"And?"

"But it's probably true."

"What's true?"

"That I do feel that way."

"It feels normal to you that nobody is interested in you."

"It does feel normal, I suppose."

"Well, I wonder whether you could just settle back and just reflect on that for a moment. It feels normal that no one is interested in you."

I obeyed. It seemed easiest.

"So, if it's normal that no one is interested in you, I am wondering: how does normal feel."

"Just ... normal."

She let me dwell on that for a minute or so.

"What if I said I was interested in you?"

That is the bit that sticks best in my mind. She is very good-looking, Ms Felicity, I think. In a Dianne Keaton, high-cheekboned, nice-complexioned, mischievous-smile-sometimes sort of way. I have always been excited by beauty in women. Excited and, simultaneously, frightened. Obviously.

"What happened then?" she asked.

"When?" But I knew what she meant.

"Just then. When I said what if I was interested in you. What happened for you?"

"I got excited. I don't know why I am telling you that, but I did."

"You felt excitement."

"I did."

"So, my being interested in you, the possibility, feels exciting for you."

"Yes."

"And how is that? Compared with normal?"

"It is good, but I don't really trust it."

"You don't trust ... the excitement?"

"No. It doesn't really feel real. Well, I don't really think you are interested. The possibility feels exciting, but I am pretty sure it won't last. It won't outlast this session, for example. You are paid to be interested. My getting excited is a bit like getting excited about meeting a prostitute, in a way. She might seem interested, and you want to believe that, but you know she isn't, or probably isn't anyway. She's interested in what you're paying her."

"How does that feel, telling me that?"

"It feels quite good, actually. Like I'm punishing you for making me think you were interested. For a few seconds. I did get quite excited there."

"We'll have to finish up," she said then. "We're out of time, I'm afraid. I wonder whether, until I see you again, you could just reflect from time to time on that feeling of excitement, and on where it came from, that you thought someone—me even, if that helps you think about it—*might* be interested in you. Just think about that feeling, feel the excitement if you can, and be aware of what else comes up for you. Just when it occurs to you. And we'll talk about that next time."

I SUPPOSE IT WAS no coincidence that not long after that session I was thinking about Jessica's party. I must have been quite nervous about going. Probably more so than I had noticed way back at the time. When the day came, it had been pissing down with rain. I had good gear for riding in rain but I would need somewhere dry to get it off, and preferably without dripping all over Bob's carpet, which began immediately you stepped in the front door. It would also be awkward to slither through a crowd at the party clad in wet, greasy bike gear so that I could get to the bathroom at the back. So that meant getting there early, before many had arrived, and I had not wanted that either: it had seemed presumptuous, given that my relationship would be just getting going again, with both of them really.

I phoned Roland, assuming he would be going, and he said he would be, with Debbie. I asked whether I might stay the night, if necessary, and after a short consultation was offered a bed on the couch. Agreed to get there about eight, after dinner. The invitation from Jessica and Bob was for eight, so we thought we would get to Bob's place at nine. Roland still had his renter at Abbotsford, less than half an hour's walk away. But of course we would be driving, which would take less than ten minutes. As it turned out, the rain had all but dried up by the time I set out, having adjudged it too early to eat, although the roads were still wet. The distraction of negotiating the slippery surfaces and myriad reflected lights on the ride down was welcome. Roland greeted me with his customary warmth; Debbie with a cheeriness I did not quite credit. "Patience will be there," she said at some point soon after I had removed my all-weather suit. I am sure she said it so that she could enjoy my discomfort. Possibly her cheeriness had been connected solely with her anticipating that before long she would be able to tell me that. I replied that it would be good to see Pash, but I suspected that my response sounded hollow. "I'm having a bourbon," Roland said. "With Coke. Want one?" We sat at the dining table and he pulled out a joint. "I've got two for when we get there," he confided, opening his golden packet of B&H tailor-mades so that I could see two rolled joints inserted among the cigarettes. "But I thought we would have one beforehand. Is it a while since you've seen Bob?"

A joint often seems like a good idea before a party that you are nervous about, and as I was nervous about most parties I would have been agitated by then about this one, having thought it possible Pash would be there and having just had that confirmed. Debbie had also commented sceptically on my clothing: I was wearing bike boots under jeans and, I am pretty sure, a sloppy pullover. A jacket would have suited the weather and the occasion better, but I did not own one except for bike jackets. I was conscious, as so often before social occasions, of my resistance to shopping for garments, a resistance reinforced by my history of penury. Debbie was wearing a neat black cardigan over a dress—I have an intimation of the dress having been green—her diminutive, somewhat plump frame looking quite well turned out with black heels. "It's an engagement," she reminded me, in a tone that suggested amusement. "All Bob's doctor friends will be there." Roland, more comfortingly, had on a cheap-looking casual zip-up jacket and—although I would not swear to this—newish blue jeans. I trusted him to blend the joint mildly so that I would not be walking into the party already raving, and anyway it was not a bong and so could be savoured more gingerly.

"It's ages," I said, having taken up Roland's invitation to begin on the joint. "I don't think I've seen him since we were all here last time."

"Wow," Roland said. "More than a year."

"It is much more than a year. Mmm, this tastes pretty good. Feels like you've rolled it just right."

"We've seen them a few times," said Debbie, who had sat with us to await our departure. "What did you get them?"

"A gift? I thought about it. I don't actually have one. Should I have one?"

"Ye-e-s!" said Debbie. "It's an engagement."

"What have you got them?"

"Glassware," said Roland. "Bob still likes a red now and again. And Jessica likes her wine."

"Do *you* see them?"

"Every now and again. They came to a barbecue we had with a few people. That was funny. Jessica likes a bit of a smoke."

"We've had them for dinner," said Debbie. "I like Jessica."

"But we do wonder what she sees in Bob," Roland said, giving a smirk and a significant glance.

"Roland!" Debbie scolded.

"No," said Roland. "Bob's all right."

"They make a very good couple," Debbie insisted. "I think she's good for Bob. Takes the sharpness off him. Makes him more tolerant."

"You mean tolerable," Roland said with a giggle. "What has he got to be tolerant about? She makes *us* tolerate *him*."

"Roland! Don't be mean about Bob. They're a good pair. What time is it? It's time to go. Shall we go?"

"Let's just stay here and have another joint," Roland said, giving another giggle. "Or a bong. Let's have a bong."

"Roland. You won't have a bong. Don't be silly. Come on, we're leaving."

"Bong?" Roland inquired of me, raising his eyebrows. "No, I'm just kidding. All right, we'll go."

THERE WAS MORE OF a crowd than I had expected, given that we must indeed have arrived about nine, which had felt early for a party. But then it was an engagement do, and clearly it was a bigger deal than I had assumed. Bob's extendable dining table had been pushed against the left-hand wall, and as well as carrying nibbles it supported at its far end a small mountain of packaged gifts, forcing me to recognise that I had been remiss in bringing nothing but a bottle of red—a double misjudgement, as clearly drinks were on the house. The room was quite warm already. I can remember congratulating Jessica, who wore a flimsy, flowing white gown and wreathe-like headdress in which she looked, I thought, inappropriately virginal, and receiving from her a warm hug in response; and that I got a less effusive welcome from Bob, equally striking in a white suit and what I would now recognise to be a Panama hat. Jessica introduced me to her parents, whom I had never met when we had been sharing at Mornington. That too was a surprise: it had not occurred to me that parents would be invited. In contrast, I had met Bob's mother before. She asked me what I had been up to, and seemed approving of my job as a sub-editor. I was aware of how much easier to negotiate were conventional social events when you could name an occupation that was known to bring in a comfortable living. From their high standards of dress—some also wore suits, but none white—I hypothesised that most of the guests present were doctors invited by Bob. Roland was not desperate to hobnob with Bob's doctor guests and their partners. He and I and Debbie drifted towards the kitchen, an open galley off the rear of the main room. From a short bench set up at its entrance, a young-looking curly-haired man in torn jeans was dispensing drinks. An earring, a T-shirt, and florid tattoos on his arms and neck completed the incongruous outfit. Already I was feeling too warm in my jumper. Jessica joined us again. "Have what you'd like," she encouraged us. "Don't worry, there will be people you know. Bob's people from work all arrived on time. My friends haven't got here yet. It's all work and family. This is Tran ... from school." She indicated the barman, who smiled at us and accepted my red, and then she re-crossed the room to welcome new entrants. "Well," Roland said, after we had exchanged greetings with Tran and had stood aside with our drinks, "we may as well use the time. Do I remember that there's a back garden?" I said that it could be reached from the door immediately to our right. Debbie followed us out. There was a small table and trestle seats in the narrow backyard, glistening wet under the security lighting. We stood outside the kitchen windows. I felt relief from the crisp, cooling air. Roland withdrew his packet of cigarettes and retrieved a joint.

"So how long is it since you've been here?" Roland asked me.

"I'm not sure. Never since Jessica lived here. Which is quite a while. A year; more than a year. Actually it was a while since I'd been round before that. Pash," I said. "I hadn't wanted to find Pash here." The joint, coming as it did on top of the joint we had smoked back at Roland's, was beginning to work its dubious magic. Roland gave me a curious look. "You remember Pash. It's been ages so I don't suppose it matters now but I was worried I might find her here. If I dropped in. When I'd thought she wasn't around to see me," I finished, doubtless suspecting this ending was lame. "Oh, you know, it wasn't really my business what she did but I just would have found that uncomfortable, too uncomfortable. I still don't really know what went wrong there. Pash was great. I liked her. Really liked her. Somehow it all went wrong and we just drifted apart. Anyway I guessed she'd found someone else she liked better than me. For a while I thought that might have been Bob. She did come round here a lot, I know that. Anyway you're probably not interested and I don't see why you should be interested. It's all in the past now anyway, but I do miss her sometimes. Although I'll admit it wasn't all her, the drifting apart. I had started to wonder whether this was really what I wanted. You know."

Roland was gazing at me inexpressively, as though he had not been following, which I suspected immediately was the case.

"Don't worry," I said. "It's all in the past. All bull really."

"Did you think Patience was seeing someone else, when she was with you?" Debbie asked. In contrast to Roland, Debbie was all curiosity.

"I did wonder," I said. "I was pretty sure. Not before. Not at first, or at least I didn't suspect at first. Sounds ridiculous, doesn't it: 'suspect'. But really I was just too glad everything was happening. Later on though I did wonder and she pretty much told me it was happening. Or had been happening. Pretty much from the start, as far as I could work out. I don't know. Maybe I'm no good in bed."

"I wouldn't have thought that of Patience," Debbie said. She sounded entertained, excited to have been offered this window onto someone else's intimacy. "Do you know she's with someone now?"

Debbie could be tactful but I think she enjoyed being blunt with me when she had the chance. Having been wounded too often by my bluntness with her, perhaps—or more accurately, by my failing to be blunt but instead colluding with Roland to dismiss passively her desires and entreaties. Many of the latter would have been founded on a prior pledge she had extracted from Roland. It struck me only recently that she must have experienced his backsliding as painful. I was not sure whether to seek from Debbie the identity of Pash's latest lover, or whether to attempt to push her question aside.

"I imagined she would be. Could be with several people, for all I know. It really doesn't matter, does it?"

"Jessica sees Pash," Roland said, displaying renewed interest in my affairs. Or perhaps the point was that this was not my affair. "We hear a bit from time to time."

"When you see Jessica? You don't see Pash as well?"

"Never," Roland said. "I'm not really part of that circle. Shooka sees her, I think. They probably still work together. I see Shooka on the odd occasion. The very odd occasion," he said, glancing at Debbie and then giving me one of his significant looks. I guessed the visits were connected with his drug supply, which once again I felt grateful for. "Shall we go in," Roland invited.

A small queue had formed at the bar. At the rear of it, I recognised the broad face of Stanley Jones. Stanley grinned at us under his lenses immediately we walked back in the door.

"Hey, how are you!" he greeted us collectively. "Holding out on me, hey?"

"You weren't here," said Roland.

"Anyway," said Stanley, "It's good to see you all. Seamus! Don't often see you down. What have you been up to?"

"Oh, you know, nothing much. Did you know? I'm a sub!"

"You're a sub! What's a sub? Sounds like you're sinking. Or a substitute. A substitute for what?"

"On a newspaper," Roland told him. "He fixes the headlines."

"Writes the headlines," I corrected. "On the local paper. And captions and stuff. You know, cut the stories. Talk to the reporters—well, we've only got one. Contributors. They call them contributors. I work with the contributors. Talk to them about what we want to do with their stuff. There's an old guy I'm learning from. Been doing it for years. He has. Doesn't really want to talk to the contributors. Says he's over it—you know, a bit sick of it. Doing it too long or something. So I'm doing that part. I don't mind it. Really don't mind it, actually."

"So! Well, it's good that you don't mind what you're doing. Are you still down at Mornington?"

"Still down there. Same house."

"Maybe I should come down there one day. See the sights."

"Maybe you should." In my intoxicated state, that seemed close enough to an invitation.

"Where is everybody?" Stanley asked all three of us. "I've never been here. Walking distance from me, if the weather was better. Cool place."

I wondered who had invited Stanley, never a favourite of Bob's, and guessed Jessica, or suspected she had extracted from Bob a list of people who he might think would grace such a gathering, and that Bob had named Stanley as a possible. The room looked much better filled as we waited to replenish our drinks. Behind us, in the corner near the door, I recognised Julia and Jodi, with a tall man whom I took to be a possible boyfriend, all talking to Jessica. Gentle jazz was oozing from a stereo on the wall to my left, parked alongside the varnished ladder to the mezzanine area. It appeared no one had ascended that stairway, as yet. I obtained a second flute of champagne and made for Julia's group, leaving Roland to entertain Debbie. At the time I did not accuse myself of acting ungratefully. Julia welcomed me, and introduced the tall man, about whose connection with her I had guessed at accurately. Jessica drifted away to greet more new arrivals. Invited, I began to tell of my subbing. There appeared to be general interest. I felt a hand on my shoulder. "Mr O," said Bob, who had appeared intent on entertaining his colleagues.

"Hi," I said. "You remember Jodi? Well, of course you remember Jodi. You invited her. Well, I suppose you invited her. I'm sorry. I'm an idiot as usual. Socially hopeless. Thanks for inviting me. I'm very pleased to be here. Quite a gathering. And growing. I'm surprised. No I don't mean I'm surprised it's growing... I mean I'm pleasantly surprised to see so many people here already who I know and like, and others who look interesting and who I'm sure I'll get to know... eventually, later if not sooner. Do you work with most of these people? I mean most of those I don't know. They look like doctors. Or like they could be doctors. Or have something to do with hospitals, anyway. No, I didn't mean that. I meant they just look well to do, comfortably off. No, I didn't mean that either. Just that they seem settled. Actually, you know what, they're bloody intimidating; I think they're bloody intimidating. So well dressed. Pleasant company, I mean present company excepted," I said, nodding to Jodi and Julia. "No, I don't mean you're not well dressed; you're dressed beautifully; I mean you're not quite dressed the same way. They look so businesslike," I said, gesturing towards the group of half a dozen men and women I guessed Bob had just come from. "I don't mean not dressed for a party, but just somehow... you know..." I realised I was being stared at and halted my attempt to categorise the group's clothing.

"A bong or two, Mr O," Bob said, as much a statement as a question. "I'm not surprised you came fortified. Must be quite an event for you, living out in the sticks. I'm delighted you chose to grace us with your presence."

"Well, thank you, I'm delighted too, as I said." I held out my hand to Bob, and after a pause Bob took it. "Congratulations," I said.

"Again. I think it's fabulous you're engaged. And to Jessica too. One of my favourite women of all time. You're a lucky man. A very, very lucky man," I said. "Isn't he lucky," I told the others. "Don't you think he's a lucky man, Jodi?"

Jodi nodded her assent, grinning: "He's *so* lucky!"

"And so well dressed," I said. "That's a fabulous outfit. You look like you're mocking the whole wedding thing."

"Well, looking at what you've got on, I think I'm taking it a whole lot more seriously than you are."

"Yes I know, I am sorry about that, didn't really get it, for some reason forgot—about engagements, I mean. You do look fabulous. You really do look fabulous. Doesn't Bob look fabulous!" I said, appealing to the others.

"You look very nice," Julia said to Bob. "Congratulations. Jessica looks beautiful. You *are* very lucky." She introduced her bloke, whose name I doubt I registered.

It is funny, I have been meaning to get to my last meeting with Pash, and all of a sudden I am recalling my feeling peculiar with Julia. Awkward, I suppose people would call it these days. It was obvious to me that she was being kind, and to me as much as to Bob. Rescuing me from a silly situation I had gotten myself into. Where I would make snide remarks to Bob when I was supposed to be celebrating his engagement. To Jessica, of all people. I wondered what Julia's boyfriend was like, and what they would talk about. Probably, not that I would have noticed this at the time, I was annoyed the boyfriend was there. Would have been happy to see Julia, and would have wanted the opportunity to chat to her at the party, where she might not have known all that many people. I could have rescued her, in a way. But then, I suppose if the boyfriend had not been there, Julia might have seemed too available. Even though she was not available at all. To me. I knew that. Or I thought I did. And as I recall that meeting, my standing around in a circle at the party with Julia and her bloke and newly engaged Bob, and Jodi, and wondering what to say next, that connection with women and interest and excitement and Ms Felicity's question comes back to me. That nervousness that I suppose I was feeling at the time. Which—and this just occurs to me now—which I suppose felt better, or at least much more comfortable, if I told myself Julia was not interested in me after all. Or if she was, it felt more comfortable if I told myself that really I was not interested.

"Shamo, it's nice to see you," said Jodi, who had crossed behind Julia so as to engage me directly. "I was hoping someone here might share a smoke with me."

"Sorry." I said. "I mean I'd love to. Just don't have any. Roland. You know." I remembered Roland might not want to be outed as a supplier of joints, and that he had claimed to have brought only two joints to the party. "I mean I didn't bring any. Just got lucky. I'm sure you know what I mean. Not that ... well, you'd be welcome, I'm absolutely certain of that. If it were up to me. I mean, if it were my place to make an offer. You know what I'm talking about ..."

"Come with me," said Jodi. "Is there a backyard?" She gave me an inquiring look, and apparently satisfied told the others: "See you soon. Congrats, Bob!"

"Congrats, Bob," I said. I followed Jodi to the back door and through it, immediately feeling guilty that I had not invited Roland, who as I passed him had glanced at me, without turning his head, from where he and Debbie were chatting with Stanley.

Jodi removed a long joint from her handbag and immediately lit up, taking two sustained drags before passing it over.

"Thought I'd never get that," she said. "Even though I suppose I'd only been there ten minutes. What a spinout. I'm happy for him, though. I think she's what he's wanted. Somehow. I'm not really sure what he has wanted. Something, though. He's been looking fairly hard." Jodi gave me what I guessed in the poor light was a wink. "Lucky girl. Sort of. Well, she might be. But you know her, anyway. Didn't you used to live with her? What's she like? Will she be good for him?"

I imagine I had taken a solid pull on the joint by this time, and had been struck suddenly with how pungent it tasted.

"My God! What's in this?"

"Just something sweet. Don't you like it? Ex-boyfriend. Another one, I suppose. No, not really. Am I jealous? No, I'm not jealous. Why would I be jealous? Have some more. It's good. I really like it."

I am making most of this up, as for obvious reasons I do not remember all that well how this conversation went, nor how often we passed back and forwards that oversized cigarette. What I do remember, and it is not a comfortable memory, is that suddenly I was feeling quite dizzy and faint. "I'm feeling a bit dizzy," I told Jodi, or something like that. If I had still been holding the joint, I would have been capable of handing it back. "Think I need a drink." But the instant I got through the door and back into that warm air, I knew it was not a drink that I wanted. I wanted to lie down. But where? I saw Roland turn to me as I re-entered, and instantly feared he would claim I was looking pale. That added a shock to my developing nausea. But I was not bad enough to head for the bathroom—was even aware it might well be occupied and that I wanted neither to be demanding urgent entry nor to be standing around at the door. Likely it also occurred to me that I could not, at this point of the evening, settle in there without attracting attention I did not want to attract. There were of course the two bedrooms but they seemed equally likely to engage me in confrontations with my hosts or their guests. And so I steered myself towards the ladder, already on my side of the room, and unsteadily made my way up to the mezzanine. I recall a lull or diminution in the conversation that I thought could have been connected with my ascent and that I hoped would go away, a hope that, for reasons I can only guess at, was fulfilled. At the top were three new-looking beanbags arranged around a TV set, lit only by a dim lamp on a coffee table and reflections from the main room. I collapsed into the farthest beanbag from the ladder and breathed a groan of relief. Hubbub from the guests below had resumed its former level, drifting up with the jazz. Immediately I felt slightly better, even if I was in no mood to move and was contemplating remaining just there for the rest of the night. I hoped I would not feel worse, as I had not noted a bucket. I considered casting about for one, on the off-chance, perhaps, that Jessica had secreted something like that in a corner, but concluded that the odds did not justify my proceeding.

I felt weak and noticed that the room had begun to revolve. Not a good sign, I knew. It occurred to me that possibly I should have had dinner. But I did not feel hungry. While lying down was more comfortable, I was not feeling better. The room continued to revolve. If I threw up, the question was where. It was very warm in the mezzanine area, located immediately under the ceiling, which followed the contour of the peaked roof. The ceiling had been painted a pale yellow. Some sort of apricot cream, probably. I decided to take off my jumper, aware that under it I was wearing only an ancient T-shirt bearing the logo of the university bike club, two ducks copulating in flight. I had not thought much about the party being so warm. The jumper came off, an activity that did not contribute to my sense of well-being, and after I settled again it occurred to me that I could throw up on the garment if necessary. That did not seem immediately necessary, but I could feel a moist area growing at the back of my throat and guessed it might be necessary soon. I noticed a head had appeared at the top of the ladder, that it was followed by a body, and that the body was carrying what appeared to be a saucepan from the kitchen. "From the bar," said Jodi. "Are you not feeling well?"

Gratefully—well, I know I was grateful, not sure whether my manner was—I retched into the saucepan. Not much came out.

"I might get you some lemonade," said Jodi.

"Do you think that would hel—" I retched again, this time bringing up a bit more, mainly liquid.

"You need something in your stomach. Don't go anywhere. I'll get you some lemonade." She disappeared down the ladder, treating me to another wink—I guessed she was trying to let me know she was not disgusted—just before I lost sight of her.

I felt slightly more healthy, if weaker, and settled back again on the beanbag. It occurred to me that Jodi might bring Roland when she returned, and so I became preoccupied with hoping that she would not.

Jodi reappeared, with a tall bottle and a glass. Behind her came a shaven head, fairly obviously female. And behind her, a darker female with a full head of wavy hair: Shooka.

"Shit!" Shooka said.

The shaven female said: "Bit of a shock?" I understood instantly from the melodic tone that it was Pash. I could even see her scar as she knelt and bent over me.

"Just a bit," Shooka said. "Are you okay?"

"No," I said. "But don't tell Roland. Thank God you didn't get him," I said to Jodi, who had begun to pour lemonade.

"He did ask how you were," Jodi said. "I told him you were fine." She handed me lemonade.

"Thanks. Clever girl. I didn't expect this. What was in that?"

"It's nice, isn't it. I've saved the rest for later."

Bob's voice said from the top of the stairs: "Is everything okay here? Mr O. Are you all right?"

"Perfectly fine," I said. "Haven't even made a mess. Ministered to by three angels. Go away and don't disturb them. They're great. I feel lucky. Great party. I'm having a really good time. Sorry about your pot," I said. "I mean your saucepan. The pot here's really good. I'm impressed with the pot here. Now go back to your party and leave me alone. I am perfectly fine and having a perfectly wonderful time. Ministered to by three angels. I think I've died and gone to heaven," I said. I drank more of the lemonade. "I am so glad to see you both," I said to Shooka and Pash. "What have you done to your hair?" I said to Pash. "You still look beautiful. I don't think I ever thought you were so beautiful. I can't say it suits you but I really think you look amazing." I sipped on more of the lemonade. "I'm feeling a bit better," I said. "It's good having you three around. I think if I had a choice I'd have felt sick just to bring you up here. It's so nice you came up here," I said to Pash and Shooka. "How have you been? I heard you had a boyfriend," I said to Pash. Pash exchanged a glance with Shooka. "I'm glad if you've got somebody," I told Pash. "Have you heard? I'm a sub. On the paper down there. So you know ... I remember you asking me, what my plans were. How it was all going to work out. Money I mean, and all that. Well, it is. Working out. I like subbing," I said. "And I think I'm pretty good at it. Getting good at it. They seem happy with me there. Oh," I said, "Zoom's moved out. I'm down there with Lisa. She moved in after Jessica left. Sandy's gone too, of course. Well, not of course, but I think he found it pretty tough there after Jessica left. Do you know what," I said, "I've missed you. It's an odd thing I know given how I was and all that but I've missed you. Not all that much, but I have missed you a bit. That's what I'm trying to say. It's really nice to see you," I said. "And you two as well," I added, glancing at Shooka and Jodi. "I feel blessed. Thanks for the lemonade. Could I have a bit more? Already I am feeling much better."

Or something like that. I cannot vouch for every word. It is sort of painful remembering. Not painful but certainly uncomfortable. Maybe the whole beanbag thing reminded me of the time when Pash first came to Mornington. Except she did not lie down with me this time, nor suggest I move over. She just came and sat on her heels, and Shooka sat on one of the other beanbags, near me, while Jodi disposed of the saucepan and then came back and fed me lemonade. Bob's head had long gone from the top of the stairs. The party hubbub had risen once again. Pash did not say anything about her boyfriend. Shooka said she could not help feeling relieved. Jodi said she had another joint anyway, so we could all have some later. I sipped more on the lemonade. Someone turned the lights lower. The music got noisier and more contemporary. "I suppose you should be getting back to the party," I told all three of them. "We're in no rush," Shooka said, after a glance at the other two women. "It's nice up here."

I suppose it took me about half an hour to recover to the point where I was prepared to return to the fray. Well, maybe forty-five minutes. Certainly it took a while. The others stayed the whole time, perhaps happy to have found one another and to have an excuse for avoiding the melee below while yet still feeling like they were a part of it. I suppose lots of people get nervous at parties. We had another visit from Bob, and the girls told him I was fine and recovering. They talked among themselves—so far as I can recall the conversation it was mainly pop and rock gossip—and I mainly listened.

I recall such details, but the sense of what I am trying most to express with this recapitulation keeps slipping away from me. I think about Pash and Shooka and Jodi, and of how they looked all that time ago dressed for the party, and of the ease with which they seemed to participate together in the unusual social environment they had created. I drift off into fantasies, remembering that I had since created for myself on many a lonely occasion an imagined post-party spree with all three. I think about Pash and wonder whether she really did have a boyfriend, and if so why he was not with her at the party, or if he was with her why she made no obvious effort to introduce us or spend time with him, instead heading out the back with Jodi for a smoke and then returning with her to the space upstairs, which by then had also gathered members of Jessica's party crowd—who thought it unnecessary to take their smoke outside. Probably they had other things too, I do not know: I had no desire to go back up that ladder.

I think about declining to leave the party with Roland and Debbie, and about getting into another conversation about subbing with Julia, and about dancing with Jessica and a bunch of her pals, and about wondering whether I could go home with Shooka or Jodi but then thinking that really this was not what I wanted. All very confusing. I had had another joint with Roland and I drank a lot of champagne, which made it easier to strike up conversations with strangers but probably helped me go down in history as the party idiot. So perhaps Marjorie, a decade and more later, had a point. I certainly felt like an idiot, walking back to Roland's on a cold night in my T-shirt to shiver for what felt like hours on his front porch. Just outside their bedroom window. Until Debbie must have heard me moving around and invited me in and took me to the couch, where she had prepared a pillow and blankets. But none of this is what I wanted to capture.

It was just the lying there on the beanbag with Jodi and Pash and Shooka around me, and of how they had come up to find me, and of how they were in no hurry to leave. Pash really did not say much to me at all. None of them did. They were just there looking after me. But they were there looking after me, that is the thing I remember. They were there, and I do not think they would have been there for just anybody. What I mean is, they were not there just because they liked playing nursemaid and it did not matter to whom they played nursemaid. They were there to be with me. And I was not in a state to entertain them or romance them. I was not capable of performing. And they were there with me anyway. That is what kept nudging me, when I thought about the party, after that session where Ms Felicity had asked me to think about how it would feel if someone were interested in me. And I suppose it is occurring to me even more now than it did soon after the session—at that time it was more of a glimmer than anything properly illuminating—that those three women must have been interested in me. And that at the time at least, there was not much in that for them. And how did it feel? The thing is, I have realised, it felt really good.

12

ALL GROWN UP

I DID NOT EXPERIENCE MUCH SURPRISE WHEN I LEARNED that Bob had succumbed. It was as though I had expected to receive that news. There is surprise and surprise. I was not surprised that this had happened. But I was surprised it had happened that week. And I would have been surprised in any week. It was more than eight years since I had seen Bob.

I had seen Bob last at a barbecue Roland had organised. It had never occurred to me that this would indeed be the last time I saw him. We had been polite to one another. I had enjoyed Jessica more. Roland had lit up a long joint, and Jessica, but not Bob, had partaken. Bob and Jessica had looked good together. They had been the power couple of the occasion. Better known than anyone else present, and probably wealthier too. Bob had not made much of his social position but I could see he thought he had something that no one else had. Jessica's success had been the more prominent but she had made nothing of that at all. I think I had been to two of Jessica's shows, and then I seemed to have fallen off her invitation list—I supposed because I had not bought anything and she could fill her list with people who would buy things. I had read about Jessica from time to time—there had been at least one piece even in our papers. Nothing had prevented me from getting along to her shows on evenings after the openings, and I am sure she would not have turned me away if I had appeared uninvited at an opening. But I never got around to doing either. Had I been afraid of meeting Bob? Or Pash even? Perhaps it was just that I had not bought one of Jessica's pictures, when I could have done so. Now she could charge more for a picture than I could reasonably pay.

SINCE I BEGAN ON this monologue I have become more attentive. I observe myself more frequently, and I inspect myself more closely. I connect my inner states more consciously to outer events. I did not want to attend Jessica's shows. It has become easier to notice, when I recall a reality of that kind, what goes with it. That inner repulsion, almost a disgust. It had always pleased me to see yet another indicator of how widely Jessica had become appreciated. But the pleasure, I know now, I was willing to experience only at a considerable remove from the work. That I had shared a house with Jessica, had got drunk with Jessica, had got stoned with Jessica, had exchanged eye-rolls with Jessica over Bob's bombastic behaviour, these facts I wanted to distinguish from the fact that Jessica could charge a multiple of my monthly earnings for a picture that you imagined she might have spent days or even weeks on, but not consecutive months. It was not that she must have become wealthy; it was that whatever wealth she accumulated had looked so easily come by. It had been as though I wanted to peer at Jessica over a tall, smooth wall with no footholds. What Jessica had done, she had done somewhere else.

The practice of attending to how I respond to events has become more familiar, and easier. I can see more the point of nurturing that awareness, even though I still find it difficult to persist in the awareness. Perhaps everybody finds that sort of thing difficult. In a way, my breakdown, if you want to call it that—and I imagine people do—has been good for me, in so far as it introduced me to someone who could construct that point for me.

I am more connected with what Bob could have meant for me. More connected with who Bob could have been for me. Indeed, with who he was for me. Bob did, after all, introduce me to Roland. And then, almost, to Pash. And if it had not been for Pash, I might not have met Marjorie. Well, I may have met her merely—assuming I would even have taken that job if I had not met Pash first. And for all that we are no longer a couple, and that I knew I would not miss her greatly and do not, I still feel grateful for Marge, and to Marge. It is impossible to comprehend the influences people have on your life, at the time when they are having the influence. I feel about losing Bob almost as though I had lost a father. But a father whose patronage I have resented.

So what do I notice as I type this account, which I expect will be the last of its kind? Perhaps I wish that I had spent more time with Bob. My merely doing so might have decided other near things more helpfully. I do feel sad about Bob. Or am I sad about me about Bob? Probably I was not very sad about Steve. I did not believe I had lost much, when Roland lost Steve. I did not even think Roland had lost much. But likely Roland had lost a great deal. Pun not intended. The loss is always more than you realise. Perhaps there is an element of the abused little kid remaining in each of us as we grow up, or in most of us. "Didn't hurt!" When it did. And what hurt more was that the universe had chosen to inflict that pain, that blow. When you had not thought that anything you were doing had deserved to be punished so grievously. Didn't hurt, but let's have a bong anyway. Let's do what we used to do. Let's remember Steve in the way that he would have wanted to be remembered. Let's get stupid, like we had wanted to get stupid with Steve. But Bob had not wanted to get stupid with Roland and me. Perhaps Bob had not wanted to reveal to us, when intoxicated, how he had felt about Steve. Or perhaps it was merely a calculation for Bob: (no bong = better decisions) + (better decisions = better performance) + (better performance = a better life) → I won't have a bong. QED.

I had always wondered about Bob's ease with Shooka. Roland would know, because Steve would have told him. More likely, Roland would have completed a trio—even a quartet. The four of them lying around the floor of Steve's flat, listening painlessly to rock guitar that Steve radiated from his ghetto blaster. But it hardly matters. These could not have been frequent occasions. Had Bob become reckless in middle age? Had he become ever more desperate? Had he feared that his much more reliable sources would be exposed? Had he planned his departure, or was it an accident?

Jessica was not able to tell me. I had been curious, and I believe she had thought that my question was fair. "I don't know, and that's about all of it." And that had been about all of it. "He certainly didn't do that with me. We used to talk about things, but I probably didn't realise he was quite that unhappy. I am not even certain he really was that unhappy. There was something that happened at work, that I knew had preoccupied him. I think he had felt quite stressed—well, he did. But I had thought he would be able to tell me. That it would come out one night. We were not talking all that much, really. I had wondered, when I started to do well, if that upset him somehow. I know he was pleased for me, but when I look back on it, I can easily think that there was some pain with that. And why wouldn't there be, in a way. He really was very talented, and he could work very hard. Being a doctor was not all he wanted. Maybe the work thing was just too much. He had always felt competent there.

"A group had wanted to buy the practice, and when we talked about it that had seemed to be a good thing. We'd seen it as a chance to have more time for other things. He wanted to play guitar again, and thought that maybe he'd write. By the way he did write some stuff—I should show it to you. And the offer he got for the business was good. I think we ended up with quite a few hundred thousand, and he still had a job."

Just what was the work problem, she had never discovered. Jamie Danielson claimed some knowledge of it. Jamie had kept up more with Bob than I had, and so maybe he did know. He would drop in on trips back from England. I imagine the two of them presenting themselves to one another, as successful men. Comparing notes, and looking back together over the profitable decades since they had met. Successful professionals, who had transcended their professions—as I suppose many do. Becoming leaders, and earning as much from the efforts of more junior professionals as from the practising of their own professional skills. Jamie much more so, but Bob to an extent. Perhaps for Bob, selling the practice had seemed to offer a way back from that, a chance to be just a physician again and no longer a boss. He would have had to get the other partners onside. I can imagine him, talking them into it, appealing to logic and leaving them without a defence that could stand up to logic. "We get now what they'll hope to get later; they carry all the risks; they handle the management; we get to go home early. And we can all still look after our patients: if they don't let us do that, then they won't get their money back. So we do just what we're doing, but less of it, for nearly as much money, and a fair bit of the money we won't get we *will* get, straight away. It's win-win." QED.

Jamie said: "I think something came up and he had a row with one of the new bosses and couldn't handle it." Typical bloody Jamie. Straight down the line. But he might have been wrong. Jamie had made a virtue of bluntness, and a vice of its absence. I can imagine Jamie sacking someone, or making a point to the board. "We had some bad PR, which wasn't remotely deserved. But you couldn't deflect it. Got onto the back foot." Jamie was fond of cricket analogies, having taken up the game when he first got to England. "Now we're behind, it's as simple as that. You guys need to get runs, or retire." I am imagining, but I do not know that I am far from the facts. Which possibly did not help with Jamie's divorce. Or his marriage, for that matter.

Jamie flew back for Bob's funeral. I suppose he saw it as a chance to catch up with the rest of us, or some of the rest of us. He had wanted to pay his respects, as they say. While he could. While those he wanted to show respect to were still living. And to take the opportunity to reconnect with the living. I gathered that the divorce had been tough for him—well, most seem to be tough, and especially for those who have children. And property. I was lucky with Marjorie. Not that we had a divorce. But there was still stuff to think about, after so much time together. I suppose she would have felt entitled to more if we had produced a child or two. Which is ironic, when you think about it, as if we had gone down that path I would have gone there for her. Or at least, that is how I would have seen it then. Maybe I am less convinced now. It is never too late, of course, for a man. In theory. In principle, maybe. But if I face facts, Jamie-like, it is too late for me. Which is just how that works. Not that I know I would say yes, even now, if a chance arose for me. That would be really silly. I would reach seventy with a teenager. Still, no kids and maybe angry about that, deep down anyway, Marjorie was remarkably fair. I still have a house, even if it is a smaller house. And, I can admit, a much lonelier house. I do not see many people. It was good to see Roland. And Jamie. And it was good to see Jessica too. I had wanted to see her. Might that have been partly because Bob was not there to intrude? I do not like to think so, but I cannot rule that out. Jamie's bluntness. He might make more of it than is good for him, but it does serve a cause.

    Marjorie did not go to Bob's funeral. We had never spent time together with Bob. Marge had been at Roland's barbecue, which had come latish on for the two of us. She had enjoyed a few drinks, but no joints by then. She was probably worried that I would get idiotic with Roland. She was probably worried when she saw I was smoking with Jessica. Maybe Marge had said something about that. I would not have let her rant on. We too would not have been talking all that much, by then. I was glad that she did not go to the funeral. I could have phoned her up and invited her, and let her know what had happened. After Roland let me know, which had come as a shock. Not surprised, and yet very surprised. His phone call itself had come as something of a shock, if a pleasant shock. I had been thrilled to hear from him. I suppose I would have thought it meant Roland was interested. Without noticing that I had thought that. I just felt pleased, I believe. I am wondering now whether I also felt, briefly, nervous.

"I just wondered whether you'd heard about Bob. I know you're not on Facebook. Have you even got a mobile? Guess what: it's 2010."

"What about Bob?"

Perhaps I had been assuming that Bob had pulled off a property coup, or had left Jessica for someone younger and more adoring. Who was already married. It is easy to see that I had always been pissed off about Bob and Jessica. It had not been that I could not understand what Jessica saw in Bob. Of course not. Bob had been an interesting guy. A powerful guy, in his way. Smart, disciplined, good with women, ready to speak his mind on all sorts of topics. A bit peculiar socially but we all are. Even Jessica. Obviously. It had been more the underhand way Bob had gone about things. I assumed that it had been underhand. It is easy—too easy—to think that it could not have been otherwise. Seeing Jessica when she went down to the city. Introducing her to Roland, so that she could pick up some dope. Making it so easy for her to slip away from Sandy. Whom I have not seen for decades, and who was not at the funeral. He could have crowed over Bob's grave, almost literally. But then Sandy would never have done that.

"Well... he's no longer with us."

"Just thought you might want to know."

"There's a service on Friday that I thought you might want to get down for."

"I'll be going. You could come with us if you like."

"You could probably stay over. We could have a drink afterwards."

Which was Roland all grown up. Another surprise, and another pleasant surprise. He would brazen it out with Debbie, or more likely he already had. Or even more likely, he had no need to. Debbie had always been good at such times. And so of course I would go down for the service. Get the day off work. We always worked Saturdays, and so if I stayed over at Roland's I could do my shift on the way home the next day. Maybe I would feel a bit hung over, but I would cross that bridge when I came to it—if I came to it. I had not seen Roland for months. Was it really only months? Maybe more like a year. I had thought I would see him more often, after I split up with Marge, but it had not worked like that. I may have seen him more often, but that still was not often. You blame your spouse for your not seeing people, but afterwards it is the same. Habits you get into are not easy to break. Especially if you have not seen them as yours. The memorial service was mid-afternoon, which I assumed Jessica had chosen so that more people could get there. But perhaps it was luck. There would be a cremation, a bit of a drive from Roland's place but not all that far. So I agreed to go with Roland and Debbie. It was impossible not to think about that night at the party. I would come down on the bike, on dry roads in warm sunshine, arriving at 1pm for our 2.15 embarkation. Roland's suggested timing, which I had had no reason to reject.

"I've rolled a joint. I thought maybe you'd like one." Said with the usual Roland smile in such circumstances. A challenging grin. Not an assuming or sneering grin. If I had said no, he would have accepted that I had good reasons, and might even have acknowledged that his own reasons for having a smoke right then were not very good.

"Would that be cool?" It is funny the way we hold on to our language.

"It's cool by me. I'm not sure how cool it would be at the venue. At the service. I'm not sure Jessica would mind if we were a little bit out of it. It's not as though we need to be on our game or anything."

"Bob's mother would be there, I suppose."

"You would think so. Depending on how she is handling it. And everyone from his practice. And a whole pile of people he knew, probably all wearing suits. And probably his patients, or some of them. The ones that had appointments with him, anyway, if there were any."

"I suppose we don't need to leave for an hour. Are you wearing what you've got on?" Roland was in a stale-looking, dark, pinstriped suit that I assumed he wore typically to the office.

"Yes. I'm ready. Are you?"

"Yes, pretty much. I've just got to change into shoes." From the motorbike boots. I had worn jeans and a near-new shirt. "Is Debbie coming?"

"Not with us. She didn't take the day off. She's going to get a tram out from work and meet us there."

"Bloody hell. We can go to town. Roll a big one!" I knew that Roland would pick up the irony.

"Shall we have a small one?" he said, retrieving as he spoke a small joint from an old tobacco tin on the table. He had given up smoking cigarettes.

"Does it have tobacco in it? No, I don't suppose it does."

The joint had been appallingly rough on my throat, and I had coughed and coughed after the first toke, and again after other tokes. Roland of course had soon suggested a second joint, and as I had insisted on its being rolled with my tobacco, in the interests of avoiding further eruptions, he had rolled me a joint of my own. We had been a little late leaving, and our drive to the service had felt very weird. I had wondered whether Roland felt more comfortable than I did. And whether he was worried about being pulled over and tested, a possibility that could not have intruded upon us twenty years earlier. But there seemed no point in asking. As I got out of the car for the walk to the chapel, I realised that I had forgotten to take off my motorbike boots. My feet felt hot, and I felt even more awkward than I had expected.

The gathering was quite big. It was a warm afternoon in November. I doubt I was the least comfortable there. I could not quite decide whether the chief mourners were Bob's very elderly mother and Julia, or Jessica and the children—Bob's son and daughter, looking grown up enough to get on without Dad. I can remember wondering, seeing them, just how they had experienced Bob as a dad. Confusion seemed to be in the air there. Doubtless Bob's mother and Julia, and Jessica and even the children—maybe the children in particular—would have wondered whether they bore a measure of responsibility for Bob's passing. Whether there had been something they could have done or said, or noticed, at some time past, that could have influenced Bob to act in some less lethal way. Assuming they all knew of the circumstances. I doubt that Jessica would have sought to hide those. Possibly she had hidden some from Bob's mother. And then questions would have arisen for the principals of the firm that had bought Bob's practice, with at least one of whom Bob had entered an angry impasse, if Jamie could be believed. They would have wondered whether to refrain from attending, and thereby to attract reproving comment on their absence, or whether to attend, in which case they risked imbuing the occasion with the tension that had led in part, very possibly, to its having arisen. Did I feel that way too? I cannot remember that I thought about that. I think I believed that my estrangement from Bob—if that is what it amounted to—had arisen from Bob's abandoning of me, and not at all from my abandoning Bob. I had remained available to Bob—that was how I saw it then. The principals did attend, it was explained to me later, and doubtless Jessica was typically gracious, but I imagine that the presence of these executives indeed added to the peculiar sense I gained upon arriving with Roland that no one felt as though they knew how to behave. A sense I recognised from occasions long past. But now we were the elders.

Sandwiches and tea were available after the service, in a big room alongside the chapel. I had thought Jessica would invite people to her home. I knew she had moved with Bob to Parkville, directly down Sydney Road on the edge of the inner city, and although I had never visited them there I had heard something of their dwelling, likely from Roland and perhaps second-hand, and had gained the impression that it was generously proportioned. Jamie had joined us before the service, along with Debbie, who had arrived ahead of us by tram. People said nice things about how hard Bob had worked. About how much compassion he had felt for his patients—panegyric that I had not found easy to swallow. It was as though they had been speaking of someone other than Bob. But even there, something tugged at me from inside: had not Bob been considerate of me, at least intermittently. I am sure I recalled then his visit with Pash to Queen Street, and considered, at least briefly, whether that visit might have demonstrated compassion. Jessica spoke about how devoted Bob had been to his family. At which point the irony of the situation overcame her—or so I guessed—and she retired from the lectern, unable to complete her tribute, the remainder of which was read for her by Julia. Who added a tribute of her own, which attributed pride, ridiculously, to her long-deceased father. I had not seen Julia since Bob's engagement party and I did not get around to greeting her. I doubted that she would remember me, and I had no desire to meet the eyes of Bob's mother.

There was the moment when Bob's body was consigned to the flames. At the few cremations I have attended, and I am thinking also of the service for my colleague Griff, I have found that moment poignant. I suppose it is the finality of that commitment. Any hopes over whether the deceased might wake up could be put to rest, finally. The flames would leave nothing worth hoping for. Debbie was wiping away tears at that point. There were no tears from Roland, as far as I could determine without staring obtrusively. Perhaps he felt about Bob much as I had about Steve. I did not feel like I wanted to cry. It was more like I experienced an ache of some kind, as the coffin disappeared. An ache, which was perhaps a fear. An apprehension. Of the kind someone might feel when they handed in an exam paper, or that I might have felt each time I approved a front page as checked. What was done was done, and nothing more would be done. If more doing was needed, well then it was too late and I must face the consequences of my omission, my insufficiency. Afterwards we stood and drank tea, and chatted together, Roland and I, Debbie and Jamie, and expressed our sympathies to Jessica, who seemed glad to see me and invited me to visit her at her home. "But not today. After a day or two, or perhaps give me a week." Stanley was in attendance also, and so we spoke too to him. He was still teaching literature. "Good to see you guys. It was hard to get the time off," he said. "What are you up to, Seamus? Still on the papers?" Funerals bring people together. But there were not many there whom I wanted to see. "Shall we go?" Roland asked. "Jamie is coming back for a drink." I climbed into the back seat of Roland's big Audi, marvelling suddenly that he drove such an expensive vehicle, and one that I had judged to be new, or nearly so. Jamie sat alongside me, leaving the front seat for Debbie.

"Well, that's the end of Bob," Jamie told us all, once we got moving.

"Yes," Roland said, "I suppose so."

"I miss him, actually," I said.

"Yes," Roland said, "I suppose so. But you hardly ever saw him."

"It was just the way it worked out," I said.

"Life is like that," Jamie said, having given me time to elaborate, time that I refrained from making use of. "It works out, or it doesn't. It works out in certain ways, and you're in control less than you think. I think it's overstated, what they say about having control. That you can take charge of your life. People want you to take responsibility, but most of the time you just do what you can. I bet Bob didn't think this was where he'd end up. How he'd end up..."

"He might have thought of it," Roland interjected, "but that's a different thing from thinking that you'd actually go through with it."

"It might have been an accident," Debbie reminded him. "We don't know what happened. People usually leave a note."

"They don't," Jamie said. "Only a third leave notes, apparently."

"I get that," Roland said. "Imagine writing a note. You'd have to be so sure you were going to do it. Well, you could always tear up the note if you didn't, but I mean your state of mind. You'd have to be more conscious about it. It wouldn't just be almost an accident. You'd have to be thinking you were going to go, and in a way looking forward to it. Rather than just feeling bad and doing it in a bit of a daze. Which is how I'd rather do it. Not that I've thought about it. Well, the idea has crossed my mind on the odd occasion but it always occurs to me that it would be a lot of trouble to go to, to make sure it all worked out. Not that I've really thought about it but, you know..."

"I've contemplated suicide," Jamie said. "But you're right. You would need to do it properly. One in ten people who shoot themselves don't die, apparently. You have to wonder about them. Presumably there is a significant number who are badly wounded but live. And that's one of the most lethal forms. Forty per cent of people who jump off buildings survive."

"My god," said Roland. "That's horrific."

"I've thought of suicide," I told them. "But that stuff puts me off too."

"At least Bob did it right," Roland said. "If he did do it. I bet the success rate goes up among doctors. He did it the right way. If I really wanted to go out and had thought about it, that's what I'd do."

"Steve," I said. "Have you ever thought about Steve?"

"I have," Roland said. "But not for a long time."

"We didn't think it was suicide," Debbie said.

"Bob, interestingly, thought it might have been," Roland said. "I didn't think so. Steve would have done that properly. And not there with Shooka. And there was no reason why he would. I did think of Steve, when I heard about Bob. I just meant I hadn't thought for a long time about whether he did that deliberately. I'm quite sure he didn't."

"I'd forgotten about Steve," Jamie said. "It is interesting, the way you forget about people."

"You hardly knew him," Roland said. "Or not well."

"It is interesting, though," Jamie said. "You know, when someone commits suicide, they probably think you'll always remember them. That you'll never get over it. But even though I will miss Bob a bit, and it was a shock to hear that he'd gone, you move on. We will get over it." Jamie paused as though reflecting on this. "But he won't."

"It will take a while for Jessica to get over it," I said. "And the kids."

"People don't get over it," Debbie said. "Not if they were close."

"But you do move on," Jamie said. "The one who's dead doesn't move on."

"You do move on," Roland said. "And here we are."

THERE WAS MY MOTORBIKE, parked inside the front yard, again recalling to me an earlier meeting in similar circumstances. The house was bigger, in a more well-to-do part of town and in better repair, and it seemed to face in a different direction. There was a veranda, like the old house had had. And a fence, taller and more secluding, and a gate. When they had renovated, extending the house to the rear, Roland had arranged for a basement to be dug underneath, which he had set up as a music room, a place where he could make lots of noise but not bother the neighbours. Inside, down a short set of stairs from the lounge, lived his collection of guitars, and his amplifiers, and some chairs and a table, and a small refrigerator. There was also a drum kit, the only instrument that I could attempt to play, and which I had attempted to play, under Roland's cynical eye, on the day when he had shown off the room to me. In theory we could have smoked bongs down there when I visited, silently and safely away from the children. In practice, we had smoked only joints there and no more than twice. Key deterrents were the litter trays that Debbie had placed in the room for the family's cats, and the poor ventilation. The trays could, however, be moved up to the rear deck. I recall a battle with Debbie over whether a door to the deck could be left open for the animals. In the basement, a fan could be switched on that in time cleared the air.

"I'm going to cook some spaghetti," Debbie said. "Would you two like to stay? You'll have to eat with the family. Well, Agnes, our middle girl, is at her boyfriend's. Yes, all right," she told Roland, in response to his inquiring glance. "It's not cold. Put the trays out. And remember you're having dinner."

"We should go downstairs," Roland suggested to Jamie and me. "I'll get it ready. Have a seat in the lounge for a minute. Scotch, Jim Beam or a beer?" He disappeared down the stairs and returned, grimacing at us, with the cat trays held at arm's length before him, placing them outside the back door and repeating his journey for the drinks. "Give it a few minutes," he said. "It will be all right. I am assuming you'd both like a bong."

"A bong," Jamie said. "I'm amazed that you've still got some dope. I haven't had a bong for an age."

"Then we'll make you an especially big one," Roland said. "And we'll watch Seamus get really silly."

"Why would I get silly. Nothing's happened that I'd want to get silly about."

"No, just the departure of Bob," Jamie said. "And I don't suppose we'll really miss him. Even if Jessica and the kids do. He was pretty weird."

"We're all weird in our own ways," Roland said. "I'd miss you. Well, I wouldn't tell you that, and I'm not telling you now." He laughed briefly. "But I would."

"But we spend no time together," Jamie said. "These days I mean. How long has it been? Five years? Did I see you when I came back here last time?"

"If you didn't, you should have," Roland said. "We can probably go downstairs."

And so we had a bong or two and a couple of drinks as the smell of cat faeces dissipated—replacing it with a pall of bong and cigarette smoke that we soon failed to notice. The others borrowed my cigarettes. We came back up for dinner with Debbie and tried to seem sober for Roland's girls, who exchanged knowing grins. And of course went back down after dinner and got a bit stupid and probably spoke more about Bob and about Steve. None of which you would expect to precipitate a decline in any participant, but I think it may have begun this for me. Not the smoking or the company but the reality of the occasion, of who was there and who was not there. Steve was not there, nor Bob. But Roland was there, and Jamie. You would think I might have taken comfort from the presence of the other two, the persistence of these relationships that we had nurtured, in our own peculiar ways, for periods long exceeding two decades and approaching three. And perhaps I could have taken comfort as well from reflecting that if Steve had scorched me with his recklessness, Bob had seemed excessively calculating and industrious. And that Roland and Jamie, by contrast with both, had seemed to walk with me a more satisfying, ultimately, middle path. But I think what struck me after my shift at work the next day, as I rode home from Moorabbin to a solitary Saturday evening and Sunday, in preparation for our usual marathon Monday, was how thin all this was. I was not conscious over that weekend that I was feeling unusually unhappy or flat, let alone having a sense of why that might have been, but I think it was from about that time that work began to seem less important. My performance at work and my status there seemed less worthy of the energy I had devoted to sustaining them.

If I reflect honestly—and as I have said, I am learning that benefits accrue from that practice—what about the same time became more important was the fact that I was not far short of turning fifty, and my hypothesising that when I reached that milestone, likely I would be celebrating with a cigarette and a drink and possibly a small joint, if I preserved a proportion of Roland's send-off, by myself. Not that I would have to do that—it was not the case that I knew nobody with whom I could celebrate, and I had a few months remaining when I could get some guests organised. But probably I would do that. That, probably, was what I would choose to do, just as I had chosen to celebrate in a similar way my past three or four birthdays since had I split up with Marjorie. Certainly, there was no one at work whom I would invite to celebrate my turning fifty. No one since Pete had left. I could have invited Pete and Roland, if Pete had still been around, and that could have been the core of a gathering. I suppose I could have spoken to Charles, but I saw him only at Christmas. Marge had never been fond of Charles's wife, Jennifer, and I had never been that fond of Charles. To have insisted they attend a very small celebration would have felt very odd. I did not want to celebrate only with my parents—that would have felt like an admission that I had failed to thrive. They would have pretended that they were pleased to see me, but mainly they would have been worried that it was just me and them and my stay-at-home sister. And possibly Charles and Jennifer, whom I could not disinvite. And then my brother and sister-in-law might bring some of their children, which would make a statement about thriving that I could not rebut. I could hardly have invited Jamie from England. Marjorie was out, for obvious reasons. And there was no point imagining that I might invite Bob. It occurred to me that I could invite Jessica. "I'm turning fifty. Come down. It's not for a party; I just feel like seeing you." I thought about Bob's cornering of the market in Jodi's best dope. Perhaps I could have invited people down for some bongs. If I had possessed enough dope to fill a few bongs. Which I did not. And if I had known anyone besides Roland who might have wanted to come down for a bong. And if Roland had ever wanted to come down, which would have given me a shred of belief that he would want to come down this time. I remembered my smoking at Abbotsford with Roland and Jessica. And then I thought about Pash, who had been at the funeral.

I did not know whether Jessica had phoned Pash, or whether Pash had heard about Bob through other channels. Likely Pash was on Facebook. For all I knew, she might have been one of Bob's patients. She had not introduced herself. I do not even think Roland had noticed her. I am sure Jamie had not, but then he had met Pash only once or perhaps twice. And if Debbie had seen Pash, she had not chosen to confront me with my ignoring of Pash. Perhaps she had not thought that necessary. In a way, Debbie had won, had overcome me. She still had Roland, had the house in Hawthorn, had her daughters. Had Roland working nine to five, still pulling in regular dollars and more of them, and had consigned the guitars to where they belonged. Doubtless that had mellowed Debbie. Or had made her more confident. Which in its own way was easier on Roland. And on me. I had thought of saying something to Pash but I had not been sure what I would say. I had not seen her for ages. Not since Bob's engagement. She had gone a bit grey—which was possibly why Roland had not noticed her. She had seemed to be there on her own, but that did not mean anything. She had dressed differently, looked more corporate, I had decided. Had grown back her hair, and probably long ago. Was wearing heels, and a skirt. Not really the Pash I had remembered. I had thought of saying hello.

I DROPPED IN TO see Jessica. I had given her a week; in fact, I think I gave her nearly two weeks. I just phoned her and said I was coming, and she said that was okay. It would have been a Tuesday, about lunchtime. The house was among several dwellings I had admired from the outside when I lived nearby in Carlton. Opposite the green expanse of Royal Park, and quite big for how close it was to the city centre. I was invited into an airy and spectacularly furnished ground-floor living area, its walls festooned with Jessica's paintings. And not only hers, clearly. The effect was crowded and yet tasteful. So striking. It felt like I was stepping into heaven, where everything was beautiful and soothing to the soul, and abundant. How could Bob have abandoned this, I wondered. Jessica offered me tea. And then a gin and tonic. And then a small joint, for which we stepped out the back door. "For old times," she said. "Lunch is quiche and some salad. It's all done; I just need to serve up."

"It's fantastic that you are so successful," I remember saying. Nestled in the carport behind the house I could see a silver Maserati, whose four doors I noted. Very Bob. But Jessica and Sandy had shared an appreciation for exotic cars.

"Once upon a time I would have told you I'm not that successful. But I am, really. That's one thing that's changed. That this has changed. It's no use saying I'm not that successful. I am. And it's good. I just hope it goes on like that."

"It will. Your stuff's great. I always knew you'd do well."

"And you? What about you?"

"I'm a sub these days. A sub-editor. Better money. Well, more immediate money, anyway."

"And your stories about your friends? What are you working on these days?"

"Nothing really. Haven't been doing that for a long time."

"You should be still writing something. I thought you were good too."

"I wasn't. It was just boring autobiography. Unless you are talking about the bikie stuff I used to do. Which was boring for other reasons."

"No, the other stuff. About the messy guy you lived with. Who was Roland, I've realised. Now that I've made the connection. And the guitars. And of course Bob. See, I remember. It was about the first thing you finished when you lived with us. I remember you were so happy about it."

"I was happy about it, then. I've still got it filed somewhere."

"Who do you live with now?"

"Just me. By myself. I used to live with Marjorie but that didn't work. Well it did work for a while, twenty years I suppose. Eighteen. In the end I don't think we were that compatible. You were lucky with Bob. Or I assume so. Sorry..." For Jessica had looked away from me and raised a hand to her face. "...I am crass. I am sorry too about Bob. Of course. I don't really know how I let things get to this point. I've missed you, too. It's been ridiculous. But I don't think Bob would have really wanted to see me. I think he was pretty annoyed, at your party. I probably should have apologised. But I was just getting stoned. It seemed like fun to me."

"It was fun," Jessica said. "I didn't mind it."

"But Bob did."

"He did a bit. Seems dumb now but he really did."

"I have missed him," I said. "I think I've missed him dropping in. Those long chats."

"Things might have changed anyway."

"You know I wouldn't have met Pash if it wasn't for Bob. Well I'd already met her, but nothing had happened. In which case I wouldn't have met Marge. I might not have met anybody."

"Did you see Pash at the service?"

"No."

"Seamus, you did see her. You must have. She told me you did."

And that was a shock.

"Well I did, but I didn't know what to say. So I didn't say anything. I don't think I really wanted to see her. Well I did, but... I just didn't know what to say."

"You could just say hello."

"Yes, but then what? The last time I saw her was at your party. Your engagement party."

"You weren't at the wedding, were you."

"You didn't invite me."

"Bob didn't. And my mum wasn't keen, when Bob told her who you were. I wanted to have you."

"I always did like you. Why did you have to take up with Bob?"

"He was real. Someone different. He had money, a house. He was fun. He loved me. It worked out."

"But not Sandy."

"Not Sandy. I missed Sandy. I missed all that stuff. But I had my work, and friends from work. And Juliet, and Cedric. It worked out."

"Have you ever seen Zoom?" I asked, wondering suddenly whether things had worked out for him, too.

"He's a curator. Or was. In Tasmania. A small gallery. He still paints. I've sent him invites to shows. He came to one a few years ago. If he hears about Bob he'll probably send me a card. Sandy sent one. You should have spoken to Pash. Anyway, let's have some lunch."

"I should have," I said. "I just didn't know what to say. Especially there. I wasn't even sure what she might have had with Bob—before you. I was with Roland. Debbie was there. I just wasn't comfortable."

"I don't think she had anything with Bob before me. Not that it matters. Especially now. But I don't think she did. Which reminds me. Bob wrote something, and I know you were in it. As the basis for a character. Serve yourself some quiche and I'll get it for you."

And so what had Bob written, printed double-spaced and apparently carefully proofed? I will not pretend I did not read some of it straight away. All but ignoring Jessica as we nibbled on quiche. "There was a point when he thought he'd write," Jessica said. "He spent quite a few weekends on this."

IT was evening. We'd been playing *Kind of Blue*, which is my favourite Miles Davis session, and which I had brought mainly for the driver, who I had offered to re-introduce to a friend of mine who spent his weekdays devising tall tales. Even if the tallness in some cases was nominal, because his characters were mere caricatures, people he knew whose flaws he exaggerated and whose strengths he made light of. He was a lonely looking person, a bit below average height, neither good-looking nor plain, his nose and lips perhaps a little too big for the rest of his face. His face was small but you wouldn't call him a pinhead. He did have a sharp eye, and a quick wit, and enough natural talent that he could get by without discipline. His hair, an unusually thin and near colourless thatch, had been receding since, by my reckoning, his 19th birthday, which was about when we had met.

He thought a lot of himself in some ways, and not much in others. He had written about the driver's boyfriend, who had died a year earlier, and who'd been a friend of mine also. Steve was restless, impulsive, and possessed of a death-wish he fulfilled via an overdose. The driver, who we called Pash, because her real name was so antiquated and puritanical, and because she encouraged that, had been stirred by the death of Steve but not shaken. I hope you'll forgive my adapting an Ian Fleming cliche. Pash was in her way quite a glamour girl, gently voiced and broadly curious. She had a long and quite visible scar on her neck just above her throat, running from about the centre to just under her cheekbone, visible but not disfiguring, where someone must have been forced to stitch up a cut that could have been deadly, and had done a very good job. While sorting through Steve's possessions, she'd come across something from my friend that had featured a version of Steve, which Steve had shown her soon after they became acquainted. It was at the funeral for Steve that she had met its author. It appeared she'd taken an interest in him, fuelled in part by this story, which had featured Steve prominently, and which embellished a real incident from several years earlier. The writer had done a good job, she thought, of representing Steve. The pages had been strewn with corrections, and she'd asked me whether Seamus would like it returned. I'd said that I believed he would, but that there was probably no rush to do so. Nevertheless, several months later we'd set out on our journey.

"He writes okay," I told Jessica. "Or wrote—I'm sorry. I am quite enjoying this. It is interesting seeing yourself written about. Things you remember. Or you remember your side of it. He is no more complimentary than I would have expected, but interesting, and you don't have to take it all on. Do you remember Bob coming down to see us when this happened? You were at work, I think. You got back much later."

"I remember. You can keep reading."

Pash had been asking me about Seamus. I'd told her what I could, holding back little. He was a university drop-out who had moved to a house by the bay, where he'd decided to live day-to-day. Where he thought his tale-telling might lead him I don't think he knew. I took the approach to life he had adopted to be a form of escapism, a way of avoiding facing up to the reasons why his academic progress had stalled—to why, given his talent, he had underachieved. I saw it as an outlook founded on myopia, but having blinded himself to its consequences he seemed unspeakably comfortable. I used to wonder how he could fail to see that rents would rise faster than the dole.

It was not clear how Seamus would haul himself out of this hole, especially given that he'd made himself so comfortable in it. He had an additional problem in that he had known no women. I could see he liked women in general; he just didn't get close to women who he thought might like him. It wasn't that he was obese or kyphotic or in any other way grotesque. It was just that he found females alarming. He'd told me that himself, in the roundabout fashion that he preferred—it was not so much that he spoke in riddles, as that you rarely felt like he was giving you all of the facts, or even that he knew what the facts would have been. "If someone likes me, then something is wrong with her," he'd said to me in the early hours of one morning, after a bottle of wine and a joint I'd supplied, summarising the sort of assessment he found himself making. He was 24 years old and had never so much as been on a date, so far as I could determine. He'd hidden himself away in his share house, and was accumulating memoirs about friends and past housemates and their consumption of bongs—the last a topic that he seemed to see as endlessly gripping.

"Is there a particular reason why you wanted me to read this?" I asked Jessica.

"I don't know. Art and life. I just thought you might like it."

"I like his style," Pash had said. "And he seems very clever. I liked meeting him. I'm excited to meet him properly, although I do hear what you say. I'm not sure anyway what plans I'd have for him. We'll wait and see, shall we?" Clearly, she'd got it into her head that he might be a challenge worthy of her talent for romance. And she was talented in that area—she certainly knew how to generate an approach from an object of interest, and how to deflect an approach. Even if she was not, on balance, my type. I'm sure she had found Steve a challenge, but it was a challenge that she'd seemed to enjoy. Nevertheless, Steve had been straightforward, I'd thought, by comparison with Mr Cullen.

"I'd be wary," I warned her. "Just in case you were thinking of anything. You might feel masterful by comparison, but it's still possible you'll be hurt. Fearful people do painful things. I keep a bit of distance from him myself. He's not exactly the faithful type. He'll be a puppy one minute and a rattlesnake the next. He'll be an uncomfortable cuddle, if that's what you're thinking. But he's easy enough to know if you don't get too near. And he's a lot less reticent when he's stoned."

All Grown Up

We get to the house in the dark, after dinner, and sure enough there were three of them there, obviously having smoked a joint recently. There was Zamyr, the house patriarch, who went by the nickname of Zoom, a connection apparently with his motorbike riding. There was Sandy, a good-natured chap who obviously liked a drink. And there was Seamus, who was showing signs of inebriation already. Pash marched in with her usual style and sat down near Seamus, who remembered her and was obviously fascinated by her in his impotent way. He quickly dropped a few repellent comments, which alone would have seen her off if she'd gone there unprepared. There was some banter based on her nickname, and somehow that offered Seamus an opportunity to ask her why he hadn't been kissed yet. Which was completely uncalled for. You could see that he couldn't help himself from doing his best to repulse her, while overtly inviting her. It wasn't easy to look at, up close like that. My assumption is that when he was stoned, he excused himself. But Pash simply hinted that he might get kissed later. She gave him an excuse for looking hard at her face, and an opportunity to defend her appearance against an injest attack from Zamyr. I am sure he found the situation unusual, this unusually attractive woman dropping clear hints to him that she fancied him. But Pash was also very much in control. From time to time he would make a gauche remark of some sort but she would just bat it away. And she continued to let him know that she found him enticing.

Pash had brought down a bottle of dissolved dexamphetamine. It had been part of her job to procure this and that for popular bands that were in Melbourne on tour. Amphetamines have a folk association with violent behaviour but in pure forms they can be calming and euphoric. Pash persuaded Seamus to take some—not unexpectedly, he didn't need much persuading. At about the same time, she presented him with the draft of his tale about Steve, and implored him to read it aloud. By this time we were listening to music in their shabby lounge room, with the rest of the household asleep. Seamus read us the story, which I think made him feel pretty good. Then Pash practically insisted that he embrace her. It was comical to watch. Seamus was stiff and resisting, as though he'd be fed to the lions in the Colosseum if he made a wrong move. But in the end, and I am certain with the help of the drugs—they'd both also helped to smoke a few joints—she managed to get him relaxed enough to lie calmly with her in his arms on a beanbag chair, and it was pretty clear he was having the time of his life. In the end I went for a small-hours stroll along the road by the seafront, and although I never asked her to detail what went down after that my belief is that she took him to bed. The two of them spent most of the next day in his bedroom.

Whether this had been Pash's plan all along I don't know, but I don't think it had been. Not that I'm certain she had made a plan. I think the idea was that she give him a taste of some intimacy as a sort of reward for his work, such as it was, and because she enjoyed exercising her feminine powers in this way. I had known her for about two years, and not for the first time it fell upon me chillingly—like an unexpected hailstorm—that Pash was addicted to lost causes. She'd picked up Steve when he was in a similar condition to Seamus—so far as I knew never having had a girlfriend before, or not for more than a week or two. I also wondered whether the stress of connecting with Pash had contributed to Steve's overdose. Even prolonged pleasure and excitement can be stressful, if it's not what you're used to or have grown up with. Steve's elder brother had been in some trouble and I think he'd assumed that at some point he'd be there too, notwithstanding his status as his family's white sheep. I don't think he'd thought he was much of a catch, or at least for the women he'd tended to meet while at RMIT doing Business. The more I think about it, the less I think Pash really expected that relationship with Steve to go anywhere. It was more of a "Yes, I've got a boyfriend" thing for all the times she was propositioned at work. But then there was also her endometriosis, which had meant she was on the pill constantly, and had developed doubts about her fertility. The doubts were not unreasonable, but I believe they loomed larger in her mind than was warranted—as tends to be reported clinically, and it's not rocket science to see why. My assumption has always been that the diagnosis, and where Pash had taken it mentally, was connected with her approach to men. She was unusually unconstrained, and yet in certain respects reserved. She was never flirtatious with me, for example. Perhaps the feeling that she was firmly at the helm was a turn-on. Or more likely, it was a precondition of her feeling comfortable, given that she saw herself as damaged goods, and damaged in a way that was very troublesome but far from standing out on the surface. That limited what she would reach for, or seemed to. Arguably, Seamus was less vulnerable than Steve had been. Certainly, he was less volatile. I thought it not likely that any intimacy Pash might advance to Seamus would endure but I could not convince myself that this would be bad for him.

"Interesting?" Jessica asked. I had not said much for a while, I suppose. "You can read to the end of it, but maybe not now. So you see, this sort of stuff can be interesting. Even helpful, perhaps—at least for the character models. Who are, in many respects, simply the characters in this kind of work. I think they call it creative non-fiction these days—in that the material is directly from life but liberties are allowed. Usually names are changed. You should do some yourself. It's like one of your sketches. I would have liked it if Bob had gone on with this. And then maybe revised it. He could easily have retired, and got into it. Perhaps made a book from it. It would have helped him, I think. It's very silly, the way he behaved. I understand it, because I understood him, but at the same time it all seems so unnecessary. We weren't getting on badly. We weren't getting on wonderfully—I think because of what he'd been going through—but I'd seen it as a temporary thing. We'd get past it. You know, I really wish you two had seen each other more often. It was almost as though I met Bob and you un-met Bob. Almost. He was grumpy about the party but I thought you were fine. Every party needs a drunk, to be worth thinking back to. Or someone a bit past it—I'm not saying you were really drunk. It could easily have been one of my friends—well, you were one of my friends, but I mean one of my friends from school. I know two of them arrived tripping. I didn't really miss that sort of thing but I still enjoy a joint. Eat your quiche. Shall I roll us another?"

I NEED TO ADMIT that my getting drunk in the morning, while looking out at my back garden, and my refraining from going in to work, and for the first time my refraining to phone, had coincided with my birthday. I had been glad there was no one who could hassle me about turning fifty. No one to ask me how I was celebrating, and who might have smiled thinly and nodded when I replied that I would not be celebrating at all. "There's nothing to celebrate." "It's time to stop counting birthdays." "I'm not that excited about it." I had thought through all sorts of responses that I could make, and none had felt very promising. I do not think that I stopped phoning in just for that reason. But it was a useful result of my not phoning that time. Which meant that I could celebrate by myself. With a drink and a smoke. I had indeed saved a smoke from that session at Roland's—or rather, from the stuff he had given me afterwards. And I told myself that I was glad to get it over with, turning fifty. A milestone you did not want to celebrate. But one that, celebrated or not, brought me to a point on life's journey that conferred certain privileges.

Indeed, I was privileged in so far as I no longer needed to celebrate significant birthdays. And I had invoked that privilege at my first opportunity. I had felt some apprehension; had thought my decision naughty, perhaps. Had felt as one might feel when unwrapping sullenly a birthday gift in advance of the date. But then, such a feeling would not be wholly unpleasant. And especially if the gift were a gift to oneself. It was as though I had embarked upon a slide into decrepitude, and had experienced it as gently exhilarating. I had felt as though I were facing up to myself, in a way. Admitting to myself that I was a certain sort of person. And ceasing to pretend that I was not that person. A person who wanted to live differently. One who did not want to do all the formal stuff, such as celebrating big birthdays. And also someone who, as Bob's narrative had made painfully plain, was mildly handicapped, and who was recognised as deficient by people around him. Most of whom refrained from overt condescension. Perhaps some people saw me as profoundly handicapped—and I would not know. Perhaps Pash had seen me that way. Bob thought she had seen me that way, as indeed he had seen me. I was a basket case. Someone who might be polished up but who never would shine. Not a whole person. Just bits and pieces thrown into a carcass, shambling confusedly about the world while composing running commentaries on activities in a very small part of it. A joke. I was a joke, and Pash had enjoyed her contact with my comical self. She had even made a comedy of me, playing expertly on my ludicrous fears so as to manufacture a fork in our paths. To push me off down one track while she took another. And to where had my track led? At the time it had seemed to me that I made the best of things. But I had been riding through desert. Little water; less nourishment. It should not have surprised me that I had wilted.

WHAT ARE YOU WAITING FOR?

I HAVE BEGUN TO WONDER WHETHER I HAVE INHERITED a foreboding. A dark apprehension, and one that connects not at all with my circumstances. Have I incubated from birth an unexamined assumption that my universe will fall apart? A suspicion that my life of ease might be a life of ignorance, and that what I am ignorant about is the insufficiency of its foundations. I wonder also whether I share this foreboding with others raised in analogous settings. Whether they too experience as primal a hankering to hide in small spaces. Nourish a belief that performance is paramount. Strive for self-sufficiency as though it were integrity. Harbour a horror of sinking to a depth of depravity at which they see no choice but to solicit donations or die. I wonder whether others too live in fear that they might burden their relatives, or their friends. Whether they hear an interior urging that they demonstrate their independence through their accumulating of expensive inessentials. All of these concerns I have come to believe that I have carried through life as I might have carried a ponderous collar, its heaviness compressing me and fatiguing me. A collar that I carry still. But a collar that from time to time seems to hover now, as though by some accident I toggle on it an anti-gravity switch, so that it no longer weighs on me, no longer chafes on me, and no longer weakens me.

For brief minutes every now and again I am free of its hindering. The prospect that some error might crush me seems at such times so distant as to be unworthy of my attending to it. It feels likely that what I contribute is plenty, even if my contribution is not superior. It feels almost as though I can do as I please.

That these intervals of emancipation resound with echoes of past periods when I submitted to intoxication among certain acquaintances is not lost upon me. I wonder whether it was Steve Hurtley who showed me for the first time how I could lay my collar, if briefly, aside. "Have another bong." "It's your bong." "You should have another bong." "You'll feel better if you have another bong." "You deserve another bong." "You will be in a much better position to decide whether you need another bong after you've had another bong." "I've had my bong, and now it's your turn for a bong." "If some's good, more's better." Steve may have extended his motto imprudently. His willingness to test his invulnerability to yet another bong might have brought him results that, tragically, he could not replicate in other spheres of his life. But he was right about bongs. There was relief for me in becoming an imbecile, and more relief in recognising that I could not, from smoking bongs, become too much an imbecile. And from experiencing this as a fact, among fellow imbeciles.

Intoxication is scorned for its diluting of judgment. But how insipid is our judgment when sober. We experience ourselves as having judged well, but as experience this is illusory. When our judgment turns out to be good, we congratulate ourselves on our foresight; when it fails us, we see wisdom in cursing our choices more than our luck. But luck has affected the outcome in either case. We cannot choose to live well and, having thus chosen, live well; just as we can risk living badly and yet find ourselves living well anyway.

Did I act well in denying, after six months of leave, that I was fit to resume my role at the office? Was that a choice that I made or a choice I discovered? A moment came when I might have returned, but I had not felt as though I could rise to the bait. Perhaps I chose not to rise. I had things on my mind. To have returned would have been provident, but I was weary of provident. Where had provident got me? It had got me to here. Yes, I was fearful that they would stop paying me. A fear that I believed was well founded. Did I foresee that Danny would propose my redundancy? I had never thought that he would. That would have been one sub fewer on the floor, because he could not replace me. But the papers were shrinking. Given that redundancies had been demanded, if not for me then for whom? I may never again have a job. But I have been here before. Not unemployed, for in recent months I have found much to do. Unempaid, as my embellishing of this record has brought me no money. It is as though I have returned to my days with the painters, in that run-down house with the grate falling out of the furnace. Except that my house is well finished. And I have been able to pay down my mortgage, so that what remains of my borrowing costs me much less than rent. Perhaps I could apply for a pension, on the grounds that I am incapable of sustaining empayment. Ms Felicity might be supportive. Is that what I will do?

The question is less urgent than it had been when Zoom said he was abandoning Queen Street. Ought I have let his looking out for me slide right on by? Would something else have come up? Or would I have faded then into a deeper dependency, begging for shelter? Collecting my dole cheques while affixed to no address, and requiring complicity from another, a parent perhaps, in my fortnightly lies to the government. Might I have moved in with my parents and Tess? Gone to work for my father? Such reflections repulse me. Sub-editing has not been so bad. I could call up Danny. Maybe offer to check just the web pages. One or two days a week, on a day rate. Or three afternoons, and maybe even from here. I might log in remotely, a feat I believe I could master. But there are other avenues to empayment, and I do not need a lot of empayment.

Empaid once again, I could look young Jack straight in the eye. "It has been quite a big day, mate. Always nice to kick back. Why don't you drop over later? Would I have guessed right if I guessed you could force down a beer?"

I HAVE SEEN SOME more of Jessica, and I've met up with Pash. Our brief dialogue at Bob's party would not be our last. I had not made much of Jessica's assessment that I should have accosted Pash at the funeral. Say hello? And then what? And what since? "I've realised you were bullshitting." "Are you finished with sleeping around?" "I got your number from Jessica. Thought you might like to talk about old times. Or she did. I'm not sure if I want to." None of those openings had sounded promising. Did I even want to see Pash? Was I assuming that Jessica would do what was needed, if she were to reach the conclusion that something was needed? I don't think so. Why would she. After all, no one was interested. And then, it was as though I knew someone was interested. Is the world produced by our self-understanding? "Can you get down for dinner? There is someone I would like you to meet." Yes, of course, Jessica, I could get down for dinner. I could do just about whatever I wanted, as long as I did it almost for free.

Jessica served tomato soup, crusty bread, cheese and spinach in fine filo pastry, chutney, and a dressed green salad. And chilled white wine—it was again spring. And two joints. And Patience. "People don't call me Pash any more. I've discouraged it. I grew out of that. It seemed, you know, childish. Patience seems right now. Seems more womanly. Pash was girlish, and I think I wanted to be girlish back then. But not now. You can cling on to your childhood, or you can understand it has passed. The only thing about Patience is that it sounds like you are waiting, and it makes me wonder sometimes whether I am waiting, and what for. Do you ever wonder if you are waiting for something? What are you waiting for?"

No immediate answer had come to me, and both questions had confronted me—had set me back on my heels. Was I waiting for something? And for what was I waiting? Introspection revealed that my first answer was yes. I was waiting. I had been waiting for months. Had I, possibly, been waiting for years? Even for decades? All of a sudden, at dinner with Pash, in that beautiful space, infused with grace from the so popular Jessica, who seemed to wear her success as though it were a flimsy and transparent headscarf that added to her only delicacy, it occurred to me that I had been waiting all my life. And so the question was for what. Was there something that would come to me if I waited? Was I waiting for an endowment—for an inheritance, say? A sum of money that would support me? That possibility, I could dismiss. Thus endowed, I would have been waiting still. I deflected. "Give me a clue," I demanded of Pash, who was transforming before my eyes into Patience. She looked much less sombre than she had looked at the funeral, which was only to be expected. And which was welcome, and yet oddly so. She had arrived in a blue denim jacket, and a knee-length blue denim skirt. A denim suit, almost. With a silky orange blouse, and black tights, and short boots. I had wondered whether she might have become decrepit like me. "What are you waiting for?"

"If I knew, maybe I'd have it," Pash said, her voice still sounding musical. A little richer, and faintly deeper I think. "To grow up? But I've grown up. It may not be that I'm waiting for anything. I went there only because of my name. I didn't insist that you were waiting for anything. I just asked whether you were."

"You're both waiting for death," Jessica told us. "And you know what? It's coming."

It was as though she were channelling Jamie, with his disdain for the layer of sugar. And Pash took up her cue as directly.

"I have stomach cancer," she told me, speaking gently and meeting my eyes. "I still have a few years, I think."

"I'm very sorry," I said. "I am very, very sorry." Of course I remember that accurately. It was only a short time ago. And then for some reason, I told Pash: "I'm perfectly healthy." And after that, as though I believed I could bury my tactlessness: "At least as far as I know."

This book has been published independently.
If you enjoyed the novel and would like to show support
for the author, consider submitting a rating or review to
your online place of purchase, or to goodreads.com.

Follow I J Baker at ijbaker.com.au

Milton Keynes UK
Ingram Content Group UK Ltd.
UKHW040434241024
450062UK00028B/94/J